Mark Chadbourn was raised in the mining com-
munities of South Derbyshire, and studied at L[
University before becoming a journalist. Now a
screenwriter for BBC television drama, he has also
run an independent record company, managed
rock bands, worked on a production line and as an
engineer's 'mate'. He is a two-time winner of the
British Fantasy Award and author of the acclaimed
The Dark Age, *The Age of Misrule* and *Kingdom of
the Serpent* trilogies. *The Swords of Albion* adventures
– of which *The Devil's Looking Glass* is the third –
were in part inspired by the famous 'Corpus Christi
portrait'. Dated 1585, this painting of a young man
bears the motto *Quod me nutrit me destruit* – 'That
which nourishes me, destroys me' – and is believed
by many to be the only surviving depiction of the
playwright and alleged spy, Christopher Marlowe.

Mark Chadbourn lives in a forest in the Midlands.
To find out more about him and his writing, visit
www.jackofravens.com

By Mark Chadbourn

THE DARK AGE:
THE DEVIL IN GREEN
THE QUEEN OF SINISTER
THE HOUNDS OF AVALON

THE AGE OF MISRULE:
WORLD'S END
DARKEST HOUR
ALWAYS FOREVER

KINGDOM OF THE SERPENT:
JACK OF RAVENS
THE BURNING MAN
DESTROYER OF WORLDS

LORD OF SILENCE

THE SWORDS OF ALBION:
THE SWORD OF ALBION
THE SCAR-CROW MEN
THE DEVIL'S LOOKING GLASS

THE
DEVIL'S
LOOKING
GLASS

MARK CHADBOURN

BANTAM BOOKS
LONDON · TORONTO · SYDNEY · AUCKLAND · JOHANNESBURG

TRANSWORLD PUBLISHERS
61–63 Uxbridge Road, London W5 5SA
A Random House Group Company
www.transworldbooks.co.uk

**THE DEVIL'S LOOKING GLASS
A BANTAM BOOK: 9780553820225**

First published in Great Britain
in 2012 by Bantam Press
an imprint of Transworld Publishers
Bantam edition published 2013

Addresses for Random House Group Ltd companies outside the UK
can be found at: www.randomhouse.co.uk
The Random House Group Ltd Reg. No. 954009

The Random House Group Limited supports the Forest Stewardship
Council (FSC®), the leading international forest-certification organization.
Our books carrying the FSC label are printed on FSC®-certified paper.
FSC is the only forest-certification scheme endorsed by the
leading environmental organizations, including Greenpeace.
Our paper procurement policy can be found at
www.randomhouse.co.uk/environment

Typeset in 12/15pt Bembo by
Kestrel Data, Exeter, Devon.
Printed and bound by
CPI Group (UK) Ltd, Croydon, CR0 4YY.

2 4 6 8 10 9 7 5 3 1

For Elizabeth, Betsy,
Joe and Eve

Go, Soul, the body's guest,
Upon a thankless errand;
Fear not to touch the best;
The truth shall be thy warrant:
Go, since I needs must die,
And give the world the lie.

Sir Walter Raleigh, *The Lie*

PROLOGUE

THE MERCILESS SUN BOILED IN A SILVER SKY. WAVES OF HEAT shimmered across the seething main deck of the becalmed galleon where the seven sailors knelt, heads bowed. As blood dripped from their noses on to their sweat-sodden undershirts, they muttered prayers in Spanish, their strained voices struggling to rise above the creaking of the hull timbers flexing against the green swell. Harsh light glinted off the long, curved blades pressed against each of their necks.

At the sailors' backs, the grey men waited in silence. Ghosts, they seemed at times, not there but there, their bone-white faces wreathed in shadow despite the unremitting glare. Oblivious of the sweltering heat, they wore grey leather bucklers, thick woollen breeches and boots, all silver-mildewed and reeking of rot. As still as statues, they were, drawing out the agony of the whimpering men before the swords would sweep down.

Captain Juan Martinez de Serrano knelt on the forecastle, watching the row of seamen from under heavy brows. Even now he could not bring himself to look into the terrible faces of the ones who had boarded his vessel. Aft, the grey sails of the other galleon billowed and the rigging cracked, although there was no wind and had not been for three days. Serrano lowered his head in desolation. How foolish they had been. Though they knew the devils of the Unseelie Court were like wolves, the lure of gold was too great. The captain cast his mind back to that night ten days gone when his men had staggered out of the forest with their stolen hoard. Barely could they believe they had escaped with their lives, and their laughter had rung out across the waves as they filled the hold and dreamed of the glory that would be lavished upon them by King Philip in Madrid. They had set sail with a fair wind and all had seemed well, until the grey sails appeared on the horizon, drawing closer by the hour.

The steel bit into his neck and he winced. They should have known better. Now, save for the last eight of them, blood soaked into the boards of the quarterdeck where they lay, each one slaughtered within moments, though they were among the fiercest fighters upon the Spanish Main.

A rhythmic rattling stirred him. Raising his eyes once more, he watched a strange figure approach. The sound came from trinkets and the skulls of mice and birds braided into long gold and silver-streaked hair. Hollow cheeks and dark rings under his eyes transformed his features into a death's-head. He wore grey-green robes covered with unrecognizable symbols outlined in a tracing of gold that glistered in the midday sun, like one of the gypsy conjurers who performed at the fair in Seville. Sweeping out his right arm, he addressed Serrano in a voice like cracking ice. 'You are honoured. Our King.'

Serrano swallowed. He sensed the new arrival before he

saw him, in a weight building behind his eyes and a queasy churn in his stomach. He closed his eyes. How long would this torment continue? A steady tread crossed the main deck and came to a halt in front of him. Silence followed.

When he had mouthed a prayer, the captain squinted. A pair of grey boots fell into view, and the fur-lined edge of a shimmering white cloak. He heaved his shaking head up, following that pristine cloth until he reached the head of the one who looked down on him. But the brutal sun hung behind the figure and the features were lost. Serrano was glad of that.

'I am Mandraxas, of the High Family, and until my sister is brought back to the land of peace, I hold the Golden Throne.' The voice sang like the wind in the high branches. Serrano could not believe it was the voice of a cruel man, until he remembered that this was not a man at all, but a creature with no understanding of compassion or gentleness or the kindnesses that tied mortals together. 'Who are you?'

The captain muttered his response, his mouth so dry he could barely form words.

'Your name means nothing,' the King replied. 'Who are you, who dares to trespass on our land and steal our gold? Who thinks you are our equal?' When Serrano failed to reply, Mandraxas continued, 'You were damned the moment you insulted us with your arrogance. Let Deortha show you what you truly are to us.' He waved a languid hand towards the main deck where the robed intruder waited. The robed one nodded, the skulls clacking in his hair, and the nearest swordsman whipped his blade into the air and plunged it into the sailor who knelt in front of him.

Serrano cried out as the seaman pitched forward across

the sandy boards. Deortha knelt beside the unmoving form, his lips and hands moving in harmony, and a moment later the slain sailor twitched, jerked and with a long shudder clawed his way upright. He swayed as if the ship rolled in a stormy sea, his dead eyes staring.

'*Por Dios*,' Serrano exclaimed, sickened.

'Meat and bones,' Mandraxas said. 'No wits remain, and so these juddering things are of little use to us apart from performing the most mundane tasks.' He waved a fluttering hand towards Deortha. 'Over the side with it,' he called. 'Let it spend eternity beneath the waves.'

The captain screwed up his eyes at the splash, silently cursing the terrible judgement that had doomed them all. 'Let this be done with,' he growled in his own language.

Mandraxas appeared to understand. 'There will be no ending for any of you here,' he said in a voice laced with cold humour. 'You, all of you, will join your companion with the fishes, never sleeping, never dreaming, seeing only endless blue but never understanding.' His words rang out so that all the sailors heard him. 'But, for the rest of your kind, their ending is almost upon them. Listen. Can you hear the beat of us marching to war? Listen.'

A sword plunged down; a body crashed upon the deck. And another, and another, the steady rhythm moving inexorably towards Serrano. He sobbed. It was too late for him, too late for all mankind if the cold fury of these fiends was finally unleashed.

'In England now, the final act unfolds,' Mandraxas said above the beat of falling bodies. 'And so your world winds down to dust.'

Serrano looked up as the shadow fell across him.

CHAPTER ONE

BEDLAM RULED IN THE EIGHT BELLS INN. TRANQUILLITY WAS for landmen who sat by warm firesides in winter and took to their beds early, not for those who braved seas as high and as hard as the Tower's stone walls. Here was life like the ocean, fierce and loud and dangerous. Delirious with drink, two wild-bearded sailors lurched across the rushes, thrashing mad music from fiddle and pipe. With shrieks of laughter, the pockmarked girls from the rooms upstairs whirled around in each other's arms, their breasts bared above their threadbare dresses. The rolling sea-shanty crashed against the barks of the drunken men clustered in the shadowy room. In hazy candlelight, they hunched over wine-stained tables or squatted against whitewashed walls, swearing and fighting and gambling at cards. Ale sloshed from wooden cups on to the boards, and the air reeked of tallow and candle-smoke, sweat and sour beer. The raucous voices sounded lustful, but underneath the discourse odd, melancholic notes seemed to suggest men clinging on to life before they returned to the harsh seas.

When the door rattled open to admit a blast of salty

night air, the din never stilled and no eyes turned towards the stranger. He was wrapped in a grey woollen cloak, his features partially hidden beneath the wide brim of a felt hat. Behind him, across the gleaming cobbles of the Liverpool quayside, a carrack strained at its moorings, ready for sail at dawn. The creak of rigging merged with the lapping of the tide.

The new arrival closed the door behind him and demanded a mug of ale from the innkeeper's trestle. A seat in one of the shadowy corners called to him, away from the candlelight, where he could watch and listen unnoticed. If they had not been addled by drink, some of the seamen might have recognized the strong face from the pamphlets, the close-clipped beard and black hair curling to the nape of the neck, the dark eyes the colour of rapier steel.

Will Swyfte was a spy, *England's greatest spy*, so those pamphlets called him, *the bane of the Spanish dogs*. Only the highest in the land knew his reputation was carefully constructed for a country in need of heroes to keep the sleep of goodly men and women free from nightmares of Spanish invaders and Catholic plotters, and other, darker things too. Swyfte cared little. He did his dark work for Queen and country without complaint, but kept his own machinations close.

He sipped his drink and waited. As the reel of the shanty ebbed and flowed, he caught snatches of slurred conversation. Tall tales of haunted galleons and the clutching hands of dead sailors. Of cities of gold hidden in the lush forests of the New World. Of a misty island that came and went as if it were alive. Of golden lights glimmering far out across the waves and far down in the black deeps. Through the eyes of the sailors, the world was a far stranger place than their land-locked fellows believed; and Will Swyfte knew the sea-dogs were correct. They had sailed to the dark shores of life, where the truth lived, and had paid a price for their wisdom. The spy noted the leather patches over missing eyes, the lost legs and hands, the scars that drew maps of the world across their skin. He felt a kinship. Like him, they were cut off from the peace and order that most experienced, although his own wounds were not so easily seen.

He thought back more than a week to Nonsuch Palace, a day's ride to the south-west from London's fetid streets. While the Queen recovered her strength in her bed, under the observance of the Royal Physician, turmoil reigned throughout the grand building. Servants scoured the chambers and searched the grounds. The Privy Council had been cloistered in the meeting room for more than an hour when the knock had come at Will's chamber door.

His assistant, Nathaniel Colt, had been waiting on the threshold, flushed from running through corridors warmed by the late autumn sun. His dark green doublet was stained with sweat under the armpits and his brown hair lay slick against his head. 'Sir Robert sent word from the Privy Council meeting to summon you to his chambers,' he gasped. 'There was fear in his eyes, and his voice wavered. Is this it, then, Will? Invasion? Our enemies are marching towards us?'

The spy hid his true thoughts with a grin. 'Nat, you worry like an old maid. Do you see me rushing to arms?' Enemies, yes, but not the ones Nat feared. Not the Spanish, nor their Popish agitators. No, he meant the true Enemy – those who lived by night, and treated men as men did cattle.

'I do not see you rushing to a flask of sack, and that worries me more.'

Will rested a reassuring hand on the young man's shoulder. 'England lurches from crisis to crisis, as always, but we stand firm and we abide. This will pass.'

His words seemed to reassure Nat a little. Will left him resting by the open window and made his way through the noisy palace. Lucky Nat, who slept well at night. He saw only glimpses of the greater war. Will sheltered him from the worst horrors for the sake of his wits, and would continue to do so while there was breath left in him.

The spymaster's door was hanging open when Will arrived. Fresh from the Privy Council meeting, Sir Robert Cecil was firing orders at a clutch of scribes and assistants as he marched around the chamber. The Queen called him her Little Elf because of his small stature and his hunched back, but his sharp wits and cunning were more than a match for any other man at court. He had a feel for the games of high office, and his ruthlessness made him both feared and powerful.

When the black-gowned secretary saw Will, he dismissed the bustling aides and closed the door. 'Gather your men,' he snapped, feigning calm with a lazy wave of his hand. 'You ride north today in search of Dr Dee.'

'You know his whereabouts?'

'A carriage was seen travelling along the Great North Road. I received word back this morning that it has taken a turn towards Liverpool.'

'You are sure?'

'Yes.' Unable to contain the apprehension he felt, the spymaster turned away to calm himself. 'Dr Dee was seen in the company of that Irish whore, Red Meg O'Shee. They must be stopped before she spirits him away to her homeland. If they reach that land of bogs and mists, we will never see Dee again. And then . . .'

England will fall, Will completed the unspoken thought. Dee was the architect of the country's defences. He worked his magics to keep at bay the supernatural forces that had tormented England for as long as men had walked the green fields, and the Irish chieftains had long envied that protection; they had suffered long and hard under the torments of the Fair Folk. But whatever wall Dee had constructed around England with his ancient words of power and candles and circles had been crumbling. Dee was the only man who could repair those defences. Without him, the night would sweep in.

'The threat is greater than you know.' Cecil bowed his head for a moment, choosing his words carefully. 'The mad alchemist has in his possession an object of great power. For years he denied all knowledge of it. But shortly before he was spirited away, he confided in me that he had used it to commune with angels.'

'Angels?' Will laughed. 'I have heard those tales, but Dee is most definitely not on their side.'

'This is a grave matter,' the spymaster snapped, a twitching hand leaping to his flushed brow. 'Should this object fall into the hands of our enemies, there will be no laughter.'

Will poured himself a cup of romney from a jug on a trestle table littered with charts and documents. 'Then tell me the nature of this threat.'

'It is a looking glass.'

The spy peered over the rim of his cup, saying nothing.

'No ordinary glass, this. An obsidian mirror, supposedly shaped by sorcerers of an age-old race who once inhabited the impenetrable forests of the New World.'

Will furrowed his brow. He remembered Dee showing him this mundane-looking object at his chamber in Christ's College in Manchester, where he had, no doubt, been tormenting the poor brothers. 'Brought back to Europe in a Spanish hoard?'

Cecil's eyes narrowed. 'Legend says it could set the world afire, if one only knew how to unlock its secrets.'

The spy drained his cup. 'Very well. I will take John Carpenter, the Earl of Launceston and our new recruit, young Tobias Strangewayes. We will ride hard, but Red Meg has a good start on us.'

The spymaster narrowed his eyes. 'You allowed Mistress O'Shee into your circle. You trusted her, though you knew she was a spy—'

'I would not use that word. Tolerated, perhaps. I understood her nature, sir, and I am no fool.'

'Is that correct? I heard that you were more than associates. I need assurances that this woman has not bewitched your heart or your prick. If that were so, I would despatch another to bring her back.'

'There is no one better.'

'You have never been shy in trumpeting your own achievements, Master Swyfte,' Sir Robert said with pursed lips. 'Nevertheless, I would rather send a lesser man I can trust to succeed in this most important . . . nay, utterly vital . . . work than one who will be led by lust to a disaster that will damn us all to Hell.'

'I am no fool,' Will repeated, setting aside his own uncertainty regarding his feelings for the Irish spy. 'There is too much at stake here for such distractions.'

'I am pleased to hear you say it.' The spymaster ran the gold-ringed fingers of his right hand across his furrowed brow. 'If Dee leaves our protected shores, he will be prey for the Unseelie Court, and the repercussions of that are something I dare not countenance.'

Will left the cold chamber with fire in his heart. Within the hour, he and his men were riding north as hard as their steeds could bear. Red Meg would expect him to be on her trail – she was as sly a vixen as he had ever known – and she would not make it easy to recover Dee. He had seen her kill without conscience. Even the affection she felt for him would not stand in the way of her carrying such a great prize back to her homeland.

Braying laughter jolted Will back to the Eight Bells. The musicians had put away their instruments and were swigging malmsey wine in great gulps. The girls flopped into laps or draped themselves over shoulders in search of the night's earnings. Arguments sparked. Punches were thrown.

Dee's knowledge was dangerous and he needed to be returned to London at all costs, that was certain. But the alchemist revelled in misdirection and illusion, the spy knew. Was this mirror truly the threat Cecil feared? Or in this time of uncertainty had the spymaster simply given in to superstition and fear? Will shrugged. The world was filled with worries, and the truth would present itself sooner or later.

Once he had drained his ale, he selected his subject, a balding seaman with wind-chapped cheeks and a scrub of white hairs across his chin. Nursing a mug, the man leaned against the wall next to the stone hearth, eyeing the flames with the wistful look of someone who knew it was a sight he'd not see again for long weeks. He looked drunk enough for his guard to be low, but not so inebriated that he could not provide useful information. Keeping the brim of his hat down, the spy demanded another drink and walked over.

Will rested one Spanish leather boot on the hearth and watched the fire for a moment before he said, 'I have never met a man of the sea who was not interested in adding to his purse. Are you that rare creature?'

'Depends what you need doing,' the man slurred.

'All I require are words.'

The sailor's gaze flickered over Will. He seemed untroubled by what he saw. 'Ask your questions.'

'I seek news of two new arrivals in Liverpool who may be requiring passage to Ireland. A woman with hair as fiery as her nature and a tongue that cuts sharper than any dagger. And a man . . .' The spy paused. How to describe Dr Dee in a way that would do the magician justice? 'White hair, blazing eyes, a fierce temper, and a slippery grip on the world we all enjoy. He may have been wearing a coat of animal pelts.'

'I have heard tell of them, an Abraham man, mad as a starved dog, accompanied by his daughter,' the sailor grunted. 'The woman cut off the ear of Black Jack Larch, so I was told. His only crime was to lay a hand upon her arm and ask for a piece of the comfort she promised.'

'That would be Red Meg.'

The seaman smacked his lips, watching Will's hand. The spy unfolded his fingers to reveal a palmful of pennies.

Snatching the coins the man continued, 'They bought passage to Ireland on the *Eagle*, sailing at dawn. Wait at the quayside and you will see them.'

'I would prefer to surprise them before sunrise. Where do they stay?'

'The woman took Black Jack's shell outside Moll Higgins's rooming house. You could do worse than to seek them there.'

'You have earned yourself another drink. Go lightly on the waves.' Will gave a faint bow of the head and turned towards the door. He found his way blocked by three men, hands hanging close to their weapons.

'What 'ave we 'ere, then? A customs man come to spy on us?' the middle one growled. His left eye was milky, a jagged scar running from the corner to his jaw. He wore an emerald cap and his voice had the bark of authority; a first mate, perhaps, Will thought.

'Why, you are good honest seamen. I could find no rogues or smugglers here,' Will replied, his tone as laconic as his gaze was sharp. 'Step aside. My business here is done and I will disturb your drinking no more.' He knew any sign of weakness would only encourage the drunken men further.

The sailor's one good eye flickered from left to right, and in an instant strong hands gripped Will's arms. Someone tore off his hat. The sailor whisked a dagger from the folds of his dirty linen shirt and pressed the tip under the spy's chin, forcing his head up. A blast of ale-sour breath washed over Will as the man searched his features. Silence fell across the rest of the inn. The other drinkers crowded round.

One of the women leaned in, her eyes narrowing. 'I know 'im,' she said in a broad accent. 'That's Will Swyfte, that is.

England's greatest spy.' A lascivious smile sprang to her lips. 'I would see the length of your sword, chuck.'

'Later, in the privacy of your chamber, perhaps. Let us not point up how dull are the blades of these fine men.' He held her gaze and her smile broadened.

'The great Will Swyfte,' the one-eyed man mocked. 'The dewy-eyed women and the witless fieldworkers might be easily dazzled by your exploits, but here you are just another sharp nose poking into our business.'

'Your business concerns me less than the contents of your privy. I am troubled by greater matters: the security of this realm.'

'Stick 'im now. We'll dump him in the drink and no one'll be the wiser,' another sailor said. 'Let 'im walk out and we'll be swarming with tax collectors like rats on the bilge deck.'

Will's dark eyes flickered over the leering, grizzled faces pressing all round him. He had been here before, too many times, and whether he was looking into the eyes of Spanish pikemen or Kentish cut-throats, he knew the signs; there was no point in further talk.

Wrenching his shoulders back, he unbalanced the two men gripping his arms. With one sharp thrust, he planted a boot in the gut of the sailor wielding the knife. The milky-eyed seaman doubled over with a forced exhalation. Will saw that the drunken sailors were taken by surprise by the suddenness of his movement, and smiled. Sober, they would be a formidable army of cut-throats. Soaked in ale, they wheeled around like small children.

Tearing his arms free, the spy lashed one foot under a three-legged stool and heaved it into the face of his former captor. Bone shattered, blood sprayed. A roar rang up to the rafters. Squealing whores ran for the rickety stairs at the back of the inn. The seamen drew daggers and hooks, each weapon glinting in the candlelight. The men surged forward.

Will felt the familiar heart-rush. He drew his rapier, enjoying the familiar feel and weight in his hand. With one bound, he leapt from a bench to the innkeeper's cluttered trestle. Cups flew. Coin jangled on to the boards.

'Who will be the first to feel the bite of my blade?' he called, kicking the barrel. The wooden tap burst free, the honey-coloured ale gushing out. The keg spun off the table and into the path of the onrushing seamen.

The spy felt no desire to kill any of these rogues; he wished to save his steel for more deserving blood. But they swarmed around him like angry bees, eager to sting him to death. It was as he searched for a route past them that the flagstones began to vibrate as though the trestle were being dragged over cobbles. The sailors came to a sudden halt, eyeing each other with unease. Across the inn, the candle flames sputtered and shuddered as one. Shadows swooped. Breath clouded as a winter chill descended. The sailors murmured, casting anxious glances all around. One by one they put away their weapons.

Through the small, square windowpanes, distorted lantern-light danced in an unnatural manner from the carrack. A moment later, the door crashed open. The master of the quay lurched into the space, his hat askew, his face drained of blood. 'Take up your weapons and any light you can find,' he croaked. 'The devil has come with the fog.'

CHAPTER TWO

THE THICK FOG MUFFLED EVEN THE CREAKING OF THE SIGN above the entrance to the inn. Nothing of the quayside was visible, nor any of the lights of Liverpool beyond. Never had Will known such a dense mist to sweep in so quickly. In the time it had taken him to push his way past the quay master and find a hiding place outside, the grey folds had billowed in from the west, consuming all in their path.

He crouched behind the dank-smelling rain butt at the edge of the stone frontage, watching the sailors flood out of the inn and clatter across the cobbles with pitch-soaked brands to light their way. The fog swallowed them in an instant. Distorted calls and responses floated back, before they too were lost. They were simple men, easily frightened by things beyond their understanding. But Will suspected that whatever it was that accompanied the unnatural mist would dwarf their present fears.

Moisture dripped from the inn sign. An angry cry rang out from near the water's edge. A dull querying rejoinder from somewhere further afield, the splintering of break-ing wood: odd sounds, incomprehensible in their muted isolation. Will waited, his fingers clenched round the hilt of his rapier.

He sensed the strangers long before he saw them. His head throbbed, his stomach churned. Blood bubbled around his left nostril. Familiar signs, all of them. They were coming, those foul things that had thrown his entire life off its course. Cold anger burned in his chest as his thoughts took him back from that misty autumn night to the hot summer day in Warwickshire that he could never escape. Jenny was there, then, as she was always in his heart, waving to him across the cornfield, her dress the pure blue of forget-me-nots, brown hair tied back with a matching ribbon. One moment, frozen for ever, along with all the promises of shared summers yet to come. In the blink of an eye, she had vanished. No trace remained behind, no path through the corn to show where she had gone, no footprints. No body. Gone as if she had been whisked up to Heaven by a choir of angels.

Will peered round the water butt at the figures emerging from the folds of grey. No, it was these devils who had stolen Jenny away, he knew now. For what reason, he had no idea, and the mystery of it still sickened him. But never would he give up hope that she was still alive, whatever his friends said. Over the years he had learned enough to convince himself that she did still live, that she was a prisoner somewhere – perhaps across the sea, in the New World where men said the Unseelie Court made their home. Everything he did, every battle he fought, every sacrifice he made, was to find some way to bring Jenny home. She was all that mattered. Not his life and not, though he would never give voice to it in public, his Queen or country.

Four figures swooped forward with near-silent tread, at first almost as insubstantial as the fog that enshrouded them. But when a sailor sprawled across the glistening cobbles, they appeared to coalesce, and take on flesh and bone. Dread crept across the still quayside. Despite himself, Will felt the hairs on the back of his neck prickle. Here they were, the sum of all human fears since the days of the Flood: the grey men, the Fair Folk, the Fay; their names seemed endless, a way for mortals to skirt around the essential horror that lay at their heart. Three were swathed in grey cloaks and hoods, cold faces as pale as the first snows of winter and eyes black as coals. The fourth was the leader, Will was certain. He sported a beard and moustache waxed into points, and his black hair was long and sleek. His eyes were lost to shadow, but hard lines edged his mouth and when he smiled he revealed sharp teeth.

'My name is Lansing,' he murmured, looming over the fallen figure. 'Others are the wits of the High Family, or the cunning. I am the blade.' And he whispered into the terrified man's ear, whispered words that were poisonous and corrupt, words that piled horror upon horror – words that would drive a man mad. Will clenched his fingers round his sword-hilt tighter still, so that his knuckles grew white. He wished he could drive his blade into Fay flesh to ease his anger, though he knew he could never defeat four of them.

When the sailor curled on the cobbles whimpered, the spy recognized the balding man he'd talked to at the Eight Bells. At the same time, he heard the Fay lord say, 'Tell me now, while you can, where I will find this man, the sorcerer John Dee. Once we have him, there will be an end to this long strife and you will know peace. All of you.'

Will cursed under his breath. The words were comforting, their true meaning deeply disturbing. If the Unseelie Court hunted the alchemist so brazenly, then the matter was more grave than he had been led to believe. He could not afford to allow the hidden Enemy to reach Dee ahead of him, for then he would have seen the last of Elizabeth's conjurer, and most likely the last of England.

As Lansing continued to question his prisoner, Will lifted down the iron lantern beside the inn door, and wrapped his cloak around it to shield the moving light. He crept along the wall to the cover of the mounds of bales and spice-scented boxes that had been unloaded before sunset.

Running feet echoed close by. Orange light flared across the wall above his head, and he dropped to his haunches just in time. He could smell the acrid pitch-smoke and hear the sputtering of the brand. Three drunken sailors argued about what devils were loose in Liverpool. They would find out soon enough, Will thought.

Sneaking to where he could hear water lapping in the shadow of the great vessels at anchor, he used his nose to find the reeking barrel of pitch the shipwrights used to seal the hulls. He heaved the heavy butt on to its side and flung the lantern into the slopping contents. As the pitch ignited and the flames roared out, he rolled the barrel hard. The blazing keg hurtled across the quayside to where the Fay were cloaked by the fog.

Cries of alarm rang out along the water's edge. Blazing brands flickered in the dense bank of grey cloud like fireflies on the wing, circling back to where the burning barrel painted the fog orange. The Unseelie Court worked their cruelties best in the shadows. No doubt they would melt away long before the fear-filled sailors discovered them. But had he done enough to disrupt their interrogation before they discovered Dee's whereabouts?

As the tumult swept towards the crackling fire, Will raced into the rat's nest of narrow streets leading away from the dock. The ghost of the Unseelie Court still lingered, a cold breath on the neck in a midnight churchyard. The town was dark, but his mood was darker still.

CHAPTER THREE

LIVERPOOL TUMBLED AWAY DOWN THE HILLSIDE TOWARDS the River Merse where the thick fog bank held its breath, waiting. Yet above the town the night was clear, the Everton Beacon stark against the starry sky. Moonlight limned the blue-tiled rooftops. Candle flames glowed in diamond-pane windows. Here was life, grubby and bloody and loud. Down on James Street, not far from the black bulk of the Old Castle, packs of sailors roamed like dogs from stew to tavern, lured by the fresh meat calls of the competing whores displaying their breasts in the lamplit doorways. Snarls and snapping punctuated the drunken laughter. Bruised knuckles crashed against jaws as rivals brawled, rolling among the contents of emptied chamberpots to the baying of their yellow-toothed fellows.

Liverpool stank of brine and cesspits and smoke.

One desperate doxy keen to earn her bed for the night ventured into the shadowed alley where she had glimpsed three men lurking. From the gloom, John Carpenter watched her approach. Pulling down the front of her dirty emerald dress, the rouge-smeared woman put on a seductive smile. 'Come hither, lads,' she called, hands on hips. 'The comfort of these thighs will give you sweet dreams when you're tossing away on the waves.'

When she saw one of the men step from the enveloping dark, she breathed a relieved sigh. Carpenter knew her thoughts: a few moments of grunting was a small price to pay for a good night's rest. And the well-cut grey doublet and grey woollen cloak, free of stains and wear, suggested a gentleman, no less. Then a shaft of light from the lantern over the door of the White Hart struck his companion's face and she all but cried out. His skin was bloodless, and his dark eyes held a hellish glow.

'Away, you pox-ridden whore,' Robert, Earl of Launceston, ordered in a voice like autumn leaves. 'Trouble us no more or feel the prick of my dagger – and not the kind you are used to.'

Realizing it was a man after all and no grim spectre, the doxy cursed at the shock she had been given. She turned to summon the sailors to teach this elf-skinned scut a lesson. Before she could cry out, Carpenter leapt from the shadows and placed one hand on her mouth to stop her. His hazelnut doublet was of a rougher cut than his fellow's, but still clean, and though his long, dark hair fell oddly across the left side of his face, he eased a charming smile on to his lips to soothe her. He pressed a silver coin into her grimy palm and released his hand from her mouth.

'My friend has poor manners, mistress. He knows not what it is like to work hard for a living,' he said, with a bow. 'Take this and buy yourself a night off your back.'

The woman giggled and curtsied, flashing one fleeting murderous glare at the Earl as she darted towards the inn to spend her earnings on drink. Once she had gone, Carpenter turned on the noble and hissed, 'Sometimes I think you are more of a threat than our enemies.'

'I am heartened to learn that you think. 'Twas my assumption that you had the wits of a hound, running round in circles yapping and baring your teeth before hunting for food and sleep.' The Earl peered past his fellow spy with studied disinterest, searching the passing faces for the missing Dee. He was a gaunt man, slim but powerful, yet even those who did not know him recognized that there was something askew, something strange about the way his cold gaze penetrated as though he were peering through skin and muscle to see the sticky organs within, or the manner in which his hand twitched towards his hidden dagger with unsettling regularity.

'I should give thanks that you did not slit her throat there and then,' Carpenter sneered. He pulled his black cap low over his eyes. 'One full day without you trying to skewer an innocent. Let us celebrate!' He felt weary from the effort of restraining his companion's murderous instincts and exhausted by the lonely, unceasing work of the spy. He wanted to be free of that world; even the mundane life of a book-keeper held its attractions, or that of a tailor. Anything. Unconsciously, he scratched the scars that marred his face beneath the fall of his hair, the mark of the thing that had attacked him in Muscovy and a constant reminder of the price this business exacted from him.

'You bicker like old women,' the third man in the alley whispered. Tobias Strangewayes was new to their band, as raw as a country apprentice. Red-headed and wiry, the younger man had fancied himself as good a spy and

31

swordsman as Will Swyfte. But when he discovered the true nature of the threat they faced, his arrogance was blunted. Strangewayes still thought highly of himself; he proudly showed off the blue silk lining of his cloak, like some fop parading in Paul's Walk, but Carpenter knew he could be relied upon in a fight.

'And you keep a civil tongue in your head or else I will cut it out,' Launceston breathed. Strangewayes scowled in response.

The strain was taking its toll on all of them, Carpenter could see, those wearying hours in the saddle riding north from Nonsuch Palace, and then the futile search for Dee through Liverpool's dingy streets. They were starting to tear at each other like caged curs. Blades needed to be drawn and traitors carved, blood stirred and thoughts that fed upon themselves driven out.

'We are all defined by our nature,' he muttered to himself.

'Since dawn we have watched these streets without any reward,' Strangewayes complained. 'That Irish slut has taken to her rooms, wherever they might be, and she will stay there until she can board the ship with her prize and gain the protection of a crew of cock-led apple-johns.'

'And then it will be too late,' Carpenter snapped. 'We will never see Dee again, and this land will be overrun by the things that walk with printless feet and cast no shadows on this earth. And then you, you red-headed puttock, will know what it is like to thrash in the throes of a nightmare from which you can never wake.'

'I am a good Christian man, and I have the shield of God above to protect me,' the younger spy announced, his chin raised in defiance of his seasoned companions.

Launceston and Carpenter exchanged a glance and each gave a dismissive shrug.

'You have no faith in anything,' Strangewayes continued, his cheeks growing red. 'You drink to excess, you gamble, you dally with whores . . .'

'The world is harsh and you must take comfort wherever you find it,' Carpenter said, secretly wishing he had the other man's spirit.

'My heart is only for Grace. I need no other woman.' The red-headed spy pushed past the two other men and strode to the edge of the reeking alley. 'I believe there is more to this life than the filth and the misery we see around us. A higher purpose, hidden yet in plain sight, if we only had eyes to see it.'

'You are a true spy,' Launceston mocked in a dry tone, 'always seeing a face behind the one presented to the world.'

'The plan has not yet been revealed to us, but that does not mean it is not there. And, yes, we are spies and we should be used to peering beneath the surface for deeper truths. But you two have been worn down by the meagre diet of deceit and death. You turn your eyes away from the light and see only shadows.'

Carpenter could not disagree.

'Hrrrm.' The familiar breathy sound, like a death rattle, rolled along the alleyway; Launceston had seen something that had struck him as curious.

'What is it?' Carpenter asked.

The Earl was looking up at the thin sliver of night sky between the eaves where a few stars sparkled. 'Someone passed overhead,' he said.

'On the rooftops?'

Launceston nodded.

Carpenter joined Strangewayes and the Earl at the edge of the alley and craned his neck up. The rooftops were a jumble of thatch and tile and plain wood, a silhouetted confusion of angular shapes against the lighter sky. Conditioned by years of strife, the spy feared the worst. The three men spun in a slow gyre, searching the eaves. 'Nothing,' Carpenter said after a moment. 'You were mistaken.'

'I am never mistaken.' Launceston stepped out into the muddy street to get a better look. 'There,' he said, pointing.

Carpenter gazed along the line of his companion's arm and glimpsed fleeting movement along the pitch of a tavern roof in the buttery glow of the moon.

'There, too,' Strangewayes asserted, waving a hand towards the roofs on the other side of the street.

Carpenter could see them clearly now. To the casual eye they could have been moon-shadows. What those flitting shapes truly were, he was in no doubt. 'The Unseelie Court are abroad in force,' he said. The cold of that long-gone Muscovy night reached deep into his bones once more.

'Here?' Strangewayes whispered. 'Though England's defences have weakened in recent times, they risk too much by being out in such a populous place.'

'Like any man, they will risk anything if the stakes are high enough,' Launceston murmured.

His words disappeared into a clamour exploding along the street at the three men's backs. Men and women rushed towards a swelling crowd near the entrance to one of the rat-runs cutting through the jumble of houses.

'What now?' Carpenter growled, his skin prickling

with suspicion. As he edged towards the churning crowd, he heard the curious queries from the front turn to fearful cries, then yells of alarm. Shadows crossed faces caught in the flickering pale light from the iron lanterns over the stew doors. Eyes widened. Lips drew back from stained teeth. At the front of the crowd, heads spun away from whatever had been discovered. The ripple of concern broke into a wave of horror, the men and women in the first ranks driving the others away from the black entrance to the alley. Crying to God, they sheltered in doorways where they watched with frightened eyes.

Carpenter and Launceston thrust the last stragglers aside and drew their rapiers. Strangewayes unhooked the rusty chain of a lantern from the wall beside the White Hart door and raised the wavering light aloft. The night swept away, but the black mouth of the rat-run remained impenetrable. The three men stood for a moment at its edge. Silence fell across the street.

Carpenter advanced with a measured step, his blade held for a quick thrust. Launceston was at his shoulder, and the younger spy loomed behind, the lantern swaying from side to side.

From the dark echoed a strangled sound that a man might make with a hand clamped across his mouth.

'Step into the light,' Carpenter called.

The snuffling grew more intense, but no man ventured out where he could be seen.

'It tries to draw us in,' Strangewayes whispered.

Carpenter wavered. A trap, perchance? Steeling himself, he stepped into the dark.

Rats scampered away from the tread of his leather shoes.

He smelled urine and rotting food scraps. Deep in the dark, a pale shape shifted. The animal noises grew louder still, almost drowning out Strangewayes' ragged breathing.

'Raise the lantern,' he ordered.

He flinched as the light danced over two forms pressed against the wattle wall. They were locked in an embrace, a seaman, his wiry hair flecked with grey, his breeches round his ankles, and a whore, her skirts pulled up, her pale legs wrapped around her partner's waist. In the midst of their coitus, their lips were forced together in an open-mouthed kiss. Creeping horror turned Carpenter's skin to gooseflesh. The man and the woman were fused together, their flesh melting into each other where he thrust into her, and where his hands gripped her white arms. *And their mouths*, Carpenter thought, realizing the source of the snuffling noise. Two heads, joined as one; their kiss would now never end. Wide eyes ranged in wild panic, pleading for help. Their combined grunts sounded more beast than mortal, but he heard their desperation clearly.

There was no helping them, he knew. The Unseelie Court left no hope in their wake, only suffering.

'Put them out of their misery,' Launceston breathed.

Carpenter raised his rapier, but could not bring himself to strike.

'I have no qualms.' The Earl pushed the other man aside. With two thrusts of his dagger, he completed his task, then stood over the fallen shape. 'The beast with two backs,' he breathed. 'They like their sport, our Enemy.'

'We will be wanted for murder now,' Strangewayes protested.

Launceston looked at him through slit eyes. 'You would

36

have left them to their agonies? We are honourable men, despite all appearances.'

'You saw the onlookers,' Carpenter muttered. 'The beadle will not be informed. They will burn the bodies and pretend this atrocity never happened, though it haunt their sleep for evermore. Now, come.' Sheathing his rapier, he prowled out of the rat-run and along the street. He felt the eyes of the silent seamen and doxies upon his back, all of them at once despising him yet relieved too.

'I see no movement now,' Strangewayes said, looking around the rooftops.

Carpenter grimaced. 'Our Enemy wished to divert prying eyes from their true intentions. We have already fallen behind.'

CHAPTER FOUR

A GLITTERING CONSTELLATION DANCED ACROSS THE WORM-holed ceiling beams. The silver-bearded old man squatted on a stool by the empty hearth, watching the shifting stars with a childlike wonder etched into his wrinkled face. It looked as if he were seeing through the upper storeys of the rooming house and out into the vast unknown. Dr John Dee, alchemist, inventor, sorcerer and astrologer to the court of Queen Elizabeth of England, wore a cloak stitched from the pelts of woodland animals, every head still attached so that he appeared to be swarming with wildlife. Beneath it, skulls of birds and mice hung from silver chains looped across the chest of his purple gown. Every time he shifted, their rattle broke the stillness of the room. His slender fingers cupped a circular mirror made of polished obsidian. As he turned it back and forth, the glass caught the flames of the candles and threw pinpricks of light across the damp plaster of the bedchamber.

From the small, square window overlooking the dark rooftops of Liverpool, Meg O'Shee studied her companion's entranced expression. Soon the herb-inflicted stupor would begin to wear off. She would need to administer another dose of the potent concoction that had kept Dee supine since she had spirited him away from Nonsuch Palace more than a week ago. She felt uneasy about stealing a man's wits for so long – she had seen others never regain them – but Dee with a clear head was too dangerous a prospect for her to consider.

The Irish spy was dressed in a bodice and skirt of black and gold, the more easily to disappear into the shadows of the filthy town's dark alleys. She hated it there, but she had suffered worse places. As she combed her auburn hair, Meg dreamed of her home, a short journey across the turbulent waters. Too long had it been since she had walked in the fields of her youth, but prices aplenty had been demanded of her since she had set out to steal England's greatest treasure. And once Dee had built his magical defences and Ireland was free of the predations of the Unseelie Court, there would be such a celebration! No more death and misery, no more crops blighted and cattle stricken for mere sport. No more children stolen from their cribs and replaced by mewling straw things. Peace, for the first time in generations.

And then all her sacrifices would be worthwhile. She repeated those words in her head, but still they did not catch fire. Her thoughts spun back to Will Swyfte, and the merry jig they had danced together while calamity unfolded on every side. Annoyed with herself, she tossed the comb aside. Why was she so loath to leave their wild courtship behind? Her life would be so much easier – and certainly much safer – if she put him out of her mind.

Lightning flashed on the horizon. The church bells clanged in the rising gale. First fog, now an approaching storm? Meg peered out of the window and murmured a prayer that the inclement weather would clear before the dawn's sailing. The end of this lethal business could not come soon enough.

She noticed that the flickering lights around her had come to a halt, and she turned back to her prisoner. Dee now sat immobile, peering deep into the looking glass. His wondering expression had grown taut. Meg felt a flutter of apprehension. Moving to the corner of the room, she opened the sack in which she kept her herbs and balm, her mortar and pestle, her lock-picks and the knotted cord she had once used to throttle the life from a man twice her size. She could have the concoction ground into paste in a matter of moments, ready to apply to the inside of Dee's cheek. One stray thought troubled her: what if Dee had been feigning his bewitchment and the effects of the potion had long since started to wear off? The alchemist was cunning, but could even he control the ebb and flow of the fading enchantment?

The sorcerer began to murmur as if speaking to his reflection, the unintelligible susurration rustling out into the corners of the chamber.

Meg tensed. Once, in a dirty tavern in some forgotten village in the Midlands, she had used her charms to encourage him to teach her simple magics, and he had shown her how to use a glass to commune with another, miles distant. She closed her fingers round the dagger hidden in the folds of her skirt. If the alchemist was using this mirror to call for help, she would take off a finger or an ear or a nose if she had to.

After a moment, Meg decided Dee was no threat. She

delved into her sack and withdrew a bunch of wilting herbs and the mortar. When she looked up again, her breath caught in her throat. Dee had stood silently and was peering at the wall as if he could see through it. The looking glass lay upon the bed.

'Stay calm, my love,' she whispered in honeyed tones, 'and I will stroke your brow and soothe away all your worries.' Usually the alchemist fell under the spell of her voice and returned to his dazed state, but this time he dropped to his knees and brushed aside the rushes on the floor with a feverish intensity. Meg watched him at work, wondering what strange thoughts were running through his head. He seemed oblivious of her presence. In all the time she had administered her concoction, never had she seen this reaction before.

Dipping into a hidden pocket in his cloak of furs, Dee withdrew a piece of chalk and began to draw a circle on the boards. His feverish fingers flew across the familiar design, inscribing inexplicable symbols at points along the arc.

Meg stroked his long hair. 'You are troubled, my love,' she pressed, her tone a little more insistent than she had intended. 'Put aside these things and return to the bed. Enjoy the pleasures of my thighs one final time before sleep.'

Dee ignored her, the first time he had refused her charms. She felt worried by the alchemist's actions now. He seemed possessed, his eyes glinting with an inner fire.

Finally he stopped his inscribing, squatting in the centre of the chalk circle. Her hand felt for her dagger once more. If she had to, she could wound him enough to incapacitate him until she had him aboard the ship bound for her homeland.

Before she could move, Dee's head jerked up and his eyes swivelled towards her. His lips unfurled from his yellowing teeth and he uttered one word, one sound that made no sense to her, but it made the heavens ring.

CHAPTER FIVE

THUNDER RUMBLED AWAY TO THE WEST. WILL PAUSED AT the end of the urine-reeking alley and glanced along the deserted high street. If the Unseelie Court were abroad there near the centre of Liverpool, they were keeping away from candles and lamps. He darted through the deep shadow under the overhanging eaves until he saw the grim faces of Launceston, Carpenter and Strangewayes. They waited for him at the assigned spot, in the lee of the silent stone bulk of the town hall.

'Good news, lads,' he said, forcing a cheery tone. 'Or not. Our Irish vixen has made her lair in one Moll Higgins's rooming house. Now the moment we dreaded must be addressed. Can we bear the lash of Dr Dee's sour tongue all the way back to London, or should we leave him to his fate? Make your case now, and be quick about it.'

'We have friends in Liverpool,' Launceston said in his familiar monotone. 'The kind of friends who would turn our bones to straw and mount us on sticks to scare the crows till Judgement Day.'

Will nodded. 'I encountered those pale fiends too. They

also search for Dee. The risks here are doubled, men. We must fly like arrows if we are to prevent this from becoming a disaster.' He looked round the solemn faces. Not one of them, not even the raw Tobias Strangewayes, gave a hint that a mere four spies was a poor force against the supernatural might of the Unseelie Court. Will felt proud of them. 'Come, then, good lads. There will be wine and doxies aplenty once this work is done.'

The spies weaved through the deserted streets back towards the jumble of stews and inns near the quayside. The night-time drunken revelry had started up again. Shouts and singing and the calls of women rang over the rooftops. Carpenter demanded directions from a whore pissing in the street and within moments they were picking their way among rat-infested rubbish heaps in pitch-black alleys where the eaves almost closed over their heads.

Moll Higgins's rooming house squatted on the edge of the dockside squalor. It was the perfect hideaway for the Irish spy and her charge, Will thought: close enough to reach the ship speedily, but far enough away from the bustle of the port to maintain a degree of anonymity. It was a tall house of four storeys, leaning in a precarious manner down the slope as if it were about to skid towards the water. Spice-smelling merchants' stores jammed hard against it.

Will looked up at the dingy whitewashed walls. Most of the small windows were dark, but a candle flickered in one on the second floor and another in the roof. The storm rolled around the town, throwing off spears of lightning and clashes of thunder. The wind tugged at his hair, slamming shutters and unlatched doors.

Beside him, Launceston and Carpenter were watching

the rooftops for any sign of the Unseelie Court. Strange-wayes stood a few paces down the slope, watching for an attack at their backs.

'They are here,' Carpenter said in a flat, low voice. Blood dripped from his nose, and Will could feel the familiar knot in the pit of his stomach as his senses rebelled against the alien presences that drew near. Across the roofs, grey shapes began to flicker against the night sky, circling, like wolves.

'No time to lose now,' he whispered, drawing his rapier. He felt comforted by the weight of the steel in his hand. 'In and out with Dee. Cut down any who stand in our way.'

'And that includes the Irish woman?' Carpenter asked with a pointed stare.

Will hesitated for only the briefest moment. 'If she stands in our way.' *Meg will not sacrifice her life for even a treasure like Dee*, he thought; he hoped.

The moon chose that instant to break through the roiling clouds, and as Will glanced up one last time he glimpsed a sight that chilled his blood. With arms and legs spread out, grey figures crawled across the tiles and down vertiginous walls like spiders, drawing in upon the rooming house from all directions.

'I wish I had a fire to burn out this infestation,' Launceston hummed, 'even if it took down all Liverpool.'

Will snatched open the door that backed on to the alley and led the way into a small scullery that smelled of lamb fat and cheap beer. Dirty cooking pots from that evening's meal were stacked on a trestle to one side. Instantly, the spy recognized an unnatural feeling to the house. A chill hung in the air and intermittent tremors ran through the walls and floor under the old, dry rushes.

'What is wrong here?' Strangewayes hissed as he darted in behind the others and closed the door. He drew the bolt with a resonant clank.

Will sifted through his impressions for some clue to whatever was unnerving him. His face hardened, his eyes flickering around for any sign of threat. Raising his arm, he flicked his fingers forward and his men followed him without question, into a silent, cold kitchen and then into a hallway that smelled of damp. Everywhere was dark. A passage ran alongside a flight of ramshackle stairs. Though the gale whistled around the eaves, inside the house was so still it seemed devoid of life. Will felt troubled by the quiet – any rooming house was filled with a symphony of creaks, footsteps, snores and conversation for most hours of the day – and he could see from Carpenter's darting eyes that his companion felt the same.

'We go up,' he said.

The first board protested like a wheezing old man. They all halted, listening. When no response came, they continued to climb.

Halfway up the first flight, a throaty laugh rolled out just above them, low and resonant. Behind him, Will felt his men bristle, their rapiers at the ready. Will's eyes narrowed. He searched the dark at the top of the stairs for any sign of movement, and listened for a soft tread on the boards. After a moment of quiet, someone began to hum an old sea-song, a man's deep voice, the melody punctuated by another laugh.

The four spies looked at each other, curious.

Will bounded up the remaining steps and rounded on to the second flight. A man in a dirty undershirt and stained breeches slumped halfway up the rise, his head against the wall. His greasy brown hair hung lankly around his un-shaven face, but his eyes had rolled back so only the whites were visible. He waved one hand in front of his face as if in time to music, and then hummed the sea-song once more.

'Has he lost his wits?' Carpenter whispered. 'The Unseelie Court have already ventured within?'

'If not yet, then soon while we waste our time here gabbling,' Will hissed. He dropped low in front of the man's face until he smelled the ale-reeking breath. 'An Irish woman and an old man,' he demanded. 'Where are they?'

After a moment the man appeared to hear and raised one finger. 'The third,' he said. As Will made to push by, the man grabbed his arm and whispered, 'The eyes are afire. Say your prayers.' Will shook him off and looked up the stairs into the dark.

At the top of the second flight, he heard a clatter on the roof high overhead. Movement flashed past the small window beside him. A crash echoed from the cobbles below; a tile had been dislodged. He raised his eyes, listening, then signalled to the other men with his eyes that the Enemy had reached the rooming house.

'They go down as we climb up,' Launceston said without a hint of fear, 'and where in the middle shall we meet?'

At the top of the third flight, Will found a plump, pink-faced woman crumpled on the floor beside a younger man with the marks of the pox on his cheeks: Moll Higgins, perhaps, and the man another lodger. Both lived, but spittle drooled from the corners of their mouths and they looked right through him when he shook them.

'What has happened here? These are all fit for Bedlam,'

Strangewayes whispered. He knelt beside the woman and took her hand.

Will had no answer. The Unseelie Court still sought entry; this was the work of another. He wondered what terrible thing had happened here to drive the wits from the occupants. In the silence, dread seemed to drift down the stairs like the unnatural fog along the river.

Mistress Higgins and her lodger began to convulse, crying out in a language that no one recognized. As he climbed the stairs, Will frowned, forcing himself not to look back. Launceston held up a hand to bring them to a halt, but Will had already felt it: a cool draught sweeping down the stairs, smelling of the smoky night air. A window had slid open. The boards overhead creaked.

Catching a glimpse of uncertainty in Strangewayes' eyes, Will whispered, 'If we walk away and leave Dee to the Enemy, all will be lost; for England, for us. There will be no coming back for a second chance. We must do what we can, though our lives be forfeit.'

On the third floor, they searched the first two rooms, small and cramped, with beds that had not been slept in. The third was larger, but also empty. 'This is the place,' Will whispered, recognizing Meg's crimson taffeta dress hanging over the end of an unmade bed. While Carpenter crouched to peer underneath, Strangewayes moved to the window and glanced out. He shook his head: the Irish woman and her prisoner could not have escaped over the nearby roof-tops.

Another creak echoed above them. Will imagined grey figures prowling around the darkened top floor. Soon those *things* would begin to descend. He stilled his thoughts and looked around. Ropes that had clearly been used to restrain the astrologer were coiled in one corner with a blue silk gag on top. The rushes had been brushed aside and a circle had been chalked on the floor with mysterious signs scrawled around the perimeter. Had Meg allowed Dee to cast a spell, he wondered? Surely she would not have taken such a risk. But there was a fat candle, half burned, and the sweet scent of incense hung in the air.

His gaze fell upon the obsidian mirror, lying on its side beside Meg's bag. Such an object of power would never have been discarded so easily. He pushed past Carpenter to snatch up the looking glass. It was insignificant enough; few would have given it a second glance. But as he stared into the surface, cold prickled down his spine. He felt the weight of a presence looking back at him. Before he could dismiss the sensation, the glass misted, and a face began to form in the depths. A part of him wanted to hurl the mirror away, but he felt strangely gripped by what was revealing itself. And then the face formed and the shock jolted him.

It was Jenny, his Jenny, staring at him with wide, frightened eyes.

Carpenter jerked up, half raising his rapier in concern, but Will was caught in the grip of that vision. No illusion, this. So many years had passed since he had seen her, and yet it was Jenny as he remembered her, from that last day in the cornfield, brown hair tied back from her pale face. He reeled from the rush of emotions that accompanied the sight, the memories of quiet conversations at dusk, the sensation of her hand in his. And yet somehow he knew that this was Jenny now, and that she could see him as clearly as he saw her. Her eyes grew wider still when they took in his face, but if he expected a smile of relief, or love, he saw only worry in her features.

She vanished as quickly as she had appeared. Will almost cried out, pleading with her to return so he could see her for one moment longer, a moment that felt richer than any he had lived in the last ten years.

'What ails you?' Carpenter growled in annoyance.

Will began to explain, then caught himself. 'At least we have the mirror now,' he whispered, slipping it into the leather pouch at his side. 'Now, let us find Dee and be away from this haunted place.'

The window rattled in the grip of the gale that now buffeted the house. 'Perhaps they are long gone, and already aboard their ship,' Carpenter ventured.

Will eyed the taffeta dress and flashed a reassuring smile. 'Perhaps.' Raising his rapier, he stepped out of the chamber and prowled towards the final flight of stairs.

For one moment, he stood, looking up into the dark. All was still.

His breath locked in his chest. He levelled his rapier, twirling the tip once, then placed his foot upon the first step.

A high-pitched whine screeched across the upper floor. Will reeled against the flaking plaster of the wall, clutching his ears in agony. Steel barbs plunged into his head. He half glimpsed the other three men stumbling back with contorted features, hands pressed against their own ears.

A moment later, a boom resounded across the floor upstairs, bringing down a shower of dust. White light flared so brightly, Will wondered whether the house had been struck by lightning or a keg of gunpowder had exploded.

Bedlam erupted before he had a chance to gather his thoughts. Throat-rending shrieks ripped through the house, sounding unnervingly like the cries of ravens. More flashes of light, a billow of acrid smoke. The very foundations of the house seemed to shake.

Will grabbed the rocking banister to keep his feet. The violent tremors threw the other three men across the landing. A body burst out of one of the rooms on the final floor and wheeled down the steps to crash in a broken-limbed heap at the foot of the stairs. Fearing it was Dee, or Meg, the spy wrenched himself round.

Will felt his chest tighten in shock. The figure crumpled in front of him wore a grey shirt and breeches silvered with mildew, the cut echoing a fashion of a time long gone. The skin was bone-white, the cheeks cadaverous. The eyes had been burned out so that only charred black sockets stared back at him. He struggled to comprehend what had happened. Never had he seen one of the powerful Unseelie Court despatched so easily, so brutally. He yanked his head back to peer up the stairs through the swirling smoke, wondering what force wreaked havoc up there.

Another figure lurched from the open doorway at the top. Will glimpsed a flash of auburn hair, a pale face, a bodice and skirt of black and gold. Red Meg O'Shee clutched on to the banister, casting one wide-eyed glance back into the room she had left. Her mouth formed an O of horror. Will felt another wave of disbelief. This spy, so hardened by the fight against the English in her homeland, who had suffered all manner of threat to her life and well-being, gripped by terror.

Before he could call out to her, she propelled herself

down the stairs in desperation to escape what lay at her back. In a flurry of red hair and skirts, she crashed into him, fleeting surprise lost to mounting panic. 'Leave!' she screamed. 'Leave or lose your soul!'

As they turned, another tremor hurled them to one side and they crashed through the splintering banister on to the flight of stairs below. Will took the brunt of the impact, pain lancing through his ribs. Meg landed on top of him, already craning her head in fear to see what followed.

Strangewayes was pointing and crying out a warning lost beneath the booming that now sounded like a cannon barrage. Cloaked in the swirls of acrid smoke, a figure was descending the stairs at a steady pace. Will felt gripped by the sight, and by the terrifying power he sensed in that apparition. It seemed he was in the centre of a storm, with lightning crashing all around and thunder breaking overhead.

And then the figure loomed out of the cloud, and Will saw a cloak made from the pelts of many woodland creatures, the still-attached heads swaying gently. White skulls of birds and mice rattled on a silver chain to the rhythm of each step. Wild silvery hair, a wrinkled face that mapped a life lived in the shadows.

'Dee?' Will gasped.

The alchemist turned his terrible gaze upon the spy. The eyes flickered with blue fire, and in them Will saw nothing that was human.

CHAPTER SIX

BLACK PEBBLE EYES WATCHED FROM THE HIGH BRANCHES. Hunched like old men, the crows perched in silent attention, so great in number it seemed the stark winter trees were flourishing with sable growth. Sweating with fear, Tobias Strangewayes wrenched his head round as he ran. Their unnatural stares chilled him. Why had they gathered? Why were they silent? Why were they watching?

Relief flooded him when he burst from the great Kentish forest and saw the large, brick-built merchant's house on the edge of the village, the family home, safe and secure. His father had made no little money, buying up the woodland to feed the endless demand for timber for the great seagoing vessels that had made England such a power across the world. His breath burning in his chest, Tobias scrambled up to the door, his only thought, odd yet somehow right, The crows shall not get me now.

And then he was in the bright morning room and his brother was there, good Stephen, strong and wise, sitting by the cold ashes in the hearth. Tobias felt a yearning that he couldn't explain. But then Stephen turned his broad, rosy-cheeked face to him and gave a sad smile, and Tobias realized that his brother was dead, overseas, as so many of his family had died.

'*There is no reward in killing a King,*' Stephen said.

Tobias felt a cold reach deep into his bones, but before he could respond the vision shattered, the glittering shards falling away into the dark.

He jolted awake. The floor where he had been lying was cold. His mouth felt as arid as if he had swallowed a hogshead of ale the night before. A shaft of early morning sun fell through the open door of one of the rooms and caught a constellation of drifting dust motes. All was still. In the autumn chill, he pushed himself into a sitting position. Launceston and Carpenter were stirring behind him, and beyond them he saw the woman they had guessed to be the rooming house owner, Moll Higgins, sitting against the cracking plaster on the wall. Though dazed, she looked as if her wits had returned.

Strangewayes struggled to think clearly. Though the unsettling dream about his brother still had its hooks in him, fragments of the previous night emerged. He recalled Dee coming down the stairs, and the terror he felt, an unnatural terror as if all his senses were warning him of something he could not see. He remembered the flashes of light, and the smoke and the booming, like the swell of the ocean against a hull heard on the bilge deck. And the last thing that sprang into his mind was Will grabbing hold of the Irish spy and hauling her down the stairs.

Strangewayes heaved himself to his feet and made his way unsteadily down the creaking wooden treads. Swyfte was slumped next to the open front door, the woman nowhere to be seen.

'Dee?' Strangewayes gasped as his companion stood up. 'The mirror?'

Will shook his head, running a hand through his tousled black hair. Gathering his wits, he spun out into the cobbled street. Liverpool was lit by a thin orange light as the sun edged up over the horizon. Across the still streets, a hum rose up from the direction of the docks.

'Zounds, what happened last night?' Strangewayes demanded. 'Dee was filled with fire and brimstone. Never have I seen him that way. Was he possessed by devils?'

'Possessed, aye, that is a good enough explanation,' Swyfte replied, distracted. 'When I looked in his eyes, I saw no sign of the man I knew. Something dark has been awakened within him.' His tone was measured, his words free of shock or unease, and Strangewayes guessed he had already started to reach some understanding of the alchemist's transformation.

'He laid low those night-things as if they were drunken apprentices. Where did he get such power? And why did he only reveal it this past night?'

'These are questions for another time,' Will replied, dismissing any debate with a wave of his hand. 'For now, we must hope we still have an opportunity to prevent a greater disaster. Let us to the docks, and pray that we are not too late.' He threw himself down the cobbled slope towards the crack of sailcloth and barked orders, the cries of the gulls and the dank smell of the wide, grey river.

Strangewayes shielded his eyes from the bright morning light as they emerged from the shadowed alley on to the quayside. The dock-workers were already hard at their labours, grunting and sweating as they heaved bales on to the backs of carts. The horses stamped their hooves and snorted, the apple-sweet scent of their dung caught in the sharp wind off the water. The steady beat of wooden mallets echoed from the shipwrights' dens. To that rhythm of seagoing life on the Merse, merchants waved their arms in the air as they auctioned their wares, haggling over prices, and sailors sang their work-shanties on board the great vessels at anchor.

Tobias followed Will's gaze along the forest of masts large and small. His heart fell when he realized the carrack had already sailed.

'We have lost Dee,' he said with bitterness, 'when we were so close. What now for us all?'

'Keep your spirits up.' Swyfte seemed oddly unmoved despite the desperate situation in which they found themselves.

'What do you suggest? That we steal a boat and sail for Ireland? We will feel the sharp edge of a chieftain's broadsword if we trespass into the interior of that benighted land.'

He felt another spike of annoyance as his companion ignored him, striding out to the edge of the quay where a black-bearded seaman knotted the frayed ends of a net. 'Tell me, friend, the carrack that sailed for Ireland,' Will asked, 'how much of a head start does it have?'

'Ireland?' The sailor's eyes sparkled. 'It's bound for farther shores now.'

'What say you?' Swyfte's eyes narrowed.

The seaman drew the final knot on his net and admired his handiwork. 'A new course was ordered before dawn, so I 'eard,' he replied, glancing out across the glassy water. 'They'll be putting in somewhere or other to take on provisions. But then they're bound for the New World.'

CHAPTER SEVEN

RED MEG SHIVERED, PULLING HER CRIMSON CLOAK TIGHTER around her. The autumn wind bit hard, lashing her auburn hair, as she leaned against the oak rail and watched Liverpool disappear into the hazy distance. How easily she had sailed into uncharted waters, with Will Swyfte once again steering the new course of her life. She smiled. Though danger awaited, better a life of adventure and romance than a slow march to a grey death. She turned, looking towards the forecastle. Ahead lay the Irish Sea with its wild storms and soaring cliffs of black water. And beyond? She pushed aside all the questions that assailed her, unable to stare into the furnace of her true motivations. Time would judge if she were fool or not.

Captain Nicholas Duncombe emerged from his cabin. He was a strong man, tall and broad-shouldered, with a quiet nature that seemed more suited to scholarly pursuits than to command. He was kind, too, kinder than any other man of the sea she had encountered, most of whom always had a lustful look in their eye when they spoke to her.

The captain saw her watching him and strode over. He

kept his eyes down, his features tense. 'Mistress O'Shee,' he murmured, not wishing to draw attention to their conversation, 'I fear for all our souls. This vessel is bewitched.' He glanced towards the helmsman who stood as rigid as an oak, oblivious of the wind pummelling his face. Meg followed his gaze across his crew, who moved as if in a dream. 'Your companion is the devil's own. I know not what spell he has woven over my crew, but only disaster can come of this.'

'I cannot control Dr Dee, captain. If you would keep your life, 'tis best to do as he commands.'

'I am a seasoned traveller on these waves, mistress, but the New World? Such a journey requires careful planning and men prepared for the rigours that lie ahead.' The captain furrowed his brow, his fears both imagined and real. 'We sail into the haven of pirates and Spanish warships and the Lord knows what else. Perhaps Hell itself, if your companion is any indication.'

'But there will be good men coming to our aid, and soon. You must trust me on this.'

Duncombe searched her face, wanting to believe her words. 'Then I will delay the taking on of provisions for as long as possible when we put in to port in Ireland, and pray to God that your good men will have a fair wind at their backs.'

Meg smiled with confidence, but she fervently hoped they could wriggle out of Dee's grasp before they reached whatever destination the alchemist had in mind. She had seen the fire in the old man's eyes and had no doubt that whatever he planned was terrible indeed.

'I have little experience of sorcery, save the dark stories sailors tell each other on the waves,' the captain went on as his fingers closed on the hilt of the dagger he wore at his hip, 'but I fear our lot on board the *Eagle* can only get worse. Find some comfort in the knowledge that if you are threatened in any way I will defend you with my life.'

Meg winced at the captain's kindness, but quickly offered her thanks. Here was a man who valued honour above all, far removed from the duplicitous and treacherous world of spies that she knew. When she peered into his weathered face, she found herself thinking of her father, though he had been gone for years now, and she felt a wave of sadness. At that moment, she feared for Duncombe more than he did for her. Could men so good ever survive in such a world?

The door to the cabins clattered open. She sensed Dee's presence before he stepped from the shadowy interior as if he blazed with the white heat of a forge. His hair was wild, his eyes drained of all humanity. 'And so we leave this world behind,' he called to the wind. He looked at Meg, and through her to the dim horizon, and gave a lupine smile.

CHAPTER EIGHT

NONSUCH PALACE ECHOED WITH THE SOUND OF FEET MOVING
through vast chambers and down winding stairways.
Candles threw swooping shadows across the stone walls as
breathless servants hauled wooden chests between them,
and dragged well-stuffed sacks, and staggered under the
weight of bales. In the moonlit inner ward, horses stamped
their hooves upon the cobbles. Blasts of hot breath steamed
in the chill air. Cart after cart creaked under the weight of
loads waiting to be transported along the highway to the
Palace of Whitehall just beyond the city walls. The Queen
and her court were returning to London.

In the ruddy glare of hissing torches along the walls,
guards watched the hasty exodus, their furtive eyes flickering from the frantic activity to the darkness that suffocated
the surrounding countryside. *Make haste, make haste*, the
orders rang out, every voice trembling with unease. The
bitter reek of sweat born of dread hung in the air.

Grace Seldon paused in the long gallery leading from
the Queen's chambers to peer through the diamond-pane
windows at the confusion in the yard below. Her arms ached

from the weight of the Queen's sumptuous dresses, each one jewelled and heavily embroidered. She was wearing her plain yellow travelling skirt and bodice, and a matching ribbon held her brown hair away from her face during her labours. Since sunset had she carried garments to the other ladies-in-waiting in the courtyard, and there would be no respite until all the monarch's chambers were bare. She had heard the tales of nameless enemies marching upon Nonsuch, the mutterings of blood and thunder and impending doom, as she had heard them so many times before. She raised her chin in defiance. These were dangerous days and she would not jump at shadows.

The murmur of familiar voices rustled along the gallery, and Grace pressed herself back into a darkened chamber before she could be seen. She bristled as she heard the arch tones of that duplicitous little man, Sir Robert Cecil, the spymaster, who had often turned his poisonous words against Will. The other was the Earl of Essex, a self-important braggart who swaggered through the palace in his white doublet and hose as if all eyes must ever fall upon him. She peered through the crack in the door as they neared.

'Too many rumours swirl around this palace. Threat, danger, death, drawing closer by the hour,' Essex was saying in a grim whisper.

'You think we should speak true?' Cecil exclaimed with contempt. 'Better by far that they have their imagined fears.'

'Though the spectre of the plague still haunts London, I will feel some comfort once we are behind the walls of Whitehall. The defences still hold there?'

'For now.'

Plotting as ever, Grace thought. Never could a word be

trusted that came out of either man's mouth. And upon their shoulders rested the future of England. As they neared, she stepped back a pace, still watching. What an odd pair they made, the tall, muscular Essex looming over the shorter, hunchbacked Cecil. Yet power resided with the smaller man, she knew.

'And have we news from Swyfte?' the Earl asked.

Grace's ears pricked and she leaned closer once more.

'As yet, no word. It sickens me to have to put our faith in such a coxcomb.'

'Elizabeth favours him.'

Clenching his fists, Cecil ground to a halt only a step away from Grace. She held her breath. 'Will our Queen hold such a high opinion of that rake if he fails to return Dee and she is tossed into a burning pit with all of England?'

'Swyfte—'

'Speak to me of Swyfte no more,' the spymaster snapped. 'He has always been one step away from turning upon us, and only his effectiveness has kept his head upon his shoulders.'

'If he learned the truth about the woman he lost—'

Cecil ground his teeth, his voice falling to a whisper. 'He will not. If he fails to return Dee to us, his life is forfeit. If he succeeds . . . He has brushed close to the truth too many times and we can tolerate it no more. Too much is at stake.'

The spymaster grunted his distaste and set off along the gallery at a fast pace. Essex hurried to keep up. Once the two men had disappeared from view, Grace eased out of her hiding place, chilled. She heard herself hailed and turned to see Will's young assistant Nathaniel Colt, red-faced and sweating, with a large sack thrown over his left shoulder and another gripped in his right hand.

'Nat!' she exclaimed, relieved to see a friendly face. Clutching the monarch's dresses to her chest, she hurried up to him and whispered, 'I fear Will's life is in danger.'

'Will's life is always in danger,' Nathaniel sighed. 'Rogues, cuckolded husbands, poor card players, jealous rivals . . . and that is even before we discuss the Spanish.' He saw her worried expression and softened. 'Tell me what you know, Grace.'

She glanced over her shoulder, repeating in grim tones what she had overheard. 'And what did Essex mean, *the truth about the woman he lost* – about my sister Jenny?' she asked as she finished. She felt a tremor of unease run through her.

'These spies would find a plot in the contents of their evening stew,' Nathaniel replied with irritation. 'They can as much trust their own as the foreign agents they presume to fight.' He set his jaw, thinking, and then replied, 'There is nothing we can do but wait until Will returns. He will be grateful for this information, I am sure, and will know the right course to take. Come, let us talk as we walk. I have a chamber full of chests and bales to empty and I would catch one wink of sleep this night.'

Together they carried their individual burdens along the gallery towards the stairs. 'Will never lost faith that Jenny still lived, never wavered even once,' Grace said, feeling the weight of this new mystery, 'and that alone was a beacon of hope in those dark moments when I feared she could only have been taken by rogues and killed that summer's day in Arden. Even after all these years, Will loves her very much.'

'More than life itself,' Nathaniel replied. 'I have seen him reading through old letters that she wrote to him in the days of his youth. He keeps them locked away in a chest beside his bed.'

Grace paused at the top of the stairs, looking down into the dark. 'I was but a girl when Jenny disappeared. That night I was woken by a sound at the well, and I ventured out to find Will returned from his long search, washing his hands. I can never forget his expression. Haunted, he looked. Broken, as if his life would never be well again.' Her chest tightened with grief at the memory. 'Will was a changed man after that night.'

'He has searched high and low for her. He will never relent.' The young assistant struggled with his sacks down the creaking wooden steps.

'Has he ever spoken of any knowledge he might have of where Jenny might be,' Grace asked, adding quietly, 'if she yet lives?'

Nathaniel shook his head. 'Will is a man of secrets. He shows one face to the world, a carefree gentleman who likes his wine, good sport and laughter, but behind that mask there are many chambers, all of them dark.' He leaned against the wall to catch his breath. 'Despite what many here think, he is a good man. I see him in his private moments, when the mask falls away, and I know the truth. And yet I fear he does not believe it himself.' Nathaniel's brow furrowed.

'What are you saying?'

'Part of his darkness is that he believes he is as base as the enemies he faces.'

Grace could not disagree. They continued down the steps in silence. Crossing the echoing entrance hall, they stepped out into the night, enjoying the cool air on their flushed faces. Nathaniel dumped his sacks upon the cobbles and grinned, attempting to lighten the mood. 'You will be awaiting the return of Master Strangewayes eagerly, I would wager.'

She blushed. 'Why, he had never entered my thoughts until you mentioned his name,' she lied. She felt surprised by her growing affection for the young spy. At first his gloating manner had only served to irritate her until she realized that, like Will, he too wore a mask.

Servants streamed around them, muttering curses under their breath as they heaved their heavy loads on to the backs of the carts. The hard work was near done. Soon the long journey through the dark countryside would begin.

'You are pleased to return to Whitehall?' Nathaniel gasped as he threw one of his sacks on to the nearest cart.

'If I call anywhere home now, it is there.' She pursed her lips, trying to identify the prickle of unease she felt. Then she had it. 'Would that I never had to venture near the Lantern Tower, though.'

The young assistant laughed. 'What have you against it?'

'It scares me.'

Nathaniel shook his head in disbelief. 'The monument our Queen built to remind her of her father? No wonder, no awe, no reflection on the achievements of old Henry?'

'What is in it?'

He shrugged. 'It is empty.'

'The other ladies-in-waiting say that all roses planted in its shadow wither and die,' Grace said. 'And Charity Gomershall declares she heard a strange sound one evening, like a mournful song, rising from the summit. Ghost-lights flicker around it—'

65

'Superstition,' Nathaniel chuckled.

'It is haunted,' she replied emphatically, 'and I will have nothing to do with it.'

As she handed the dresses to one of the other ladies-in-waiting for storage on the Queen's own carts, her gaze fell upon the spymaster and the Earl of Essex, still deep in grim-faced conversation in the shadows by the palace wall. She felt her unease grow stronger still.

Across the inner ward, the grinding of the opening gates echoed. Eager cries rose up from the crowd, keen to leave Nonsuch for the safety of Whitehall. But Grace couldn't help but wonder if worse things lay ahead.

CHAPTER NINE

GOLDEN SHARDS OF MOONLIGHT FLICKERED ACROSS THE BLACK water of the River Thames. Oars dipped and splashed, hauling the tilt-boat past the glinting lamps of London along the north bank. The night was clear and still and cool. In the back of the long, low vessel, Launceston and Carpenter nestled on crimson cushions, woollen blankets pulled over their legs. Will listened to them bickering as they continued to debate what could have transformed Dee into the horrifying vision they had witnessed in the rooming house near two weeks ago.

'Faster, lads,' Will called to the oarsmen, his voice taut. 'Time is short.'

Strangewayes brooded on the bench in front of them, his thoughts no doubt dwelling on the threat that now loomed over all England. Whenever he glanced back, Will saw the red-headed man's eyes searching the shadow-shrouded banks for what they all knew waited in the night, only a whisper away. How long before the Unseelie Court broke the last of Dee's defences? How long before they never saw another dawn?

Will turned away from his companions. His plan, so insubstantial only days ago, was growing stronger. And he would see it through to its end though he brought down the Crown, the country, even all of this world, into damnation's flame.

When the black bulk of the Palace of Whitehall loomed up out of the night, the call of the guards along the river wall echoed over the water. The master oarsman responded with a piercing three-blast whistle and guided his vessel in to the short jetty. Candles glowed in the palace windows. The Queen and her court had returned from Nonsuch in search of shelter from the approaching storm. Grasping at straws.

Strangewayes caught Will's arm as he climbed out of the tilt-boat. 'Tell me you can see a way out of this predicament. Or are prayers my only hope?' Fear flickered behind the younger spy's eyes. The new recruit had come far in the short time since he had discovered that the world was not the way he had been told since he was a child. Few coped easily with such a dark revelation, and with each passing day Strangewayes clung more tightly to God to guide him out of the horrors. Will hoped madness was not a few steps away.

'When life appears at its darkest and most desperate, Tobias, then it is time to gamble everything.' Will flashed a reassuring grin. 'Caution is our enemy, coz. We will shake this matter up, one way or another.'

He beckoned for Launceston and Carpenter to follow. He felt a responsibility to his men. Though they did not yet know it, their lives were the stake in his gamble. Was he, then, any better than the Unseelie Court?

The four men passed through the River Gate, across the echoing cobbled courtyard in front of the silent palace and into the maze of narrow passages among the towering brick and stone halls. Entering another gloomy courtyard, they came to an iron-studded oak door behind which lay many secrets. Torches burned on either side of the entrance so there would always be light even in the darkest night. Will hammered on the door with the hilt of his dagger. While the other men went in search of beef and ale after their long journey from Liverpool, a guard in a burnished cuirass led him inside and up a spiral staircase to the Black Gallery. The walnut-panelled room echoed to the rhythm of his leather heels. Shadows danced away from the light of the logs burning in the stone hearth.

At a long, heavy table in the centre of the hall, Sir Robert Cecil looked up with a startled expression as if he feared he was about to be attacked. His features were drawn, the result of long nights without sleep, Will suspected. The Queen's Little Elf took his work as spymaster seriously, but not as seriously as his personal advancement. He was a humourless man, who spent his days weaving webs and his nights dreaming of what life would be like if his hunched back were straight and true.

When the spymaster recognized his guest, he scowled and covered the charts before him with a book. *Always a keeper of secrets*, Will thought. Cecil wheeled around the table with his rolling gait and peered up at the spy. ''Tis true, then?'

'It is. I am adored by all.'

Cecil bared his teeth. 'Swyfte, what others think charm, I think callow. So, you have failed? Dee has been spirited away under your very nose?'

Will perched on the edge of the creaking table and pushed the heavy tome to one side so he could eye the charts. With an incensed snort, the spymaster snatched the stained and creased maps and rolled them up.

'Dee is gone, yes, but not to Ireland,' the spy said with a bored shrug. Cecil had a temper much larger than his stature, and Will knew how to play him to achieve the best advantage.

'Then he *was* taken to the New World?' With a trembling hand, the Little Elf tapped an insistent finger on the table to gain the spy's attention. 'To what end? Hugh O'Neill needs Dee now, to protect Ireland from our great Enemy.'

'It seems that Red Meg O'Shee bit off more than she could chew when she stole Dee from under our noses. This detour was not planned by the Irish.'

'And the mirror?'

'Gone too,' Will lied. Before any further questions came, he moved on to describing the alchemist's dreadful trans-formation in the rooming house, and watched the blood drain from the spymaster's face.

Cecil prowled to the fire and watched the flames for a long moment. 'Is this the work of the Unseelie Court or of some other agency? Or has Dee himself finally gone mad?' he uttered in a low, strained voice.

'The doctor always skirted the edge of sanity. Whatever the cause, this matter is not yet over.'

The spymaster spun round, his eyes narrowing. 'Have you lost your wits?' His hands flew to his head. 'We stand on a precipice. Without Dee, what hope do we have of fend-ing off the bloody revenge of the Unseelie Court?'

'You and I are not alike.' Will sauntered from the table

to pour himself a flask of sack. 'You surround yourself with shadows and see only the dark. But the more I move into this night-shrouded world we have created for ourselves, the more I look towards the light.'

Cecil snorted. 'Then you are a fool. Or you are ignorant of the true state of England in those days before our Queen encouraged Dee to build his defences, when our Enemy had full, brutal rule over all corners of this land.' He perched on a stool, a hand across his eyes, looking like a child at prayer. 'When I was a boy of no more than seven years, I travelled with my father and three servants to Child's Ercall in Shropshire, where we had family.' His hoarse voice rustled out in the still room. 'While my father was at business, the woman who cared for me, a kindly soul, Jane . . . Jane . . . I cannot recall her full name! Oh, how poor are my wits! How broken am I.'

As his troubled memories rose, Cecil seemed to have forgotten Will was there. The spy thought how sad and small his master now looked, all the hardness of the court manipulator stripped away to reveal the infant that lurked at the heart of everyone.

'Jane, goodly Jane, she never once mocked my misshapen back, never raised a hand to me or called me fool or jester or . . . or Little Elf. She would tuck me up at night and brush the hair from my brow and whisper "Sweet angel" . . .' The words choked in his throat for a moment, but then he gathered himself and rose, turning back to the fire in the hope that Will would not see him blinking away tears. 'There is a pond on the edge of Child's Ercall, surrounded by willows and reeds, the water black as night. The local people say there is no bottom to it. Indeed, that it reaches down to

71

Hell.' He gave a hollow laugh. 'Despite the warnings of the villagers, I played along the edge of that foul place, chasing dragonflies in the sun. Jane, who was wiser and more fearful than I, came to fetch me back to the house. At once there was music in the air, pipes and fiddle, a reel that tugged at the heart and spun the head. I saw Jane stop and stare and her face freeze in terror, and I followed her wavering gaze to a beautiful woman with hair like the sun and skin like milk, rising from the water. A part of me knew, even then, that it was not a woman, and that that face was not the one Jane saw. A dreamy state came upon me, all sun on water and lazy, buzzing flies, but I recall as clear as day Jane's visage as she walked towards that woman. She looked as though she made her way to the executioner's block. The one in the water spoke with a voice that rang through my mind like a bell, though I understood not a word. And Jane continued to walk, into the pond, sinking deeper with each step until the black waters closed over her head. The woman who had summoned her turned to me and nodded slowly, her face growing paler by the moment, her eyes darker, her cheeks hollow, and she reached out her arms to me. I ran crying back to my father, and told him all that had occurred. But there was no comfort for me. He chastised me and sent me to bed, because he believed every word I said and was afraid of it.'

Cecil fell silent, watching the flames dance. Will felt moved by the intensity of his master's feelings. Cecil had always seemed cold and untouched by the suffering of others, but perhaps they had more in common than he had come to believe.

'Jane's body was never found,' the spymaster continued.

'No search was made of that pond for her drowned form. Three nights later, I woke from sleep and went to the window. Jane stood below, her dress sodden, her hair plastered to her head and filled with rotting pond leaves, and she reached up her arms and silently called to me. And I wanted to go, God help me, for I knew from that moment I would be alone in the world. But then I saw the shapes dancing in the night beyond her, and I was filled with such dread that I thought I would die. I ran back to my bed, but for nights after I sensed her out there, calling to me, and I thought how could one so kind become so cruel. And that notion told me all I needed to know about this world.'

He turned back to Will, his face drawn. 'We have all had our lives blighted by the Unseelie Court in some way. You . . . it was some village girl, was it not?'

'A childhood friend,' Will replied, feigning disinterest, but the vision of Jenny in that haunted cornfield blazed across his mind.

Cecil stalked forward, his hands raised and clutching in the grip of his passion. 'Think, then, sirrah, what England will be like without Dee to offer a modicum of protection against those night-terrors. When the Unseelie Court have freedom to do as they wish, my nightly visits from Jane will be nothing compared to the horrors foisted upon every man, woman and child.'

The spectre still visited Cecil? Will reflected on the scars that must have been inflicted upon his master through that relentless haunting by the only one who had ever been kind to him. 'Yes, for the Enemy will want even greater revenge for England's betrayal,' he snapped, surprised by his own rush of emotion. 'For stealing their Queen and holding her prisoner when they thought we were offering the hand of peace.'

Cecil gulped like a codfish. 'You are never to speak of that thing!'

'Why? We are among friends, are we not?' Will swigged back his sack and tossed the flask aside. Cecil squirmed under his cold gaze. 'Despite the play you make to the world, there are no heroes here. We are all tainted.'

'England had no choice, you know that. Our "betrayal", as you define it, was a matter of survival—'

'And that is justification?'

'Yes!' Cecil roared. 'The survival of our Queen, of England, of us all, a life free from the shackles of fear. That is worth any action. And you know, too, that the Faerie Queen is the heart of Dee's defences. The power that rages within her like a furnace burns the night away from this land.'

Will's thoughts returned to the story as he had been told it, his own Queen Elizabeth meeting the Faerie Queen on windswept Dartmoor to seal a pact that might end the long years of conflict between the two races who lived side by side on England's green land, though one in day and one in night. The meeting had been hard-won, the mistrust both sides felt barely overcome. But after that night the Unseelie Court would never trust the mortals again. England's forces emerged from their hiding places among the gorse and granite, slaughtered the Fay cohort and took their Queen prisoner. And in her meagre cell she had resided for more than thirty years, her miserable incarceration keeping England safe. Will shrugged, fighting to contain his simmering anger. 'Let us not squabble,' he said, pretending he cared little when in truth he found it harder by the day to tell friend from foe.

Cecil rested both arms on the table and released a weary sigh. 'Oh, for your simple world, Swyfte, where the only concerns are fresh wine, doxies and a bowl of the ordinary.'

The Secretary of State searched through the heap of yellowing charts until he found the one he wanted. Will recognized the outline of Europe stretching to the far Orient. 'We now know the Unseelie Court have been planning for this moment for many a year. Word has reached me of the Enemy's maintaining positions of influence in the great courts. One of those fiends advised the rebel leader Severyn Nalyvaiko as he led his Cossacks through Galicia, Volhynia and Belarus in his struggle against the Polish-Lithuanian commonwealth. Another has the ear of the Doges in Venice and Genoa. Philip of Spain, I fear, is still troubled by Malantha of the High Family. The story is the same in Hungary, in the whispers that prompt the Serbs to rebel against the Ottomans, in Tuscany, Austria, Malta, even in Rome itself. All around us, they move their pieces.'

'Their aim?'

'To burn this world. After the indignities they have suffered – yes, at our hands – they have decided the time of man has passed.'

'Then all of humanity will pay for England's grand be-trayal.'

'Leave it be!' Cecil's spittle flew across the stained chart as he roared. 'If I did not know better, I would think you revel in the suffering about to be inflicted 'pon us. That is treason.' The spymaster sagged. The hopelessness he had tried to contain rose in his features and he flapped a feeble

75

hand towards Will. 'Enough. This tires me. I do not know why you wish to provoke me in this dreaded hour, but . . . enough.'

Calming himself, Will walked round the table to the fire, remembering all the times he had seen Dee trying to warm himself but never being able to drive the cold from his bones. 'I hear plenty about the monstrous acts of the Unseelie Court,' he murmured, prodding a log with the toe of his Spanish leather shoe, 'but never anything about what manner of beings they are.'

'What do you mean?'

'What is their true nature? Their essence? What do we know of them?' Will turned back to the spymaster, tugging at his chin hair in thought, but he kept one eye fixed on every subtle movement Cecil made. 'Do they love? Do they care for their children? Do they have children? Or art and poetry and learning—'

'They are monsters who wish us all dead,' Cecil interrupted. 'That is all we need to know.'

'And you are aware of nothing more? They are what they seem, these pale creatures of the night?' Will narrowed his eyes, watching the faint muscle-tremor around his master's mouth.

'I know nothing more.' The spymaster looked away at the last, unable to hold Will's unflinching gaze. He turned back to his charts and pretended to sift through them while he sought to change the subject. 'For all your many flaws, you have a sharp wit, Swyfte, and you have played your public and private role well in service to the Queen. Tell me your thoughts, for at this moment I would clutch at even a thread to draw me out of the dark.'

Will felt the weight in his chest lighten. Everything was unfolding as planned. 'We feared Dr Dee had been stolen by the Irish. We came close to losing the mad alchemist to the Unseelie Court, but his transformation saved us from that fate, while at the same time denying us the opportunity to reclaim him. But we must not lose sight of the fact that, at the moment, Dee is free—'

'Yes, somewhere in the wide Atlantic!'

'Nevertheless,' Will replied, throwing his arms wide, 'he is, for now, at large, and with a fair wind at our backs and the will to achieve it, we can bring him back.'

'How so?' Cecil snorted. 'Do you know where in the New World he travels? Or why?'

Warming to his performance, Will smiled. 'I know we are in a race, Sir Robert. The Unseelie Court will be in pursuit. Whoever finds Dr Dee first, wins.'

Cecil weighed the words, his furrowed brow revealing the hopelessness he felt.

'Dee's carrack will have need to take on supplies for the long ocean voyage,' the spy continued, 'and the vessel I saw bore no comparison to our own race-built galleons. Across the stretch of that vast ocean, we can catch up. And,' he added, 'I may . . . perchance . . . be able to uncover some clue as to the course Dee's vessel takes.'

The spymaster's eyes narrowed. 'Even if you found the route the doctor has taken, you would have to fight off the full force of the Unseelie Court. You, and a handful of mere men. That is madness. You would be sailing to your deaths.'

'My life means nothing,' Will said in all honesty.

Cecil paced around the table, kneading his hands together in thought. 'But can we prepare a galleon for an Atlantic voyage at such short notice? The cost of food and munitions – England's coffers are already bare – the shortages of meat and grain after this long, plague-ravaged summer . . .'

'You will be counting gold when the Unseelie Court arrives at your door?' Will said with a wry smile.

'The *Tempest* is moored at Tilbury. Our best ship—'

'Not the *Tempest*. You may need her to defend London, should I fail. Requisition another ship, in the Queen's name. After the poor trade of this year, there must be many a merchant keen to be reimbursed.'

'I will see what I can do.'

'One other thing.' Will strode to the window and peered out across the moonlit roofs of the Palace of Whitehall. Not far away, a faint crackle of emerald light sparkled in the sky. 'If I am to risk my neck, I would arm myself with any information that might help.'

'A reasonable request. Ask of me what you will.'

'Not you. There is one other who has all the answers I could ever need.' Will rested an arm on the window frame and pressed his forehead against the cool glass. 'Take me to the Lantern Tower. I would question the Faerie Queen herself.'

CHAPTER TEN

EMERALD FLAMES CRACKLED AROUND THE TILED ROOF OF THE stone tower like marsh lights. Far below, a swaying lantern echoed that glow as a knot of six men processed across the courtyard. Beneath the gentle soughing of the night-wind, the click of their leather heels on the cobbles was the only sound in the still palace. At the oak door studded with black iron, the group came to a halt. The four armoured guards gripped their pikes, their stern faces revealing that they had no notion what was contained within the Lantern Tower. Sir Robert Cecil lowered his eyes, but Will gazed up to the spectral display, his brow knitted. His great gamble began here.

'Do not let anyone else inside the tower,' Cecil barked at the guards, looking each man in the face in turn. 'Defend it with your lives.' He removed a large iron key from a velvet pouch and unlocked the heavy door. The tumblers clanked into place. Taking the swaying lantern, he stepped inside and closed the door behind Will. The candlelight illuminated stone steps spiralling upwards into the dark. 'Dee's magical defences have been disarmed,' he whispered. 'We are safe to proceed.'

'Safe. An odd choice of word.' Will began to climb the steps. The air was dank and smelled of tallow and burnt iron.

'Do not concern yourself. She cannot escape.'

'None of us can escape, Sir Robert.'

The spymaster did not query his charge's enigmatic response. Perhaps he understood, for he was no stranger to prisons and bars and duty and fear.

They climbed through floor after floor, with the Secretary of State growing more anxious with each step. 'Who feeds her?' Will asked.

'She takes no sustenance as you and I know it,' the spymaster muttered. 'In the early days of her imprisonment, I am told attempts were made to bring her meals, but the food rotted in the bowls and was returned untouched.'

'She has guests?'

'Rarely. Though Dee has ensured his sigils and spells keep her trapped in place, still all who encounter her fear her power. Sometimes . . .' Cecil smacked his lips with distaste. 'Sometimes you can feel her words deep inside your head, like a maggot burrowing. Only that fool Spenser has dallied here awhile, until my father sent him away for fear he had fallen to her wiles.'

Alone, in a cell, for so long. *How hot must her rage burn*, Will thought. How terrible would be her vengeance if she ever escaped.

The steps ended at another heavy oak door marked with mysterious whorls and symbols inscribed in red paint. Cecil hesitated, looking up at the portal with dread. Will thought his trembling master was about to fall to his knees and pray for their salvation. The silence was heavy, but it was not the silence of emptiness. Will sensed that the cell's occupant waited on the other side of that door, listening, dangerous, poised, perhaps, for any opportunity that might arise.

'Go, then. Ask what you will,' Cecil whispered. He held up the lantern so that Will's shadow swooped.

The spy leaned in, his nose almost brushing the wood. He couldn't imagine the prisoner's terrible beauty, though he had heard stories: a beauty that could drive a man mad or blind. But he imagined her lips parting in a dark smile.

'Your Highness,' he began.

Her laugh sounded like an echo in a deep well.

He dabbed the side of his right hand to his nose where a droplet of blood had formed. 'My name is Will Swyfte,' he continued. 'I am in the employ of Queen Elizabeth of England, and I have dedicated the last ten years of my life to fighting your people for the tragedy you inflicted upon me.'

Another uncaring laugh punctuated by a low scraping. Will pictured her drawing her long nails over the rough oak, perhaps imagining, in her turn, his skin peeling, his eyes being drawn out.

'I have killed your kind,' he said.

Silence.

'You think yourselves greater than mortals, but your lives still pass on the end of cold steel,' he continued.

After another moment's lull, her musical voice rolled out. Though muffled by the wood, her words were laced with humour but had a cold, cold core. 'You speak boldly. Would you do the same if you stood beyond the protective sigils, deep within my cell?'

'I would. For I speak truly.'

'Very well.' Her voice hardened. 'Is the indignity of my imprisonment not enough, that you have come to taunt me further?'

Will reached his fingertips towards the surface of the door. Just as they were about to brush the wood, something crashed against the exact spot on the other side and he snatched his hand back involuntarily. 'I have no interest in cruel sport,' he replied. 'That is the province of the Unseelie Court. I hold myself to higher standards.'

'Indeed, you *do* think highly of yourself. That a mere man should speak to a Queen of the Unseelie Court like an equal,' she mocked. 'Were you here beside me, I could, if it suited me, peel away your flesh to the rough construction that is your essence. But we are craftspeople, delicate and skilled, and we can find subtler ways to teach harsh lessons.'

'I have seen some of those ways. One whisper in an ear that can turn thoughts in such a way that it drives a man mad.'

'We see the weakness in all men's hearts. That one flaw that we can prise apart with a few words until it becomes a yawning chasm. I see into your heart.'

Will glanced back down the steps to his master, assuring himself that Cecil could not overhear the conversation. 'I know my own heart well enough.'

'No, you do not. No man does. You only think that is the case, and that is why the truth drives you from the illusion you all hide behind to stay sane.' Beyond her muted words, he heard a faint scraping as if she were stroking the door. He imagined a lover's caress and shivered, despite himself.

'You waste your breath—'

'I see sadness, a deep, abiding sadness.' The Queen rolled the words around her tongue with pleasure. 'I see the pain of loss and separation, a life that has become corrupted by mystery to such a degree that it can no longer be lived. You would rather know the truth and be destroyed than live in this twilight world any longer.'

Will raised his head in defiance. 'And I feel anger,' he replied in a low voice, 'for you stole from me the only thing I ever valued.' He shook his head and his blood spattered across the door.

'I hear the impotent cry of the wounded child.' Her breathy words sounded low and closer still. He presumed she had pressed her cheek against the wood. Now they were barely separated, like two lovers teasing towards an embrace, her seductive voice luring him in. The hairs on his neck tingled as if she had brushed his skin. He should break the enchantment and leave that place without a backward glance, he knew, but the rage in his heart held him fast. He sensed her smiling. Yes, she knew his weaknesses well.

'You see sadness,' he whispered, 'you see rage, I know, but you do not see fear.'

She laughed again. 'Fear is the sane response to us.'

'Then I am not sane, and proud of it. Tell me *your* weakness.'

'The very definition of insanity. You presume I would bare my throat to you.'

Will glanced back at Cecil who had retreated further down the steps. The spymaster quivered in the wan light of the guttering lantern flame. 'You will tell me.' Will kept the confidence in his voice, luring her in as she had attempted to ensnare him. 'For sport. A mere man is no threat, you have said so yourself. What have you to lose by indulging my desire to seek my own destruction?'

'You think yourself clever. Perhaps you are, by the standards of man. Yet there is much you do not know — about the Unseelie Court, about yourself, and your place in this world. Nevertheless, I agree. Our weakness is something your kind would never understand — honour. Our word is unbreakable, even though it mean pain, or loss, or defeat. Do you find any gain in that knowledge? Does your kind even understand what honour means? I think not,' she added with cold contempt.

Will folded the information away and continued lightly, 'Is it true that you have made your home in the New World?'

'Would you visit my palace, O man?' she enquired. He heard a crackle of dark humour in her voice.

'I am sure you would offer me all the courtesies extended to every mortal who has crossed from this world of hard things into your moonlit realm.' He waited a moment and then added, 'Yet perhaps I could offer a few common courtesies of my own.'

The Faerie Queen laughed. 'Oh, what sport that would be. Would you wave your sword at us? Would you rage and curse and threaten? Before we fell upon you like wolves?'

'We have more steel in us than you imagine, Your Highness.'

'Then I extend an invitation to you, should you wish to prove yourself,' she replied with cruel glee. 'Damn yourself. Sail to the New World. Cross the gulf between our realms, if you can find a gate, to the place where both lands exist as one, and then follow the great Orinoco until you reach the confluence with the Caroni. Along that river you will discover the fortress of the Unseelie Court.'

Will felt a squirming sensation deep in his head. He reeled away from the door as his mind's eye was flooded with a vision of startling richness. At first he struggled to comprehend what he was seeing. A monstrous black spider as big as Hampton Court Palace squatting on a verdant landscape, where green hills rose above the treetops of a mighty forest. Iron cartwheels wider than the grey Thames, revolving within a sphere. And then he found himself looking down on a grim fortress with soaring walls of black basalt and gold.

The Fortress Crepuscule, the Faerie Queen's voice echoed in his skull. *Your kind will always find our home, should that be your wish. But it is much harder to leave.*

His gaze drifted down a vertiginous cliff, across a stone labyrinth set in the forest to a high tower with a soft white glow emanating from the summit. He heard himself murmuring, 'What is that?'

The Tower of the Moon. The beacon that illuminates the way between our worlds. As long as the light shines, the paths remain open.

'Swyfte!' Will heard Cecil's strained voice as if it were rising from a deep well. 'Take your leave now before she steals your wits!' The spy snapped out of his delirious vision into the cold grey of the Lantern Tower.

The Queen of the Unseelie Court scraped her nails down the door. 'While you mortals are base lead, my people are gold.' For the first time Will heard a hint of yearning in her voice. 'And our home is gold. A golden city, which the men of that hot land call Manoa. The wonders you would see there, mortal. It would drive you mad.'

'One day, Your Highness. One day I will sail there and bring the vengeance of the English to your doorstep.'

'And as your life ebbs away, try to read some meaning in the entrails of your suffering. There will be none.'

Will forced himself to break her spell and turned away from the door. 'I have purpose in my life, Your Majesty. I will never be deterred from finding the truth.'

'Truth?' she repeated with dark humour. 'Would you know the greatest secret of all? We are all in cells, to greater or lesser extent. This world you see around you is a prison, though the bars and locks are hidden. But who is the gaoler, ask yourself that? And what does it take to escape?' Her voice grew fainter. Will imagined her drifting away from the door into the confines of her dismal cell. 'Even as we speak my people rise from their silent chambers under hill and under lake. I hear them in my heart, drawing nearer. One vow is on their lips: to stop you recovering the mad magician, who is your final hope. You will never set sail from this city. You will die here, all of you. The end is close. Say your prayers. Kiss your loved ones. The end is close.'

A laugh, like cold crystal, fading away into the lonely dark.

CHAPTER ELEVEN

THE MAN SURGED THROUGH THE SEA OF BODIES FLOWING along Cheapside in the wan morning sunlight. Furious servants heading to the market yelled curses and apprentices searched for stones to hurl at his back, but still he ran, casting anxious glances over his shoulder. He was swarthy-skinned, the wide-brimmed felt hat he had used to hide his identity long since lost.

Will thundered in the running man's wake. 'Queen's business,' he bellowed. The crowd peeled away on either side. He was lighter on his feet than the other man, stronger and faster, though he had barely slept since his haunting conversation with the Faerie Queen.

Sensing his pursuer was closing the distance, the fugitive threw himself into a flock of geese, kicking wildly until he drove them into a frenzy of honking and beating wings. The birds scattered across the street in Will's path. Without missing a step, the spy vaulted on to the back of an apple cart trundling through the flock, scrambled over the seat beside the startled carter and leapt across the flapping obstruction, allowing himself a tight smile. His prey was oblivious of what lay ahead. As they passed the towering five-storey houses near the Great Conduit where apothecaries sold herbs and spices, he watched the runaway glance round in shock. At the eastern end of Cheapside, at the Stocks Market confluence of three great thoroughfares, an army of labourers was milling around with armfuls of cordwood for the ring of beacons that were to be built beyond the city's northern wall, while men in sun-burnished burgonets and cuirasses looked on.

The swarthy man put his head down and tried to weave his way through the confusion without drawing attention, but the towering heap of firewood blocked most of the trivium and the three streets were choked with jumbles of carts and frustrated merchants. As the fugitive stumbled, trying to force his way through the throng, Will called out again, 'A traitor to the Queen! Stop that man!'

Three pikemen swung their weapons towards the runaway. When he veered away from them, Will sprinted the last few yards and hurled himself forward. The two men crashed across the cobbles. Will leapt up in an instant, drawing his knife and pressing the tip against the fugitive's neck. The man snarled in Spanish. Will only grinned.

Through the gathering crowd, Cecil barged his way from where he had been overseeing his hastily planned gathering of fuel. 'What have we here?' he snapped.

'A Spanish spy.' Will sheathed his blade as the pikemen levelled their weapons at the prisoner. 'Our earthly enemies see an opportunity to make mischief while we are so distracted.'

The spymaster leaned in close and whispered, 'Prompted by the Unseelie Court, no doubt. That witch Malantha of the High Family is working her wiles upon Philip of Spain.'

'Threats wait in all quarters. We must never lower our guard.' Will's attention was caught by Grace and Nathaniel pushing their way through the throng. Grim-faced, they stopped beside the labourers unloading the wood from the carts, their eyes urging him to come over.

'To the Tower with him,' Cecil barked. 'We will see how loose his lips are after he has rested 'pon the rack.'

As the spymaster directed the pikemen, Will made his way over to his two friends. 'Grace, I know I have not seen you since my return from Liverpool, but now is not the time—'

'This is not a social visit,' she interjected, clasping her hands together against her emerald skirt. 'I have grave news.'

'Give her a moment of your time, Will,' Nathaniel put in. 'You will not regret it.' The spy had rarely seen his assistant looking so serious.

'Speak, then,' he said.

Grace glanced towards Cecil, still strutting along the ranks of pikemen. 'When I was at Nonsuch, I overheard your master speaking . . .' she paused, blanching, 'of Jenny.'

Will furrowed his brow, remembering Cecil's mention of Jenny the previous night. 'He knows little about her.'

'Not so.' Grace recounted what she had overheard as the court fled Nonsuch. Will felt his pulse quicken. Could this be true? Cecil had some knowledge of what had happened to Jenny that day so long ago? The spy looked over to where the Queen's spymaster bustled about, gesticulating at the assembled troops. He felt a cold nugget of anger form in his stomach. Were that so . . . should the spymaster have kept such information from him . . . he could not be held responsible for his actions.

Always the voice of caution, Nathaniel said, 'Perhaps Grace misheard. And it is often hard to divine the truth from eavesdropping.'

'Perhaps.' Will continued to watch Cecil, now in deep conversation with the commander of the pikemen. He knew the nature of the man, and all the things of which he was capable.

Grace leaned in and whispered, 'This business you are involved in in Liverpool, and here in London, does it concern Jenny?'

'I cannot say,' Will replied truthfully, for anything involving the Unseelie Court was linked to his love's disappearance.

'Do not treat me like a child.' Grace raised her chin in defiance. 'She is my sister, and I would know what you know.'

Will could barely draw his gaze from Cecil. He felt the anger starting to burn through him. 'You know you must not ask me these things,' he said, more sharply than he intended. 'We will talk later.' Unable to contain himself any longer, he strode over to the spymaster. 'I would have words,' he said curtly.

Cecil began to dismiss him, until he saw the cold look in Will's eyes. The spymaster edged to the lee of a cart where they could not be overheard, and nodded.

'I am told that you have information about my Jenny's disappearance,' Will said, as calmly as he could.

Practised at revealing nothing of his innermost thoughts, Cecil only pursed his lips in thought.

'Last night you feigned ignorance of her,' the spy snapped. 'You know more than you are saying.'

'I know nothing.'

'Do not lie to me!'

'Or what, pray tell?' Cecil blazed. 'Are you doubting my word?'

Will steadied himself. This was not the time. 'If you know anything of what happened to Jenny, tell me now.'

Cecil snorted. 'What has come over you? You conjure these suspicions out of thin air. Why should I know anything about your woman? Walsingham was spymaster when she disappeared, was he not?'

Will searched his master's face for a long moment. Grace had been adamant in her assertion of what she had overheard, and Cecil was a man enveloped in secrets. There was a mystery here, for sure, but Will could see he would get no joy from the other man. He frowned, weighing his options, his suspicion of the spymaster grown a hundredfold.

'I know no more than you,' Cecil pressed through gritted teeth. 'Why would I?'

Will felt queasy at the thought that his masters might have known something about Jenny's disappearance for all these years and told him nothing. What reason could they have? Unsure of his ground, he stalked away, though a part of him wanted to drag Cecil to one side and beat the truth out of him.

Beside the pile of cordwood, he glanced back. The spymaster was watching him intently. Will knew that look and realized he should be on his guard from now on. He pressed on into the crowd, his shoulders heavy, and didn't stop until he rested in an alley beside a grocer's shop. Leaning against the damp wall, he closed his eyes, trying to calm his churning thoughts. If Cecil kept many secrets, he had a few of his own. Dipping into the leather pouch at his hip, he pulled out Dee's obsidian mirror, which he had wrapped in a thick velvet cloth to keep safe. He studied the glass for a long moment. He would find the answers he needed whatever the cost.

CHAPTER TWELVE

AN ARC OF FIRE BLAZED ACROSS THE NIGHT-DARK FIELDS surrounding London. Spirals of gold sparks, whipped up in the breeze, rose from the beacons enclosing the city from the marshy western reaches by the grey Thames to the riverside woods beside the eastern city wall. Carpenter leaned on the battlements at the top of the White Tower and felt the acrid smoke sting the back of his throat.

It had been four days since the Faerie Queen had issued her hate-filled warning, four long, wearying days of organizing the militia, spinning a web of deceit to sustain the rumour that the suspected attack came from Spanish agents, surreptitiously spreading a long line of salt and protective herbs among the beacons to bolster Dee's failing defences. Four days of hope and worry.

'Will our preparations be enough?' he asked, rubbing at the scar tissue under his hair. It was an unconscious tic in moments of anxiety, harking back to that bitter night in Muscovy when the bear-thing had left him for dead.

'Hrrrm,' Launceston murmured, acknowledging the question without answering it. He looked across the slow-moving river towards an orange glow in the east. Another ring of beacons surrounded the docks at Greenwich where men laboured through the night to provision their requisitioned galleon, the *Gauntlet*, for its long ocean crossing.

'Can you not offer me even a crumb of comfort?' Carpenter snapped. He fought down his bitterness.

'What good would that do?' the Earl breathed, his dry voice almost lost to the wind.

Carpenter prepared to give a barbed response, then thought better of it. What was the point in wishing his companion could comprehend such trifles as human feelings? Instead he muttered, 'We are modern men, not superstitious fools like the country folk, and I have long since discarded the Bible's cant. But sometimes I hope . . .' The word caught in his throat. 'Tell me, Robert, do you think there might be a God?'

'If there were a God, would He allow a thing like me to exist?'

Carpenter heard no self-pity in his companion's voice, only an acceptance of his unnatural urges. For a moment, he recalled the diabolic vision of the Earl drenched in blood. He felt surprised that the emotion it stirred in him was not disgust, but sadness. 'I have had my fill of this business,' he sighed. 'It wears me down by degrees, and seals me away in a dark place where I fear I will never see the sun again. I would break away . . . and soon.'

'Where would you go?' The Earl drew his grey woollen cloak around him and stepped beside his companion to look out over the jumbled roofs of the city. 'This business has stolen your life. No family, no woman, no friends, no trade. We company of travellers are all you have.'

Carpenter gave a bitter laugh. 'This is it, then? You are my family, and Swyfte, and that red-headed maggot-pie Strangewayes? Kill me now and be done with it.'

'The Enemy will come soon enough,' Launceston said, looking up to the billowing smoke from the bonfires. 'Even when Dee's defences were strong, they still wandered across our territory. The alchemist only kept them from attacking in force. Now not all our charms will hold them at bay for long. We must hope that we can be at sea before they strike. At least if we can regain Dee we stand a chance of repelling them.'

And without Dee there is no hope at all, Carpenter thought.

Cries of alarm rang up from the dark of the water's edge far below them. Frowning, Carpenter stifled his pang of anxiety as he peered over the battlements. Some waterman in distress, he tried to tell himself. The sound of running feet echoed. More cries.

'The river is protected by the charms on the wherries working their way back and forth between the banks,' Launceston said, as if he could read the other man's thoughts. 'All is as Dee prescribed.'

'I can see nothing,' Carpenter snapped. 'Come.'

He wrenched himself away from the battlements and ran down the winding stone steps, Launceston only a few paces behind. In the ward he shouted to the guards to open the gates. Out of the fortress they raced, and along the grey walls to the river's edge. The cries of fright had ebbed away. Only the lapping of the Thames broke the silence.

Struggling to see in the thin light of the crescent moon, Carpenter found the muddy path by the black water. It was low tide and the river reeked from the stink of offal dumped unlawfully in the flow by the city's butchers after night had fallen. On a small stretch of gravelly shore, he glimpsed the flare of torches bobbing in the dark. He cast an uneasy glance at his companion, but the Earl's sallow face was impassive.

Carpenter crunched across the slick stones, feeling colder by the moment. His hand searched for the hilt of his rapier for security. Nearing the crackling torches, he made out a group of six watermen in caps and thick woollen cloaks to keep them warm in the chill of the open river. Their attention was gripped by something he could not see. The Earl had drawn his dagger and was keeping it hidden in the folds of his cloak.

'We are on the Queen's business,' Carpenter announced with a snap in his voice, grabbing the shoulder of one of the watermen and easing him aside. 'What is the meaning of this outcry?'

Six faces turned towards him in the dancing light of the torches, each one etched with fear. One of the men stretched out a trembling arm to point. The spy followed the line of his finger.

Hunched on the edge of the cold, black water squatted a man clad in the filthy corselet of an old soldier. His breeches were coated with river mud, his hair and beard wild, his face drawn from a life lived in hedgerow and street. He had the thin frame of a man who went too long between meals. Beside him, a rod and line was set in the mud and gravel and a small fire had been built with driftwood, ready to be lit. The figure didn't move, his gaze fixed on the eddies lapping against the shore.

Dead, Carpenter thought. But even as the notion crossed

his mind, he found himself unsettled by a faint shimmer across the man's body.

Launceston must have seen it too, for he grabbed one of the torches and held it over the still form. The old soldier all but glowed, like some apparition.

Carpenter took an unconscious step back. The dead man was rimed with frost, his hair and beard white, his skin gleaming with ice crystals as though he had spent a night out in a Muscovy winter. 'What is this?' the spy exclaimed. An autumnal chill hung in the air, but nothing that could account for such a state.

Launceston squatted beside the soldier, moving the torch around so he could examine the frozen face for some clue as to what had occurred.

A murmur washed around the huddling watermen as if a dam had broken. One blamed the devil, another the Fair Folk, a third some curse or other.

The Earl withdrew his dagger and jabbed the point against the man's cheek. A *clink* echoed above the gentle lapping of the river. 'Solid,' he mused. 'Like ice.' He jabbed harder and the side of the soldier's face shattered. Shards of frozen flesh rattled on the gravel. The squatting body teetered for a moment, then fell back, cracking into a hundred hard fragments.

The watermen cried out as one and fled back along the river's edge towards their boats.

'Zounds! What evil is this?' Carpenter gasped.

'I fear it is the beginning of something,' Launceston breathed, rising to his feet. He waved the torch over the glistening remains one final time and then turned to the water. 'Of what, I am not entirely sure.'

'Would the Unseelie Court attack a starving soldier fishing for his supper? There must be some other answer.'

'If you leave this work, if you flee into a new life, I will come with you,' the Earl murmured in a distracted tone. Gripped by the sight of the shattered body, Carpenter barely realized what his companion had said before the Earl added, 'In this mystery lies the key to what we will face in the days ahead, if we can only divine it.'

'And if we cannot?' Carpenter asked.

'Then winter comes early for all of us.'

CHAPTER THIRTEEN

CANDLES SUMMONED GLITTERING JEWELS FROM THE STAINED glass window above the altar. The Lady's Chapel in the Palace of Whitehall had heard the whispered devotions of monarchs, lords and ladies, but this night it was Strangewayes' low voice that rustled up into the shadows. Head bowed, he knelt on the cold flags, hollowed by too much doubt and fear.

'Dear Father, hear my prayers,' he entreated, his pressed palms shaking. 'Deliver us from the evil that draws nearer by the day.'

The only answer did not come from God. 'Tobias?' His name echoed from the dark at the back of the chapel.

The young spy stumbled to his feet, running one trembling hand through his auburn hair. 'Who goes?' he snarled, shock adding a crack to his voice.

A hooded figure stepped into the candle glow. His heart leapt when he saw that it was Grace, wrapped in a thick woollen cloak against the growing chill. She folded back the cowl and forced a weak smile. 'Come back to the fire. You have been here in the cold for too long.'

'Soon,' he said. 'I find some peace here in the midst of all this turmoil. And if God hears my pleas, then we have hope in the struggle that is to come.'

Her brow furrowed. 'We have defeated the Spanish before. Surely we can again.'

Strangewayes felt a pang of regret that he had to lie to her. It seemed a betrayal of the love they shared. And yet how could he not deceive her, when her sanity, perhaps even her life, was at stake? Swyfte had warned him time and again how many others had been driven mad by knowledge of the Unseelie Court. 'You are the voice of reason, Grace. I worry for naught, I am sure,' he replied, putting on a confident smile. 'It is in my nature to grow anxious before a battle.'

'Then you must listen to Will,' she said with a warmer smile. 'He is always as calm as a millpond.'

The spy flinched, but he nodded politely. ''Tis good advice. I will be along once I have finished my devotions.'

Her face darkened. 'We have only been close for a matter of weeks, Tobias. I miss your gentle words, and I would enjoy your company before the Queen's business calls you away once more.'

Once she had left, his heart grew heavier. All his sacrifices were for her alone. He would do anything to keep her safe in the face of the supernatural threat that circled all their lives. After a moment, more footsteps disturbed his thoughts and he was surprised to see Sir Robert Cecil emerge from the gloom. The spymaster gave a faint nod of greeting. Tobias, as always, found his master's eyes unreadable.

'Sirrah, I must apologize,' Cecil said. 'It was only my intention to pray awhile here. Like you, I am a godly man.

I could not help but overhear your exchange with your woman.'

'Grace and I have nothing to hide.'

'I would think not.' Cecil knelt before the altar and made the sign of the cross upon his chest. 'Pray with me,' he said, beckoning the other man to join him.

Strangewayes knelt, his uneasiness in his master's presence giving way to the churn of his own troubles.

'You have been a loyal and trusted servant since you joined my band, sirrah,' Cecil said, his head bowed. 'That has not gone unnoticed.'

'I do whatever is required of me in service to the Queen.'

'Of course, of course.' The spymaster nodded. 'And I would be remiss if I did not reward you for that service.'

'A job well done is its own reward. That and the knowledge that I serve God.'

'You would do well to accept this reward, Master Strangewayes, for it is only a small thing. A warning.' He paused for one moment, allowing the weight to build. 'I fear for the safety of Mistress Seldon.'

Tobias jerked his head towards the spymaster. 'Grace? What are you saying?'

'You must beware of Swyfte. He is always scheming to his own ends, and he cares little who gets hurt in the process.'

'What do you know?'

Cecil closed his eyes, muttering a prayer.

After a moment, Strangewayes shook his head. 'There is no love lost between Swyfte and me, but I cannot believe he would allow Grace to suffer unnecessarily. Indeed, he has protected her since her sister, Jenny, was lost.'

The spymaster shrugged. 'If you are certain—'

'You must tell me. If Grace is in peril, I will do whatever is necessary to protect her.'

A small smile flitted across Cecil's lips, gone before Strangewayes could be sure he had seen it. 'All I can say for now is that you must keep close watch on our friend, Master Swyfte,' the older man repeated. 'At this time of greatest threat he is at his most dangerous, and he will do aught to save his own neck. Even sacrificing those closest to him. Never let him out of your sight. Listen to his weasel words. Judge him. You do not have to accept my account. Trust your own heart. And if you feel he is about to betray us to save himself, you must be prepared to act in an instant, for to tarry for even a moment could cost us all dearly, including the life of your woman.'

Strangewayes bowed his head. A part of him had always feared that Swyfte could not be trusted. 'What should I do?' he whispered.

'There is only one course. You must slay him before he drags us all down to Hell.'

CHAPTER FOURTEEN

GREY MIST ROLLED ACROSS THE RIVER. THE NIGHT-SOUNDS of sleeping London whispered through the fog like the breath of a child at sleep: the calls of the beadles, the hoots of owls from the wooded shores, the splash of oars and creak of rigging. Along the quayside at Greenwich, pikemen in burgonets appeared to glide out of the folding cloud. Darting eyes searched for the foreign agents they had been told were preparing to attack. They glowered at the boys heaving cordwood to the beacons, hurling abuse to mask their fear. Beyond the circle of light cast by the sizzling lantern over the inn door, two men huddled together in intense conversation. Both kept their heads down to obscure their identities.

Will Swyfte glanced suspiciously at a merchant's cart further along the quay. The horse snorted and stamped its hooves as the bleary-eyed driver nodded in his seat. Two bickering labourers heaved an oak cask of salt beef off the back of the cart. Cursing, the men lowered the barrel to the cobbles and then trundled it to the winch beside the *Gauntlet*. The provisioning of the galleon was almost complete, salt fish, biscuit, wine, water and rice all stored in the hold. They would be set to sail at dawn, as planned. Will hid his unease. It had been seven days since the Faerie Queen's warning, three since Launceston and Carpenter had discovered the frozen soldier on the river bank, with nary a sign of the Unseelie Court.

'Then we have agreement?' the other man enquired. Sir Walter Raleigh was many things – explorer, occasional spy, soldier – and famed at home and abroad, yet since he had fallen from the Queen's favour he had spent his days skulking away from attention. Under his cloak, his fine midnight-blue doublet with jewelled buttons showed he had not lost his taste for flamboyance, Will noted, but his refined features had hardened.

'You have met your side of the bargain. It seems your secret society can achieve great things, and with speed.'

Raleigh turned his face away as one of the labourers strode towards the inn. 'In the ranks of the School of Night we have many men of wealth and influence,' he whispered. 'Your request was difficult at such short notice, but not impossible.' He held his hands wide. 'See, Master Swyfte. *Together* we can achieve great things.'

Will's mind swam with the faces of the men he had learned were part of Raleigh's conspiracy: Henry Percy, the Wizard Earl, and Dr Dee himself; George Chapman, the playwright, Thomas Harriot who studied the stars and numbers, and good Kit Marlowe. Raleigh had hinted that there were many more besides, men of good standing who showed one face to the Queen and another in their private meetings, nobles and educated commoners, and the brave explorers who had uncovered the darkest secrets of the

New World. The School of Night wished to chart a course away from the never-ending war between England and the Unseelie Court, but Will suspected the conspirators had a further agenda that had grown out of their love of forbidden knowledge. But that was a consideration for another day.

'And your aid is given freely and without obligation?' he asked with a wry smile. He did not wholly trust Raleigh, nor feel any desire to be indebted to him. Indeed, at that moment, he felt there was barely a man in the world that he could trust.

'I am a genial fellow, Master Swyfte, but I did not achieve my place in the world by being naive. *Quid pro quo*. That is how every man does business.'

The spy's attention was caught by a golden glow deep in the mist over the river. It moved steadily towards them.

'You seem unsettled, sir. You fear the attack is imminent?' Raleigh asked. He followed Will's gaze, but appeared untroubled.

'I prefer not to lower my guard at this late stage. Our defences hold for now, but the Unseelie Court are as cunning as snakes.'

The hazy light became a lantern swinging on a pole at the prow of a wherry. Two oarsmen heaved in unison. They were both bearded, in the manner of watermen, their thick woollen cloaks wrapped tight against the night's chill.

'The Charm Boat?' Raleigh asked.

Will nodded. 'It sails an unceasing course between the twin banks with Dee's magical concoctions and amulets aboard. The Unseelie Court will not be able to use the wide Thames as a route into the heart of London.'

He thought how desperate they had all become. Dee's

protective magics had given them the illusion of security for so long, they had grown to think they were immune to the terrors that waited in the night. Now they had all been revealed as frightened children, from the lowest in the land to the Queen herself.

As the wherry eased out of the grey curtain, he saw it carried three passengers on the benches near the stern. The small, hunched shape in a hooded black cloak could only be Cecil, come to inspect the provisioning of the *Gauntlet*. Will watched the figure coldly. The other two men had the look of guards: implacable stares, broad shoulders, hands hidden inside cloaks where their daggers lay.

'I must away before the Little Elf sees me,' Raleigh said with a grimace. 'That befanged spider squatting in the centre of his web is an echo of the Queen and she sees me as betrayer, though in truth it is more a matter of wounded pride. But quickly, our bargain. In return for the aid given to you by the School of Night, we require your loyalty.'

'Treason, then?'

Raleigh shrugged. 'Matters are never so bald. It is my intention to launch another expedition to the New World shortly. I would meet with the Unseelie Court. Perhaps common ground can be found. We may learn from their vast knowledge of the mysteries that underpin existence, and thereby enrich the lives of all men.'

'Or the Enemy may eradicate you in the blink of an eye.'

'Nevertheless, it is a risk worth taking. I would ask that if you return from the New World, you relate to me personally all that you learned there. Elizabeth does not need to know.'

Will nodded, but kept his eyes guarded. 'I have served the Queen well for many years, but the time has come for hard choices. The ceaseless scheming of monarchs and men of power grows tiresome. There are other matters of greater import to me.'

'Very well.' Raleigh nodded, taking this as acceptance. 'Then let us say farewell for now.'

The wherry crunched against the side of the quay and one of the guards called out for the oarsmen to take care. Will guessed the watermen had been drinking to numb the boredom of their repetitive journey. When he turned his attention back to Raleigh, the other man had melted into the mist.

Striding to the river's edge, Will put aside his suspicions about the spymaster and hailed him. Cecil's head jerked up and he glowered, anxiety drawing new lines on his face. But he took the hand offered him and clambered up the stone steps to the cobbles. 'The Queen is safely ensconced in the Palace of Whitehall with two hundred good men to guard her,' he said. 'Though she is still recovering from her recent ordeal, she is determined to lead her people in the defence of England.'

'I would expect no less. But for now she can only wait and worry. If all goes well, our sailing will take the heat away, for a while at least.'

Cecil glanced towards the men rolling barrels up the planks on to the *Gauntlet* and gave a relieved nod. 'Wait and worry, indeed. Our sentries round London report that all is calm. No hint of threat, no sign of anything out of the ordinary. Perhaps the Faerie Queen sought to frighten us with lies.'

'She has no reason to lie.'

Cecil clenched his teeth, peering into the mist over the

water. 'Let them strike, then. We will show them what fire burns within us.'

It was then that one of Cecil's men in the wherry half stumbled as he edged towards the stone steps. He clutched on to the side to stop himself from pitching into the drink, but his velvet cap fell on to the water. 'Steady-o!' the older waterman called in irritation, spluttering through a mouthful of sack he had swigged from a skin. The burly guard growled a curse under his breath and leaned over the side to reclaim his sodden headgear from where it floated on the black water.

Will felt his chest tighten, though he did not know why; some instinct perhaps, honed in his constant fight for survival. 'Leave it,' he yelled. He felt Cecil's reproving gaze upon him, but his own was fixed on the guard's hand reaching towards his hat.

As the man's fingers brushed the inky surface, the river boiled all around. The man gaped at the churning water that rocked the wherry, and then sudden, rapid movement erupted. Screaming, the guard pitched on to his back in the bottom of the boat. The senior oarsman dropped his skin of sack, whirling. Now Cecil gaped. 'What in God's name—'

The waters became as calm as they had been a moment earlier, but the guard continued to scream and thrash in the bottom of the wherry. The waterman leaned over him, his eyes widening in horror. Will bounded down the stone steps and leapt into the rocking boat, thrusting the oarsman to one side. He knelt beside the guard, whose struggles were easing as shock took hold of him.

The man had lost his right hand. He pawed feebly at the stump with his left, moaning. Teeth had ripped through flesh and bone, Will saw. He had heard tell of a pike in a pool in Kent that could consume a man, and of sharks, the wolves of the sea, one of which John Hawkins had brought back to a horrified reception in London after his second expedition. Yet such a monstrous creature in the peaceful Thames? Never had he heard of such a thing.

As he inspected the wound, he realized there was no flow of blood and the surrounding skin had taken on a greyish cast. Puzzled, he brushed the forearm with his fingertips only to recoil in shock. The flesh was frozen solid. He recalled Carpenter and Launceston's account of the soldier turned to ice at the water's edge only a few nights earlier and felt a sick realization dawn inside him.

'What is wrong with the fool?' Cecil barked, a faint tremor lacing his words.

Will peered over the side of the wherry, his skin prickling. The still water was black and impenetrable.

Turning to the oarsman, he said, 'See this poor soul is cared for. I fear he will not survive this torment.' With renewed purpose, he leapt back up the stone steps and raced past Cecil, who waved his arms in confusion. Catching hold of one of the labourers, he snapped, 'Find Captain Prouty. Tell him the plans have changed. The *Gauntlet* must be made ready to sail as soon as possible. If we are short of provisions, so be it. We will have to survive with empty bellies until we reach our destination. But dawn is too late. Do you understand?'

The labourer shook off his slow-witted expression, nodded earnestly, and ran towards the inn, his shoes cracking on the cobbles. Will turned as Cecil hurried up to him, breathless and angry that he had been ignored. 'I must take the Charm

Boat back to the other bank,' Will said before the spymaster could speak. 'I have urgent business to conclude before we sail.'

'Speak to me, Swyfte,' Cecil roared, shaking his fists in the air. 'What is happening?'

Will looked towards the mist-shrouded water but thought only of the silent night-world beneath its surface. 'We thought ourselves untouched. We believed we had time on our side. But the war is already under way and our advantage long since gone.'

CHAPTER FIFTEEN

'DO YOU UNDERSTAND, NAT? LIVES ARE DEPENDING ON YOU.'
Will tried to keep the crack of disquiet out of his voice. His
young assistant blinked, bleary-eyed from being woken, and
turned away from Will to find his shoes at the end of the
bed.

'Riding hard, I will be at Tilbury in no time,' he said. He
glanced back at his master, stung by what he perceived to be
an understated criticism. 'I have never let you down before.'

'I could not have wished for a better assistant. The need
for urgency is more to do with the severity of unfolding
events than any reflection on your abilities.' Will softened,
thinking back to how inexperienced his assistant had been
when his father had entrusted him to the spy's employ.
Angry at being torn from his village life and thrust into
a dangerous world where he was never allowed to ask any
questions, Nathaniel had grown into the job, and learned a
maturity beyond his years, though his tongue remained as
sharp as ever. Will trusted him more than any other man,
and took his vow to protect him with the utmost serious-
ness. Never had he revealed any hint of the Unseelie Court

or the threat they represented. For Nathaniel, the world was still a sunny place where things happened as they ought, and in that way he was kept from a life of madness in Bedlam.

Nat perched on the edge of the bed, still eyeing his master askance. 'It troubles me when your tongue is not sharp. Am I still lost in dreams? Or are you awash with sack and still seduced by the honeyed words of some doxy at Liz Longshanks's?'

'I can find some words to lash you with, if that gives you comfort, Nat.' Will strode to the window and peered out over the palace, no longer sleeping. Candlelight gleamed in window after window, with new flames flickering to life by the moment. The fog hung heavy over the secret courtyards and maze of shadowed paths among the grand buildings, muffling the shouts of the sentries on the walls and the tread of marching pikemen preparing for a threat that none of them truly comprehended.

'No, let me savour this moment.' His shoes on, Nathaniel rose and took a steadying breath. 'Yes, this must be how employment is for every other man. Apart from the being woken in the middle of the night to risk my life on rogue-infested byways without a crust to break my fast.'

Will looked back at the young man and saw the inno-cence that still nestled in his heart. He almost remembered how that used to feel. 'Nat, you have been a good and loyal servant . . .' he began.

Nathaniel's eyes narrowed with suspicion. 'And there you go again. What, have I been consigned to the block and no one told me?'

'Hear me out. I promised your father that I would guide you and keep you safe. In truth, I have learned as much from you and your honest, hopeful nature as you ever have from me,' Will said, choosing his words carefully. 'But now I have taught you all I can, and after this task is complete I release you from my service.'

Nathaniel looked as if he'd been slapped. 'Have I wronged you in some way?'

'You have exceeded all expectations, Nat. This is a reward, not a punishment.' Will smiled to soften the blow, but he felt a pang of sadness that he had to turn his back on his faithful assistant after all they had shared.

'What if I do not wish to leave your service? Do my views matter?'

Will turned back to the window to avoid his assistant's hurt gaze. 'I plan to write a letter of recommendation that will gain you any position in London that you would wish for,' he continued. 'You have lived with danger long enough. You deserve to make a life for yourself where there is some material reward. A wife, children. Peace. Not this business of sweat and blood and shadows.'

Nathaniel started to speak, but Will silenced him with a hand and sent him on his way. He knew the curt dismissal had wounded Nat, but if he had allowed any space the young man would have woven a tissue of words, of argument and protest. There was little time for that, and no point. Much as he would miss his friend, and he would, greatly, he had spoken truly; this was the best reward he could offer Nathaniel: hope, freedom and the opportunity for a fresh start.

Drawing a stool to the trestle in one corner, he took the quill and ink-pot and by the light of the candle flame wrote the letter of recommendation. His name at the bottom, alone, would buy Nathaniel a good future. Even that did not feel enough.

Once done, he put aside his regrets and raced to the Black Gallery, where Carpenter was drinking sullenly by the roaring fire. Launceston paced the room in silence like some ghastly revenant. Will told them what had taken place at Greenwich. The two spies grasped the implications without any need for explanation and together the three men made their way through the fog to the palace's River Gate.

Kneeling on the jetty, Carpenter peered at the black ripples lapping against the posts. 'What foulness now resides here?' he asked.

'Something with teeth which carries with it the bitter cold of winter,' Will replied. 'You would do well to keep your face away from the water if you do not wish to be left with a permanent grin. Find Strangewayes, and then make ready a wherry to take us to Greenwich. I have one final piece of business to attend to, and by then Captain Prouty should be ready to sail.'

'Hrrrm,' Launceston mused as he peered into the fog. 'Is it wise to take to the water?'

'We do not have the time to cross the bridge and ride along the bank to Greenwich. The river is faster, and no vessel has been disturbed.'

'So far,' the Earl replied.

Will left the two men to select one of the boats tied to the pier and went in search of Grace. But as he hurried through the still palace corridors to where the Queen's ladies-in-waiting slept, she found him first. He saw in an instant that trouble awaited him. Her cheeks were flushed and her eyes blazed. Wrapped in an emerald cloak, she strode up to him and snapped, 'I have just seen Nat. He is concerned for you. I fear for your sanity.'

'Grace—'

'Do not play games with me. I am no fool.' She thrust her face towards his. 'Nat is a good man, and although he has spent long years at your side he has not grasped the true twisted paths your own mind follows.'

'And you have,' Will said, remaining calm.

'At some level, we were joined by the tragedy of my sister's disappearance, Will Swyfte. That terrible event set us apart from the rest of the world, yet in its shared misery bonded us. Yes, I do know how you think. I know what shapes you, what drives you, whatever face you present to the world: a hero loved by all; a drunken fool; a rake who fornicates with doxies. I see the sadness and the hardness and the determination. And when you give Nat such a *glorious reward*, I know it means only one thing: that you believe you are sailing off to die.'

Grace's perception caught Will off-guard and for a moment he could not find the words to respond. A bleak smile leapt to her lips when she saw that she was right, but her expression quickly darkened.

'Grace, do not make this more difficult than it needs to be.'

'You have dwelt in the shadow of Jenny's disappearance for so long that you can no longer see the light. You welcome death as a release from your pain.'

'I sail to rescue Dr Dee, not to end my own existence.'

He saw the determination in her face, the echo of the elder sister he loved, and that only lacerated him more. 'We have been close, you and I, and there was a time when I

115

wished us to be closer still,' she said. 'And now you would come here and bid me farewell as if you were only crossing the river to drink in Bankside? I deserve better.'

'You always did, Grace, but I gave you only what I could. Let us part in a manner that will bring us both some comfort in the weeks and months ahead, not with harsh words that we will come to regret.' He would miss her, and Nat too, and all of London, but he had lived in the half-world for too long. He could not go on that way. For good or ill, there had to be an ending.

'Very well,' she said, stepping forward to kiss him on the cheek, 'but you must vow to do all in your power to return to me—'

'Step away from her!'

Will turned to see Strangewayes standing at the end of the corridor, his rapier drawn. The red-headed spy looked furious. Will sighed.

'Tobias, it is not as it appears,' Grace began, but jealousy seemed to consume the other man. He ran towards them.

Will drew his own blade and parried the younger man's wild thrust. 'Sheathe your weapon. You are acting like some wounded child,' he snapped, adding, baffled, 'Why do you behave in this manner?'

That merely drove Strangewayes to greater rage. 'You know Grace keeps a flame for you in her heart and you trifle with her affections to swell the head of the great Will Swyfte. Do you care for no one but yourself?'

'Curb your tongue. You will regret this outburst.'

'England's greatest spy,' Strangewayes sneered. 'What a confection that is. You are a wastrel and your time is done. I am the future.' He thrust again, with more care this time.

Will deflected the attack once again. The other spy had some skill, Will saw, but it was still raw. Given time he would be as great as he imagined himself to be now.

'Tobias, if you love me as you say you do, end this,' Grace demanded angrily. 'You are mistaken in your suspicions.'

But Will saw that Strangewayes' hurt pride would not let him back down. In a flash, he clashed rapiers, spinning the other man off-balance, and then cuffed him on the right ear. Strangewayes crashed against the wall, dazed. 'Your heart is in the right place, if your head is not,' Will said. 'I am glad you love Grace enough to risk your neck, but this is a futile display. Everything we have fought for now hangs by a thread and I do not have the time to knock sense into you. If you continue to fight, I will run you through and leave you here to die, though Grace hate me for evermore. Do you understand?'

Strangewayes glared, but the defiance had been knocked out of him. Will turned back to Grace and took her hand. 'Fare you well, Grace. I hope we will see each other again.' Tears sprang to her eyes.

'Tell her,' Strangewayes pleaded when he saw her sadness. 'Tell her what we face.'

'Silence,' Will snapped, allowing the threat to surface in his eyes.

'She deserves to know the truth. No stories for children. No false comforts. Tell her, so she can put her thoughts in order if we do not return—'

'I said silence.' Will flicked the tip of his rapier to Strange-wayes' throat. 'You are young. You have only just learned the secret knowledge that we share, the knowledge that can destroy good-minded people.'

'I have considered this matter greatly while at prayer. Grace is strong enough.'

Will dug the tip of the blade deeper, raising a bubble of blood. 'You think you are doing her a kindness, but it is only cruelty. I say one final time, silence.'

'Very well. But now it is my turn to say goodbye.'

Will watched the other man's face. He wondered briefly if it wouldn't be simpler to kill him there and then, but then Grace took his wrist and gently eased his sword away. 'He will not tell me your secrets, dear Will,' she murmured. 'I will not allow him to.'

Will held her gaze for a long moment. He felt a deep affection, and only wanted her to be happy. He thought that perhaps she understood. Putting up his sword, he walked away without another word. In the shadows at the end of the corridor, he glanced back. Strangewayes held her in an embrace, whispering in her ear. He was not the man Will would have chosen for her, but he loved her, and at that moment, that seemed enough.

Back at the jetty, Carpenter and Launceston argued, pacing around each other like dogs preparing to fight. They grew silent when they saw Will and clambered into the wherry, where a lantern glowed on a pole in the prow. Carpenter eyed the water with unease. The Earl hummed tunelessly as he selected an oar. A moment later, Strangewayes joined them in sullen silence, flashing one unguarded look at Will as he found a place beneath the lantern. He pulled the hood of his cloak up and kept his head down.

'Take us out into the current,' Will said, 'but have a care as we ride the fast water at the bridge. A dip will bring more than a chill to our bones.'

'Do you lie awake at night searching for increasingly elaborate ways to kill us?' Carpenter grumbled, undoing the rope tied to the quayside ring. He grasped another oar and pushed the wherry out into the flow.

'My intention is to keep your days interesting, John.' Will crouched in the bottom of the wherry and peered into the dark water.

The bank faded into the fog. As the grey enveloped them, the lapping of the river grew muffled and distorted. Will cocked his head and looked around, but he could neither see nor hear any sign of the greatest city in Europe. They could have been alone in all England, drifting through a wilderness.

Carpenter and Launceston heaved slow, measured strokes, each man watching the point where his blade dipped into the river as if he expected the oar to be torn from his grasp.

When they had moved downstream in silence for a few moments, Strangewayes wrenched to one side and pointed. 'There!'

Will felt an eddy that rocked the wherry.

''Twas the length of a seal at least,' Strangewayes said with unease. 'Perhaps larger still. I saw grey skin just break the surface.'

'There too.' Launceston pointed on the other side of the boat. 'It swims fast, to circle us so quickly.'

'No,' Will said, looking around. 'Not one. Many. See.'

In the circle of lantern-light round the prow, they saw repeated rapid movement at the surface. The wherry rocked more vigorously. All around, the sound of splashing echoed.

'They are like salmon at spawn,' Carpenter said. 'Have we disturbed them in our passing?'

'Not fish,' Strangewayes whispered, leaning back.

Will moved to the prow and leaned over the edge. Grey shapes flashed past, arching their bodies and rolling near the surface before diving down. He fixed his gaze until one passed in front of him. He saw a face that was human in shape, though longer and thinner than most men's, with hollow cheeks and huge, lidless eyes. Straggly hair, like seaweed, streamed down from the top of the skull-like head. Yet it was the mouth that burned in Will's mind: lipless, with two rows of needle-sharp teeth forming a permanent grimace.

Sharp enough to tear off a man's hand, he thought.

The skin was pale, merging into mottled grey. And as the unearthly creature darted from view, he caught a glimpse of an eel-like lower body ending in fins.

'Neither man nor fish, but both,' he said in a cheery tone that belied his unease. 'Row a little harder, lads.' He still could not guess what the Unseelie Court hoped to achieve with these creatures. Although they buffeted the wherry as they swam past, they made no attempt to overturn the boat.

'In the taverns around Tilbury, seamen tell of such things swimming in northern waters. It is considered a bad omen to see one,' Launceston informed the others.

'It is a worse omen to see one if you are in the water,' Carpenter muttered.

They fell silent, watching the churning river. Will began to count the number of times the creatures broke the surface, but soon gave up. And then, as suddenly as it had begun, the disturbance in the water ended and the Thames was quiet again. Carpenter and Launceston bent to the oars vigorously. The wherry forged on.

When the current grew stronger as they neared London Bridge, Strangewayes shivered and said, 'Has winter come early?'

Will knew what the younger spy meant. The air had become distinctly colder. His breath misted. He peered out across the water, puzzled, and thought he glimpsed something that troubled him. Strangewayes passed him the lantern and he stood in the stern and held it high. The light glinted off the river. Now he understood the purpose of the swimming creatures and why the sailor and Cecil's guard had seen their flesh turn to ice.

'Row faster,' he called with urgency. 'Ride the fastest current under the bridge, never mind the danger. Our time is running out.'

The Thames was freezing.

CHAPTER SIXTEEN

ICE GLITTERED AROUND THE STONE PILLARS RISING FROM the river. In the growing cold, the fog was thinning. The narrow arch of the bridge supporting its jumble of merchants' houses and shops began to appear out of the grey. The night was filled with the thunderous rush of water between the supports as Launceston and Carpenter heaved on the oars to guide the wherry to the centre of the flow. Will watched their labours, shouting encouragement or guidance when they drifted too far to one side or the other. He had seen more than one vessel dashed to pieces on the bridge pillars. Most watermen would not risk the turbulent currents and dropped their passengers short of the bustling bridge to walk to where they could hail another boat on the other side. The spies did not have that luxury, and now the risk was even greater. The briefest dip in the water would see them torn to pieces by the creatures that swam there, just out of sight.

Despite the chill, sweat glistened on Carpenter's forehead. His long hair flicked back with each jerk of his shoulders, revealing the pink scarring along the left side of his face.

'Heave to the right!' Will yelled as he watched the wherry swirl towards the nearest pillar.

His face impassive, Launceston pulled on his oar. The boat continued to swing in the violent current. As the vessel swept into the dark beneath the bridge, Will inhaled a blast of dank air. The lantern-light flared up the stone support, the high tide mark now glistening with hoar frost.

'Tobias! To me!' he called.

Throwing off his hood, Strangewayes lurched along the yawing wherry to Will's side. As the boat skewed towards the bridge, the two men swung their legs out over the side of the boat and pushed them off the pillar. Carpenter jabbed his oar against the wall, and the three of them steadied the drift. Together they heaved the vessel away. Will and Strangewayes teetered over the churning river until Carpenter snatched two handfuls of damp cloak and yanked them to safety.

The current caught the wildly rocking wherry. When it hurled the vessel across the roiling water, Will crashed on to his back on the bottom. By the time he had managed to raise his head they had shot like an arrow out at the other side.

Here the mist hung in wisps. He could glimpse candle-light in the windows of the large merchant houses that lined the northern banks. A bitter blast of air struck him. Bony fingers of ice reached out from both edges of the river, clutching for the wherry.

''Sblood! How fast it freezes!' Strangewayes exclaimed.

Glancing back, Will saw that a white sheet now covered most of the Thames. The ice appeared to be spreading from upstream where they had witnessed the frantic activity of the pale fish-creatures. He imagined their ritual dance through the dark depths, drawing up the cold power as they weaved together the final strands of their supernatural masters' scheme.

Will began to grasp the true scale of the Unseelie Court's plan. Dee's tattered defences were still strung out invisibly across London, reinforced by the wards Cecil had put in place round the city's boundaries and the quay at Greenwich. But the Thames – a silver lance piercing through to the heart of London – had always proved the most difficult to protect.

As they rounded the bend of the river along the narrowing black channel, Will's worst fears were confirmed. The Charm Boat was locked in the ice not far from the north bank. The two watermen were futilely hammering their oars on the white glaze. It cracked like dry wood, but held firm. No longer able to maintain the ritual path, the frozen wherry had left the river route open to the Enemy.

Carpenter, Launceston and Strangewayes saw the icebound boat and looked back to Will with unease. He nodded. 'They will soon be here.'

The other men's heads fell, but only for a moment. Carpenter and Launceston threw themselves into their oarstrokes, driving the wherry forward.

'The *Gauntlet* will be trapped at the quay,' Strangewayes called. 'What chance have we of freeing it from the ice before the attack comes?'

'We will do what we must.' Will's voice was grim. He pulled his cloak around him against the cold and rested one foot on the side as he searched the sky for the ruddy glow from Greenwich's beacons.

A band of orange sky flared behind the silhouettes of trees, houses and the great bulk of the Palace of Placentia. Wrinkling his nose at the ash caught on the breeze, Will finally saw the stark outline of masts and felt a surge of hope. But only a thin black strand of water stretched out ahead. Their hair and eyebrows white with frost, Carpenter and Launceston shuddered as they struggled to get good strokes with their oars. The wherry bumped against the encroaching ice on either side time and again. Finally the boat came to a juddering halt. The keel groaned from the pressure of the rime forming around it.

'Abandon ship, lads,' Will called.

The shivering spies hauled themselves out of the wherry, each one gingerly testing the ice before putting his full weight on it. The frozen river crunched underfoot. Will scrubbed the white glaze off the surface with the sole of his shoe. Through the near-transparent newly formed ice, he glimpsed movement. The fish-creatures glided just beneath their feet. As if it could read his thoughts, one came to a halt in the space Will had created and peered up at him with those unblinking eyes. It gnashed its needle-teeth once and then swam away.

On the river they could have been in Muscovy in winter. Putting his head down into the chill wind, Will headed towards the silhouetted masts. The crunch of his footsteps echoed across the still waste. The other men followed, their breath clouding. After a few moments, the golden lights of the quayside inn glittered through the stark trees and Will could make out the shape of the *Gauntlet* leaning askew under the force of the ice that had formed around it.

Before he could take another step, Strangewayes called out, 'The fog returns.'

Will turned to see a low wall of mist reaching from bank to bank at their backs. But this fog was a pearly white and seemed to glow with an inner luminescence. It rolled towards them as if a tailor were unfurling a bolt of cloth. Faint stars twinkled in its midst.

'Make for the quay as fast as your legs will carry you,' he urged.

The spies raced towards the inn's lights, slipping and sliding with each step so that Will feared they would fall and break their necks. When he could smell the acrid stink of the pitch on the *Gauntlet*'s hull, he paused and looked back. Tall, grey figures were emerging from the mist, cloaks billowing behind them. They stalked towards Greenwich, grasping swords, spears and axes.

Will felt a chill sweep through him even deeper than the one brought by the frozen river. A droplet of blood fell from his nose and froze before it hit the ice. The Unseelie Court were in opposition to nature, and every sense rebelled whenever they were near. Their clothes had a timeless feel, bucklers and leather belts, breeches and boots, all of them silvery grey as if they considered colour too much of a celebration of life for things that flirted with death. Long hair lashed in the wind. Their faces were the colour of frost, shadows pooling around their eyes. Scanning the steadily advancing group, he counted around thirty, small in number yet devastating in force.

'We have a fight on our hands.' The wind plucked his words away. 'And if we fall this night, England is lost.'

He turned and raced up the icy stone steps that led up to the quay where a crowd of puzzled onlookers had gathered to see the frozen Thames. At his back, the winter storm swept in.

CHAPTER SEVENTEEN

WILL BOUNDED ON TO THE QUAYSIDE, CALLING TO THE pikemen Cecil had set to guard the *Gauntlet*, 'Gather your weapons and prepare for the fight of your lives!' He knew he was probably sending them to their deaths, but their sacrifice would not be forgotten if the ship could be freed from its icy prison. He caught the officer of the guard by the arm and leaned in to whisper, 'Tell your men not to look those bastards in the eye, nor listen to their words. They will undermine you with lies and deceit. Keep your eyes on their weapons and kill without mercy.'

The captain nodded, running towards his men, barking orders. Their cuirasses rattling as they ran, the defenders hurried down the stone steps on to the ice.

'Should we join them in battle?' Launceston peered towards the pale figures drawing in on the quay.

'I need you here to help marshal the crew and these labourers. We must break the ice around the *Gauntlet* and carve a path out to where the river remains unfrozen.'

Unsettled whispers rustled across the quayside. The crowd grew in number as attention fell upon the Unseelie Court.

Will beckoned for the other spies to gather closer. 'We must prevent these good men from having their sleep ruined for evermore – however long that might be after this night,' he whispered. 'Spread the word that it is Spanish agents who approach. We need all good Englishmen to do their part in standing firm against the invaders. Keep them occupied.'

'How do we do that?' Carpenter asked.

'Tell them to collect all the pitch from the shipwrights in Greenwich and carry the barrels down on to the ice. One of you find Captain Prouty and order him to prepare to sail.'

'He will think you mad,' Strangewayes complained.

'Mad, I am. For only one of Bedlam's Abraham men would dare to do what I plan.' Will grinned. 'But this is why the Crown selected us for our work. We are all mad, and, as you well know, the gods protect fools and lovers.'

He spun round, shouting, 'Come, lads!' to draw the attention of the gathered crowd. Carpenter and Strangewayes followed suit, whipping the men up with shouts and cheers and sending them off to the shipwrights' stores marked out by piles of stone ballast along the quayside. Emerging from the inn with Launceston, Captain Prouty tossed aside a mug of ale and bounded up the plank to his ship. His orders rang out through the night as he moved across the deck. At the mainmast he paused to point up towards the yards.

Will ventured to the edge of the quay. On the river, the Queen's men edged away from the safety of Greenwich, pikes levelled and swords drawn. Before them, the Unseelie Court advanced with long, determined strides, heads down into the wind, like wolves preparing to fall on a wounded deer.

Will forced himself not to rush to the aid of the men.

Their sacrifice had bought him time. Turning back to the frantic activity along the dockside, he jumped on to the plank leading up to the galleon and demanded more haste in a voice that carried across the docks. As the labourers trundled the barrels of pitch from the stores, the spy directed them to carry their casks down the steps to the ice and there lay them in a line from the ship's prow out into the river. Carpenter and Strangewayes marshalled another group of men to collect axes and the long-hafted hammers that the boat-builders used to drive wedges to split timber.

'Captain Prouty insisted I inform you that he does indeed think you are mad,' Launceston murmured as he urged the men on, drawn sword in his hand.

'Then we are all in agreement. This is not a place for sane men. Bring the others and let us wallow in our madness.' Will eased into the flow of men trudging down on to the ice.

Once the barrels of pitch were laid out in a line, he ordered a labourer to stand beside each cask with a hammer or an axe and, on his signal, smash it open. When his arm fell, the crashes of splintering wood drowned out the clash of steel and tormented cries echoing from the battle on the other side of the galleon. The pitch spewed out across the hoar-frost from barrel after barrel, flowing stickily into a black line pointing the way to freedom.

'Bring me the brand,' Will called. A workman thrust the spitting torch into his hand, and he lowered the flame to the sable stream. The fire licked at the pitch, raising bubbles that spattered and crackled. After a moment the tar caught. Acrid smoke whisked up, then an orange wall of fire racing out into the middle of the Thames. Cracks like cannon-fire boomed out into the night as the searing heat met the biting cold of the frozen river.

'Do not wait for the ice to melt,' Will roared as he marched along the line of workmen. 'Take your hammers and your axes and smash it to pieces. But take care not to fall into the water.'

Red-faced from the sweltering fire, the men rubbed their hands and spat, grasping their tools and swinging them over their heads. The iron came down like thunder. Chunks of glittering ice flew. Will felt a swell of hope as he saw the jagged cracks race out. Man after man repeated their strikes until the ice shattered and the spy could glimpse lines of black water.

'Keep at it until a channel forms,' he yelled. Twirling an upright finger, he summoned the attention of Carpenter, Launceston and Strangewayes, then flicked his hand towards the galleon. They raced for the steps. On the quay, Will glanced back as a blazing pool of pitch slid into the water with a sizzle. A cloud of steam billowed up. When it cleared, he saw a trail of broken ice reaching out to the unfrozen channel in the middle of the river.

Launceston gave a satisfied nod. 'Let us hope that is enough.'

Cheers rose from the labourers as they swung their tools to break more of the ice. But then, with a resounding crack, a large section broke free and turned vertical like a platter tipping off the edge of a table. Three men standing upon it plunged into the water. Will closed his eyes, knowing what was to come, but still he jerked when the screams tore out.

The dark pool boiled. Labourers inched towards the edge of the cracked ice, reaching out axes towards the thrashing arms. But the limbs fell away at odd angles, and the churning water turned red. After a moment, the river calmed as the feeding ended. The surviving workmen gaped in horror.

Will stifled his dismay at the deaths and ran up the planks leading on to the galleon.

'Master Swyfte, let us see if this wild plan has found its legs,' Captain Prouty boomed from the quarterdeck. He was in his fourth decade, his face pockmarked, and his curly hair streaked with grey. At his barked orders, crewmen scaled the rigging to unfurl the sails.

On the forecastle, Will saw that a clear channel now reached out through the shattered ice, widening by the moment. Would the water freeze over before they could set sail, he wondered?

On the poop deck, Carpenter called out. He leaned over the rail, his mouth a grim slash in the flickering light of the ship's lantern, pointing across the wastes upstream. Will followed the line of his arm. Bodies littered the frozen river, the white now stained with pools of blood. The Unseelie Court had torn through the resistance. The last few pikemen fought on bravely, thrusting with their weapons, but they seemed like statues against the mercury of their foes. The Fay whirled, their blades slicing open throats, lopping off hands or arms or opening up bellies. The last man fell like a strand of barley before a scythe. As one, the Unseelie Court turned towards the galleon and stood motionless for a moment, the bitter breeze whipping their long hair.

Will felt their cold gaze upon him. He sensed their contempt for lesser beings, and their urge for vengeance and hot blood.

The moment passed and the grey figures strode forward

together, slow, relentless, as if they knew no prey could ever escape them.

'Time has run out,' Carpenter said flatly.

'Not yet,' Will growled. His rapier sang as he drew it from its sheath. 'Let them earn their victory.'

With a deep rumble, the sails caught the wind and the *Gauntlet* jerked like a horse under whip. The hull protested, the wood flexing against the hard ice. A loud grinding echoed through the night as the vessel pulled free. Will wondered if the keel would survive its ordeal.

Launceston and Strangewayes darted to the rail. The younger man glanced up at the billowing sails and uttered a prayer.

'You waste your breath calling to your God,' Carpenter snapped. 'We will not escape Greenwich without being tested.'

'What hope do we have?' Strangewayes replied in a small, wavering voice.

'They die on the end of cold steel, like any man,' Will said, trying to reassure him. 'Whatever they are, they breathe, their hearts beat, their blood flows . . . and it can be spilled.'

Strangewayes nodded, hiding his fear. 'I am keen to earn my first kill.'

Carpenter gave a sarcastic grunt and Launceston hummed, one eyebrow raised.

'Let us put our differences aside,' Will whispered, resting one hand on the youngest spy's shoulder. 'Tonight we watch out for each other.'

The Enemy had advanced to within a stone's throw of the lurching galleon, which seemed to be moving through molasses. The cracking and rending of the ice against the hard oak of the hull resounded through the haunted night. At the last, the Fay warriors broke into a run.

Strangewayes was chilled by the sight of the shadowy faces and the silence of the speedy attack, Will could see, but still he grinned, believing the Fay were incapable of boarding the galleon from the frozen river. Will knew better.

'Prepare to repel the Enemy,' he called. 'Hold them off until we reach open water and that is victory enough.'

Before Strangewayes could question the order, the first line of the Enemy reached the side of the galleon. Simultaneously, the Fay leapt. The thuds of the bodies hitting the wood echoed through the vessel. The next line of warriors followed. Peering over the side, Will and Strangewayes glimpsed the Fay clinging to the hull like grey spiders. Their heads swivelled up as one, their eyes glowing. Uttering an oath under his breath, the younger spy crossed himself.

The Fay began to climb.

'For England!' Will called, his voice rising above the shattering of the ice.

Along the rail, any crew members who could be spared drew their swords. Carpenter moved along their ranks, reassuring them with a clap on the back or a touch to the arm. Will could almost hear his quiet urgings: *Do not look in their faces. Strike fast. Whatever you might think, they are Spanish agents in disguise.*

And then the first head appeared above the rail, the skin near as white as the frozen river below, the face blessed with high cheekbones and a straight nose yet made like a rose rotting on the stem by the cruelty glittering in the dark eyes. Before the nearest seaman could even raise his sword, the Fay warrior lashed out with his left hand. Talons ripped through the seaman's pale throat. Blood sparkled like rubies in lamplight.

As the gore-spattered Fay warrior leapt on to the rail, the other men rushed forward, levelling swords and swinging cudgels. Sheer weight of numbers dislodged the boarder. But then the silent Fay attack erupted in force all along the rail.

A grey figure swung in front of Will. The spy parried one strike and pivoted to ram his shoulder against his opponent. For a moment, they hung together against the rail, enveloped in the loamy odour of dark tunnels far underground. Their eyes met. Will saw no compassion there, only contempt for some rough beast that was almost beneath its notice. And then the Fay fell backwards and down towards the ice.

The cries of wounded men echoed across the deck, the iron tang of blood caught on the cold breeze. When a man fell, Will darted into the space, thrusting with his rapier as each new bone-white face heaved into view. He glimpsed Launceston, a curious expression on his face as he studied the deep wound his blade had made across the neck of his opponent: a lick of his lips, a flicker of a smile. Carpenter swung his sword like a butcher carving a cow with strong, hard blows, his lips curled back from his teeth. And Strangewayes darted fast and low, each thrust made with grim determination. Yet the wave of Fay warriors seemed as if it would never end.

Lost to the delirious whirl of swords and bodies and the cries and screams and oaths, Will barely realized the galleon was gathering speed until it lurched free of the ice with such force that it almost threw him from his feet. 'Almost there, Master Swyfte,' Captain Prouty bellowed from the

135

quarterdeck. 'Hold them off a moment longer and we will be away.'

Will caught Carpenter's eyes and they nodded. Renewing their efforts, they yelled encouragement to the men. The Enemy's attack appeared to falter, then die away, and the spy dared to hope. But the resonant cracking of wood signalled a new approach. Throwing himself to the rail, Will peered down the hull to where the remaining warriors clung like spiders. Another crack echoed as a Fay tore off a gun port and flung the shattered oak behind him. Twisting like a snake, he slithered through the black square into the vessel.

'To the gun deck!' Will cried, beckoning his fellow spies as he raced past the bewildered crew and ducked down through the door in the forecastle. He understood the cunning of the Unseelie Court. In the dark, cramped gun deck, filled with cannon, there would be little space for swordplay. The Enemy's speed and strength would give them an even greater advantage.

He slowed as he stepped into the pitch-black of the lower deck. The steely taint of powder hung in the air. Holding his rapier in front of him, he allowed his eyes to adjust to the dark. At the far end, the lighter night intruded in three shafts where the gun ports had been wrenched off. All was still. Will waved his blade from side to side, searching for the attack he knew would come.

'They would lure us into their midst so they can slit our throats, unseen,' Launceston breathed at his shoulder. 'Let them come to us.'

Though the Earl's words made sense, Will felt a tingle of apprehension. His worry was answered a moment later by a flaring light. A flint had been struck. A candle flame flickered into life in the open door of a lantern. White faces appeared from the gloom like pale fish rising from the sightless depths. Will saw a triumphant smirk spread across the lips of the Fay warrior who held the lantern and he knew what was to come.

'Back,' he yelled, keeping his rapier levelled as he urged the other three up the steps. 'We are too late.'

The powder barrel lay on its side, its granular, black contents flowing across the boards. Two of the Fay warriors darted past the cannon and wriggled out the way they had entered. The third stood against the open gun door, his gleaming eyes locked on Will. With a flick of his wrist, he released the lantern. The guttering flame arced.

Will pounded back up the steps after the others. The blast ripped through the heart of the vessel, flinging all four spies through the forecastle door and across the main deck. His head ringing, Will felt the ship lurch to one side beneath him. Grey smoke billowed out of the open door. The roar of the raging fire below deck drowned out the terrified cries of the crew.

Will hauled himself on to shaky legs. Flames were already licking up the side of the stricken vessel, curls of sparks whisking towards the sails. He reached out a hand to drag Carpenter to his feet. Launceston and Strangewayes staggered behind.

Another blast tore open the main deck. An orange sheet of flame rushed up through the fissure, catching stays and canvas and lines as it swept along the vessel. A sailor was caught in the inferno and, screaming in agony, hurled himself overboard in a bid to quench the flames. Will choked, holding up an arm to protect his face from the searing heat pressing in on every side. They had perhaps only a moment before the powder store blew, taking the galleon and every man aboard to kingdom come. Yet the fire beat him back at every turn.

'Is this how it ends, then,' Strangewayes gasped, his face ruddy in the light of the flames, 'for us, for England?'

Will spun round, searching for a path through the conflagration. Then, as the mainmast cracked with a sound like cannon-shot, the blazing sailcloth plunged down towards them.

CHAPTER EIGHTEEN

FLAMES ROARED UP INTO THE NIGHT. DANCING ORANGE light flared across the frozen river as the listing galleon was consumed in the jaws of the conflagration. Blackened wood cracked and spat. Black snow fell across the icy waste, flakes of charred canvas swirling in the breeze. In the trees on the far bank of the Thames, Sir Robert Cecil watched from under lowered brows and thought of the midwinter fire festivals in the far north. No celebration here; it was a bonfire of all their hopes. After so long holding the Unseelie Court at bay, England was lost.

Sickened, he reined in his skittish horse, no longer able to see a path ahead. What would he tell the Queen? That Dee was lost to them? That they should free the Faerie Queen immediately and plead for mercy from the Fay when they came like a storm in the night?

His bodyguard shifted uncomfortably in his saddle. He was a big man, his face a map of scars, but he sensed his master's dismay and had grown scared. 'Swyfte and his men?' he asked.

'Dead and gone. They failed us all.'

The galleon's powder store exploded, the deafening blast a bitter punctuation to his comment. A plume of fire soared high above the treetops. Shards of smouldering timber and burning sailcloth rained down. The spymaster's horse whinnied in terror and reared up, almost throwing him from its back. With a curse, he fought to bring it under control. When the fog of smoke cleared, nothing of the *Gauntlet* remained save a few burning staves slipping below the black water.

Cecil covered his eyes, hoping the soughing of the wind in the branches would soothe him after the din. Yet when he raised his head to survey the dismal scene, he felt as if despair would be lodged in his heart for ever. Damn Swyfte for raising his spirits! After such hope, this failure tasted even more bitter.

'Back to the Palace of Whitehall,' he snarled to his bodyguard. 'I must give the Queen my counsel.' He urged his mount back on to the lonely road to London.

As he rode, his gaze flickered towards the white ribbon of the Thames glimpsed through the trees. He could no longer see any sign of the misty figures he had witnessed sweeping towards the galleon. From a distance, they had looked like moon-shadows, but he knew their true nature. Even if he had raised the militia, they would have stood little chance of repelling the invader. The tales of the days when the Unseelie Court roamed across England without hindrance haunted him, and always would. The ruined lives, the lost souls. *Jane, poor Jane.* Still visiting him every night without fail.

As the two riders thundered towards London's walls, the bodyguard bellowed to the sentries to open the gates. Inside the city, their hoofbeats rattled off wattle walls. Candlelight gleamed in windows here and there, but the cold streets were empty. Cecil had thought the explosion at Greenwich would have brought the curious and fearful out into the night, and he wondered if somehow they all sensed that grim atmosphere. *Stay with your families and pray for all our souls*, he silently implored.

And on they rode, out of the West Gate and up to the Palace of Whitehall, ablaze with lanterns to hold the night at bay. Within the walls, Cecil felt the tightness in his chest ease a little. An illusion, he knew. He took in the pikemen marching in their ranks and the sentries lining the walls in preparation for what was undoubtedly to come, and then he hurried towards the Black Gallery. He dreaded giving the Queen the news that he had failed her – Elizabeth's temper burned hot – and he had resolved to lay the blame squarely at Swyfte's feet, when a woman darted out of the shadows to confront him. It was the spy's mare, Grace Seldon, the one Swyfte had sworn to protect and who mooned over him like a girl who had yet to bleed. She was wrapped in a cloak the colour of forget-me-nots, but her eyes were pink from lack of sleep. Her hair had been pulled back with little care and tied with an old ribbon.

'Sir, pray tell me news of William Swyfte.' She lifted her fine-boned face up to him, as pale as the moon. 'He came to me in a manner that suggested he feared he would not be returning—'

'Then you should have listened to him,' the spymaster barked, trying to push by the lady-in-waiting. 'Master Swyfte has passed from this world, God save his meagre soul.'

141

The woman's eyes widened for a moment as she clutched her fluttering hands to her lips before falling back in a swoon. Cecil regretted his cruel response for the inconvenience it had caused him. Turning, he beckoned to his bodyguard. 'Take her to the physician so she does not clutter up this place, and do not allow her near me again.' Women were a mystery to him, and a weakness to all men. Swyfte had been proof enough of that.

He hurried into the Black Gallery, hoping for a moment to order his thoughts before he faced the Queen. Instead, he found the Earl of Essex pacing the chamber. In the candlelight, the Earl was all aglow in a white doublet and half-compass cloak and breeches the colour of snow. *A fine show*, Cecil inwardly sneered. *So wealthy and gallant and charming, no smuts would ever dare taint his attire.*

'At last,' the Earl snapped, stabbing a finger towards the spymaster. 'Hiding yourself away to avoid all blame while England burns?'

'Someone has to keep the wheels of government turning in this time of trouble.'

'I suspected you were arranging a ship to flee to Flanders, or France.' Essex narrowed his eyes.

'You think we can run from them?' Cecil snorted.

The Earl slumped on to a bench, head in hands. The spymaster glanced at the other man askance, surprised to see the usual swagger stripped away.

'We have lived fat for so many years, we have forgotten what it was like. The bodies in the ditches leaking pus and shit. The children stolen from their cribs. Women turned to stone, and men left blind or mad.' Essex ran his fingers through his lustrous hair. 'Perhaps we should run, whatever you say. They will come for us first, the ones who kept them at bay and colluded in the imprisonment of their Queen. Not the ignorant common man who goes about his life with eyes only on the next meal. If we earned ourselves even a day more of life, that would be of some value.'

Cecil lumbered to the hearth and tossed another log on the fire. It had grown chill in the room. 'I would hold your tongue, sir,' he replied with unconcealed disgust. 'We do not run like rats. We have sworn an oath to stand by the Queen, and England.'

Essex stared into the corner of the chamber, unable to meet the other man's eye.

'The Privy Council?' Cecil asked.

'Has gathered, as you requested. What will be your advice to the Queen?'

Before the spymaster could answer, pounding feet drew nearer and the door crashed open. A pikeman lurched in, his helmet askew and his cheeks flushed. The spymaster could see the flames of fear licking in the man's eyes. 'I plead indulgence for this rude entry, sirs,' the man stuttered, 'but your . . . your attendance has been requested.'

'By whom?' Cecil snapped.

The pikeman moistened his dry mouth. 'Men wait upon the frozen river. Men . . .' His voice trailed away and his blank gaze roamed the room as he recalled what he had witnessed.

'The Spanish,' the spymaster said. 'The ones who plot against the Crown?' It was a small kindness, he knew, but it allowed the pikeman an opportunity to pretend.

The man nodded. 'They would meet, upon the river, to discuss the terms of England's surrender.'

Cecil threw a hard look at Essex. 'Fetch the Privy Council. We should face this rabble shoulder to shoulder and show what Englishmen are made of.'

Essex bowed briefly and left. The pikeman followed. Once he was alone, the spymaster threw his head back and sucked in a gulp of air, trying to stop the shaking of his hands.

He found the Privy Council gathered near the River Gate, beady-eyed and grey-bearded, like a murder of crows in their black gowns, shivering in the chill coming off the river. Cecil flapped a hand to urge the sentries to drag open the gates. He stared at the widening crack with mounting dread, feeling his heart beat in rhythm to the creaks and groans of the protesting hinges. Finally the gates crashed wide with a resounding *thoom*. Cecil's breath caught in his throat.

At first the expanse of white river appeared empty. A cold wind moaned over the icy wastes. The stark branches of the trees across the Thames on Bankside whisked. But just as he began to hope that the Enemy had departed, he glimpsed movement, as if a hunting party were emerging from a thick fog. Grey figures appeared in the centre of the frozen river, silent sentinels watching him with hate-filled eyes. Long hair and bone-white faces. Doublets and bucklers and breeches silvery with mildew as if they had been stored in dank cellars. On either side and behind the tight knot of the main group of ten or so, warriors waited. They appeared misty, their features hidden, as if glimpsed through a haze.

Cecil swallowed. Then he pushed up his chin and marched out. He prayed the Privy Council were following him. Resisting the urge to look back, he walked out along the jetty and climbed the short wooden ladder down to the ice. Through clear patches around his feet, he could see pale shapes swimming near the surface of the river beneath. He shivered, feeling himself moving into a world he no longer understood.

The spymaster came to a halt four sword-lengths from the Unseelie Court's representatives. He turned a cold face towards them, but would not – could not – meet their gaze. At the centre of the group was a tall figure with long black hair, a sallow complexion and a beard and moustache waxed into points. Beneath a felt cap, shadows pooled in the eyes, but Cecil noted a cruel turn to the pursed lips. *This one is the leader*, the spymaster decided.

'I am Lansing of the High Family,' the Fay said in a whispery voice that somehow carried over the sighing of the wind. 'All you hoped for has turned to ashes. These are the final days. Have you made your peace with your God?'

'We are not afraid of you.' Cecil hoped the defiance in his voice rang true.

'Your last hope has died with the burning of your ship,' the Fay continued as if he had not heard the spymaster's comment. 'This moment was inevitable, from the instant you betrayed us and stole our Queen. I find it laughable that you ever thought otherwise.'

'We held you at bay for many years.'

'The blink of an eye in the way we see time. We are eternal. We watch and we wait and we make our plans and when the time comes we strike, be it years or decades.'

'How you must hate us,' Cecil sneered.

Lansing knitted his brow. 'Hate? Do you hate the beasts of the field? They are to be herded, and punished when

145

disobedient, and slaughtered should we see fit. Is that not how it is in your fields?' He looked across the troubled faces and then raised his gaze to the lights of the palace. 'You lived in caves once. You hunted with stones and sticks. You whispered oaths to the moon and the trees and the wind. We watched you as you sat around your fires, praying the night would end. When you sowed your seeds, we were there. When you raised the stones and built your homes of timber and turf. When you tamed the horses and made weapons of iron. Always a whisper away.' One corner of his mouth crinkled in a puzzled smile. 'And then you challenged us.' He looked directly in Cecil's face. 'I have peeled back your skin, and your flesh, and broken your bones and delved into the smallest part of you, and I have found you wanting. This judgement has been made. And now the time for talk is done, and silence must fall. Bring me our Queen and prepare for the harrowing.'

The spymaster sifted through Lansing's words, seeing meaning hidden in the shadows behind them as only a spymaster could. He smiled, quick and fast. 'No,' he said. The Fay's eyes narrowed. 'If you want her, take her.'

In a single fluid movement the Earl of Essex drew his sword in readiness for a fight, as did a number of the younger Privy Councillors. Yet the Unseelie Court remained as still as the ice beneath their feet. The cold wind tugged at their hair, its whispers the only sounds across the desolate river.

As he searched those unreadable faces with their un- blinking eyes, Cecil felt a moment of satisfaction. He spun on his heel, turning up his nose at the aged members of the Privy Council who had been cowering behind him. 'Follow me,' he said to them with only a hint of contempt, and strode back towards the jetty. Even at such a moment, he found himself smiling inwardly at the notion of the deformed little man he knew himself to be piping on the rats who had always secretly mocked him.

He felt the Fay leader's cold gaze upon him, but he did not look back. Once he had passed the River Gate, he leaned against the stone wall, shaking, yet proud of himself.

Gathering himself, he turned to the other men. 'We die with dignity, not as cowards. Let us to the Queen and see if we can find a sliver of hope in this time I have bought us.' With that, he marched away, head high.

CHAPTER NINETEEN

SILENCE HAUNTED THE DUSTY PRIVY COUNCIL CHAMBER. In the candlelight, the blank face of Elizabeth, Queen of England and all its dominions, glowed as white as a death mask, the make-up so thick to hide the ravages of age and high office that flakes intermittently fell to the lace ruff round her neck. Her eyes, though, were black pebbles of despair, Cecil thought. She saw the end of her reign, of all England. She folded her hands in the lap of her golden skirts and looked around the sallow faces of her councillors. Few would meet her gaze. Finally her eyes alighted on the spymaster.

'Sir Robert, it seems only you have the courage to speak. Throw me some crumbs of comfort.'

Cecil bowed. 'Your Highness, these are indeed the worst of times. Our hopes of bringing Dr Dee home to bolster our defences have been dashed by our Enemy's cunning. We feared an impending invasion.' He moistened his lips, measuring Elizabeth's mood from half-lidded eyes. 'And yet in my encounter with those black-hearted fiends 'pon the frozen Thames, I spied a sliver of hope. Or, at the least, a moment to catch our breath.'

'You almost lost all our lives there and then with your play of defiance, you fly-bitten whey-face,' Essex muttered just behind the spymaster's shoulder.

Ignoring his rival, Cecil continued, 'In recent times, our Enemy have shown no desire to negotiate. They take what they want. And yet they come to us demanding that we bring their Queen to them. Why do they not storm this palace and seize her themselves?' He paused for effect, raising his chin. 'Because they cannot.'

'If the threads of Dee's defences still hold, they will not do so for much longer, Little Elf. The inevitable has only been delayed.'

'That is true, Your Majesty.'

'Then what use is the time you have bought us?' The Queen leaned forward on her throne, her brow knitting beneath her auburn wig.

'Majesty, I would suggest a final, desperate gamble.' Cecil had thought long and hard about the options left to them while he waited for the Queen to make her way to the council chamber. He knew Elizabeth well. She was not weak. In times of anger or fear, she had a strong stomach for courses that would be unpalatable to many.

'Speak,' she said. 'Even dry bread is a feast to a beggar.'

'You are right to say our defences will crumble soon, without Dr Dee to bring his magics back to them. Yet we have one thing of value, one thing only, but it is a jewel beyond measure: the Faerie Queen herself.'

'She will not offer us mercy,' Elizabeth snapped.

'No. But she has one other thing to offer us . . . her life.' A shocked murmur ran through the black-gowned men at his back. Cecil watched the same shock light Elizabeth's eyes. Yet she had steeled herself once to order the execution of another Queen, and that Queen her cousin; could the removal of one as despised as their immortal Enemy really be a step too far? Certainly, they had never encountered a more desperate time. 'My counsel, Your Majesty, is that we build a pyre to the very top of the Lantern Tower. Should the Unseelie Court threaten us further, we set it alight and burn their Queen alive in her prison.'

'And watch her die as we ourselves go down in flames?'

'The Unseelie Court would not risk losing the only thing of value to them. It is a balance—'

'It is a foolish notion!' The Queen's eyes blazed. 'Do you think we can keep the Unseelie Court at bay for ever while our men stand by with brands? Once the defences collapse, they will be working their magics in every corner of the land. They will attempt to steal me out from under your nose, Sir Robert, and place *me* on a pyre, tempting you to blink first.'

Cecil bowed his head for a moment, allowing the monarch to calm, and then he replied in a quiet voice, 'It is all we have, Your Majesty.'

Elizabeth slumped back in her throne, her chin falling to her chest.

'This may not hold for ever, Your Majesty. In the end, we may all go down in flames, though knowing we have inflicted a wound that will burn our Enemy for all time. And yet, the Unseelie Court are cautious. Time, as their representative told me, means nothing to them. They will not take rash action. And so we may earn respite for a day, a week, a month, a year, while we search for some new defence.'

'And live in dread? Never knowing if each night will be our last? I would rather . . .' The Queen caught the word in her throat and shook her head. 'While there is life there is hope. But only Dr Dee has ever found a way to shut out those foul creatures. Where will we turn in this hour of need?'

Cecil knew he had no answer, but he was spared a hollow reply. Outside the door, argumentative voices could be heard. Elizabeth scowled at the disturbance. 'What is the meaning of this intrusion?' the spymaster called. With a flamboyant sweep of his white cloak, Essex strode over and threw the door open. The two pikemen who guarded the entrance to the chamber had crossed their weapons to bar a young man. It was Swyfte's assistant, Nathaniel Colt, flushed and sweating, his forehead streaked with the dirt of the road. Behind him, the spymaster glimpsed the young woman Grace Seldon. The news of her friend's death had clearly sloughed off her with surprising speed, for her face had hardened and she looked to have recovered her fire. She pressed the assistant forward against the pikes. The young man saw the Queen on her throne and bowed his head. 'Your Majesty,' he murmured, playing with his cap.

'Have you lost your wits?' Cecil demanded. 'Do you wish to call the Tower home?'

'Sir . . .' Nathaniel stuttered, 'I . . . I must speak to you.' He glanced back at Grace and found new strength in her determined look. 'On a matter of great urgency,' he continued with a deep bow. 'I have a message from my master.'

CHAPTER TWENTY

THE RISING SUN HAD SET THE SKY ABLAZE. GULLS WHEELED in the salty wind blowing from the east, greeting the morn with hungry cries. The forest of masts silhouetted against the red glow swayed as the great vessels strained at their anchors in Tilbury docks on the wide, grey Thames. The slap of sailcloth and the crack of rigging accompanied the shanties of the sailors on the only galleon abuzz with activity. To most of those who crowded into the taverns lining the quay, the *Tempest* was a ship of mysterious purpose. None knew the vessel had been set aside long ago for use by the secret service, a ghost in the ledgers of the quay master and the Queen's tax men, often coming and going under cover of the night with a crew that rarely mixed with the other sea-dogs.

Shielding his eyes against the brassy dawn light, Will Swyfte allowed himself a tight smile of approval. His black and silver doublet was still smeared with ashes and soot from the fire aboard the *Gauntlet*, and the ends of his hair were singed. A small price to pay, he knew. 'You have done us proud, Sir Walter,' he said with a nod.

'And you are a cunning dog, Master Swyfte, and a man after my own heart.' Raleigh clapped his hands together, grinning at the success of the deception. In his lime-green doublet and ochre cloak, he looked out of place on the quayside with its barrels of stinking pitch, dusty piles of ballast and heaps of dung from the merchants' carthorses. 'Two ships provisioned, one by the Queen and one by the School of Night, one in full view and one in secret.'

'Keep a door open for a quick exit, that has always been my code.' Will closed his eyes and saw once again the wall of orange flame that had engulfed the *Gauntlet*. But they had been ready. The rowing boat towed along behind the galleon had always been their planned escape route should they come under concerted attack. While the other seamen leapt into the river, only to be consumed in a white-water frenzy by the ferocious creatures swimming there, he had battled through the flames with the other three spies. At the sterncastle, he, Launceston, Carpenter and the young spy, Strangewayes, had slid down the oiled rope into the dinghy and rowed away, an insignificant speck beside the blazing ship. The fast current had swept them towards Tilbury where Nathaniel awaited them, ready to be despatched to the Palace of Whitehall.

Raleigh eyed the other man askance. 'You knew the Unseelie Court would be lured by the *Gauntlet*. And once that vessel was destroyed, they would have no reason to believe you had prepared a second ship. A strong plan, a winning one.' He paused. 'Have you made your peace with the loss of the good men who died in the attack?'

Will raised his head to watch the sailors climbing the lines like monkeys, as if he had not heard. 'Every war has its

153

casualties. Their sacrifice will not be forgotten,' he said after a moment. Though Raleigh nodded, the spy could hear the unspoken codicil: the men had not been asked to give up their lives, and would not have accepted if they had. With each day, it seemed he made another accommodation with his conscience. How far was he prepared to go to bring Jenny home; how many lives was he prepared to sacrifice? He had no answer, though he wondered if the Unseelie Court's bleak judgement of human nature was true. He cast an unsettled glance back along the winding Thames. 'I fear I must take my leave. Time is of the essence. Our Enemy will not be blind to my guile for much longer and we must reach open water before they give pursuit. But I thank you for your aid. I am in your debt.'

Raleigh tugged at his beard and smiled. 'You are indeed, Master Swyfte. Do not forget our agreement.'

Raleigh played a long game, not so far removed from the machinations of the Unseelie Court, Will realized. The information he brought back from the New World – should he ever return – would be more valuable than gold to the School of Night. The great men who made up the numbers of the secret society could translate knowledge into power with ease. But what were they plotting? Why was the New World so important to them? Raleigh would certainly never tell. With a smile and a nod, the explorer slipped into the shadowy alley beside the shipwright's workshop where he had tethered his horse.

Turning back to the *Tempest*, Will pushed past the queue of men carrying the last of the provisions up the plank. At the poop deck rail, he searched the broad river to the west where the grey fug of London's home fires tainted the sky.

No sign yet of any pursuit, but it would come. The wolves of the Unseelie Court would sniff the wind and know their prey was loose.

'Master Swyfte. We are ready to sail.' The booming voice cut through the raucous singing of the labouring sailors. Captain John Courtenay was a giant of a man, seasoned by the sun and the salty wind, his brown beard and hair proudly untamed. No other could be trusted to lead the expedition into the dangerous uncharted waters that lay ahead. A veteran of the New World, he knew all that had yet been learned of that mysterious place. He knew of the trade routes where they might encounter heavily armed Spanish galleons bringing their rich hauls of silver and spices back to Europe, and of the river inlets bristling with fleets of small boats filled with Indians with blowpipes. He knew, too, of the plants that brought sickness and death, and of those that supplied bountiful fruit; of the taste of the wind that heralded a tropical storm. He had helped claim Nova Albion for the Crown and had been at Sir Francis Drake's side during the sacking of Cartagena and the capture of San Augustin in Spanish Florida.

And yet there were some who believed him quite mad. Bloody Jack, they called him, the sea-dog who tore out the throats of his enemies with his teeth and dyed his beard blood-red before every battle. Will wondered if that wild nature was the result of the torture the captain had received at the hands of the Spanish, his mind as scarred as his face, which was marred by a ragged pink X that ran from temple to jaw. Yet for what lay ahead, a madman was the sanest choice of all.

'Unfurl your sails, captain. We cannot depart soon enough.'

'Do ye have a course for me yet?'

'Soon. Take us out of the Channel and into the wide Atlantic, and then I will have what you need. But I must warn you – we venture close to the very home of the Unseelie Court.'

He waited for the captain to berate him for embarking on a quest that could only be suicide for every man aboard. Instead, Courtenay laughed, too loud. 'Finally we shall take the battle to those pale bastards. Too long have we cowered, Master Swyfte. Let them come in their thousands, with their magics and their creatures and their phantoms, let them drag me down to Hell, I will take down a hundred for every man we lose and die with no fear in my eyes.'

Will saw the unsettling gleam in Bloody Jack's eye. No other man would go so willingly to the source of the nightmares that had plagued humankind since Eden. He knew then he had made the right choice. Bloody Jack threw his arms wide and burst into song, striding back to the main deck to watch his men swarming up the rigging to the yards.

Will stared into the distance, the hairs on the back of his neck prickling. The sun was turning gold in a cloudless blue sky and haze hung over the river where it flowed towards the sea. It was a good day, and likely to be warm for the season. He frowned. His spirits should have been soaring, but all he could sense were the shadows closing in on every side.

On the quarterdeck, Carpenter and Launceston stood against the rail, bickering. Will had seen the signs and he feared Carpenter's mood was growing darker still. The Unseelie Court had a way of infecting men with a creeping despair that usually ended in death. Carpenter should have been stripped of his duties and given time to recover, yet here Will was, taking the wounded man to the very heart of the thing that was slowly destroying him. As for Launceston – who knew what moved in his dark depths? Yet did that give Will the right to lead the Earl by his nose to his potential doom? And there on the forecastle was Strangewayes, still struggling to come to terms with the haunted world in which he found himself. Will had stolen him from Grace, denying two people happiness in one fell swoop, and hurting one whom he had professed to protect.

He turned away from his men, feeling the weight of his decision. Had he damned everyone he knew and his own soul in the process? He wondered if it was the natural order for men to become as terrible as the things they fought. Yet the stakes were high, and no reward was easily bought. This was the path he had chosen and no other would lead to victory.

As the wind filled the sails and the anchor rose from the river in a cascade of glittering jewels, the *Tempest* began to pull away from the quay, gathering speed. Will leaned on the rail, watching the fields move away from him, and the oaks and elms, and all that he knew. And he wondered if he would ever see England again.

CHAPTER TWENTY-ONE

THE POOP DECK HEAVED ON THE HEAVY SWELL AND A GOOD wind filled the sails. Under blue skies, the *Tempest* scudded towards the New World, bearing down hard on the darkness and the mystery. Yet Will and Captain Courtenay stood at the rail and looked out across the choppy water at their back. They watched a wall of grey cloud rolling across the white-topped waves on the eastern horizon, keeping pace with the galleon. Both men felt uneasy.

'Master Swyfte, I fear we have a problem.' Captain Courtenay removed the beechwood and brass tele-scope from his eye. 'If that is a natural formation, then I am a toad-spotted skains-mate.'

Will took the tele-scope and studied the drifting fog. Even so powerful a tool as Dr Dee's most recent invention could not pierce that dense cloud. No sign of pursuit had troubled them as the *Tempest* sailed out of the Channel, past southern Ireland and into the wide Atlantic. But when that strange cloud appeared one hour ago, Will had felt the first prickle of unease. 'Does it appear to you to be drawing closer?' he asked.

'Hard to tell. The ocean plays tricks on the wits. I have seen seasoned sailors look at the green waves and believe them the fields of their home. They step out to walk a while and sink straight to the bottom.' Bloody Jack took back the tele-scope and shoved it into the waist of his salt-stained breeches. 'And islands that seem a cannon-shot away can take days to reach.'

'Then there is little we can do but watch and wait,' Will replied. 'And if it is some threat unleashed by the Unseelie Court, we must be prepared to act.'

Courtenay threw his head back and laughed. 'You have indeed led us by the nose into Hell, Master Swyfte. Should we fight the devils at our back or flee towards the devils that lie ahead? Now that is a choice!'

As the captain made his way to the main deck, angry cries rose up from the crew. A hooded figure wrapped in a plain brown woollen cloak flew out of the doorway to the lower decks and sprawled across the sandy boards. The first mate prowled out a moment later, a swarthy man with a drooping black moustache and only one eye. Brandishing his sword, he loomed over the fallen figure.

'A stowaway, lads, stealing the food from our barrels,' he roared. 'Over the side with 'im!'

'Stay your hand.' Will bounded down the steps from the poop deck. With the cold efficiency for which they were known, two sailors had already hauled their captor half over the rail. They glanced back towards Will, unsure.

'Do as 'e says,' the first mate muttered. He eyed the spy from under low brows, making no attempt to hide his irritation at being overruled.

The sullen sailors dragged the writhing stowaway back

from the brink and threw the cloaked figure to its knees. When the first mate yanked back the hood to reveal the stranger's identity, a shocked murmur ran through the watching crew.

'A woman!' the first mate exclaimed.

'Grace?' Will uttered, stunned.

The young woman looked up at her former protector with defiance. 'I could have remained hidden for days longer, if not weeks, if that rat had not startled me. What a foolish girl I am.'

The spy reeled. 'Are you mad?' He couldn't help but think of the dangers she now faced.

At the outcry, Strangewayes, Launceston and Carpenter stumbled from below deck where they had been drinking sack and playing cards in the captain's quarters. The young spy gaped when he saw his love.

'Say nothing,' Grace snapped, eyes blazing, 'or I will be forced to show you the edge of my tongue.'

Launceston shook his head, bored. 'I thought this would be a matter of interest that might relieve the tedium of this long journey. Who would choose a life on the waves? Only jolt-headed malt-worms, that's who.' He eyed the crew with contempt, either oblivious or uncaring of the murderous glances they shot back, and sauntered below deck once again.

'This woman of yours will not be satisfied until she has ended all our lives,' Carpenter blazed. 'I knew it from the moment I first laid eyes on the reckless sow.'

'Still your tongue,' Will ordered. Grace feigned an air of haughty indifference and looked away.

'From this day on, we will have to risk our own necks

to keep her safe. As usual,' Carpenter continued.

'I said, be silent.' Will's voice crackled with anger.

Strangewayes' face had drained of blood. He held out a hand to help the woman he loved to her feet and she took it as if she were accepting an invitation to dance. 'Why did you do this, Grace?' he murmured.

'I am no weak little thing,' she said with defiance. 'If this matter concerns my sister, I would be a part of it.'

'Your sister?' Carpenter said, baffled. 'Have you taken a knock to the head?'

Will's heart sank. Was that what she had taken from their parting words? His conscience was already on its knees, and here was another burden for it.

Strangewayes stepped closer to her and hissed in her ear, 'You are aboard a ship full of lustful seamen who will not feel a woman's soft embrace for many months.' He looked around the silent crew. 'But that is the least of your worries. Do you have any notion of the terrible situation you have placed yourself in?' His voice cracked with despair, and he looked at Will. 'We must turn back.'

'No,' Grace exclaimed, her eyes widening. 'You cannot abandon this voyage because of my . . .' Will watched her choose her words carefully, 'foolishness. Too much is at stake. Too much invested in this expedition. You would not be able to raise the funds for another voyage for months, if at all.'

'She is right,' Carpenter whispered in Will's ear, bracing himself against the movement of the deck beneath his feet. 'If we turn back, we lose everything. You have no right to make that decision to save this woman, however much she means to you.'

'Please,' Strangewayes begged, arms outstretched. The

161

word was almost lost beneath the creak of the rigging and the boom of the wind in the sails. 'Grace *has* been foolish but she should not pay for that error with her life.'

Will hid his dismay and beckoned to Grace. Carpenter was correct; he had no choice. Holding her chin high, she followed him back on to the poop deck where the crew could not overhear their conversation. 'What have you done, Grace?'

'I can cope with any hardship. I have in me the heart of a lion, like our Queen.' She turned away from his damning gaze and looked out over the heaving blue-grey swell.

'You have led a sheltered life—'

She spun round, her cheeks colouring. 'Sheltered? My life was destroyed when my sister was torn from the heart of my family, as was yours. If I can survive that misery, I can survive anything.'

Will saw her pain, still raw after all those years, and changed his approach. 'I know there is steel in you. But even with all that you have endured, you have barely scraped the surface of the dangers that exist in the world. You must trust me on that.'

Seeing that he had only her well-being at heart, she softened. 'I know you wish to protect me, as you have always done, but I have had my fill of being pushed aside like a girl and told only what is good for me. I believed Jenny dead, but your unwavering faith has given me hope and that, somehow, is more painful by far.' Tears stung her eyes. 'Over the years, I have grown to understand the secrets hidden in your words, and between your words and behind them.' She laughed, brushing the teardrops aside. 'Perhaps I would make a good spy.'

'And what secrets have you learned?'

She lowered her eyes and whispered, 'The ones in your heart, the ones in mine. I would rather be dead than suffer any longer in this twilight world filled only with ghosts and what-might-have-beens.'

Will understood, completely, and hated himself for it. 'You vex me, Grace,' he sighed.

She smiled, taking it as a compliment. 'When Nat returned to the palace with your message, I made him tell me what you had planned.' She saw his face harden and added hurriedly, 'Do not blame Nat. He is a good soul and I can twist him round until he tells me anything. He thought he was doing me a kindness by telling me you had survived, but while his back was turned I took a carriage to Tilbury.'

'And you crept on board and hid away.'

'On the orlop deck, sneaking down to the bilge when anyone came.'

Despite himself, Will felt some admiration. 'You are very determined,' he said, showing a stern face. 'But now you have created a great problem for me. I fear what you might see on this terrible journey. And whatever you may say, my men cannot help but try to protect you when danger arises, and by doing so they will put their own lives at greater risk.'

'I would not see any of them hurt on my behalf.'

'Nevertheless, that is the grave situation in which we now find ourselves. How to proceed?' His brow knit, he glanced out to sea, but saw only that strange, troubling cloud on the far horizon. What had already seemed dire was now fraught with even greater dilemmas. 'I must think on this awhile. Go to Tobias, but do not distract him from his duties. He will find you a berth in the captain's cabin and curtain it with sailcloth. You must stay away from the men at all costs, do you understand?'

She nodded. In her brightening eyes, he thought he saw a glimmer of excitement. For all the danger, she was enjoying her great adventure. At the top of the steps, she glanced back. 'Will, I am sorry if I have angered you, but to ease this pain in my heart, I would risk anything.' He held her gaze for a long moment, and then she descended to find Strangewayes, ignoring the lingering stares of the crew.

'Master Swyfte,' Courtenay bellowed from the main deck, 'I would have that course now. The Atlantic is not the pond at Baldock Green. We can sail around here till Doomsday without ever stumbling across our destination.'

'Prepare your charts, captain,' Will called back. 'I will have your settings in no time.' His hand fell to the leather pouch hanging at his side, feeling the weight of the secret he had concealed. All the risks he had taken, all the deceptions, and all the plans he had made, were coming to a head. This ship of fools had passed the point of no return and only darkness lay ahead.

CHAPTER TWENTY-TWO

THE NAKED WOMAN BUCKED AND WRITHED ABOVE THE OLD man. The rhythmic creak of the narrow bed echoed around the captain's dusty cabin, accompaniment to a symphony of moans. The waves lapped. The hull groaned. Flushed from their ardour, Red Meg O'Shee wiped the sweat from her pale forehead with the back of her slender hand. Beneath her, Dr Dee grunted, his grey eyes glassy. Though she ground her hips and swung her breasts and used every love-making skill she had mastered in her hard life, the Irish spy felt that the magician was almost oblivious of her presence. She knew he was aroused; his hardness inside her was testament to that. Yet his gaze searched only an inner horizon and his lips moved in whispered conversation with things she could not see. Sometimes she thought she heard responses from the corners of the cramped cabin, and then her arms prickled into gooseflesh.

She hid her distaste for what she endured. This was business, no more, and she had long since grown inured to the demands of staying alive in a trade not known for the longevity of its practitioners. But she wondered how much longer she could continue this way. Since she had stolen Dee from under the noses of the English, she had kept him bewitched with her thighs and the stupor-inducing concoctions she had been taught to mix by the wise women in the green hills of her homeland. But after Liverpool, other devils rode him.

She had watched him weave his magics with mirrors, hunched over their glittering surfaces uttering a guttural language that sounded like pebbles dropped on wood. In response, she had seen the shadows seem to lengthen around the cabin, and move of their own accord. And as of that moment he had been like a man drifting through a dream, ignoring her honeyed whispers as he took command of the vessel. The crew had fallen further under his insidious influence, going about their work in silence with the same glassy-eyed distraction. Captain Duncombe had stood by her at every turn.

As the west coast of Ireland faded from view, she sensed other, unseen passengers aboard, voices whispering down in the bilge or on the gun deck or the orlop deck, although each proved empty whenever she investigated. Flickers of movement in shadowy corners, gone when she looked directly. The nights were worse, until she had become afraid to sleep. A haunted ship carried her away from all she knew, she could deny it no longer.

She felt Dee's muscles grow taut and raised herself off him before he spilled his seed, finishing with her mouth in a manner that would have drawn admiration from the doxies along Bankside. Once done, she whispered in his ear, 'You have made my head spin, as always, my sweet. I am caught in your spell.'

'I have business on deck,' he muttered, pushing her aside. Meg flashed a murderous glance, but hid it before the doctor saw, though she doubted he would have cared; he already appeared to have forgotten her.

'Where do we sail, my love?' she asked, as she had many times, in her gentlest voice.

'West,' he grumbled, distracted. 'Where the dead live.'

She sighed at his usual reply, climbing off the bed to tie back her red hair with a green ribbon that matched her eyes. While she pulled on her white linen smock, Dee prowled around the cabin with the vitality of a man half his age. At ease with his nakedness, he tugged at his beard as he examined charts, then stood at the window and watched the white wake trailing from the carrack's stern. 'I know,' he snapped to no one she could see. 'We will be there when we are there.'

Mad, she thought, eyeing him as she slipped on her black and gold skirt and bodice. *Mad and drunk with power. A lethal combination.*

When he had pulled on his purple robe, he stepped out on to the deck, his silvery hair flying in the salty ocean breeze. Meg followed. No eyes flickered her way. She was unused to that, for she had worked hard to learn how to draw men's attention, then steal their gold or their papers or their life while they were distracted. In dreamy silence the crew went about their tasks, mending sails, climbing the rigging to the yards, or drawing the lines to bring fresh fish aboard. No singing, no ribald laughter. Duncombe was caught up in his duties, not trusting these jolt-heads to keep them on a safe course.

Never had she felt more alone, though she had been

a solitary soul since her chieftain had decided to utilize her natural talents for the good of Ireland. It felt as though she was condemned to purgatory aboard a ship of ghosts.

On the forecastle, Dee peered down at the magic circle he had inscribed in scarlet paint. She watched him take position in the centre of the strange symbols, untroubled by the rolling sea as if his legs were affixed to the deck. For long moments, he bowed his head, beginning one of his monotonous incantations, his words lost beneath the wind.

Red Meg's chest tightened and she shivered, not with cold but with unease as the shadows thrown across the deck by the masts and the rigging shifted without explanation. Behind her, she thought she heard a sound like a giant snake coiling on the poop deck. As Dee threw his head back and raised his arms, the wind grew stronger. It lashed his hair and whipped the deep sleeves of his robes. Overhead, the sails boomed as they filled to their limit.

She watched the doctor as the carrack surged across the waves, and then, satisfied that he would be distracted for a while, returned to the cabin. Sliding the bolt across the door, she hurried to the chest under the window and searched through the jumble of contents until she found one of the gilt mirrors Dee carried with him for his divinings. In her time with him, she had learned some of his tricks.

When she had studied the charts scattered across the trestle, she set the looking glass in the centre and peered into its depths. The words seared through her mind with such force that she almost recoiled and was momentarily disoriented. Then the mirror clouded over, clearing to reveal a familiar face peering up at her.

'Will Swyfte,' she said with a seductive smile. 'How I have missed those dark eyes.'

CHAPTER TWENTY-THREE

GOLDEN SPIKES OF MORNING SUNLIGHT GLINTED OFF GLASS. Across the low ceiling of the captain's cabin, shimmering pools flickered as Will peered into the depths of the obsidian mirror set unsteadily on the trestle table. The pounding of the waves on the hull throbbed through the stifling stale air, loud enough to hide any conversation from prying ears.

In the looking glass, Meg's lips and eyes teased him as always. Will felt relieved to see she was well. Yet if anyone could survive in that perilous atmosphere, it would be Red Meg O'Shee.

'This merry ocean jaunt is to your taste?' he enquired.

'I see no reason to wallow in gloom, my sweet. There is always pleasure to be found in every situation.' The smile was just one of many masks that prevented any man from knowing her true thoughts, he knew. She was a strange woman, the Irish spy. Duplicitous on so many levels, as lethal as any opponent he had ever encountered, yet at her core he had found some well-protected part of her in which he felt he could place some trust.

Will's thoughts rushed back across the waves to Liverpool and to that tumultuous night when he had seized the opportunity presented to him and embarked on this desperate gamble. Driven mad by the rush of his new power, Dee had raged through the upper floors of the rooming house while Will and Meg fled down the wooden stairs to the front door. Meg was terrified by the inexplicable transformation she had witnessed and had been gabbling about the alchemist's ordering her to accompany him on some mysterious journey to the New World. It seemed even her charms no longer had any effect on Dee, and she feared for her life and her sanity.

How Will's mind had whirled with the opportunities that chance had suddenly presented to him. Snatching at a single straw, he had decided at that moment to risk everything. From that point on, he knew there could be no going back, though his very life, the Queen and all England, were forfeit.

When Meg had recovered her wits sufficiently, he had offered her a harsh choice: stay by Dee's side and glean whatever information she could from him, or be taken back to London to face punishment for her crimes. If the dilemma troubled her, she didn't show it; indeed, he thought she seemed almost relieved that she would not have to return to her homeland, and she had even suggested how they could make his plan work.

They hid while Dee thundered out into the night, raging about his missing looking glass, which Will had hidden in his pouch. In whispers, Meg quickly related the secrets of mirror-communication that the sorcerer had taught her; though half a world lay between them, they would be able to speak through Dee's glass, she insisted. And then, her eyes bright, she had kissed him with surprising tenderness before darting out into the street to accompany the alchemist to the quayside.

Will smiled at the memory of that kiss. He could only presume she saw some advantage for herself in his plan, for Meg was not a woman spurred on by the kindness in her heart. She could not have returned to Ireland if she had failed in her task to kidnap Dee. And Cecil would have ensured there was no safe haven for her anywhere in England. Perhaps she felt the dangers of a sea journey with the doctor were preferable to a flight across Europe, where the malign influence of the Unseelie Court would still be felt.

Will had not told her that what lay ahead was far worse than she could ever imagine. It was but the first of many quiet betrayals that would no doubt see his soul damned. But it was a price he was willing to pay.

'What news?' he asked.

The Irish woman's beautiful features darkened. She glanced over her shoulder towards the door, and then whispered, 'I must speak quickly, for Dee will only be briefly distracted, and if he finds me here my punishment will be terrible indeed.' She paused, biting her lip. 'He is much changed.'

'Have you learned what has possessed him?'

She shook her head. 'All I know is that he uses his mirrors to speak with angels, as he did on the road to Liverpool, even when he was under my spell.' Her brow furrowed. 'Though now he rages against them like a madman. They must be the ones who ride him.'

Angels! Will was struck by the irony and grimaced. *Devils, more like.* He thought back along the years, to all the times when Dee had believed his magics had allowed him to commune with those higher beings. He claimed to have learned the Enochian language from them and had filled vast journals with their messages. All of it had been the manipulation of the Unseelie Court, there was no doubt now. Long had they played him, posing as angelic guardians whenever they appeared in his mirror, luring him into false security, subtly subverting his suspicions, until they could exert their control. Dee's increasingly erratic behaviour, the voices that only he heard, his inability to find warmth even in a hot room: each a sign of the Unseelie Court's influence which Will had witnessed before.

Yet why did they now pursue him, if they were close to having him in their thrall?

'Whatever afflicts the old man has spread to the crew,' she continued. 'They drift through their chores as if they are in a dream. Only Captain Duncombe retains his wits, and though he is a good-hearted man, there is little he can do.'

'Have they harmed you?'

'It is as if they do not even know I am aboard,' she replied, with a note of indignation. 'Dee tolerates me, I think, as long as I offer him comfort, but I know my influence is waning.'

'And your destination?'

She held out her hands. 'As agreed, I have the course here, for you to follow. Perhaps your own captain can plot our eventual port of call.' Glancing at the charts and captain's journal on the sea chest beside her, she passed on the bearing. 'Dee works his magics to try to speed us on,' she added. Will saw unease flicker across her features. 'Keep a steady course, my love. I would not have you lost to me.'

He smiled as reassuringly as he could. 'There will be

good sack and a merry jig waiting for you when we finish this business, Mistress Meg.'

'Oh, I expect much more than that, Master Swyfte,' she replied with a twinkle. Some noise off caught her attention and she leaned in and whispered, 'I must go. Soon, my love.'

The mirror clouded over and Will's own dark features loomed up in the glass. He bowed his head, hoping he had not doomed Meg as he had doomed so many others. With the passing of each day, he moved further away from the light, he realized. In the end, was he so different from the Unseelie Court?

For a moment he struggled with his conscience, listening to the roar of the sea and the bright singing of the *Tempest*'s crew. Putting aside his doubts, he strode out of the cabin in search of Captain Courtenay.

CHAPTER TWENTY-FOUR

THE TRADE WINDS HAD STILLED. BECALMED, THE *TEMPEST* simmered under a merciless sun. On deck, sailors squatted, sullen-faced, in what little shade they could find, their sodden shirts clinging to their skin. Captain Courtenay brooded in his cabin, loathing the inactivity that left his crew with too much time on their hands in a heat that always spawned arguments and blood. Strangewayes and Grace sat under a makeshift sailcloth shade on the forecastle, engaged in intense conversation. Launceston roamed around the hold, a ghost who could not face the sun. From the poop deck, Will watched the grey cloud on the horizon through Courtenay's tele-scope in what had become an hourly ritual. He wore his white linen undershirt open to his breeches, but still felt no respite from the heat. Peering through the glass, he had started to believe he now saw something hiding within that swirling grey miasma.

'If there is some ship within that fog, it is becalmed as we are. A small mercy,' Carpenter muttered at his side. He was stripped to the waist, his lean form tanned by the tropical sun.

Will shrugged, unconvinced. 'Then let us concentrate upon catching Dr Dee,' he said.

He thought back to how the cold November of the English Channel had gradually given way to the December heat of the Canaries and how they had been forced to put into port to pick up fresh water and victuals. His cap pulled low against the hot, dry wind, Will had prowled the docks, questioning the dark-skinned men in their white tunics selling wooden cups of sweet wine and skewers of spiced lamb meat seared over charcoal. They had told of a carrack that had moored there two weeks gone, with a strange, devil-haunted crew who moved as if through a dream and spoke in slow, measured tones as they resupplied their vessel. The carrack had remained in port for near twelve days, and the dark-skinned men spoke of seeing strange lights around its mast at night and hearing disembodied voices echoing across the water. No one had been sorry to see it sail back to sea. Their tales had raised Will's spirits. He was certain that they yet had a good chance of tracking down their prey, and much to the English crew's annoyance he had encouraged Captain Courtenay to put back out to sea after barely two days.

They battled squalls along the tropics and sweltered in the relentless heat. Christmas came and went with Courtenay ladling cups of festive wine to a long queue of his men, and prayers at dawn and song at nightfall. And when the top-men spotted a Spanish treasure galleon they fought their natural instincts and veered off course for a day to avoid a confrontation. And then, just as the end of their journey was in sight, the winds had dropped one week out of the West Indies.

For two days now they had drifted, watching for what might lie at their backs while tempers simmered. Courtenay had taken to wandering the deck with lash in hand, his gimlet eyes offering a warning of what lay ahead if any man dared cause trouble. No clouds marred the blue sky. Not even the faintest breeze wafted across the water. How much longer could they endure this cauldron of heat before something broke, Will wondered?

He sensed Carpenter shifting uncomfortably beside him and put down the tele-scope. 'What is on your mind?' he asked.

The other man ran a hand under his hair to rub the pink scar marring his face. 'The woman is no business of mine,' he began, 'but we have had words, Launceston, Strange-wayes and myself, about your delay in instructing her in the true nature of the threat we face.'

'And they sent you to speak to me?'

'I came of my own accord,' Carpenter snapped. 'We all know what happens to those unprepared for their first meet-ing with those pale-skinned bastards. Even foreknowledge is not always enough to offer protection for some, as you well know, but she deserves a chance to steel herself, does she not?'

Will flinched inwardly. He knew he had been remiss in not revealing to Grace the secrets of the Unseelie Court the moment she had been found aboard. But she had shown such spirit in coping with the privations of the past weeks, never complaining, always bright, ever offering a kind word when she saw the other spies in a gloomy mood, that he hadn't the heart to bring darkness into her world. He looked towards the main deck where she walked among the sweltering crew with a leather pail of seawater with which the sailors could mop their burning heads and necks. She reminded him still of Jenny, and the life she might have had if she had not been taken from him. He had no desire to see Grace's innocence tainted, her hope and her future stolen as her sister's had been, and he would protect her until the last possible moment.

'The more you delay, the more danger you put her in,' Carpenter pressed, as if he could read Will's thoughts.

'I will deal with her when I am good and ready,' he said, ending the conversation.

Already irritable, the other man flushed with frustration. He gripped the rail and hissed, 'Will you take no advice from anyone? The great Will Swyfte, England's greatest spy! Who knows better than all others . . . until disaster strikes, and then he throws his friends to the wolves.'

'What happened between us is long gone, John. Will you not let go of it?'

'Easy words for you. You do not see the results of that betrayal every time you look in a mirror.'

Will grunted. What could he say to ease the other man's pain that he had not said a thousand times? He thought back to frozen Muscovy and the flight through the stark woods where they were attacked by the nameless creature that had been summoned by their enemies. He had thought Carpenter slaughtered in the assault. If he had returned to search for his friend, he could well have lost not just his own life but all they had gained for the Queen during their expedition. For a while Carpenter seemed to have come to terms with what he saw as a grand betrayal. Clearly, resentment still simmered inside him, but Will had a greater fear.

'John, when this business is done . . . should we survive . . . you must ask for time away from your duties,' he said. 'I sense the taint of the Unseelie Court in you, that creeping despair that afflicts all of us eventually when we have spent too long battling those things.'

Carpenter looked over the water, not meeting Will's eyes. 'Time away? I am sick of all this. Sick to the heart. I would leave the service of Sir Robert Cecil for ever and seek a new life for myself where there are no nightmares walking under the sun.'

'You know Cecil will never sanction that,' Will said gently. 'You are too valuable in this long fight—'

'This never-ending fight!'

'Few others have your expert touch, John, your knowledge of the Enemy, your ability to look them in the eye and survive. The Queen needs you.'

'Enough,' the other man snarled. 'I tell you now that I will be gone from here, sooner or later. I deserve a life of my own, and by God I will take it, if I have to cut my way through a hundred colleagues to get it.' He rounded on Will, his eyes narrowing. 'See to the girl. Do not let her days be blighted as mine have been.' He stalked away from the rail, clattering down the steps to the main deck where he shoved aside any who crossed his path as he made his way to his berth.

Before Will could consider whether he truly was betraying Grace, a cry rang out from the topman. Looking up to the top of the mainmast, he saw the lookout pointing towards the north-east where lightning crackled from a looming black cloud. Captain Courtenay bounded up the steps to the poop deck.

'Storm's coming,' he barked, clapping his large hands together. 'In these waters, that could be good or ill. It'll blow some much-needed wind in our sails and speed us on our way. But in the tropics, storms can come down like a hammer on an anvil, with us caught between the two.'

'I will gladly take our chances, captain. I have had my fill of stewing here waiting for something to happen.'

'Be careful what you wish for, Master Swyfte.' Courtenay laughed, his eyes reflecting the crackles of lightning. Before he had even roared his orders, his men jumped to their posts, as eager to return to activity as Will. The spy watched them scramble up the lines, ready to react to any sudden change in the elements. He knew that if the storm struck hard, a full sail could tear off the mainmast and drag them all down to the bottom of the drink. Yet if they were not ready to take advantage of glancing winds, the weather could turn just as quickly and leave them becalmed once more.

He raised his head to the roiling clouds and felt the first hint of a breeze on his face. He closed his eyes, enjoying the relief.

'Will?'

Grace waited at the top of the steps, her hands clasped in front of her. Her skirts flapped in the strengthening wind and her brown hair whipped around her face. He thought how much she had grown in confidence in recent months, no longer the young girl he had played with in Warwickshire. Yet he still saw only Jenny, in her eyes, her smile, her bearing. That had always been the problem.

'Return to the cabin, Grace,' he said, not without warmth. 'It will be safer there.'

'I shall, soon. But Tobias and John both insist that I speak to you, though neither will say why. Even Robert urged me to come, and normally he acts as if I am a dog yapping at his heels. They seem angry with you.'

Will set his jaw, wishing the others would leave well alone. 'This is not the time, Grace, but, yes, we must have words about a matter of great importance.'

'Is it about Jenny?'

He hesitated, watching the hope light in her dark eyes. 'In part.'

She forced a wan smile. 'Our friendship has been tempestuous since Jenny disappeared,' she said. 'We have fought and bickered, though I . . . I always looked on you fondly, Will, you know that.'

They both knew her feelings had been deeper than she implied. She was confused, he had always recognized that. In truth, she had seen him as the only pillar of stability in a world gone mad. He had felt proud to offer her the protection she needed, and he would never have abused that position. And he had always believed he could save Grace as he had been unable to save Jenny.

She seemed to sense some of the thoughts that passed through his head, for her brow furrowed. 'I have never thanked you for all that you have done for me,' she said, grabbing hold of the rail as the ship began to heave beneath them. 'But more than anything, I would thank you for keeping the promise of Jenny alive when it would have been so much easier to let her go and return to your life.'

'Jenny has always been my life,' he replied, feeling all the pain wrapped in those few words.

'We will talk soon,' she said, 'but tell me one thing before I go: do you truly believe we will ever find answers to any of the questions that have haunted us these past years?'

'I believe we will find an ending, Grace, for good or ill. Whichever it may be, I hope there will be peace.'

That seemed to satisfy her. She gave a faint smile, then skipped down the steps and fought her way across the rolling deck. He watched her until she disappeared from sight into the captain's cabin beneath him.

As the clouds marched overhead, the sky darkened until it felt like dusk aboard the rolling galleon. The sullen sea began to protest, low waves turning to a heaving swell the colour of old ivy. Sails boomed and the rigging cracked. The wind howled, tearing at hair grown too long and wrenching men from side to side with every step. When lightning flashed, the world turned white.

Will began to fight his way through the grim-faced sailors swirling across the deck, each one concentrating on his own well-rehearsed task. They danced to Courtenay's tune, his orders booming like the thunder tearing through the half-light. Hands on hips, he threw his head back in insane laughter as he felt the first spatters of rain on his face.

'This is a contest, Master Swyfte,' he roared, 'between men and the gods of the storm. Shall we see who wins?' If any man could battle the elements and win, it would be Bloody Jack, Will agreed. It took a madman to face a tropical storm without a flicker of fear in his heart.

The spy gripped the slick rigging as the deck bucked beneath his feet like an unbroken Barbary steed. The rain was starting to come in harder on the gusts. Wiping his eyes clear, his gaze flickered out to sea as a bolt of lightning lanced down. In the flash, he glimpsed something that should not have been there. Wrapping one arm through the rigging to steady himself, he pulled out the tele-scope and attempted to place it to his eye. The view through the lens danced across the green ocean and darkening sky. Cursing under his breath, Will moved the tele-scope in incremental steps until a dark shape appeared before him. A galleon. The grey cloud bank that had followed them across the Atlantic was dissipating in the storm, and the ship sailed out of its billowing depths like a shark. A row of white diamonds had been painted along the castle. On a standard flapping from the mainmast was a black bird – a crow, Will thought. The galleon surged towards them, sails full.

Our Enemy are revealed, Will thought, *and they have skilfully chosen this moment of confusion to attack.*

Cupping his hand to his mouth, he yelled for Courtenay. The captain saw the spy's urgency and bounded over. Snatching the tele-scope, he studied the ship for only a moment and then turned to Will, his features dark. 'I know that flag. All sailors do, and they would sell their own mothers to avoid the misfortune of encountering it across the Spanish Main. The ship is the *Corneille Noire*, the cursed barque of that cut-throat Jean le Gris.'

Will knew well the bloody reputation of the French pirate who had plundered the trade routes for five years now.

'And he is not alone,' Bloody Jack added, answering the spy's unspoken question. He handed the tele-scope back.

Will frowned, looking once more. This time he alighted on the galleon quickly as it bore down on them. When the crew swam into view, shock flooded him as he saw the haggard faces of the men, the hollow cheeks, the grey skin; each one looked dead apart from a tall, sinewy man with an eye-patch and a wild black beard whom he took to be the captain. Other, shadowy figures drifted in the half-light, pale spectres, like fish from the deep. Will held his breath as he watched Lansing and the Fay overseeing the ship like a court from Hell. A part of him had expected no less, but the evidence of his eyes still felt chilling.

'The question now, Master Swyfte,' Courtenay boomed, 'in the middle of this godforsaken storm, is do we run like dogs and pray for the best, or stay and fight and risk a slow death in the deep?'

CHAPTER TWENTY-FIVE

THE STORM ENGULFED THE *TEMPEST* IN A HELL OF FIERCE wind and driving rain and walls of black water. Cresting mountainous waves, the galleon plunged into deep, midnight valleys where the sailors feared they would never see the sun again. Barbs of lightning lanced down. Booming thunder throbbed into the roar of the sea. Will clung on to the rigging for dear life, barely able to keep his legs from the deluge sluicing across the deck. He glimpsed Carpenter, and Strangewayes with one hand gripping a stay, sodden and gasping, and Launceston, seemingly unmoved by the terror of the gale, one hand twirled around the rigging as he observed the fearful antics of the crew.

Courtenay, too, looked untroubled by the elements as he barked his orders. Though the ship was tossed this way and that, he strode through the ankle-deep brine on the deck as if on dry land. 'Those that can, man the guns,' he roared. 'We have a fight on our hands, lads.'

Will craned his head to look over the crew with even greater respect. He knew the risks of opening the gun ports in a storm; the waves could flood in and take the ship to the bottom. But there was no choice. Putting aside their fear, seamen scrambled down to the gun deck, obeying their captain without question. Though it was hell above, he wondered how much worse it was below in the confined night-dark space, deafened by the hammers of the waves, thrown around by the pitching and yawing and fearful that every plunge would end on the seabed.

Peering into the face of the storm, he glimpsed the swinging lanterns of the *Corneille Noire*. The pirate vessel drew ever closer, despite the wild seas. He had seen before how the Unseelie Court's ships defied the very elements, and he understood now why the Enemy had chosen this moment to attack. In the tumult, the *Tempest*'s guns would be nigh-on useless.

Carpenter clawed his way to Will's side, both men's hair and beards drenched. 'This is why I turned my back on a life at sea,' he raged. 'Damn all this hell! Give me dry land and I would fight an army.'

'It could be worse, John.'

'How could it be worse?'

'There could be two ships filled with those Fay bastards determined to send us to the bottom.'

Carpenter cursed loudly. 'You find this sport? You are as mad as Bloody Jack. There are times I think you are seeking out ways to die.'

The *Corneille Noire* swept across the waves, a single-minded predator with the *Tempest* caught in its cold glare. Courtenay waited with one foot on the rail, one hand gripping a line, his grim gaze fixed on the other galleon's progress. As it swept alongside, he raised one arm.

Will stared at the Enemy ship, frowning. In the light of

its swinging lanterns, the grey-skinned, unblinking crew seemed like statues, oblivious of every sensation. Even from that distance, Will could tell they had the taint of rot about them. But if the captain Jean le Gris was troubled by what had happened to his men, he showed no sign of it, levelling his sword at Courtenay and shouting abuse into the roaring gale. Behind him, the pale sentinels of the Fay waited for the bloodletting. Will sensed their terrible gaze upon him.

'Let us not wait for them!' Courtenay bellowed. 'Send them a greeting from Hell!' He slashed down his arm.

The message darted from man to man until it reached the master gunner on the gun deck. A rolling wall of fire erupted into the watery world. From bow chasers to broadside cannon to stern chasers, the booming of the guns thundered out, louder even than the storm. Plumes of white smoke whipped away in the wind. Most of the shot plunged harmlessly into the towering walls of black water as the squall flung the two vessels around the high ridges and deep valleys of the swell. But one smashed a hole through the pirate ship's castle to where the captain's cabin would have been and another tore rigging from the mizzen top. Bloody Jack shook his fist and roared his jubilation, leaning so far over the rail that Will thought the waves would pluck him away.

'No cannon will drive them off,' Carpenter shouted, his brow furrowed. 'They will not rest until we go down.'

'If our only choice is to take them with us, that is what we shall do,' Will yelled back. 'Though in these turbulent waters, it will take an age to whittle each other to pieces.'

The *Tempest* rolled at an alarming angle as another wave

187

crashed across the deck. Will swallowed a mouthful of brine. Only his grip on the rigging saved him as his legs flew out beneath him. When the galleon righted, he saw the *Corneille Noire* broadside on, its gun ports open. The captain was waiting for the swell to draw the two vessels in line before giving the order to fire.

'Heads down,' Will called. The fire spewed out of the pirate ship, and the cannon cracked. He flung himself on to the deck as red-hot shot screamed by. To his right, the rail disintegrated. A sailor slow in dropping low disappeared in a red mist. Another screamed, his leg gone. Deadly shards of timber flew around, and the cacophony of cries of men in agony echoed along the length of the galleon.

Courtenay hung over the rail to survey the damage inflicted on his vessel's hull. 'All above the waterline,' he concluded with a pleased nod. 'Then let us not stop there.' As the swell lifted the *Tempest* high, he bellowed the order to fire again. Thunder rolled all around. The acrid stink of burnt powder whisked in the wind.

Sizzling shot tore through the Enemy vessel, more by good fortune than judgement. Seasoned oak as hard as iron burst into shards. Rigging tore free, lashing across the deck. The mainmast cracked and skewed at an angle. Bloody Jack made his own luck by throwing caution to the wind, Will knew: any other captain would have taken the decision to flee rather than fight in those seas.

At the pirate captain's orders, his grey, dead men clambered up what remained of the rigging to cut loose the mainsail before it dragged the mast over the side and the ship to the bottom. Jubilation flooded Will. The gamble had worked and the pirate ship had been crippled. But the triumph was short-lived. Even without its mainmast and sails, the Enemy ship swept closer.

'They are going to ram us,' Carpenter yelled.

'Board us, more like,' Will corrected as he watched the frantic activity along the other ship's deck. The rotting crew lined the rail with grapnels and rapiers in hand. Behind them, the Unseelie Court waited to seize their moment.

'Prepare to repel boarders,' Bloody Jack roared, striding along the deck. His men wrenched out their own rapiers and daggers and scrambled to the rail. Will hauled himself up, drawing his blade.

'This is more like it.' Carpenter grinned without humour. 'Now I can put my idle hands to good use. A hogshead of sack to the man who carves the most.'

The *Corneille Noire* swung close. Will braced himself for the impact. Whatever magics were at play brought the galleon firm alongside, despite the heaving swell. It was as if they were locked in congress, rising and falling with perfect rhythm.

The grapnels flew out across the black gulf, catching in the *Tempest*'s rigging. The pirates gripped their ropes and kicked away from the rail. Some of Courtenay's men attempted to cut the lines, pitching a few of the swinging figures into the roiling sea. They went down without a cry, sucked under the black water in an instant.

Will blinked away the driving rain. He glimpsed the bloom of decay on the grey, dispassionate face of the once-man swinging towards him. Yet another of the Unseelie Court's crimes against the natural order, he thought, glowering. As the pirate's feet crossed the rail, Will lunged. Cold steel plunged through the thing's chest, yet still it came. He withdrew his rapier and slashed down. The face peeled open from temple to chin, but still the wide eyes stared. As the pirate dropped to the deck, he swung his knife high. Will threw himself forward so that his shoulder rammed into his dead foe. The dagger whisked a hair's breadth from his cheek as he drove on and pitched the pirate over the side.

Along the rail blew a smaller storm of steel and curses and spattering blood. Blades clashed as Courtenay's men wrestled with their dead counterparts. One sailor barely twenty summers old went down in a gout of crimson from a slashed throat. Without pause, his staring attacker plunged his gore-stained dagger into the chest of the seaman fighting beside him.

In the confusion of the battle whirling across the storm-lashed deck, Will lost sight of his colleagues. He thrust himself into the melee. When the fighting was too close to use his rapier, he lashed out with elbows and fists and knees and feet. He glimpsed Courtenay roaring with laughter as he plunged his dagger into a grey face. A moment later the mad captain lifted the corpse over his head and pitched it into the sea.

Beyond the frenzy, Will sensed movement as fluid as the brine washing across the deck. His nerves jangled. Shadows flitted, here, there. When a lightning flash froze white faces, he realized that some of the Unseelie Court had boarded the *Tempest*. They kept to the gloom on the fringes so that it was impossible to tell how many there were.

Will tore himself away from the fight and made his way, stabbing and hacking as he went, to where Launceston was tipping a pirate over the side. 'Leave the men to fight these dead things,' he ordered. 'The Fay are aboard, and they are our business. We must find John and Tobias now.'

He darted to the other side of the deck. In the half-light, he glimpsed shapes creeping low like wolves at night, lips pulled back from sharp teeth. As a hand flicked towards the hilt of a rapier, Will sucked in a sharp breath and leapt for a rope dangling from a grapnel in the rigging. Bracing himself, he swung both feet into the nearest Fay's chest, propelling it over the rail.

Another attacked the instant he dropped to the boards, slashing with fast, controlled strokes. When a dying seaman stumbled back into his grim opponent, Will seized his chance, thrusting through the heart with one fluid strike.

Somewhere nearby Strangewayes yelled an anguished warning. Will wrenched around. Tobias was pointing at the door to the captain's cabin. It swung wildly in the lashing gale. The Fay lord Lansing, whom Will had seen drive a man mad on the Liverpool dockside, now had Grace pinned to his chest with his left arm as he eased her out on deck. The Fay lord turned his cold face towards Will, and called in a clear voice, 'Lay down your weapons.' As the other Fay circled, Lansing drew his slender fingers along the curve of Grace's neck, pushing her head back.

'Resist him,' she called in a defiant voice. 'My life means nothing when all of England is at stake.'

Will knew she was right, and so did Strangewayes.

'Kill them,' Lansing said to the other Fay. 'Kill them all, and let us be done with this rabble and return to the Golden City victorious.'

Before the first of the Unseelie Court could attack, Grace hammered her heel on to Lansing's foot. In the shock of her attack, he loosened his grip and she wrenched herself free, throwing herself among the battling sailors.

'We play for high stakes here. Win all or lose everything.' Courtenay's gruff voice boomed through the storm. The captain stood at the end of the main deck with a powder barrel over his head. Beside him, a shaking crewman held a burning fuse, spitting in the rain. 'There is no room for any middle ground,' Bloody Jack continued, a light gleaming in his eyes. 'Get off my ship, or I'll blow us all to Hell.'

Will saw the Unseelie Court weighing up whether Courtenay would go through with his mad threat. He had no doubt. If they faced defeat, better to take a few Fay bastards along with them.

Bloody Jack roared, shaking the barrel with the fury of a goaded bear.

The Fay had seen enough. Will stifled his relief as they ghosted away into the shadows by the poop deck, moving towards the rail and the grapnels. Courtenay raised the barrel high in triumph and bellowed, 'We must seize this moment, Master Swyfte. Once back on their ship, they will loose their guns again and blow us out of the water.'

Will fought to stay on his feet as the galleon spun like a leaf on a stream. Walls of black water smashed down, pitching the ship at such an angle that the hull groaned like a dying man. He fell, cursing, and skidded across the briny deck. He glimpsed Lansing by the rail, one hand on the rope that would swing him back to the *Corneille Noire*. The Fay had hold of Grace once more. He dragged her into a cold embrace, clearly intending to take her back to the pirate ship with him. Strangewayes lay dazed at his feet, blood streaming from a gash on his forehead.

The Fay lord stared at Will and yelled some threat, but the fury of the gale tore his words away. Lightning flashed

192

white overhead, making stark the fear in Grace's wide, dark eyes. Her mouth was a wide O, a cry of anguish perhaps, or a plea for Will to aid her.

Thrown around by the pitching deck, Will could only watch as Lansing pressed his mouth to the woman's ear and began to whisper. Desperation rushed through him. Grace's eyes widened for a moment, the terror in them plain to see. Her head fell slowly back on to Lansing's shoulder, her lids flickered, and she collapsed limply into his arms. Gripping the rope, the Fay placed one foot on the rail of the *Tempest* as he prepared to swing himself and his captive across to the other ship. Devastated, Will knew he could not reach Lansing, or Grace, in time.

Yet as the dead pirates responded to some silent signal and turned back towards their vessel, Will sensed movement at the edge of his vision. Carpenter was perched on the poop deck. With a snarl, he leapt. He slammed into the Fay, wrenching Grace free of Lansing's grasp. The two men careered over the side.

Will staggered his way to the rail and peered down into the roiling sea. Surely no man could survive in that cauldron? For a moment, he saw only slate-grey water, which rose up higher and higher still until it towered above him before crashing down with a sound like a thousand hammers. A moment later he spotted a figure in the water, but only for an instant before it disappeared beneath the surface.

Behind him, he heard Courtenay bark orders to the helmsman to try to move the galleon away. The storm was already starting to ebb, and if the captain caught the last of the strong winds he could put space between them and the Enemy.

Launceston appeared at his elbow, his ghastly face made starker by the gloom. 'We must save him,' he cried with an edge of emotion that Will had never heard in the aristocrat's voice before. 'Tell Courtenay to hold fast.'

Swyfte blinked rain out of his eyes as he looked into the other man's face. 'Robert, I would not leave a friend to die in such circumstances. But if we tarry here, we all die, and so too the hopes of England.' He felt sickened to hear the words come out of his mouth.

Launceston nodded in acceptance, and without another word stepped on to the rail and dived into the boiling sea. Will's cry rang out, but the man disappeared and however desperately Will searched the waves he saw no further sign of his friend. The spy cursed to himself: what had possessed Launceston to throw himself after Carpenter?

The rain eased and a glimmer of silver light broke through the thick clouds on the horizon. With a boom of filling sails, the *Tempest* pulled away from the crippled Enemy galleon.

Desolate, Will tore his gaze away from the angry sea and knelt down beside Grace. He took her in his arms. She was still breathing, but that was but a small mercy. He had seen the corruption of the Unseelie Court worm its way into even the strongest mind and consume it from within until only a shell was left.

'Grace,' he whispered in her ear, 'speak to me.'

There was no response; she might have been sleeping, though he would not wish her dreams upon another living soul. Will bowed his head. So much had been lost, yet the worst still lay ahead.

CHAPTER TWENTY-SIX

THE STORM HAD BLOWN ITSELF OUT BY SUNSET. UNDER HEAVY clouds, the *Tempest* sailed through a night as deep and dark as any the crew had ever experienced. With no stars to guide them, Courtenay stowed away his compass and charts and concentrated on putting distance between them and the pirate ship. On deck, the subdued singing of the seamen raised no spirits. They mourned the eight of their companions lost in the attack, as Will mourned Carpenter and Launceston. Sails hung ripped and yards broken. Two sailors hauled planks of wood, fresh rigging and sailcloth from the store below, while a gang of five cut and shaped to start the repairs. Even the sound of the mallets had a funereal beat. 'We lick our wounds and we move on,' Courtenay growled in passing, the closest he would come to words of commiseration.

By dawn, the skies had cleared to a perfect blue and the sea was calm. With his astrolabe, Bloody Jack shielded his eyes against the merciless sun and began to calculate the latitudes in order to discover how far they had been blown off course into dangerous, uncharted waters. His mood darkened by the hour.

Grace had not yet regained consciousness. Her breathing shallow, her eyes motionless beneath the lids, she lay on her berth in a sleep akin to death. Will sat over her through the long night, watching for any sign that she might recover, afraid what would be left of her wits if she did. Time and again he cursed himself for his failings, haunted by his vow to protect her at all costs.

Strangewayes would barely look at him, and when their eyes did meet, Will saw only simmering hatred. He felt angry at the young spy's attitude, but held his tongue. As the stifling heat rose in the dusty cabin, he realized he was only making matters worse by being there; it was now Strangewayes' responsibility to care for Grace. Will left him there, cooling her brow with a damp kerchief and muttering constant prayers.

Will asked the captain if he could be left alone on the poop deck for a few moments. Once he had assured himself he couldn't be overseen by the other men, he squatted down at the far side of the castle and pulled the obsidian mirror from his pouch, laying it on the deck. As he hunched over the glass, he whispered the words Meg had taught him and waited.

Long moments passed. It was the agreed time, and Meg had not yet disappointed him. He uttered the incantation once more, and again. Yet the mirror remained clear, and he began to fear that the Unseelie Court had claimed another life. Wearily, he bowed his head and closed his eyes.

When he looked again, the black mirror had clouded over. Yet the face that was gradually appearing in the misty glass was not Meg's. He felt his heart begin to beat faster, though he scarcely dared hope. Yet the familiar curve of the lips emerged, and the bright, clever eyes, and the tumble of brown hair, just as they had that night in the rooming house in Liverpool.

'Jenny,' he murmured, uncontrolled joy rushing through him. She still wore the blue dress she had on when she vanished from his life all those years ago.

Her eyes widened and he knew she could see him too. But then he saw the worry in her face. With apprehension she glanced nervously over her shoulder in the darkness, and then leaned closer to the glass.

'Will. It is you.'

He recoiled at the shock of hearing her voice after so long. There was so much he wanted to say to her; he had played this moment through a thousand times or more in all the years of longing. How could he ever begin to express the emotion that had been stirred in that seeming eternity of time apart? 'Jenny,' he began, struggling to find the words, but she silenced him with an insistent shake of her head.

'Will, there is very little time,' she whispered. 'When I saw you before, I barely dared believe you still lived . . . that you remembered me—'

'I would never forget you.' He could barely stop his voice from breaking. Her features softened, and he saw the affection in her smile. 'Not a day has passed when I have not searched for you in some way.'

'And you must abandon the quest,' she sighed. 'That is the very reason why I have reached out to you. You must put me out of your thoughts, and out of your heart.'

'Never.'

'You must.' He saw the tears begin to run down her cheeks. 'Will, please . . . do this for me, if you love me still—'

'I do!'

'Then forget me,' she implored. 'There is no time for explanations. You must trust me on this matter. To find me could cost you your own life, and I will never allow that to happen . . .' She half turned as if she had heard someone approaching, and then added in a hasty tone, 'I must go.'

'Wait,' he called out, too loud, but the looking glass had already misted over, and a moment later it showed only blue sky. Will slumped back against the rail and closed his eyes, turning her words over in his head, listening once again to the music of her voice. He felt afraid to stop in case he could no longer remember how she sounded. And yet Jenny lived, there could be no doubt about that now. His heart leapt, and it was all he could do not to shout to the heavens. Her warnings meant nothing to him. How could he accept her plea for him to stay away? Nothing would deter him from bringing her home.

He inhaled a draught of salty air and took a moment at the rail, looking out over the blue waters. Though his spirits now soared, he yet felt doubt. What of Meg? Did she still live? And without her to guide them, what chance did they have of reaching their destination?

He was in reflective mood as he descended on to the main deck, and barely noticed Courtenay beckoning him to enter his cabin. Strangewayes knelt beside the still-prone Grace, so intent on his prayers he seemed unaware that the two men had entered. Will followed Bloody Jack to his trestle where his dog-eared charts were scattered, the astrolabe weighting them down. Keeping an eye on Strangewayes, the captain whispered, 'Do you have a new course for me?'

'Not yet. Soon,' Will replied. 'You have identified our position?'

Courtenay jabbed a finger on the chart. 'Right where we shouldn't be, Master Swyfte. We've already had our fill of the horse latitudes, where the wind comes and goes like a woman's affections, and you can drift becalmed for days under a sweltering sun. Aye, that's bad enough, but that damnable storm has dumped us back in it, and worse. Here . . .' he drew a filthy nail along the chart, 'is a sea within the sea. Cursed, it is. Good ships disappear without a sign. Pirates, some say.' He shrugged, not believing. 'Other vessels are found deserted, with treasure still in their holds and food and water in their barrels. Every captain knows to steer well clear—'

'You did this.' The low growl of Strangewayes' voice rustled across the cabin. Will turned to see the red-headed spy confronting him, rapier drawn, his face flushed with an anger that must, Will surmised, be born of despair. 'If you had taken even a moment to prepare her for the horrors of the Unseelie Court, she might have survived the encounter. But no, the great Will Swyfte had better things to do with his time.'

'Put your sword away, boy,' Courtenay growled. 'You're making a fool of yourself.'

'England is littered with dead and wounded men who have made your acquaintance, oft-times decent-hearted, God-fearing people you have used and discarded once they have served your purpose, so I have heard,' Strangewayes continued, not taking his gaze off Will. 'You care for no one but yourself. And yet you are tolerated because, in your cunning way, you offer a service to the Queen and her government. But you must be held to account sooner or later – if not by God, then by me.'

''Tis true that I am not a good man, but I am an effective one,' Will replied in a calm voice. He could see the hurt burning in the other man's face. 'And you are mistaken on one count. There are people dear to me, and I would defend them even at the cost of my own life. I would never see Grace harmed—'

'Lies.' Strangewayes thrust with his rapier, missing Will by a hair's breadth as the older man stepped aside at the last moment. Will could see there was no reasoning with him. His passion burned too strong for that. Snarling, Tobias thrust again, and this time Will's sword was at the ready and he parried. The clash of steel rang through the cabin.

Red-faced and puffing, Courtenay looked fit to burst at the display of disrespect upon his ship. 'Shed one drop of his blood and I'll have ye keel-hauled,' he roared.

Strangewayes thrust again. Will deflected the tip of the sword with a flick of his wrist. Though he had some skill with the rapier, the red-headed spy was too raw, too consumed with emotion in a way that no true swordsman would ever be, Will saw. His bravado and arrogance had always seemed a shield to protect his insecurities, traits Will had presumed he would eventually grow out of, given time and experience. Now he wondered if they would be the death of the other man before he had a chance to learn.

Driven by anger, Strangewayes prodded with his rapier as if he were poking a smith's forge. Will parried, once, twice, and at the moment when he could have easily disarmed the

other man, he let his rapier fall. Courtenay gasped. Strangewayes' blade thrust true towards Will's heart. At the last,
the younger spy caught himself, the tip of his rapier piercing
linen. A rose bloomed on Will's shirt. Tobias's hand shook
as he tried to drive the blade on, but in the end he could
not bring himself to kill. 'Damn you, Swyfte,' he muttered,
blinking away tears of frustration.

'I am already damned. Would I be here watching friends
suffer and die were that not so?' Will bit down, forcing
himself to ignore the pain from the sword digging into his
flesh. 'There are few friends in this business, but we are all
brothers. The bonds run deep. We would give our lives for
each other, as John gave his life for the woman you love. No
one would ever have called him a good man, but he was an
honourable one, yes, even to the end. And honour has more
value than gold, for it buys a man a clear conscience and a
light heart.'

'And you think you are honourable?' Strangewayes spat.

'We all try to do our best in hard times. And sometimes
we fail. That is the nature of men, is it not? And our failures
are greater than others' because we play for high stakes, and
we feel them more acutely. Know only that I would die for
Grace, as would you.'

Strangewayes hesitated, torn between his impotent rage
and his sense of honour. In the lull, Courtenay cursed,
snatched up the cudgel he kept by his trestle and clouted the
younger spy round the head. Strangewayes pitched to the
floor in a daze, his sword clattering across the boards. 'Let
that knock some bloody sense in ye,' the captain thundered.

'Leave him. He is heartsick and worried for the woman
he loves,' Will said, aware of the irony in his words.

'This is my ship, not a Bankside stew,' Courtenay snapped. 'My rules, Master Swyfte.' He paused, eyeing the fallen spy. 'Yet I will show a little kindness on this occasion, as he's a friend of yours. But if he raises his blade in anger to one of us again, it's over the side with him.' He grabbed the scruff of Strangewayes' undershirt in his meaty hand and dragged him across the cabin, flinging him out of the door with a boot up his arse. Will felt concerned that the humiliation might only make Strangewayes angrier, but he had more pressing matters to concern him.

'Keep an eye on that one,' Courtenay rumbled as if he could hear Will's thoughts. 'He's still got too much of the spoiled child in him. If his temper gets the best of him again, you might find that steel going right through ye.'

Will shrugged, feeling the weight of his responsibility to Grace. 'We will shape him to be a man, one way or another.'

Bloody Jack grunted dismissively.

A warning call rang out from the topman and Courtenay and Will stepped out on deck to find the men leaning over the starboard side, pointing, brows furrowed. The captain barged his way among them, making a space for Will. For a moment, shock lit Will's features. The ocean had turned brown as far as the eye could see, and the air was thick with a stink like wet dogs. Peering closer, he saw that the *Tempest* now sailed through a dense bank of seaweed, the glistening tendrils tugging at the galleon's hull.

'Avast,' Courtenay bawled to his men. Once the sailors had trudged away from the rail, the captain leaned in to Will and whispered, 'I told ye: right where we shouldn't be.'

CHAPTER TWENTY-SEVEN

THE SEA OF STINKING BROWN WEED SEEMED TO STRETCH TO the blue horizon. The *Tempest* sailed through the boiling heat as if she were ploughing a furrow in an autumn field. The seamen lined the rails, watching with uneasy eyes while they recalled all the fearful tales of that place they had heard in quayside inns across Europe.

Leaning out, Will glimpsed dark shapes weaving sinuously among the floating clumps of seaweed; eels, he thought. He glanced around for the land he presumed must be near.

Bloody Jack shook his head. 'No land here,' he said. 'Not for days. This is the great Sargasso, a sea within a sea. All around, the currents are the strongest you will ever encounter, but here ships drift in this forest of weed, and grow becalmed. It is a strange place, sailors tell, haunted, and most give it a wide berth.'

'The weed will not hold us fast?'

'The wind, or lack of it, is the greater problem. The weed can snarl a rudder, at worst. It floats on the surface in vast mats. I have fathomed it meself here, and there is no bottom.

A Spanish sea-dog told me how his vessel was becalmed for weeks in the middle of this stinking sea. To conserve their water, the crew were forced to throw the war horses o'erboard and feared they would not get out with their own lives. There is nowhere like it in all the oceans.' His brow furrowed. 'And yet . . . My mind plays tricks with me. The last time I skirted the Sargasso the weed looked different . . .' His voice tailed off. 'It remains a mystery to me how that storm blew us so far off course.'

Will heard a troubled note in the captain's voice, but his attention was caught by the swimming shapes. One broke the surface, black skin glistening in the sun. As thick as a man's arm, the eel seemed to have a face akin to a baby's, with wide eyes and full lips that revealed a hint of sharp teeth. A strange mewling sound rose up, cut short as the thing darted back below the surface.

Courtenay recoiled. 'God ha' mercy,' he hissed under his breath.

Will thought back to the white men-fish that swam beneath the surface of the frozen Thames and asked, 'You have seen the like of that before?'

'Never. Nor have I heard word of such.' He crossed himself. 'I do not believe this is the Sargasso at all. It is some devil-haunted place we have sailed into.'

The sun beat down; the breeze began to fail. An uneasy mood descended on the men as the *Tempest* drifted through the reeking seaweed. Eyes flickered up to the sagging sails, watching for the moment when the breeze finally died and the galleon would be stranded there. The sea-hardened crew pretended not to notice those mewling noises rolling across the gently lapping swell. And with each hour that passed the weight of apprehension grew until every man was suffused with a deep dread of what lay ahead.

When the sun was at its highest point, the lookout called. Three dark smudges emerged from the heat haze over the seaweed ahead. Shielding his eyes against the glare, Will saw that they were barques. As the *Tempest* neared, he realized that there was no movement aboard. Two were little more than rotting hulks, listing low in the water, the sails but tatters. He did not recognize their design, but the crudity of the build suggested great age. Courtenay tugged at his beard, his brow creased.

The third ship sported a Spanish flag, hanging limply from the mainmast. Brown weed swelled up its hull. 'I would investigate that barque,' Will said, pointing.

Bloody Jack sighed. 'I had a feeling you were going to say that, Master Swyfte.'

All eyes remained down when the captain asked for volunteers to board the Spanish vessel. Roaring in anger, he chose three men at random and they shuffled off to lower the rowing boat. As Will prepared to climb down the rope ladder to where the vessel bobbed, Strangewayes stepped up. A bruise bloomed on the side of his forehead. 'I would accompany you,' he muttered, his expression sullen. After a moment's consideration, Will consented with a nod.

The seamen sculled away from the *Tempest* with hesitant strokes, their unsettled eyes darting around the waves of brown vegetation. Will sat at the prow, studying the path ahead. The weed bundled up ahead of the boat, the choking stink of it even thicker now they were surrounded by it. One of the sailors, a pockmarked, pink-faced man, cried out as one of the eel creatures leapt out of the water, disturbed by the oars. Its jaws snapped and its eyes swivelled towards them as if it knew what it was seeing. The men muttered prayers, rowing faster, but that only disturbed the creatures more. The sea on either side churned as they leapt up, mewling and crying in tones that were unsettlingly human.

'Fish, nothing more,' Will called out in a reassuring voice, keeping his eyes fixed on the Spanish ship ahead. 'Only fish.' The seamen continued to mutter. Strangewayes withdrew his hands from the sides of the boat and clasped them between his thighs.

In the sticky heat, they pulled alongside the larger vessel and one of the seamen hurled a grapnel over the rail. One after the other, they climbed. The ship was still, the only sounds the whispers of the hull. Will wrinkled his nose. An odd smell hung across the stained deck, like a butcher's shop on a summer noon. 'Search below,' he said to the three men, who looked as if he had ordered them to leap into the sea. 'Call out if you find anything of note.' He beckoned to Strangewayes, and strode to the captain's cabin, his hand resting on his rapier's hilt.

The cabin was no cooler. He sucked in a mouthful of stale air, casting an eye over the berth and the chart-covered trestle. By the compass a half-eaten biscuit lay in its crumbs next to a cup of wine. Strangewayes prowled around the trestle, eyeing the food as if it would bite him. 'The captain left in a hurry,' he said.

'Abandoned his own ship?'

'Taken, then. By pirates.'

'Perhaps.' Will looked round, seeing no signs of a struggle. Dropping to his knees, he traced his fingers across the dusty boards, but found no bloodstains. He flicked open a chest under the broad window to reveal the gleam of gold plate, cups and coin.

'I do not like it here,' Strangewayes said, looking round the hot, gloomy cabin. 'It feels haunted.'

At the trestle, Will pushed a quill and ink-pot aside and opened the captain's leather-bound journal. He ran one finger under the florid scrawl, silently translating the Spanish entries. 'He speaks here of an isle of devils, and hearing the tormented cries of lost souls in the night.' He skimmed the pages and read on. 'A city of gold. Manoa, he calls it. "No man may escape it, save that he traverses the labyrinth before the Moon-Tower."'

'If this city of gold exists, Philip of Spain will have sent a fleet of galleons to loot it,' the younger spy said.

'Perhaps.' Will recalled the Faerie Queen's words from her cell in London and her mention of a Tower of the Moon which kept open the way between their worlds. He continued reading the journal. '"Long hours were we caught in that maze, fearing what was at our backs. And yet the way became clear. Twice stare into the devil's face, then bow all heads to God. Thrice more the unholy must call. Again, again, again until the end."' Will reflected on the message for a moment, then tore out the page, folded it neatly and slipped it into his leather pouch.

Strangewayes wandered to the window and peered out into the west. 'God has abandoned us,' he said in a low, desolate voice. 'I fear what lies ahead.'

The pounding of running feet echoed across the deck, accompanied by the frightened cries of the seamen. Will stepped out to meet them. Eyes wide with fear, they gibbered and plucked at their clothes with anxious fingers. Will glanced towards the dark entrance to the lower decks, the door swinging slowly shut. 'Survivors?' he enquired in a calm voice, his fingers folding round his sword-hilt.

'Voices,' the pockmarked man said breathlessly, looking over his shoulder at the closing door. 'We were on the orlop deck and we 'eard 'em.'

'From the bilge?' Strangewayes enquired.

'From . . . from the other side of the hull.'

'In the water?' Will demanded.

The man nodded. 'We heard their nails scratching on the keel, and their whispers—'

'What did they say?' Strangewayes snapped, grabbing the sailor by the shoulders.

'"Join us",' one of the other sailors whispered. His hands were shaking. '"Join us."'

Will pushed Strangewayes to one side and leaned in, tapping his head. 'The mind plays strange tricks,' he said.

But the seaman shook his head furiously, having none of it. 'This is a ship of ghosts,' he insisted. 'We are doomed if we stay here. They will come for us—'

Will felt Strangewayes' eyes on him, but he did not acknowledge the look. 'Let the dead whisper to the fishes,' he interjected. 'We are done here.'

Sweating and red-faced, the seamen heaved the rowing boat back to the *Tempest* with furious strokes, their gaze never leaving the drifting seaweed. Will himself half expected to see hands rising from the surface or dead faces looking up from the pools of dark water among the vegetation.

Once they were back on board the galleon, Courtenay set the helmsman to steer a steady course west through the strange dead sea. The deserted Spanish ship fell behind them, but even then Will thought he could feel eyes on his back. For the rest of the day they creaked along under the unforgiving sun, and as twilight began to fall they broke out of the bank of vegetation and into open water. Will felt the mood lift, and not long after he heard Courtenay's throaty laughter rumbling across the deck as the crew began to sing.

Yet he found himself haunted by what he had read in the Spanish captain's journal. An isle of devils. Lost souls in the night.

With the red sun low on the horizon, he found his worst fears confirmed. Wreckage drifted on the swell ahead: a shattered hull, chests and barrels, masts tangled with rigging and ragged sailcloth. 'Caught in the storm?' Will asked as Courtenay joined him at the rail.

The captain tugged at his beard in his habitual manner as he studied the shattered remnants. 'Mayhap.'

They watched in silence until Bloody Jack caught sight of a torn flag floating by: a red cross on a white background. 'One of ours, then,' he said. Neither of them needed to express what lay heavy on their minds. The captain sent two of his men out in the rowing boat and in the dying light they returned with a sodden remnant of the captain's log bearing the ship's name: the *Eagle*, the carrack which had carried Dee and Meg. Will felt a momentary pang of despair.

Strangewayes appeared at their side, fresh from ministering to Grace. He looked tired and drawn; Will had not seen him eat since the storm. There had still been no improvement in her condition and Will's mood darkened further.

'Can there be survivors from such a wreck?' Strangewayes asked. 'If Dee is lost—'

'This is not the time to speculate,' Will said, a little more curtly than he intended. For a moment, his thoughts turned to Meg, but he set them aside when the lookout cried, 'Land ahoy!'

Courtenay's brow furrowed. 'There is no land in these waters.' Yet when they rushed to the forecastle, they saw white-topped waves crashing against a jagged reef, and beyond it the hazy outline of an island in the dying ruddy light. 'Hard a starboard,' the captain bellowed to the helmsman, adding with a growl, 'We'll not end up on the rocks like those other poor bastards.'

Will gripped the rail, peering towards the island. He could make out a hilly, tree-covered central area, and grey cliffs to the south and north with a stretch of sandy strand directly ahead. 'Dee could have washed up there,' Strange-wayes said in a hopeful tone.

'Aye,' Bloody Jack growled, raising the tele-scope to his eye. 'He's as tough as a tanner's hide, that one. Wring his scrawny neck and he'd still keep on breathing. And I've wanted to do that a time or two. We'll sail to the north and drop anchor. Only a madman would try to cross that reef with night coming in,' he added without a hint of irony.

Will watched the darkening waves as the ship sailed astern. So much misfortune had afflicted them in recent days, he barely dared to hope for some small relief. Beside him, Courtenay cursed. 'What afflicts that fool at the helm?' Once more, the island lay directly ahead. He snatched the tele-scope from his eye and roared to the helmsman, 'I said, hard a starboard!'

The *Tempest* turned a starboard again, but within moments Will blinked his eyes in the growing gloom and saw the island ahead of them once more. Courtenay's face darkened. 'Will we never be out of these cursed waters?' he muttered.

Three more times they attempted to sail round the island's northern edge, and three more times they failed. 'It seems,' Will said, 'that this island is waiting for us.'

CHAPTER TWENTY-EIGHT

STREAMS OF TORCH-FIRE BLAZED THROUGH THE DARK OF THE London night. Alarmed cries rang off the high stone walls of the Palace of Whitehall as the guards raced across the courtyard, their boots clattering, weapons clanking as they ran. In the flickering light of the brands worried white faces were caught, eyes urgently trying to pierce the deep gloom around the Lantern Tower.

'Find it!' Sir Robert Cecil bellowed. A sheen of sweat glistened on the spymaster's forehead despite the wintry chill that had reached long into spring. 'Slay it without a moment's thought.'

He whirled as a low snarl rumbled out from a corner of the courtyard, a sound that would not have been out of place in the Queen's menagerie but which he knew came from something that walked like a man. A moment later the growl echoed from the other side of the square. *So fast*, he thought, quaking.

The torches whisked around in confusion. In the gloom, stars of ruddy light danced off burgonets and cuirasses. The spymaster glimpsed a pale face frozen in the wavering flames, mouth ragged with horror, but it was gone in an instant. Another man dashed past him, yelling in fear. Round and round he spun, caught up in the visions flashing before his eyes – a stabbing pike, a guard staggering back, clutching his head, a blood-spattered burgonet bouncing across the cobbles – until he grabbed at his chest where his heart was pounding fit to burst.

Those inhuman snarls seemed to be echoing all around, as if there were a host of the things and not just one.

Another face flashed by, torn and bloody. The guard stumbled in the dark and lay still.

Cecil cried out in a fury born of fear, demanding his men do something, anything, to end this slaughter.

And then, as the snapping and snarling reached a new pitch, the bestial cry was cut off with a strangled gurgle.

'To me,' the spymaster bellowed. As the surviving guards gathered around him, their combined torchlight lit a chaotic scene. Fallen bodies, gleaming pools of blood and scattered cordwood where the intruder had attempted to tear through the towering bonfire surrounding the Lantern Tower to free the Faerie Queen. 'Is it dead?' he barked. He needed to show that he was not afraid, but his hands would not stop shaking.

''Tis gone.' The voice floated out of the dark. Cecil snatched a torch and stalked towards the sound. The flames lit a man dressed in a costly sapphire doublet and breeches, the face half turned away. He gripped a rapier dripping black blood and his cloak covered a still form on the cobbles. 'Send your men away. They should not see this.'

The spymaster recognized the intruder and waved the unnerved guards away. Once they had gone, Sir Walter

Raleigh stepped out of the shadows into the circle of light from Cecil's torch.

'If Her Majesty knew you were here . . .' Cecil began.

'And will you tell her, so that I can relate how I achieved what your impotent band could not?' The adventurer stooped to wipe his blade on the already bloodied cloak. 'A foul thing,' he said, turning his nose up at the twisted shape beneath the folds. 'There have been many of them?'

'In recent times, too many.' Cecil pressed the back of his quivering hand against his mouth, steadying himself. 'The Unseelie Court may not be able to set foot upon this still protected part of England, but that does not prevent them from sending their agents in to engineer disaster.'

Raleigh sheathed his rapier. 'But the Faerie Queen still resides in her tower-prison and the bonfire is still piled high to roast her like a suckling pig. All is well in the world.'

Cecil snorted, his laughter bitter. 'How much longer can we go on? Those fiends whittle us down by degrees. And now you are here.'

Raleigh bowed, sweeping one arm out with ironic flamboyance.

'Your secret society, your School of Night, seeks to use this calamity to your own ends,' the spymaster continued with contempt. 'While the Queen's government is distracted and out of joint, you step in and seize power. Is that how it is?'

'Sirrah, you wound me. We in the School of Night are all good Englishmen, loyal to the Crown.'

Cecil paced around the other man, looking him up and down. 'Then why are you here, risking the wrath of the Queen? You have not yet earned your way back into her favour.'

'In these darkest hours, the School of Night will stand shoulder to shoulder with you—'

The spymaster laughed again. 'To worm your way into the heart of government. To learn our secrets, things that you can put to good use should we survive this catastrophe.'

Raleigh tapped the form under his cloak with the toe of his shoe. 'And that matter of survival is still in doubt. For now, can you refuse our aid? We have knowledge, we have wealth, when the coffers of England are near empty. And we have some skills you may be able to use.'

Cecil's eyes narrowed. 'Go on.'

'Dr Dee is one of our number—'

'I knew it!' The spymaster clenched his fist.

'Some of his occult knowledge was passed to other members – not all of it, by far, but enough perhaps to be of use in keeping the Unseelie Court at bay. This will buy Her Majesty . . . and England . . . time for Swyfte to succeed in his quest.'

'You know of that?' Cecil turned away, pretending to examine the huge pile of kindling in the wavering torchlight. 'Of course you do! Yet how can I ever trust the School of Night when you have been secretly working against us for so long?'

Raleigh gave a tight smile. 'How can you trust us? We believe in the power of knowledge, sirrah, in natural science and the occult arts coming together for the good of all men. And a new way in this never-ending war with the Unseelie Court, one that will not tarnish our integrity and may yet save the lives that are so regularly sacrificed. And we believe in honour above all. Can you say the same?'

Cecil refused to meet his gaze.

'I have heard tales,' Raleigh continued, lowering his voice. 'If they are true, you would do well to hope Master Swyfte does not discover what happened to his lady love. He is a man of some fame with a powerful voice . . . and a powerful temper. His rage would be a fine thing, if he were to learn the truth. I would not put money on any man standing in his way . . . or upon the survival of those responsible.'

This time Cecil whirled, a cold anger lighting his eyes. 'You have the luxury of honour, sirrah. You hold no power. You are not faced with harsh decisions on a daily basis, where choices must be made in sacrificing one life to save two, or ten to save a hundred. Do you think my life peaceful? Do you think my soul remains untainted by those choices? Forget Master Swyfte. He will never be allowed to foment rebellion here. He will die on foreign soil once his quest has been accomplished, or he will die when he sets foot back in England. Either way, there will be an end of it.'

CHAPTER TWENTY-NINE

THE LANTERN GLIMMERED DEEP IN THE GLOOM AT THE FAR end of the orlop deck. Carpenter felt little comfort from the tiny speck of light in the stifling heat and stale air of the dark space. The cargo hold throbbed with the rhythm of the waves pounding against the creaking hull, and sometimes, when the din diminished a little, he could hear the scrabbling of rats in the bilge beneath him. He grimaced as he sucked in a breath heavy with the stink of rot and worked at the greasy ropes binding his aching wrists behind his back.

Here, on this ship of the dead, the spy fought back his fear. He had been in many tight spots in his life, but few as desperate as this. His plunge from the *Tempest* into the violent sea had smashed the breath from him. Brine had flooded his nose and mouth, the undercurrent sucking him into the black water below. Swept back up to the surface, he had seized a fleeting chance to gulp one last gasp of air, and as he did so he glimpsed the white face of the foul thing he had dragged into the seething cauldron. If Lansing of the High Family had been swept to an agonizing death at the bottom, his own passing would have been worth it. The last thing he remembered was feeling arms close around him as Launceston attempted to keep him afloat. He marvelled: Launceston, who had no feelings for any living thing, who slaughtered innocent and guilty alike with the dispassion of a butcher preparing meat for the table.

Carpenter screwed his eyes shut. For some reason, the hated Enemy had saved him and stowed him away here in the filthy, stinking hold. Why did they not kill him and be done with it? He was no use to them; he knew nothing. Perhaps his suffering was simple sport, or revenge against a man who had been a thorn in their side for years, however ineffective.

'Do you miss your friends? Your family?'

He flinched at the voice and almost cried out. His senses had told him that the hold was empty, but he should have known better; the Unseelie Court were like ghosts. The voice was that of Lansing. He was disappointed that the hated Fay had survived too, but he should have expected it.

The Fay asked his question again, his voice measured.

'I have no family,' Carpenter spat, 'and no friends either. I have nothing in my life except the work I do, so do not think you can torture me with false hopes.'

'We are not the monsters here.'

The spy laughed long and hard.

Footsteps echoed as Lansing drew closer. Carpenter tensed, expecting to feel a blow or the prick of a dagger, but instead he heard the Fay's passionless voice at a lower level as if he were crouching to look his prisoner in the eye. 'There is great beauty in our world. Music that can move men to tears. Art. Philosophy. The joy that comes from being at the centre of life and all the wonders it offers. You think us

218

demons, but we are not so different, our two people.'

'And yet you have treated men like cattle, ready for the slaughter, since the beginning of time,' Carpenter sneered. 'Stolen our children for sport, or our youth or our lives. Turned women to stone, destroyed families and whole villages, blighted lives for amusement or because we did not bow and scrape before you.'

'And men are so different? We do not hurt our own kind. Can the same be said of your privateers in Africa, or in the New World? Of your own Queen, in her own homeland? So much misery inflicted on those who worship by another creed – and yet pray to the same God!' An incredulous laugh rolled out from the dark. 'Since man walked tall, the world has been awash with blood. Not one race, not one country, has never raised a weapon in anger against another. Those who have suffered at your own hands far exceed the number we have tormented. And we are the monsters?'

'You twist things to seduce me with words,' Carpenter said. He let his shoulders sag.

'Nothing is as simple as it is made out to be by men of power. They always twist things to achieve the outcome they require. But I do not have power. I am just a warrior, like you, in this ceaseless shadow-conflict those greater than us have carved out.'

'Like me? I think not. For all my flaws, I have honour.'

'Then you have not had your fill of this battle, as I have? You do not wish to see it end and return to your home and your life? If this war were over, I would go in an instant and hold no hatred in my heart for any man. That is my most fervent wish.'

The spy did not reply at once. The Fay's words struck a

note deep within him. He had been left for dead, scarred, betrayed, deceived; had seen the woman he loved murdered and been denied the opportunity to walk away from the business of spying. Cecil would never let him leave. All the secrets he knew were too valuable, he accepted with bitterness. 'I have heard of your plans,' he said at last, giving no sign of his true thoughts. He pushed his head up in defiance. 'You would wash us all away in a tide of blood. You want to win this war by leaving no trace of men upon the earth—'

'We want only one thing,' Lansing interrupted in a soothing voice, 'the return of our Queen, my sister, taken from us in an act of grand betrayal when all we wished to do was make peace.'

'Do you think I can trust a word you say? Your very existence is based upon deceit and lies.'

Carpenter felt icy breath on his ear and recoiled in revulsion. He smelled strange spices. 'One more time,' Lansing whispered. 'We are the same.'

The spy wanted to feel anger, but the Fay's calm words seemed to have sapped his rage. He sagged back against the damp boards, dreaming of a home that had not existed for many years.

'Do you ever feel lost?' Lansing continued. His soles scraped on the boards as he began to circle his prisoner. 'If that word chimes with you ever, then you know my people. We are lost, all of us. Wanderers who travelled from four distant cities, Gorias, Murias, Finias and Falias, four places of such wonder and enchantment they could bring any who laid eyes upon them to tears of joy. But our way was lost, and we could never find our way home, and for as long as we have known we have been yearning for those magical, fabled cities. No peace in our days, no contentment, only endless searching. Our sadness eats into our hearts and turns our thoughts grey. But one day, we believe, we will finally find our way back and then, and only then, will we find peace.'

Carpenter felt a dismal mood descend upon him. He closed his eyes, letting his thoughts float back through the years and across the miles, to his father, in his cups and laughing by the hearth, and to his mother, wearing her best mustard skirts and white apron as she trudged through the snow to church on Christmas Eve. What uncomplicated lives they led. If only he had recognized that before he had left in search of coin in the Queen's employ. Other scenes marched through his thoughts: the fields around his home where he knew every bird's nest, how every shadow fell in the autumn twilight; the sound of the men singing as they drank their apple-beer after a hard day bringing in the harvest. He bowed his head. *Lost*, he thought, with such poignant regret it made him wince. 'Did Launceston survive?' he croaked.

'Your friend is safe.' Lansing's footsteps retreated a few paces. Carpenter wondered if the Fay was drawing his blade for the first of many cuts and realized he cared little. 'You may see him again soon,' the Fay continued. 'If only there would come a time when this war no longer tore friends apart.'

The spy read what his opponent was saying. 'I will never betray my Queen,' he muttered.

'Nor would I expect you to. You are an honourable man, as am I. But there are steps we foot soldiers can take which could free us all from daily suffering, steps perhaps unseen by our masters caught up in their grand visions.'

Carpenter allowed himself a moment to imagine what

life would be like without that struggle. He did not hear Lansing approach again.

'We need no grand betrayal to end this war,' the Fay was saying. 'Only one thing, one small thing. The sorcerer, Dee.'

The spy snorted. 'Without Dee, England falls. You will be able to do whatever you want with us.'

'As I said before, all we want is our Queen returned. When she is seated once again upon the Golden Throne, there will no longer be need for struggle. We are no different, you and I. We want the same things.' Lansing repeated the sentiment in a honeyed voice, the words almost dreamlike as they wove among Carpenter's thoughts. The spy felt himself falling under their spell. *We are the same. We want the same things. Lost.* 'Dee's hands are drenched in blood. You know as well as I that few would call him a good man. He has no honour. What a small sacrifice he would be to achieve such a great end.'

And on Lansing spoke, the steady beat of his quiet words an enchantment that swept Carpenter's wits away. Little of what followed did the spy recall, only the great swell of his yearning as he thought of fleeing his blood-drenched work for a simpler life.

And then he heard Lansing say, 'Will you help end this war?'

And he replied, 'I will.'

Though it was dark, he was sure the Fay was smiling. 'We would join you with us, so we can whisper our secrets. Guide you. Comfort you.'

'Why do you need me?' he murmured. 'You can raise the dead to do your bidding. You have your Scar-Crow Men. I am but one man, and a lowly one at that.'

'One man who gives himself freely can achieve greater things than an army of mere flesh devoid of thought.' Lansing's footsteps drew closer once again. 'Do you give yourself freely?'

'If it will bring an end to this war and this suffering. If we can have peace once more, and lives without strife.'

The Fay lord knelt beside him and struck a flint. Carpenter screwed up his eyes as the white light blazed in the gloom. Once a candle had been lit, he saw that Lansing held a silver casket in the palm of one hand. 'This path must be chosen,' the Fay said. 'We can no more enforce it than we can turn back the wind.'

Carpenter shook his head, trying to dispel his hazy stupor. An insistent voice echoed deep inside him, but it was too faint to comprehend the words.

Lansing flicked open the casket lid to reveal a silver egg lying upon folds of purple velvet. 'It is a Caraprix,' he said with an odd hint of fondness. 'So simple in appearance, yet containing such great power.'

'It lives?' the spy asked.

Lansing's lips twitched. 'Yes, it lives. It will be your most trusted companion, should you let it. Oh, the things it will whisper to you, the wonders it will unfold.'

'And it will help me achieve the ends we both want so fervently?'

'It will.'

'Then free my hands, and let me hide it in my pouch. I would be away from here and bring an end to this madness sooner rather than later.'

'You do not need your hands,' the Fay said in a calm voice which Carpenter found inexplicably troubling. Before

223

he could probe further, Lansing delicately lifted the silver egg out of the casket and balanced it on his palm in front of the spy's eyes. The unblemished surface gleamed in the candlelight.

'We will become one,' Lansing said with a cold grin.

Legs sprang out of the Caraprix's side. Like a beetle, it scurried across the Fay's palm and leapt on to Carpenter's face. He cried out in shock as the sharp tips of those legs bit into his flesh and held fast. It crawled down, and though he clamped his mouth shut the spindly shanks wormed their way in between his teeth and forced his jaw apart. As it wriggled past his lips, he felt its smooth surface as warm and yielding as flesh. Sickened, he tried to yell, but only a strangled cry came out.

The Caraprix forced itself further into his mouth, towards his throat, filling up every space until he choked. Darkness closed around his gaze. As Lansing's emotionless face filled his vision, he could only think how weak he had been, and what terrible things were now to come.

CHAPTER THIRTY

NIGHT HAD FALLEN, AND THE SEA BELLOWED ITS FURY. IRON waves hammered the *Tempest* as it crashed towards the rocky fangs protruding from the swell. Wrenched back and forth in the grip of turbulent currents, the galleon seemed caught in a battle it was impossible to win. 'Hold fast to the course,' Courtenay bellowed, his gaze fixed on the flashes of white water ahead. Sparks of orange light glittered across the dark sea from the vessel's blazing lanterns, yet the channel ahead remained pitch black.

'God save our souls,' Strangewayes called to the heavens. He clung on to the rigging for dear life, his shirt and breeches sodden from the surf gushing over the rail with every dip and crash.

'Only Bloody Jack can do that now,' Will shouted back. His fingers ached from gripping the greased rope.

The ship careered into the dark like a leaf caught in a flood. For one queasy moment, the prow pointed towards the glittering stars, then plummeted down into a sable valley. A deluge thundered over the prow. Before the brine had sluiced across the deck, the ship crested another wave.

Seasoned crewmen flew from their feet. Had the island lured them in, only to dash them on the rocks, Will wondered?

His ears rang from the thunderous roar as they neared the long line of white-topped breakers crashing against the lethal rocks. It seemed there was no path through, but Courtenay stood like a sentinel on the forecastle, unmoved by the furious heaving.

'This is madness. We will all die,' Strangewayes cried. 'I should be at Grace's side—'

'There is nothing you can do for her now. Hold fast or you will be thrown over the side,' Will called back.

The galleon heaved as a loud grinding echoed through the hull from the rocks scraping along the side. Any moment Will expected the jagged reef to tear through the pitch-covered oak. In those violent currents, the ship would break up in no time.

He gritted his teeth as the grinding grew louder, until he feared the end had come. The *Tempest* lurched. Men crashed to the deck. Then, suddenly, the grating sound stopped and the galleon swept free of the clutching fingers of the black rocks. Relieved grins leapt to the harrowed faces of the seamen caught in the wildly swinging lanterns. The violent shaking faded, the seas grew calmer, and a cheer rang out from all on deck.

When the *Tempest* reached placid water, Courtenay gave the order to drop anchor. As he strode the deck, the men showed him their respect with broad grins or bowed heads. Bloody Jack only laughed louder, clapping his hands together in triumphant glee. 'We have stared death in the face, and once again the bony bastard has backed down,' he bellowed as he passed.

The night was cool and smelled sweetly of fresh vege-tation. Now the danger had passed, Will wondered where his plans would take him next. He found his thoughts swinging wildly between hope that one day he might see Jenny again and dread that Grace had been lost because of his own failings.

Strangewayes cast one eye towards the island. 'Is this the place mentioned in the captain's journal 'pon the abandoned Spanish galleon?'

'We will find out in good time, Tobias, but there have been tales of many a devil-haunted island in these parts. Perhaps the influence of the Unseelie Court grows stronger with each step closer to their home.'

'Then let us pray we draw no nearer.' He glanced up, past the men hooting and chattering as they scrambled up the rigging, and then strode towards the captain's cabin to see how Grace fared.

Once the sails had been furled and calm had descended on the galleon, Will sought out Courtenay on the poop deck, where the captain was swigging from a cup of wine by the light of the moon. Aware of the dangers that might lie ahead, they agreed no landfall would be made until sun-rise. Eager as he was to discover Dee and Meg's fate, Will took the opportunity to snatch a few hours' rest in a corner of the main deck while the men played cards and drank in the berth.

Sleep came quickly. Through the dark he sailed, deep into dreams.

Once again, he walked with Jenny through the garden of the cottage she shared with her father and mother and Grace in Warwickshire.

In the sun, honey bees buzzed lazily past the marigolds on their way to the hives at the end of the garden. Purple-topped lavender swayed past their legs. His gaze flickered towards the dark band of woods ahead, like a storm cloud on the horizon, and he felt uneasy as he sensed that something watched him from their depths. Though he could not see it, for some reason he couldn't fathom he believed it to be a raven. Those black glass eyes lay upon him, heavy with judgement, he was sure. And then he realized that Jenny was speaking to him, her voice insistent, and when he turned he saw worry in her features. She was telling him not to go on, to turn back, forget everything, live life, for the west was where the dead went. Turn back. Turn back.

The world skewed and shadows rushed out from those dark woods to swallow him. When his head had finished spinning, he somehow knew it was the night of Jenny's disappearance. He had spent hours searching the lanes and fields around her home, desperation, then fear, then grief, burning a hole in his chest. No sign of her anywhere; no sign of her ever again in Arden. And he was washing his hands by the well, washing furiously to rid himself of the stain, but he knew that it would never go, that it lay deeper than flesh. He was changed for ever. No longer William Swyfte the poet, with a fine career ahead of him after he departed the debating halls of Cambridge University. No longer innocent. And then he turned, as he had, and Grace was there, little Grace, pleading for news of her missing sister. He tried to hide his hands so she would not see. He tried—

Rough hands were shaking him awake.

His eyes snapped open and he peered into Strangewayes' face as the spy loomed over him in an excited state, his fists gripping Will's shirt. 'Come,' he urged with passion.

'Come.' Shaking the last of the dark dream from his head, Will staggered after the other man. His heart beat faster when he saw Tobias dash into the captain's cabin. Inside, Grace was sitting up in her berth, her head in her hands, her lank hair falling across her face. When she looked round as the two men entered she appeared baffled and Will feared the worst, her wits burned away by the searing touch of the Unseelie Court. His breath caught in his throat. Yet after a moment she forced a weak smile and said, 'You both look so troubled! What is wrong?'

Relief flooded Will. 'You gave us a scare, Grace,' he said, beaming. 'You have been a bundle of trouble as long as I have known you.'

She rolled her eyes and sniffed. 'Men call a woman trouble when she does not dance to their tune. I am proud to be so described.'

The two men laughed, their moods lightening for the first time in days. Will knelt beside Grace and tested her memory and her wits with several questions. She answered every one clearly, her puzzlement moving to annoyance until finally she told him she had had enough of being mothered. Promising he would explain everything to her soon, he insisted she rest and build up her strength, for there were more tribulations ahead.

Outside the cabin door, he closed his eyes and put his head back, letting his relief show. 'Never would I have hoped for such an outcome,' he breathed.

'It seems Grace is stronger than you think,' Strangewayes said, his voice hard. 'You see the little girl you first knew. But she has grown into a woman as courageous as any man.'

'In that, you are correct. I have misjudged her. When she

has regained her strength, I will reveal all she needs to know about the Unseelie Court and their foul ways.'

'Do not expect forgiveness,' Strangewayes said. 'This time we were fortunate, but Grace should never have been placed in that danger.' He stalked away before Will could respond.

The night drew on, and on. Will climbed up to the forecastle and watched the shore, feeling unease begin to replace his jubilation. When footsteps drew near, he turned. Men slept on the decks under the lit lamps. Courtenay strode past them, his brow furrowed, and the spy knew he was not alone in his worries. 'The sun should have been up long ago,' Bloody Jack said, eyeing the full moon and the milky sweep of stars as he neared, 'yet this night stays and stays. How much longer are we to be tormented by strangeness?'

'It is a strange world, captain, and an island where night outstays its welcome is not the worst thing in it.'

Courtenay shrugged. Vertiginous seas and blood-crazed pirates were as nothing to him, but Will could see that the unnatural dark troubled him deeply. 'Well, we can't sit here waiting till Doomsday,' the captain muttered. 'I'll assemble the shore party. But you must watch yourself out there, Master Swyfte.'

CHAPTER THIRTY-ONE

THE ISLAND BROODED IN THE DEEP DARK. NO FIRES OR lanterns glimmered, no voices carried, no sign of human habitation showed itself anywhere. There was only the creak of the *Tempest* at anchor and the wind across the waves.

Uncommonly subdued, Courtenay disappeared below deck and returned with ten of his fiercest men. Will watched the rowing boat pull away as it ferried the sailors to the shore. It disappeared into the dark, and after what seemed an age, lanterns flickered to life in a circle on the beach. He joined the last boat with Strangewayes, who would not meet his eye. 'You must put aside your feelings until we are back aboard ship,' Will said in a low voice. 'Our survival could depend on us looking out for each other.'

Strangewayes did not reply.

Through the gloom they could make out white-topped waves lapping on to a small beach which led up to a dense line of trees silhouetted against the night sky. The dark beneath the canopy was impenetrable. The sweet scent of cooling vegetation drifted on the night breeze.

'Make a fire here on the strand,' Will ordered when he

stood in the circle of lamplight. 'It will be a beacon for us as we explore the island.' While the men collected driftwood and dry brush from the treeline, Will clambered over the rock pools at the edge of the horseshoe-shaped cove. Though he gained a different perspective of the island, still he could see no sign of life.

Once he had glanced towards the beach to ensure he had not been followed, he crouched down and removed the obsidian mirror from his leather pouch. It felt cool and comforting in his hand. How much he had gambled, bringing such a powerful object so close to the redoubt of the Unseelie Court. And yet it had proved the source of such hope.

He laid the looking glass on a seaweed-covered rock and peered into its depths. It seemed to glow of its own accord. Long moments passed, but just as he began to lose hope the mirror clouded and Jenny appeared in the glass once more. She smiled but her eyes looked unaccountably sad.

'You knew I was here, wishing to speak to you?' he asked.

She nodded. 'The mirror is powerful. It calls out to . . . to this place. And . . .' she lowered her eyes, trying to hide the depth of her feelings, 'I look out for you, Will. To see you again . . . after so long . . .' She shook her head, grimacing. 'No. I am being weak. You must ignore my words. Stay away, Will. There is too much at stake here. I am worth nothing.'

He shook his head with vehemence. 'You are everything to me. And I will risk everything to bring you home.' Her tears welled and she screwed up her eyes to stifle them. Will felt overwhelmed by a rush of memories, sensations and emotions: crunching through crisp gold and orange leaves in the woods with Jenny beside him; their eyes meeting at the Christmas feast amid the scent of cloves and hot, sweet wine, and the world seeming to hang though the dancers whirled around them; a kiss, on the day he left for Cambridge, thinking that surely there could be no worse pain than this parting. If only he had known.

'I have many questions,' he continued, aware that time was short, 'but first: tell me, have they harmed you in any way?'

'I am well,' she replied, so quickly that he knew she was lying and his blood boiled.

'Who took you, Jenny, and why?'

'Why? Who can fathom the minds of these creatures?' she replied in a strained voice. 'Who?' She paused, swallowed. 'I was taken on the orders of Mandraxas, the King of these people, and the first of the High Family.'

'Then he is the one who must feel the bite of my blade,' Will replied, his voice cold. 'One day I will find my way to you, and then—'

'You can never do that,' she said, her voice breaking. 'This fortress is impregnable. High, strong walls and many guards. And to enter this land of the Fay, you must first pass through one of the gates into the place where the two worlds overlap.'

'How will I find them?'

She sighed. 'Will—'

'Tell me, Jenny,' he pressed.

'The Unseelie Court say you will find the gates if you ever need them, though it is much harder to leave. Twin pillars of stone, they are, in the sea around the New World. You will surely know them, for the rules of the natural world do not hold sway around them.'

While he reflected upon her words, a cry of alarm rang out. He looked round, and when he turned back the looking glass was clear. His heart sank, but only for a moment, for he knew now that Jenny was looking out for him too.

Another cry rolled across the strand. Will stood and saw Strangewayes lit up by the ruddy flames of the crew's bonfire, beckoning him back. One of the men was pointing out to sea. Following the line of the man's arm, Will discerned lights bobbing far out on the dark ocean beyond the reef. Another ship was sailing towards the island. When the *Tempest*'s gun cracked, Will could only imagine that the new arrival was Jean le Gris's devil-haunted pirate galleon. The warning shot from Captain Courtenay would let their enemies know they had little hope of sailing through the rough waters beyond the reef in one piece.

At the bonfire, the men had made burning brands with pitch-soaked sailcloth wrapped around fallen branches to light their way through the thick woods. 'We must use well what little time we have,' Will told them. 'Search for any paths leading away from the beach. But stay in sight of each other's torches.'

'And if we find nothing?' Strangewayes muttered.

'Pray that we do, Tobias.'

As they moved into the trees, the dancing torchlight glowed like fireflies through the branches. A symphony of subtle sounds surrounded them: the whisper of leaves, the groan of dry wood underfoot, and the distant call of some night bird. Soon the dark swallowed the beach and the bonfire. No one spoke.

Will imagined Dee and Meg and the other survivors clawing their way out of the surf and staggering up the beach and into the woods. It gave him hope where he knew there should not be any.

The ground sloped steadily upwards towards the centre of the island. In the sultry heat, sweat dripped from brows and soaked shirts. The men's breath rasped with the exertion.

'If the Unseelie Court find another cove to put into, how long before we encounter them, I wonder?' Strangewayes thought aloud. Will noticed he kept one hand on the hilt of the dagger tucked into the waist of his breeches.

Ahead, one of the men whistled, and the torches swept through the trees in the direction of the call. The two spies found the other men gathered in a clearing looking up. On the side of the hill at the heart of the island, a tower stood silhouetted against the starry sky.

'Curious,' Will said, stroking his chin-hair. 'Now who would call this dark place home?'

On the far side of the clearing, one of the men waved his torch. Cracked flagstones marked a path leading up through the trees, so worn and overgrown they suggested great age. Strangewayes flashed a questioning look.

'If I had survived a shipwreck, a stone tower would have seemed a perfect shelter,' Will replied. Holding his torch high, he stepped on to the path, happier now he had a destination in mind. Yet only a moment later, a blood-curdling howl echoed across the island. Uneasy, the men huddled together, eyes wide and darting around.

'What was that?' Strangewayes hissed. 'Man? Or beast?'

Will drew his dagger. 'Cold steel cuts either one.' He continued along the path, more cautiously this time.

The path wound round the contours of the hill. Even

with the torches Will found it impossible to see any distance ahead. When he paused to get his bearings beside a craggy-barked tree, the baying rolled out again, so close this time that several men cried out in shock. The sound stirred ancient fears in his head. Yet another yowl came a moment later, behind them this time.

'Circling us,' Will said.

'Hunting.' Strangewayes whirled, brandishing his dagger in front of him.

Behind them, along the path, the baying changed into a low growl, the sound of some beast preparing to attack. 'Stand your ground,' Will called, but the fearful seamen ran as one towards higher ground. Realizing they had no choice but to follow, the two spies raced after them.

The frightened men burst out of the trees into another clearing at the foot of a rocky outcrop. The torchlight glittered across the surface of a black pool fed by a spring trickling from the glistening cliff face. 'Make a stand,' Will shouted, putting away his dagger. 'There will be no better place.'

Blades bristled out as the men formed a circle, their drawn faces stark in the flames. Will snatched out his rapier and turned to look back down the shadowy path.

A snapping and snarling rang out, but then a familiar woman's voice called out, 'Leave them, Mooncalf. They are not your prey.' Silence fell across the woods. When Will's pounding heart had slowed, he raised his torch and searched the dark beyond the pool. In the wavering light, a grey shape appeared, coalescing into Red Meg. She was barefoot, her dress smudged and worn. A grin sprang to the spy's lips and he ran over to her.

'It does me good to see you well, Meg,' he said with relief. 'I had feared the worst.'

Her eyes narrowed as if she were trying to recall his face. 'Will Swyfte?' she enquired with a faint, baffled smile.

Had she taken a knock to the head in the shipwreck, he wondered? But then her eyes sparkled and her smile broadened and she almost hugged him in her joy. 'Will Swyfte! After so long, I never dared hope I would see your cocky face again.'

'Ten weeks since Liverpool is long indeed, Mistress Meg, but it could have been eternity—'

'Ten weeks?' She shook her head, puzzled once more. 'Since the storm washed us up on this island, twelve years have passed.'

CHAPTER THIRTY-TWO

THE STIFLING DARK ENVELOPED CARPENTER. COARSE SACK-cloth scratched his face as he stumbled along blindly at the bidding of his captors. His breath rasped against the covering that had been thrust over his head aboard the galleon, but sounds came to him clearly: the whispering voices of the Unseelie Court speaking in their strange, bird-like language, the splash of the oars in the rowing boat, the crash of waves and the crunch of sand underfoot as he lurched up the strand. Blood dripped from his stinging wrists where the rope chafed him, but the pain only focused his mind. With an effort, he drove out the sickening sensation of the thing forcing its way down his throat and thought simply that he still lived.

When he came to a swaying halt, rough hands yanked the sack off his head. He stood on a small beach edged by steep cliffs facing a wall of dark, spiky-leaved trees. Torches hissed and spat in the hands of the dead pirates, their grey-green skin peeling away to reveal the bone beneath. The stink of rot floated on the breeze. Beyond the circle of light, he could just discern the spectral faces of the Fay in the gloom, their fierce, unblinking stares locked upon him.

Reeking of unfamiliar spices, Jean le Gris, the pirate captain, peered into the spy's face with his one good eye. Scar tissue marred much of his skin above his wild black beard, but Carpenter saw that this man wore his wounds with pride. With a gap-toothed grin, the pirate tossed the sack away and said in heavily accented English, 'Savour your few last breaths, dog. Your time in this world is done.' He swept a hand across his throat and laughed.

Carpenter shrugged, refusing to give the other man any satisfaction. 'How can you throw your lot in with these foul creatures?' he said with contempt.

Le Gris's grin faded. Leaning in closer, he hissed, 'Do you think I had a choice? If I had resisted, I would have become like them.' He nodded towards his dead crew.

'So you sacrificed your men to save your neck. There is no honour among pirates, it seems.'

Le Gris snarled and Carpenter felt the prick of a knife-point at his neck. A bubble of blood rose up. 'They came like wolves in the night as we sailed down the Channel. Ten men were dead before we even knew they had boarded us. A cur like you cannot judge me.'

The Unseelie Court never lost their ruthlessness, the spy understood. They needed a galleon that could survive an Atlantic crossing and took the first one they found that would not be missed. 'You survived that encounter because they needed your skills,' he said, 'but soon you will have outlived your usefulness. What then, Frenchman?'

Le Gris's blade moved back, ready to cut Carpenter's throat, but the Englishman saw the other man's eyes flicker towards something further down the beach and the foul-smelling pirate stepped back. Propelled by unseen hands, another hooded prisoner lurched beside the spy. Le Gris snatched off the sack to reveal Launceston, his deathly pallor aglow in the torchlight.

'You live,' Carpenter said, surprised by his rush of relief at his companion's survival.

'Little good it does us,' the Earl breathed.

The Fay lord Lansing sauntered past the men, carrying a small, gleaming chest a hand larger than the one that had held the Caraprix. He nodded for the pirate to follow him. Glowering at the two spies, le Gris took the chest and followed the Fay like a servant. Carpenter imagined the Frenchman's searing resentment at the humiliation, and smiled to himself.

'Did they harm you?' he asked Launceston.

'They were poor company,' the Earl replied with a shrug, 'but I have endured worse. When I was a child, my father sealed me in a hole in the cellar with three rats for company, to teach me a lesson, he said.' He looked round the beach, his voice unnervingly quiet. 'I learned how to kill rats.'

A little way away, the silver box had been set on the sand. Lansing knelt down and flicked open the lid, drawing out a glass ball like the ones Carpenter had seen in Dee's chambers. He held it gently in the palm of his right hand.

'Four times Lansing came to me. His words were sugared, but each one hid a demand for betrayal. What could he offer me? I have all I need now. Satisfying work, companionship.' Launceston paused. 'We all have a place in this world and I have finally found mine. I would not let him take that away from me.'

Carpenter hid his guilt, pretending to be engrossed by the Fay, who was dismissing le Gris with a lazy flick of his hand. Muttering under his breath, Lansing gestured as if drawing a silk kerchief off the glass ball. A flood of colour rushed out.

The two spies recoiled as one. 'More magics,' Carpenter spat.

The shifting colours coalesced into a plane on which formed a relief chart of the crescent-shaped island, with a stone tower standing on the hill at the centre. Carpenter gaped as he saw thick woods and paths running through them, valleys, pools and streams and grassy clearings. Lansing crooked a finger at the pirate and then pointed to the tower. 'The magician hides away here. Find him and bring him back, and kill anyone who stands in your way.'

Le Gris nodded, his one eye wide with amazement.

'Here,' the Fay continued, moving his finger to a faint red glow following a path to the tower, 'are the English spies.' He traced a line along a deep valley. 'If you follow this route, you will shave hours off your journey and, perhaps, reach the tower before our foes.'

'And this?' The pirate pointed to a single red spot keeping pace with Will and the others.

Carpenter saw Lansing's brow furrow. The Fay shook his head and turned back to the silver chest, removing a gilt-edged mirror. Holding it up, he whispered a few words and the glass clouded over. Gripped now, Carpenter's eyes narrowed as a hawk-like face appeared from the mist: one golden eye, one purple, wide and unblinking under arched brows, a long pointed nose ending at bow-shaped lips that added a feminine touch to the strong features.

241

'Mandraxas, brother,' Lansing said, with a curt bow of his head. 'All strands come together, here on the edge of the great everlasting.'

'You have the Ortelgan Mirror?' The voice rolled out from the glass, high and sweet.

'In time,' the Fay lord responded. 'First we will snare the magician, Dee. Once we have brought him home to endure the pleasures of Fortress Crepuscule, all things must follow.'

'And so we make our plans, brother. And so we make our plans.'

Carpenter felt his stomach knot, queasy with fear. Yet with the Caraprix nestling deep inside him, he knew there was no going back. He set his doubts aside and wondered why that face in the mirror frightened him so. It was as if his senses understood the essence of the creature and rebelled at the contact.

Once the face had faded and the looking glass had clouded once more, Lansing returned it to the silver box with the glass ball and flipped the lid shut. He stood, saying to le Gris, 'Organize your men, or what is left of them, while I see to the prisoners.' With his chin raised, the Fay wandered behind Carpenter and Launceston. 'Your time here is done,' he said in a quiet voice, 'but your passing will not be painless, for what would be the point? We all have our skills, my brothers and sisters and I, our strengths, our joys. Mine is the taking of a human life. Sometimes I come like a ghost. Men fall in a court in a foreign land, their blood pooling around them, and those standing beside them know not how their companion came to be dead. Sometimes I linger, drawing out long-held secrets or cries or vows, for the benefit of my people or for pleasure. Sometimes I slaughter wantonly, allowing men to sink into the fierce beauty of my face, the mere sight of me adding another subtle layer to their pain, another delicate seasoning to my rapturous feast. The High Family knows my expertise and they use it well. I am their sword, enforcing their will in the world of men.'

Carpenter wondered, then, why Lansing had not tortured him, or Launceston, to achieve his ends. He had used only words. Perhaps he had spoken truly when he expressed his desire for the peaceful return of his sister.

'Come to it, then,' Launceston said as if he were calling for another cup of sack. 'I have no fear of death. We are old friends.'

Carpenter heard Lansing pass by the Earl and step up to his back. He felt cold breath upon his neck. 'Our agreement stands,' the Fay whispered so Launceston could not hear. 'Find the magician first and deliver him to me and no one will suffer. You will be free to return to your life and this long war will be over.'

The spy felt the kiss of cold steel against his skin as Lansing slid his dagger under his bonds and slit the rope. 'Choose your moment well to flee,' the Fay added before saying loudly, 'I will leave the thoughts of your passing to settle deep into you and thereby make the experience all the richer. Soon, now. Soon.' He strode across the dry sand to where le Gris directed his men. They appeared to understand his meaning.

'Robert,' Carpenter whispered from the side of his mouth, 'I have worked my bonds free. When I make my move, follow my lead.'

The Earl inclined his head in assent, giving nothing away.

Carpenter watched Lansing guide the pirates until their

243

backs were turned, and then he grabbed Launceston's arm and drew him silently into the trees. When they were deep in the dark and running as fast as they could, he heard le Gris's cry. 'Too late to raise the alarm,' Carpenter said. 'Once we have put some space between us, I will free you from your bonds, Robert, and then we shall bring this matter to a close.'

His chest swelled with exuberance. Soon he would be going home.

CHAPTER THIRTY-THREE

BLACK CLOUDS LOPED ACROSS THE SKY, DEVOURING THE STARS and the moon. Branches thrashed in the claws of the wind raking through the trees on the hillside. The torches roared and spat as the frightened men of the *Tempest*'s shore party forced their way through the rising gale towards the tower where Dee and Meg had taken shelter. With the storm, they could sense something darker coming too, long fingers of shadow reaching across the tropical island to snuff out their lives as easily as the lights that guided their way. When the howl of the Mooncalf rolled out near at hand, they jumped and cursed. Death lay everywhere.

'What is that thing?' Will asked, his shirt damp against his hot skin.

'Dee's watchdog,' Meg replied. She lifted the hem of her grey skirt as she climbed the overgrown stone steps of the narrow path. Occasionally she would flash glances at her companion that ended with a puzzled smile as if she still could not believe he was there. 'The alchemist made it . . . made it out of . . .' She paused, looking away into the dark under the trees. 'No matter.'

Will still hadn't decided whether her suffering on Dee's haunted ship and in the wreck on the reef had driven her mad. Her ship had been at best only two weeks ahead of the *Tempest*. How then could she believe she had been upon that island for twelve years? He had not yet broached the subject for fear the questioning would unbalance her further, but he needed answers if he were to snatch a victory from the coming conflict.

Strangewayes strode up behind them from the rear of the column. 'How long before the sun comes up?' he snapped. 'I have had my fill of this night.'

'Put aside any hopes of feeling the sun on your face,' the Irish spy responded. 'That will not occur until Dee decrees it.'

'The doctor holds the sun at bay?' Will said with incredulity. He had seen the alchemist at play with charts of the stars and potions and incantations, but never had the old man displayed the kind of power that could shake the heavens.

'Dee has gone quite mad,' she said, 'and in his madness he has found a way to tap into forces that should never be conjured by mortals. This island too is a special place, where strange and troubling things occur, and whatever qualities it possesses only seem to serve to add to the old man's magics.'

'But holding back the sun,' Strangewayes gasped. 'Why, that is the remit of God alone.'

'Then god he is.' Meg looked up as the first fat drops of rain began to fall. 'When he senses threat, he brings the night to confound his enemies, or calls storms to dash ships upon the rocks. And,' she added, 'the Mooncalf hunts better at night.'

Will heard the unseen creature snuffling and snorting in the undergrowth, breaking branches as it kept pace with them. It terrified the men with every step. But whatever it was, it seemed to obey the woman's every word, so they were safe for now. 'Men are not as easy to control as the Unseelie Court believe,' he said. 'They think they can run us like rats, but Dee has confounded them.'

'How so?' Strangewayes asked. 'In posing as the angels he believed he contacted, he was lured away from the path of light, and eventually, when they were ready, they sent him spinning off into the dark. He took with him our last hope to repair our defences against them. And in their hands—'

'But he is not in their hands. In Liverpool, the Enemy thought they could spirit him away as easily as they steal babes from their cribs. But they have been forced to chase him across half a world, right to their very doorstep. 'Twould seem to me that Dee had long since prepared his own defences, anticipating that the Fay would one day attempt to take him. And when they did try to exert their control, he unleashed his moon-side, which still holds sway.' Will wiped the raindrops from his eyes, enjoying the cooling touch on his skin. 'In his madness, he is unpredictable and uncontrollable, and, he would hope, beyond their reach.'

'Then why come so close to their home?' the other man asked. 'Surely he would flee *away* from them.'

'Dee is cunning. If he is here, there is a reason for it.'

The path wound round the hillside as it rose towards the tower. Emerging from the thickest part of the woods, they saw lightning crackling along the horizon and bands of heavier rain marching across the treetops towards them. In one white flash, Will found Meg staring at him and asked what troubled her.

'You still look as young as that last day I saw you, so long ago, in Liverpool,' she replied. 'How can this be?'

'And you have not altered one whit.' He watched her face, ready to change the subject if she became distressed.

'No,' she said with a shake of her head, rubbing her fingers over her smooth cheeks.

''Tis true. Can you not see it?'

'Dee allows me sight of no mirrors 'pon this island. The windows of the Unseelie Court, he calls them.' Her brow furrowed. 'You say the years have not taken their toll 'pon me?'

'There have been no years, Meg,' Will said gently. 'For us, only ten weeks have passed since Liverpool.'

The Irish woman bowed her head, struggling to comprehend what she had heard. 'This cannot be. My memory is filled with so many things happening here . . . so much struggle and misery, such loneliness that at times I thought I could not bear it. Coping with the old man's caresses while my stomach turned, and listening to his ramblings about magic and philosophy and history. And yet . . . He told me once that in the home of the Fay, time did not march as you and I know it. It hovered or folded back upon itself. Ofttimes the sands did not run at all. That is why, he said, the Fay never aged, and why their schemes run over years, and centuries, even. Perhaps this island has similar qualities.'

'Perhaps so. If not the home of the Fay, mayhap it sits upon the borderlands in the shadow of that place.' Will felt his heart go out to her as he saw her troubles laid bare in her face. 'The other members of your crew?'

'Those who survived the wreck died over time. The Mooncalf has a taste for human flesh, and in those early days, soon after he was created, Dee struggled to control him. He kept one mirror in those first months on the island and taunted his enemies through it. One Fay of fierce beauty, a witch by any other name, attempted to seduce him with her charms. Her name was Malantha, one of the High Family, and she and Dee battled wits for long weeks while the Mooncalf stalked the island, killing men. Dee's weakness was always the pleasures of the flesh, and the Unseelie Court see every man's weakness clearly. Malantha spun a web around him with her seduction, and only when the old man appeared on the brink of revealing the location of this place did he break free of her spell and shatter the mirror.'

'This island was hidden to the Unseelie Court? That is why Dee settled here?' Will brooded for a moment. As he thought he played the Fay, had they in turn played him, pretending to try to stop him reaching Dee while in truth following him to the prize? He silently cursed himself for his overconfidence. Where the Unseelie Court were concerned, nothing could be taken for granted; he should have learned that long ago.

Thunder cracked overhead and rain sheeted down, forcing the sailors to move under the canopy of leaves to prevent the torches from being extinguished. Meg seemed oblivious of the downpour. 'After these twelve long years, I am weary,' she admitted. 'I yearn to be free of this business, to walk once more across Ireland's green meadows and hear the songs of my people.'

'Twelve years on an island with only Dr Dee for company

might have seemed like an eternity, Mistress Meg, but the world still waits for you, just as it always was. Nothing has been lost.' Will understood well her doubts and sorrows – they were too much alike, the two of them. 'That is a second chance few people get.'

For a moment longer, she kept her head down. But when she looked back at him with a seductive grin and the fire alight in her eyes once more, he saw the Meg he knew. 'Then let us waste no more time on miserable thoughts. The sooner we can overpower the mad magician, the sooner we can return home. And then we can dance and make merry and . . . perhaps . . .'

He smiled at the promise in her eyes. Before he could reply, calls and the sound of running feet echoed from the path ahead. As the sailors drew their knives and rapiers, two men careered out of the gloom and the wall of rain. Will recoiled, fearing he was seeing ghosts. Hair plastered to their heads and clothes sodden, Carpenter and Launceston skidded to a halt. Will stared for a moment, stunned.

'At last,' Carpenter said, breathless. 'I could not bear to run another mile.'

'John!' Will exclaimed, grasping the other man's shoulders. He beamed, barely believing his own eyes. 'Robert! You survived.'

'The Unseelie Court took us aboard their ship,' the Earl replied, his whispery voice almost lost beneath the pounding of the rain. 'But we escaped them.'

Will laughed, relief flooding him. His conscience had been stained by many things, but here was one that would no longer haunt him. 'Fortune indeed smiles on us. Grace has recovered, and Meg here and the two of you have wriggled out of death's grasp. Only a day ago, I never would have believed it possible.'

'Pfft. We have survived worse,' Launceston sniffed, wiping the rain from his face.

'Let us save our tales for another time,' Carpenter insisted, glancing over his shoulder. 'Lansing marches towards the tower to seize Dee, with the pirate le Gris and his dead crew alongside him. We have little time – they know a short cut.'

Will felt on fire. His spirits had been low, but now it seemed as if no obstacle was too great. 'Come, then, lads. Now we are reunited, let nothing stand in our way. For England!'

Even as the other men gave full voice to his cheer, another oath seared through his mind: *For Jenny. Soon now*, he thought. Soon he would have answers, and then revenge.

CHAPTER THIRTY-FOUR

FROM OUT OF THE DRIVING RAIN, THE DARK FINGER OF THE tower appeared. Thunder boomed and lightning flashed, turning the world white. The column of sodden men raced up the final steps of the crumbling path into a forecourt of broken flagstones where yellowing grass pushed through the cracks. A low wall ran round the edge, overlooking a deep drop down the rocky hillside to the woods below. One by one the torches fizzled and went out in the deluge until they had to splash through pools to cross the final few feet to the foot of the soaring structure. Will looked up, but the summit was lost to the dark. No lights gleamed from the slit windows. Worn by the elements, the tower looked ancient, as old and rough as the stones standing in circles on England's moors. Above his head, he could just glimpse carvings running round the periphery, their original shapes lost to the slow erosion of the years so that it appeared strange creatures were being birthed from the rock itself.

Carpenter returned from a circuit of the tower's foot and yelled above the gale, 'There is no doorway.'

'Dee has hidden it since I departed,' Meg shouted, 'with his magics.'

'The good doctor is greatly changed by his experiences,' Will explained to the other men, his words barely audible above the blasting wind, 'and he has powers now that allow him to walk with the gods. We must not underestimate him.'

'All well and good,' Strangewayes bawled, 'but how do we get inside before the Enemy get here?'

Meg peered up the vertiginous walls of the tower, pointing. 'Up there, at the height of five men, there is an arched window.'

'Are we apes?' Carpenter raged. 'You expect us to climb that smooth wall, and in this storm? Even if we could find finger-holds, we would be dashed off by the gale in moments.'

The Irish spy narrowed her eyes at him. 'Then it must be my second suggestion: ram your hard head against the wall enough times and you may batter your way through.'

When Carpenter bristled, Will rested a calming hand on his shoulder. 'What choice do we have, John? Cup your hands for my shoe – I will try first.'

'How high must one climb before bones break in the fall, I wonder?' Launceston mused, stroking his chin. 'Before organs burst?'

'Curb your hunger, Robert,' Will said. 'You may find out for yourself once the rest of us have failed.'

'Wait.' Meg stepped forward, pressing the palms of her hand together as if in prayer. 'There is another way. But it has many dangers—'

'More dangers than climbing this tower in the storm?' Strangewayes growled.

'More suffering before you die,' Meg said, arching one eyebrow. 'The Mooncalf could climb this tower with ease. Indeed, I have seen him do it many a time. He could carry one of you on his back. But at any moment he might unleash the savagery in his breast, and rip you limb from limb and eat your heart before it has stopped beating.'

Will nodded to Meg. 'Very well. We cannot be defeated at this stage. I will take that risk.'

'Why not let him try?' Meg said in a wry tone, pointing at Carpenter, who glowered back.

'I have asked you all to put your lives in jeopardy in recent times. Now it is my turn,' Will said. 'Summon Dee's beast.'

He instructed the *Tempest*'s crewmen to guard the perimeter of the courtyard, thus sparing them the sight of what might be to come. The sailors were only too ready to comply. The five spies stood shoulder to shoulder, peering into the dark as Meg called out to the creature. The howling wind dropped for an instant and the sound of snuffling and growling drew nearer. Will sensed the others grow tense. The reek of bloody offal whipped by on the wind. A low, hunched shape, darker than the clustering trees, appeared at the top of the steps leading to the courtyard. Loping forward with a rolling gait, it gathered speed, snarling as it bounded towards Will.

At the last, Meg stepped in front of him. She held her head up in a commanding stance. 'Mooncalf, heed me,' she called out into the night. 'Do not harm these men. You will have other food soon enough.'

At the crack of her voice, the beast slowed and came to a stop two sword-lengths away. 'She controls it like a prancing pony,' Strangewayes hissed. 'How so?' The spies took a step back as they took in the horror before them.

Will studied the shadows pooling in Meg's face and thought he glimpsed the softening of her features. As the Mooncalf raised itself up on powerful legs, he caught sight of the outline of a broad, flattened head that reminded him of the bulls baited in the bear garden on Bankside. The skin was blacker than the night and seemed to gleam as it moved, like pitch. White eyes burning cold moved across the spies. Strangewayes gasped as a lightning flash revealed a face like melted candle wax, the flesh running down to the broad shoulders. The mouth was a black gash showing a hint of sharp, stained teeth. The strong body looked twisted, as if the Mooncalf had been tortured on the rack, yet its muscular power was unmistakable. Despite its terrifying appearance, though, Will sensed something oddly human about it.

'Do not harm them,' Meg repeated as a threatening growl rumbled deep in its throat.

'You are mad to risk your life with that thing,' Carpenter whispered. 'It is a wild animal, barely tamed at all.'

'I would be mad to stand here and do nothing,' Will replied.

Meg flashed him a look of concern, but then put on a confident face and spoke to the Mooncalf so quietly that none could hear what she said. The beast lurched forward, its breath reeking of meat. It flung its arms round Will and lifted him effortlessly. Pinning him in the crook of its right arm, it bounded at the tower wall. Taloned feet and the long fingers of its left hand found cracks and crevices barely visible to the naked eye in the dark. With a rolling movement, the Mooncalf began to climb.

Pressed tight against the leathery flesh, Will glanced sideways and saw those eyes flicker towards him. In them, he recognized some semblance of intelligence, and it troubled him. What was this thing, not beast, not man? With a snarl of warning, the Mooncalf's lips curled back from its yellow fangs, forcing Will to look away.

The anxious voices of the other spies slipped beneath the howl of the wind and the rattle of the driving rain. The dark closed in around them, an endless chasm threatening to suck them down. Higher the Mooncalf climbed, seemingly up into the very heart of the storm. Just when Will feared he would be dashed on to the courtyard far below, the beast's fingers closed on the crumbling lip of an arched window. Heaved inside, Will crashed on to dry flagstones, the rainwater pooling around him. The creature crouched by the window, watching the spy through slit eyes. Its low growl echoed through the still chamber.

'If you can understand my words, I thank you.' Though Will was hesitant to turn his back on the beast, he felt along the wall until he found an extinguished torch and lit it with the flint from his leather pouch. The darkness danced away from the flame, and he saw he was in a bare stone room with an empty hearth. Two arched doorways led out of it. Though the tower was silent, he felt that it was not empty, as if someone waited only a chamber away. He imagined Dee sitting in the dark somewhere above him; not the Dee he knew, the wildly inventive but mad scholar who had devoted his life to holding the line against the forces of the moon that threatened to usurp the sunlit world, but a brooding Dee, corrupted by a different kind of madness and consumed by the well of power into which he had tapped, who saw all as his enemy. He had built his fortress here on this island, with the only human who meant anything to him, and he would not easily be shifted.

Edging along the wall with one eye on the Mooncalf, Will ghosted through the nearest doorway on to a spiral stone staircase leading down into shadows.

CHAPTER THIRTY-FIVE

HARD RAIN LASHED THE KNOT OF SPIES HUDDLED AGAINST the tower wall. Suspended in a sea of night, they could have been a thousand miles away from any other living soul as they searched the dark for the coming attack. But the wind-thrashed trees sounded like waves crashing against their small island of stone, drowning even the noisiest approach, and the gale snatched at their hair and clothes to distract them.

Strangewayes gripped his rapier, remembering his days learning the blade in the precinct of Chelmsford Cathedral, under the tutelage of the master Adam Abell. A good student but hot-headed; that had always been his teacher's assessment. And over the years, as he had earned his reputation and joined the employ of the Earl of Essex's newly minted band of spies, he had fought hard to control that simmering temper. But now it burned hotter than ever. When he had left Essex to join Cecil's more seasoned group, he had hoped to learn more at the feet of the lauded Will Swyfte, *England's greatest spy*, but Swyfte had proved a straw man. He was only concerned with his own needs, caring little about the harm he caused to others. Even Grace; especially Grace. Strangewayes would never have survived his first brush with the Unseelie Court if Grace had not been his rock, and for that alone he would give his last breath to save her. If Swyfte placed her in danger one more time, Strangewayes would kill him, with no qualms. He thought back to the accusations the spymaster, Sir Robert Cecil, had made in London and realized that this battle was no longer between human and Fay, but between himself and Swyfte, for the soul of the woman he loved.

For an instant, the wind dropped, and in the space a low, unearthly moan rolled out across the courtyard. Strangewayes felt the hairs on his neck prickle. 'What devilry is that?' he demanded.

Launceston ignored him, as graven and unreadable as ever, and Carpenter only swore at him to stay silent. 'Conjure up no nightmares,' Meg told him. 'There will be time enough to face our fears.' Though they all treated him like a child, it was the Irish spy he hated the most. She acted as brazen as a Bankside doxy, spinning men round with her wiles. Of all of the spies, the Irish woman was the least trustworthy, he had decided.

'I am not scared of anything,' he replied.

'Then you are a fool,' she came back as quick as a flash.

Strangewayes felt stung for only a moment before movement away in the dark caught his eye. A figure lurched towards them. It was one of the crewmen, and his gait was as rolling as if he stood on deck in a storm. The spy grew cold, though he did not know why. The staggering sailor seemed to glow in the dark, as pale as Launceston, his clothes as well as his skin. The sight reminded the spy of the fish he had once seen swimming in a cave pool. He swallowed, uneasy.

'The Unseelie Court have arrived,' Launceston intoned.

As the man stumbled nearer, a lightning flash lit him clearly. He was white from head to toe, as if encrusted in salt, his eyes staring in terror from his scabrous face. Mewling, he reached out to the spies with one clutching hand, which seemed to diminish with each passing moment.

The rain is washing him away, Strangewayes thought, horrified.

In the deluge, the sailor dissolved piece by piece, a part of his jaw gone here, an arm there, his body dissipating yet still alive, still calling out in that incomprehensible whine. The flood of white crystals frosted the rain pools in the courtyard. Barely able to believe what he was seeing, Strangewayes watched as the man sank to his knees, which melted away to leave the torso flailing from side to side, until finally only a crumbling face peered up from the wet stone, still crying.

When that too was gone, Strangewayes reeled out of his sickened trance. Shadows whirled in the rainswept night, the remnants of the shore party fighting with le Gris's decaying crew. The spy watched one of the *Tempest*'s men hacking into pieces an unrecognizable but still quivering piece of dead flesh. Strangewayes would have run to the aid of the men, but a hand fell hard on his shoulder.

'They need our aid,' he protested.

'Set aside feelings and be cold. We have work to do,' Launceston replied.

Struggling to ignore the cries of the dying, Strangewayes reminded himself that returning Dee to London was all that mattered; all their lives meant nothing in the pursuit of that aim. Then le Gris emerged from the dark, and three other grey pirates followed, one missing an arm, another an eye.

'Once your entrails hang from my sword, I can claim the treasure I have been promised,' le Gris yelled above the cacophony of the storm. He levelled his rapier, daring one of the spies to confront him.

Carpenter broke away from the others and leapt to cross swords with the French pirate. 'The Unseelie Court jangle shiny things in front of weak men, but they are as insubstantial as rainbows,' the spy said with a vehemence that puzzled Strangewayes. 'They can never be reached and men waste a lifetime trying.'

Le Gris only laughed. As the two men danced around each other, thrusting and parrying in the downpour, Strangewayes glimpsed a figure bearing down upon him. Spinning, he swung up his rapier just as a dead pirate hacked with its own blade. A dull ache burned in his shoulder from the force of the walking corpse's blow. Choking on the stink of decaying flash, he easily sidestepped the next thrust. Yet what the thing lacked in expertise it made up for with untiring force. The unblinking face loomed closer, ragged lips hanging off clenched teeth, fat white maggots at play on exposed cheek flesh. When the spy pierced the heart for a second time, he grasped the futility of his strategy. Before he could find another approach, he saw Carpenter slip to one knee on the wet stone. Defenceless, the other man could only look up as a leering le Gris levelled his rapier for the killing stroke.

Without a second thought, Strangewayes dropped his own defence and parried le Gris's thrust. He sensed the dead pirate swing for his neck, and screwed his eyes shut in the certain knowledge that his life was over. When the blow failed to strike, he looked round to see Meg whisking her dagger back as the pirate's entrails splashed into the puddles. Sweeping an arm out, the Irish woman gave Strangewayes a theatrical bow.

Carpenter recovered and thrust his blade into le Gris's thigh. The pirate howled in agony and staggered away, blood seeping between his fingers as he clutched his leg. Brushing back his wet hair from his pink scars, Carpenter turned to Strangewayes and gasped, 'I owe you my life.'

'And I owe mine to . . . her,' Strangewayes replied, masking his irritation that the woman he loathed had saved him. 'We keep no score here.'

'Very well,' Carpenter replied, looking round. Two other bodies lay writhing in black pools. Launceston loomed over them, his sword dripping gore and a hungry gleam in his eyes as he examined each man in turn.

'You have done your work there, Robert,' Carpenter called with a weary shake of his head. 'Let it be.'

The four spies backed against the wet stone of the tower. One by one, the cries of the dying seamen ebbed away beneath the howl of the storm until no human voice remained. Strangewayes squinted, trying to pierce the night. He saw misshapen heaps that had once been human, innards turned to straw or faces twisted into twirls of blackthorn, all the monstrous work of the Fay. He felt sickened by the atrocities committed by their Enemy. Beyond the bodies, grey shapes flitted like moon-shadows. The Unseelie Court began to creep forward.

'Stand firm, lads,' Meg called, twirling her dagger. 'We'll show them some cold steel before we take our bows.'

Strangewayes gritted his teeth and thought of Grace, until the rattle of a bolt at his back distracted him. A door that he could have sworn was not there before swung open at the base of the tower. A torch flared in the dark interior.

'Better late than never,' Swyfte said with a grin. 'Step lively now. This door will not hold them off for long.'

CHAPTER THIRTY-SIX

SHADOWS SWARMED AWAY FROM THE HISSING TORCH FLAME as Will bounded up the worn steps two at a time. At bay beyond the thick walls, the storm was barely more than a susurration. The other spies followed, their breath rasping. 'They will keep coming,' Strangewayes wheezed, his gaze downcast. 'They always do. Always. Nothing can hold them back.'

'Let us hear no signs of weakness.' Launceston had an edge in his voice.

Will felt relieved to see they had all survived, though from their drawn faces he could tell they had all fought hard. He would have liked to know the fate of the sailors who had accompanied them, but decided that question could wait. Constantly glancing back in case Dee's twisted creation, the Mooncalf, attacked, he had taken what seemed like an eternity to navigate the tower's vertiginous and winding steps and he had feared the worst. 'Yes, like the tides they come and they come, but they have not overwhelmed us,' he said with determination. 'We must use our wits and our guile to stay one step ahead, and soon the time will come when the tide will be turned.' After travelling half the world, he could scarce believe they were so close to their goal. He would not allow the Fay to stop him laying claim to Dee at this late stage.

'Such fine swordsmen have nothing to fear from any Enemy. Why, your prowess melts a woman's heart,' Meg teased, but her next words were edged with caution. 'But the alchemist will have protected himself. If he hides in the highest room in the tower, he will be unreachable. In his madness and fear of attack, his mind has turned in these past years to fiendish traps which he has secreted on the approach to his chamber.'

'Dee's inventions were mad even when he professed to sanity,' Carpenter muttered. 'How can we outwit such a man?' He paused, then added, 'Strangewayes, you should lead the way.'

The younger spy glowered, but said nothing.

Will threw up his left arm to halt the others, cocking his head as he listened. Whispers floated all around, sounding like the voices of the dead piercing the thin veil between their world and his own. When he realized the eerie voices came and went with the strength of the draught whistling down the steps, he raised the torch to reveal carvings of grotesque faces following the curve of the wall just above their heads. Small holes had been fashioned in them. As they caught the air currents, they produced the unsettling whispers.

'In our first years here, Dee spent some time attempting to discover who built this place.' Meg's deep, sing-song voice drowned out the ghosts. 'Gods or Fay or men, he never found his answers, but they left many wonders behind.'

265

Will began to climb once more, torn between caution towards what lay ahead and haste from what was behind them. 'Watch our backs, Robert,' he said to Launceston. 'If you have even the slightest suspicion the Enemy are coming up, sing out.'

As they climbed, the bare walls became covered with faded tapestries or shelves of mouldering tomes, muffling the echoes of their tread. They passed bolted doors hiding silent chambers. Strange scents drifted on the dry air, some sweet and spicy, others with a bitter tang, but Will could smell no hint of any man. Just as he was beginning to wonder if Dee had hidden himself away somewhere else, he was confronted by a flare of light and a dark figure. It was his own reflection in a gilt-edged mirror that filled the width of the passage.

'The way is barred?' Strangewayes asked. 'Have we wasted our time?' He turned his narrowing eyes on Meg.

Her brow creased. 'No. Dee told me another chamber lay at the top of the tower.'

Will traced his fingertips across the smooth, cold surface of the glass and after a moment gently applied pressure. A click echoed and the mirror pivoted to reveal a space a sword's length square bounded by three more mirrors. On the low, vaulted ceiling, more twisted faces whispered their unsettling entreaties. 'It seems,' he said with a hint of a smile, 'we are now playing Dr Dee's game.'

As the five spies pressed into the tight space, the mirror pivoted shut behind them. Launceston pressed his shoulder against it, but it held fast.

'Trapped,' Carpenter grumbled.

'Or not,' Will said. 'That would be too simple for a man

like Dee. Tricks and puzzles and games are what fire him, and in them he finds his own kind of torture.' He peered into each of the three facing mirrors in turn, then said, 'I would wager we are in a maze.'

Meg nodded, understanding. 'Each mirror opens on to another space like this one. We lose hours, if not days . . . if not our wits or our lives . . . finding a way through.'

When Carpenter reached out to press one of the mirrors, Will caught his wrist. 'We should choose carefully, John. If I know Dee's cunning, he will have arranged it that once a choice has been made, neither of the other two ways can be opened. Otherwise, it would be a matter of simply searching all possible paths.'

'And no going back,' Launceston mused, studying his reflection. He smoothed one eyebrow with his index finger.

'We have no time to dawdle. Let us make our choice and move on,' Strangewayes snapped. 'They are all the same. How can we know which way to go?'

The younger spy was correct, Will accepted. They could not afford to tarry. He selected the mirror to his left and swung it open. As he had expected, another square of mirrors confronted him. Once the others had squeezed in, he heard the mirror at their backs close with an echoing click.

'This is madness,' Carpenter exclaimed. 'We will be lost in this hell until Judgement Day.'

For long moments, they passed through an endless procession of themselves, their faces seeming more haunted in each new space they entered. Will found his head swimming with flashes of reflected torchlight, sparkling eyes and the constant whispers from the carvings overhead.

He shook his head, trying to dispel visions of other shadowy figures looking over their shoulders. He could see that the others also struggled with the assault upon their senses in the confined spaces.

'There is more at play here than mirrors,' he said as he stepped through another opening. The words had barely left his lips when the door jerked from his grip and slammed with surprising force, separating him from the rest. He hammered on the glass, but it seemed unbreakable. Through the barrier, he could hear Carpenter's muffled curses, but after a moment they died away. Only silence remained. Perhaps this too was part of Dee's trap. Divide, and conquer.

With grim determination, he turned to move forward alone.

Time seemed to stretch out in a constant parade of mirrors and doors. In every space, images of himself reached out for ever, an unending but insubstantial pageant of Will Swyftes ineffectually fighting a battle that would never end. He began to notice that the incomprehensible droning whispers were starting to make a kind of sense, urging him on towards despair. The mirrors themselves pricked his unease. The Unseelie Court communicated through them, lived within them, for all he knew. Were they now watching his every move? Laughing at his failures, luring him on to his doom?

Barely had the thought crossed his mind before he saw his reflection melt away. In its place loomed up the yellowing and hideous skull beneath the skin. *Death is waiting for you*, it told him, *and it is closer than you think*. His heart began to pound and a sheen of sweat glistened on his brow.

Reeling, he tore open another mirror and stepped

through to the next small chamber, and the one after that. He felt hours pass; days; years. His reflection aged, the skin hanging from his face in loose folds, until it crumbled to dust, then became young and vital once more.

Wrenching open one mirror, he was greeted by an image of Dee. The old man sat in a high-backed wooden chair that resembled the Confessor's throne in Westminster Abbey. His eyes were black pebbles in a frozen face. Brooding, he was, plotting death; not the Dee that Will knew at all. The vision vanished in the blink of an eye, but not before Will felt it sear itself upon his mind.

More mirrors glittered, endless Will Swyftes.

As he stumbled into another chamber, the glass showed no reflection, nor a hint of what might be, but a memory. It was night, and he stood by the well in Arden on the day and night that had changed the course of his life for ever. It was the day Jenny was stolen from him, but that had not been the only assault upon his life. He was there, washing his hands over and over again, desperately trying to rid them of the blood that now turned the water brown. And he heard the soft tread of small feet at his back, and knew that it was Grace. He could not let her see his crime, his failure. And so he turned to her and smiled and spoke as sweetly as he could. But that was the moment he knew he was not a good man, and could never be again. Redemption would never come for him. All that remained in life was saving Jenny. If he could do that, at least he could achieve something good in his miserable existence.

And then, in his befuddled mind, a single clear thought surfaced. It felt like a revelation, a burning truth. *The Unseelie Court steal our innocence*, he thought. *That is their greatest crime.*

They corrupt our highest aspirations and force us to be base and grubby.

With shaking hands, he ripped open the mirror and teetered on the brink of a pure black abyss. Buffeting wind lashed rain into his face. Somehow his fingers clutched on to the jamb. The door had opened in the wall of the tower and he half hung over a vertiginous drop into the night. The blast of air and the wet cleared some of the delirium from his mind, and he understood what a trap Dee had set. Only reactions honed by a lifetime of battle had prevented him from plunging to his doom; others would not have been so fortunate.

As he dragged himself back, he glimpsed movement below him. Even in his feverish state, his senses jangled. Gripping on to the jamb, he leaned out into the storm once more and peered down. Squinting, he could just make out shapes shifting on the sheer wall. Like fat grey spiders, the Enemy scaled the tower, clinging on to the gale-lashed stone with supernatural skill.

Bypassing the mirror maze, they would be upon Dee in no time at all.

CHAPTER THIRTY-SEVEN

THE MIRROR SWUNG OPEN WITHOUT A SOUND. BLINKING IN the glare of candlelight after so long stumbling through the dark, Carpenter looked round a small antechamber lined with leather-bound books. On a trestle in a corner stood rolls of yellowing charts, a human skull with a fragment of pate missing, an ivory-handled knife with a curved blade and a small silver casket. He could still smell the sweet aroma which had hung in the air since they had entered the mirror maze. But over the top of it now drifted the reek of human sweat.

His head swam from the visions that had floated across his mind's eye since he had become separated from the others. His love, Alice Dalingridge, calling to him, still as beautiful as when she had been alive. His father, now so long in the grave, showing him how to chop wood behind the thatched cottage in the forest clearing. And that thing tearing at his face in the frozen Muscovy woods, when Swyfte had left him for dead and he had felt all hope desert him. Time no longer meant anything to him. He might have been in that black, glass world for years.

With a shaking hand, he wiped the sweat from his brow and steadied himself. At least that damnable whispering had left him in peace. Creeping forward, he listened at the door to the next chamber. When no sound reached his ears, he opened it a crack and peered inside. Amid shelves of books, Dee sat on a stool in front of the cold hearth, his back to Carpenter. The old man had his head in his hands, deep in thought.

The spy drew his dagger in case he had to prick the alchemist to urge him to obey. As he prepared to step into the chamber, a hand fell on his shoulder. He almost cried out and lashed out with his knife. The steel whipped a hair's breadth from Launceston's throat. Pulling the door shut, Carpenter pushed the Earl to the other side of the antechamber and whispered, 'You fool. I could have killed you.'

He flinched at the other man's penetrating gaze. 'What was your intention?' the Earl asked in his blank, emotionless voice.

'To capture Dee, of course.' Carpenter's gaze flickered away from the other man's probing eyes.

After a moment, the Earl spoke, his tone measured. 'I have had little comfort in my life, despite the land my family has owned, and the wealth we have amassed – or perhaps because of it. My father was not a man given to sentiment. Ledgers and balance sheets prescribed the limits of his life; the cold stone of our castle, rarely heated even in winter, was the womb of his existence. He sought to teach me harsh lessons, feeling, mayhap, that it would best prepare me for the kind of life he lived. Cellars and drains and holes were my billet. Days spent in dark and damp, with only rats and beetles for friends. Blood and bruises and broken bones. No traitor in the Tower fared worse. I wonder sometimes if God made me the monster I am, or if it was my father.' He wrinkled his nose and shrugged. 'It matters little. We are what we are.'

Carpenter glanced towards the door, half expecting Dee to come out and cast some vile spell on them. 'Why are you telling me these things?' he asked in irritation.

'I killed him. My father. He was my first. At the time I thought it would ease the ache that reached deep inside me.' Launceston cocked his head, narrowing his eyes as he stared into the middle distance. 'It only increased my appetite. When something has been taken away, we try to replenish the space left behind with other things, but that is like filling the sea with sand.'

'You are a madman. Why speak like this, now, here?'

'You have lost the woman you loved, seen your face scarred and the very foundations of your life shaken. You are trying to fill the sea with sand,' the Earl said.

Carpenter furrowed his brow, trying to tease out the meaning in his companion's words. He sensed a weight there and it puzzled him. Launceston rarely spoke, and never expressed his innermost thoughts or feelings. Indeed, Carpenter had come to believe the Earl had none.

'I know not what Lansing offered you when you were his prisoner, but it was a deal with the devil,' the aristocrat said, his voice now a whisper. And then Carpenter understood: no one saw into the Earl, but Launceston had seen into him. 'Your belief that you can achieve your heart's desire has blinded you to the truth.'

'The bastard offered me nothing,' Carpenter lied, with a

derisive laugh. 'I resisted all his attempts to torture me.'

'The Unseelie Court rarely have need to torture. And I know you better than you know yourself,' the other man replied, turning his gaze towards the candle flame. Carpenter thought he appeared to be trying to dredge up the remnants of whatever human emotion had survived from his earliest days; a monk trying to comprehend the ways of a Bankside doxy might have looked equally baffled. 'The decision you make this day will define the course of the rest of your life,' Launceston continued. 'I will not stand in your way, whatever you choose. You have stood by me when most other men would have walked away in disgust – that is something I have never known in my life, and I value it more than you could understand. For the first time in my dismal existence, I have found a place where I am at ease, here among men who deal in false faces and deceit yet hold themselves to a higher standard than most honest men—'

'I made no deal with Lansing,' Carpenter interrupted, trying to hide the bitterness in his voice.

Launceston continued as if the other man had not spoken. '—and I feel there is a place here for you too, if only you would open your eyes to it. In the midst of all this strife, we can find peace – yes, and Swyfte too – to replace the things that have been stolen from us. Seek out the morals that have always guided you—'

Carpenter laughed. 'I am being lectured on morals by a man who has killed children.' If he had expected the Earl to be stung by the gibe, Launceston did not show it.

'We must not become the men the Unseelie Court believe us to be,' the aristocrat ended. His searching gaze fixed upon the other man's face.

Carpenter felt the guilt rise inside him. How weak he had been, and he had known it and tried to deny it. Yet here was a man without a heart refusing to judge him and wanting him to aspire to greater things. What a mad world they had entered when they had stepped within the tower.

'I made no deal with Lansing,' he repeated, adding in a gentler tone, 'and I would never have given Dee up to them. Let us work together to capture the old man and deliver him to the *Tempest*. Then perhaps we can escape this steaming hell and return home.'

But as they crept back to the door, he felt his falsehoods lying heavily upon him. Amends would need to be made. He shook his head to dispel the bitter taste of failure and saw traces of candlelight stream through the air. 'There is still magic at play here,' he muttered.

Easing open the door, he peered through the crack. Dee still sat in the same position, bowed in front of the hearth. Carpenter wondered if the old man had died, so still was he, but he drew his dagger none the less. With a man like Dee he would take no chances. Holding his breath, he eased towards the hunched figure. His head throbbed and his mouth felt dry. When he crooked his arm to slip it round the alchemist's neck, he suddenly felt a fist grab the back of his shirt and drag him backwards.

A breeze whisked past his face as an axe-blade swung from the shadows above and smashed into Dee's side, throwing him to the flagstones. Carpenter gaped. One step further and it would have been his head rolling across the floor. Launceston knelt and picked up a thread that had been broken as Carpenter entered. Another of Dee's traps, but with this one *he* had paid the price.

Yet as Carpenter whirled back to the fallen figure, he saw the truth in the shapeless robes. Pulling them to one side, the spy revealed a frame of twisted saplings. 'How could I ever have believed that was Dee?' he muttered.

'You were entranced by whatever spell the alchemist has woven here,' Launceston said. His tone was flat, but he clearly did not want Carpenter to blame himself.

Carpenter sighed. 'So the old man still hides away. We must resume our search.' He turned towards the door so that the aristocrat would not see the worry in his face. Deep inside, he could feel the Caraprix wriggling, and whispering its seductive words. Deep inside, he could feel himself dying by the moment.

CHAPTER THIRTY-EIGHT

THE TORCH GUTTERED AND HISSED. WILL WATCHED ITS END-less reflections in the glittering mirrors, deep in thought. No shadows could exist in that blazing world of light, and for the first time the spy thought he could see clearly. Outside, the Unseelie Court still climbed the tower, drawing closer by the moment. He pushed his anxiety to one side and remained calm, focused.

When he had slammed the door and escaped back into the mirror maze, he realized the blast from the storm had cleared his head. The whispers from the carvings washed around him, but now he paid them attention. The dancing light of the torch flame was no more a mere distraction. He sucked in a deep breath, letting the sweet smell with its bitter undertones envelop him. All he needed had been there from the beginning, but as Dee had no doubt suspected, his attention had been elsewhere. The alchemist was a man of intellect, given to rigorous thought and reflection. He enjoyed his games of strategy, his chess, his nine men's morris. Puzzles with solutions that could be extracted through reflection. Will nodded to himself, ignoring the call to urgency.

Kneeling, he waved the torch close to one of the mirrors. Around the area where a hand would push the door open, a faint, sticky residue smeared the surface. Will smiled. Cunning Dee, who loved his concoctions, his herbs and clays and bubbling pots of lamb fat. In times past, the wise man had demonstrated the mysterious but effective potions he had brewed in his chambers. Some had been poisons with rapid lethal effect. Others sent a man to sleep, or made them foam at the mouth in a wild rage. And some turned wits to quicksilver and conjured visions out of thin air.

The spy stripped off his sodden shirt and flicked it round his right hand. With his skin covered, the paste would not seep into him and he would have time to recover from earlier contact. He held the torch high and watched the flames whip away from the hollow mouths of the whispering carvings. The unsettling sound had been designed to add to the off-kilter effects of Dee's paste, he realized, but they required a strong draught to work. The torch flame pointed away from the source. He lowered his eyes, refusing to look into the mirrors as he fought to overcome the subtle effects of the drug. Then, when he was ready, he pressed open the door with his covered hand and began to follow the trail back.

Watching the torch as he progressed through the mirror chambers, he saw the draught grow stronger. When the whispering became the chattering of madmen in Bedlam, the dancing light revealed the edges of a trapdoor in the vaulted ceiling. The breeze blew through small holes on each of the four sides. Will reached up to a shallow indentation in the centre of the trap and pressed. With a click, the door swung down followed by a coiled rope ladder. He squinted into that dark square and thought he could see a distant glimmer of faint light.

Determination burned through his foggy thoughts. The time of confusion had ended. Laying the torch on the cold flagstones, he set one foot on the ladder and began to climb into the dark.

He found himself at the foot of a flight of narrow stone steps, leading up to a small arched door standing slightly ajar. Candlelight gleamed through the crack. The sweet fragrance of incense drifted on the draught, and he could hear faint mutterings of incantations in Latin. Drawing his dagger, he crept closer. Through the slit of open door, he could just discern a small circular room. On the wall hung a purple tapestry covered with magical symbols of crescent moons, stars, runes, circles and squares in gold. Open volumes with stained pages were scattered across the flagstones.

Dee stalked past, his gown swishing across the floor. The animal skulls clinked on their silver chains at his chest. His wild mane of silver hair swung as he flung out his arms, gesticulating at invisible companions. Now he was near, the spy realized that what he had taken for Latin incantations was gibberish. The old man was lost to his world of madness.

As soon as the alchemist's back was turned, Will kicked open the door and barrelled inside. Dee let out a bestial howl of rage. His eyes glinted with insanity, his lips pulling away from clenched teeth. The spy crashed into the older man, knocking him across the carpet of mildewed tomes. Pinning him down, Will pressed the tip of his dagger beneath Dee's eye and said, 'I will not insult you by treating you like a frail old man.'

Dee thrashed like a wildcat in a sack, but as the spy dug the steel deeper into his flesh he quietened. A trickle of blood ran down his ashen skin. Yet still his eyes ranged with madness and he snarled animal sounds.

'What have you done to yourself, doctor? Where is that sharp wit that could cut a man half your age?' Acutely aware of the Fay drawing nearer, Will searched the alchemist's flickering gaze for any sign of comprehension and began to wonder if all their sacrifices had been for naught. 'Let us talk, you and I,' he said, 'as we did so many times in the Black Gallery, and perhaps the echoes of those days will stir some sense within you.'

In a calm voice that belied the urgency he felt, Will recounted how Dee had taken him under his wing when he had first arrived at the Palace of Whitehall from Cambridge within days of Jenny's disappearance. Though as gruff and uncompromising as always, the doctor had shown him some kindness then, recognizing the scars that had been inflicted and the worse things that lay ahead. Patiently, he had instructed Will in the ways of the Unseelie Court, and the horrors they had perpetrated for generations, and their wiles and their magics, and over days he had led the freshly minted spy to an accommodation with his new life.

'Remember, doctor, how you spun your fable of an English empire, stretching across the shining seas, a world lifted free from the yoke of the Unseelie Court?' he continued, lulling the old man with his steady tone. 'Remember how we stood side by side at the court of Stephen Bathory, when you conjured the ghost of the Polish King's long-dead father? How he trembled.' Will smiled at the memory, another of Dee's tricks to bend the foreign royal to the will of the

English. 'And how you poured a flask of sack over the head of that preening popinjay, the Earl of Leicester. What a waste of good wine.'

His soothing voice worked its spell and the old man calmed. Cautiously, Will removed the dagger and stood up, unsure if Dee would slip back into his madness. His heart pounding with awareness that time was slipping away, he looked around the small, windowless chamber until he found an ink-pot and a quill. Hastily, he sketched a few lines on a page torn from the front of a book. Once done, he dangled his work in front of Dee's face. It showed a horned circle with a dot in the centre, a cross beneath and under that a wavy line, a representation of a devilish man.

'Do you recognize your glyph, Dr Dee, the one you described at such length in your vast tome, the *Monas Hieroglyphica*? You see the astrological symbols? The power it represents? You laboured over this design for years, did you not? You told me how this glyph showed the true secret of all there is, how everything is connected at the smallest and highest levels, and that all we see around is illusion, a stage on which we are the players. Once this wisdom, this glyph, is understood true power comes, you said. Here is your great work, doctor. Here is you, in essence. Remember.'

The alchemist's eyes widened and the page was reflected in their depths. His madness was no natural loss of wits, Will felt sure, and if anything could breach his defences and reach the Dee that was, it was his true obsession, his life's work; the source of all his beliefs, and, perhaps, his powers. The old man's gaze swam, and for a moment Will felt sure he had failed. But then a mist appeared to rise in the depths of those eyes, and the brows drew together. Dee blinked once, twice, and his gaze drifted to Will. He scowled. 'So, I am in Hell,' he croaked.

'As are we all, doctor,' Will replied. But his smile faded as the lilting strains of pipe and fiddle floated through the smoky air like the waking echoes of a dream. The scent of honeysuckle wafted on the draught. When a drop of blood fell from the spy's right nostril and spattered on the flags, Dee closed his eyes and mouthed a silent curse.

The spy drew his rapier and backed against the wall. His gaze drifted up as he heard a clattering overhead. 'Time to leave, doctor,' he called.

Amid the sound of rending, a hole appeared in the ceiling as tiles and wooden laths were torn away. Rain gusted into the dry atmosphere and the crack of thunder rolled all around.

'Too late,' Will said through gritted teeth. 'If your wits have fully returned, now is the time to use them.'

CHAPTER THIRTY-NINE

THE CANDLE GUTTERED. SHADOWS FLEW ACROSS THE CHAMBER as the storm crashed against the tower like waves against a reef. In the flickering light, Will levelled his rapier and waited for the first of the Unseelie Court to crawl through the holes in the shattered ceiling. He could sense them, clinging to the rain-lashed roof as they waited for their moment. And then they would come like the storm, he knew, teeth and swords and talons, wild eyes and blood.

Dee clambered to his feet and lurched to an iron lever protruding from a slot in the flagstones. Gripping it with both hands, he wrenched it back. A deep grinding reverberated through the walls. 'There,' he exclaimed. 'The path through the maze is open.'

'Go, then,' Will replied. 'The *Tempest* waits in the cove. I will hold them off.' Though death was closer than it had ever been, he set aside fear and doubt. He breathed deeply, bringing the stillness inside him. The storm faded away. The flickering light troubled him not. He was ready.

As Dee stumbled through the door, Will heard a distant shout, and another answering. Tapestries flapped in the gale. Rain pooled on the flags, soaking the age-old books. Still the Unseelie Court waited. Were they taunting him? Trying to frighten him? They knew what strategies worked from generations of torment at lonely farms and on paths through dark woods, but this time they would be disappointed.

The door crashed open and Carpenter and Launceston burst in, blades drawn. Behind them, Strangewayes stumbled, delirious. 'Ignore him; he is less than useless,' Carpenter sneered with a nod. 'He failed to discover Dee's paste upon the mirrors.'

'Ah, John, you are sharp as a knife, as always,' Will said with a flourish of his left hand.

The other man shrugged. 'Only a fool would have failed to find it, sooner or later.' Muttering to himself, Strangewayes stumbled back out of the door.

Launceston eyed the holes in the roof. 'So, they wait for their moment, like rats in a barn at night.' He shook his head and called, 'You waste our time. Come now and be done with it.'

The candle guttered one final time and then winked out.

As the dark swept across the chamber, Will braced himself. He had the door at his back, Carpenter to his left, Launceston to his right, but they were at a disadvantage. The Fay always wrapped themselves in the night.

When the wind dropped for a moment, he heard the soft thud of someone dropping to the flagstones, then a second. He could sense the other presences in the room, like a yawning grave, but how many had entered he did not know. Gooseflesh prickled on his skin as the chamber grew colder.

For too long a moment an unnatural silence hung and

then Lansing's icy voice floated through the void. 'This is what awaits you, a mere taste of death. No heavenly reward, no soothing fields of green or long-lost loved ones. An endless nothing.'

'Reassuring words from the masters of deceit,' Will replied, one eyebrow arched. 'Why, whatever I hear from your lips, I believe the opposite.'

'We speak the truth when it suits us,' Lansing replied. 'What say you, Master Carpenter? Shall I tell a tale of weakness and betrayal? Or—'

'Your lies are wasted on us,' Launceston interrupted, unfamiliar passion edging his voice.

Will swished his rapier from side to side. He was ready should the other Fay creep forward in the impenetrable dark. If he could keep Lansing engaged, at least he could pinpoint the Fay lord's position in the chamber. 'What are you?' he asked. 'In all the stories we are told, your form and nature change with the teller. Imps, sprites, spectres, bloodsuckers. Fallen angels and demons from the depths of Hell. Are you the devil's children?'

In the ringing silence that followed his question, Will thought he was being ignored, but then Lansing began, 'You think this world belongs to man? We were here first.' Bitterness swelled his voice. 'No man could ever understand our pain, our grief, our loss. You call us devils, but in truth we are angels. Saviours—'

Carpenter snorted with derision. 'Our saviours?'

'This world's saviours. From our new homes under hill and lake and sea, we watched your slaughters and your brutality, the destruction you set in motion with barely a thought for consequence. When you put women and children to the spear, and burned others at the stake, and seared flesh with hot iron and put out eyes and lopped off limbs, we saw you were unworthy of this land that you inherited.'

'All men are flawed. But we deserve the right to aspire to greater things,' Will replied. Sensing a presence only a hair's breadth from his cheek, he whipped his rapier around, but the steel met only thin air. He felt cold eyes upon him nearby, and flexing fingers keen to tear out his throat or turn his innards to straw or stone.

'It is too late for that,' the Fay lord replied. 'Perhaps . . . once . . . before you stole our Queen and meted out your atrocities upon our kind. But now this world will be better without the infestation of man.'

'A fight to the death, then,' Will said.

''Twas always going to be that way,' Launceston sighed. 'Could you imagine our two races living side by side? Let us be done with it, though the world burn down in the process.'

'And there is man in essence,' Lansing whispered. '*Let us be done with it.*'

Trusting his instincts, Will lashed his rapier downwards. The blade sliced into one of the Fay creeping towards him through the dark. A furious howl filled the chamber. Beside him, he could hear Launceston and Carpenter putting their blades to work, and cursing at their inability to see. As he swept his sword back and forth, a haunting song reached his ears from the stone steps beyond the door, the words growing clearer as the singer neared. A woman's voice, it was, and it could only be Meg.

'There were three ravens sat on a tree,
They were as black as they might be.
With a down, derry, derry, derry, down, down.'

Dee's potion still gripped her, Will thought, and he called out to warn her away, but still she sang.

'Then one of them said to his mate,
Where shall we our breakfast take?
Down in yonder green field,
There lies a knight slain under his shield . . .'

Notes of sadness and regret drifted out through her lilting voice. Even the Unseelie Court seemed entranced, for Will sensed them pause in their attack. When the door swung open, candlelight glowed. Glancing back, he saw Meg framed in the archway. Bafflement filled him; he saw no trace of stupor in her face. But then he noticed her smile, darkly triumphant, and he recognized the Meg of old, when such a smile preceded a length of bloody steel. Yet her eyes were filled with the deepest sadness, and that puzzled him.

'His hounds they lie down at his feet,
So well they can their master keep.
His hawks they fly so eagerly,
There's no fowl dare him come nigh . . .'

. . . she sang, and then she raised her candle up so her red hair was all aglow, and beckoned behind her. The roar that echoed up the stairs would have chilled even the most hardened warrior. Will thrust Carpenter and Launceston to one side. On the other side of the chamber, the Fay crouched like cornered animals, mouths black slashes in their bone-white faces.

Something thundered up the stone steps. Will glimpsed only a flash of oily black skin and fierce white eyes as the Mooncalf bounded past him with a full-throated roar that made his ears ring. No male could fail to be entranced by Meg, he laughed to himself, and even this wild beast danced to her tune.

As a tumult of rending and tearing, howls and shrieks erupted, the three spies tumbled from the chamber. 'Your surprises always come with a sting in the tail, Mistress O'Shee,' Will murmured.

'You can thank me later, my sweet,' she replied, 'and fulsomely, I would hope. But let us not tarry here. Fierce though the Mooncalf is, I fear he is still no match for a pack of those predators.' A shadow crossed her face, and Will thought he glimpsed there a hint of regret, or guilt, that she had sent the beast to its doom. Perhaps her heart was not as hard as she liked to pretend.

Carpenter and Launceston hauled the barely conscious Strangewayes to his feet and the five spies made their way down the steps to the mirror maze, each trying to shut out the awful sounds — as if a bear were being set upon by a pack of dogs — coming from the chamber above.

'Fear not for Dr Dee,' Will told the others. 'He has gone on ahead, safe and sane, I would hope.' But as they passed the final looking glass, he grabbed Red Meg's hand and slowed her descent. 'What was that creature?' he asked.

The Irish spy looked away, her voice but a whisper. 'The

captain of our ship, transformed by Dee's deviltry to be his servant when first we washed up on these shores.'

Now Will thought he understood her dismay. What suffering had that man endured, should his wits have remained in his new misshapen form? And what corresponding monster lurked in Dee's heart that he was capable of such a thing?

Launceston caught his arm. 'We have an opportunity here,' he breathed. 'Our Enemy are engaged at the summit of this tower. It would be good if they could not leave. I have little stomach for nigh-on three months of sea battles all the way back to England.'

Will understood the Earl's mind. He turned to Meg and asked, 'Would there be such a thing as a powder store in this place?'

She smiled.

Down winding steps and into the dank cellars, they ran in her wake. And in the lowest point where water pooled and rats as big as cats ran from the light, she threw open a door to release the bitter reek of powder. Six barrels stood by one wall. 'Where they came from, I do not know,' Meg said. 'Many things were left behind by whoever occupied this place before us.'

''Twill suffice,' Will said with a grin. He nodded to Carpenter and Launceston, who found a chest containing ample fuse. Once they had laid a long strand, Will took out his flint. 'Now,' he said, 'let us see how hot those devils like their Hell.'

CHAPTER FORTY

WILL AND THE OTHER SPIES RACED FROM THE DOOR AT THE foot of the tower into the blustery night. The rain had stopped, but the encircling trees thrashed in the gale. As they splashed through pools of rainwater, the spies saw torches dancing in the dark along the edge of the courtyard ahead of them. Will caught a momentary glimpse of Dee sweeping towards the lights. Courtenay's voice boomed out: 'Finish off those dead bastards. Hack them to pieces.' Swords rose and fell, glinting in the flickering light. Without the help of the Fay, the remainder of the ghastly pirate crew didn't stand a chance.

'Take cover,' Will yelled as he ran. The captain and the crew gaped. Waving his hand to force them away, he shouted again, and this time the men scattered beyond the lip of the courtyard. When Meg struggled to keep up in her skirts, Will swept her into his arms without missing a step.

'How dashing a protector,' she teased, flicking her hair away from her face.

'Even in the face of death, Meg?'

'Especially then.'

As they reached the edge of the courtyard, the night cracked in two. Fire blazed across the sky, the earth shook and the thunderous explosion sounded like a hundred cannon. The force of the blast flung the spies down the incline from the courtyard. Chunks of masonry rained about them. Ahead of a wave of smoke and dust, fire-flakes of wood and parchment spun by.

Coughing, Will staggered to his feet, throwing one arm against his face as protection against the choking fog. He found Meg, leaning dazed against a tree, and dropped beside her, taking her slender hand. He felt his fears subside as her eyelids fluttered open. She smiled when she saw his face. 'The angels have come to claim me,' she said wryly.

The spy pulled her to her feet and she half fell into his arms. 'Our lives are hard fought, Meg, but the richer for that,' he said. Blowing a strand of auburn hair from her face from the side of her mouth, she rolled her eyes, feigning aloofness, but Will sensed the warmth between them.

As the smoke and dust cleared, they searched in the gloom among the trees until they had rounded up everyone and gathered at the end of the courtyard. From somewhere in the trees, Courtenay's bellow assured them that he too was hale and hearty. Will turned to survey the wreckage of the tower. The wavering torchlight revealed a jagged stump licked by flames beneath a plume of black smoke reaching up to the lowering clouds. Of the Unseelie Court and the Mooncalf, there was no sign, nor did he expect one.

Courtenay strode into the circle of torchlight with Dee and Grace by his side. He raised an eyebrow when he saw Will's accusing glance and said, 'She insisted on coming ashore. Filled with fire, that one.'

'I am glad to see you well,' she said as blithely as if she had met him in the palace gardens.

'Grace,' Will sighed, 'you are a fine bundle of trouble. Can you not stay out of harm's way just once?'

'I can well look after myself, Master Swyfte,' she snapped, stepping past him to tend to Strangewayes, who sat on the low stone wall with his head bowed. 'A fine thing to be scolded for worrying about close friends and loved ones,' she called back.

Will shook his head wearily and turned to Dee, who seemed to have recaptured some of his vitality along with his wits. His back was straight, his eyes flashing with intelligence, his stride purposeful, but still Will worried that he might slip back into insanity. 'I have had enough of cowering away like a whipped cur,' the alchemist exclaimed, jabbing a finger at the spy. 'My blood is up, and I am ready for the fight with those pale-skinned bastards back in England.' He paused, then added, 'If Elizabeth will have me, and if that hunchbacked plotter Cecil isn't whispering in her ear to have me sent away to the darkest parts of the realm.'

'We need you, doctor. And the Queen needs you,' the spy reassured him.

Dee nodded curtly, satisfied. 'I need the sun on my face.' Glancing up at the clouded night sky, he spun on his heel. Off to work his magics, Will guessed. The island mirrored the alchemist's mood.

While Courtenay's men took the captured pirate Jean le Gris, still limping from the wound in his thigh, back to the *Tempest* to face justice, Will sat with Carpenter and Launceston, watching the dark sky. Steadily, the wind dropped until an eerie stillness lay over the woods. It

292

seemed that all of nature was holding its breath. The storm clouds overhead scudded away without a whisper of a breeze and after a moment a silvery glow lit the sky on the eastern horizon.

'At last,' Carpenter muttered. 'I thought this night would never end.'

Launceston pursed his lips, watching the light shade to gold. 'Four hours, I would say.'

'Four hours until what?'

'Until I have to listen to you bemoaning the oven heat that beats you down to the deck and wishing it was night again,' the Earl sniffed, walking away.

Carpenter hurled a stream of abuse at the other man's back. Laughing to himself, Will stood and went in search of the sorcerer. As he walked, he sucked in a deep breath, relieved that this long night had ended far better than he could have hoped when he first set foot upon the island. Along the path to the beach, he found Dee resting beside a moss-draped statue of a nymph. 'You have completed your ritual, then, doctor?' he asked.

'That business came so much easier when I was hiding behind the walls of my madness,' the old man grumbled.

To the west, the lightening sky flickered with folds of a rainbow of illumination. Will felt reminded of the green lights he had seen in the northern skies in Scotland. 'What is that strange display?' he asked, his brow creasing. 'More of your magics?'

Dee glanced up, the odd radiance playing in his eyes. 'This island stands on the boundary between the world we know and whatever lies beyond.'

'The place where the dead go?'

'Some call it such. Since our most ancient times we have always looked to where the sun sets . . . the light fades . . . and thought it the home of those who have moved on. When I was a boy, my father told me about the boat that waits by the shore to ferry the souls of the newly departed across the great wide ocean for judgement. And then, on the night he died, I saw the boat waiting and his own pale shade walking the lane from our house.' He shook his head as if to dispel the memory, and looked away. 'It is the home of the Unseelie Court,' he said in a quiet voice.

Will sensed a confusion of thoughts in the old man. Dee had spent his days probing the great mysteries that enveloped life, and here was one of the greatest, a puzzle that wrapped up life and death and grief and yearning, the promise and threat of greater powers than man's, and all man's fears about the purpose of life.

'What if,' Dee had said to him once, staring deep into the blazing fire in the Black Gallery, 'man was only placed upon this world as sport for higher powers?'

Without another word, the old man trudged down the path towards the shore. Will was about to follow, but heard Courtenay calling him. With a sigh, he returned to the courtyard where a few men had been sifting through the wreckage of the tower for anything that could be salvaged.

'Le Gris's men have been released from their torment and can now face their just rewards in Heaven or Hell,' he said, cracking his knuckles. 'Another triumph for England's finest. By noon I will have charted a course for the island of Hispaniola to take on fresh water and supplies. And if we encounter any Spanish dogs, it will be a joy to despatch them after the things we have battled these past weeks. And then to fair Albion. With a good wind, Dee can be rebuilding our defences with his cursed sorcery before the bluebells have gone from the woods in Kent.'

'May good fortune watch over you, Captain Courtenay,' Will said, clapping a hand on the other man's arm. 'You and your crew have earned the Queen's gratitude, and a joyous release in the stews of Bankside.'

Courtenay's eyes narrowed. 'You speak as if you are not sailing with us.'

The spy glanced back to the dancing lights in the western sky. 'It was never my intention to return to England. I am a lost soul, captain, and I must find my way to the land of the dead. This morning I will take le Gris's ship and a skeleton crew and sail to the home of the Unseelie Court. Nothing shall stop me finding the answers I seek. And then I will bring the walls of that fortress crashing down, though it cost me my life.'

CHAPTER FORTY-ONE

THE RIBBON OF WHITE SAND GLOWED IN THE MORNING SUN. Sparkling blue sea lapped in the cove and a cooling breeze rustled through the woods as the two men wandered along the shore. The intoxicating scent of the large pink flowers on the spiky-leaved shrubs along the treeline drifted down to meet the salty air.

'You are a fool,' Dee growled. The skirts of his purple robe swept a wide path along the beach.

Will felt an unfamiliar lightness now he had finally given voice to the inevitability of his destination. 'If it is foolishness to want an end to the torment of unanswered questions, then so be it.'

'The answers may be worse. Have you thought of that?'

Will shrugged. 'It is a gamble I am prepared to take.' If only the alchemist knew how much he had risked, he thought. How long it seemed since that night in the Liverpool rooming house when he had first started to form his plan. The sight of Jenny in the obsidian mirror had let loose a rush of desperate emotions and thoughts, as if the dam holding back all those years of misery had suddenly broken. He still felt surprised how little it had troubled him to put the Queen, and all England, up as his stakes in his great gamble. Never would he alone have been able to amass the fortune necessary to fund a galleon to sail to the New World in search of Jenny. But once Meg had told him that was Dee's destination, he knew he could trick the Crown or the School of Night into giving him what he needed. And so he had let the alchemist go, knowing full well that the old man could have fallen into the Unseelie Court's hands and everything he held dear been washed away in a tide of blood. All for Jenny.

'You have always been a gambler, Swyfte, with your own life and with others'. That recklessness will be your downfall.' Though the tone of his voice was accusatory Dee's look was not unkind.

'My life was blown off course that day – the day the person I cared for more than any other disappeared,' the spy replied, looking to the far horizon. 'I have made do as best I can, but not a day has passed when I have not thought of her. I am trapped in a maze where my mind keeps me in one place, and I would be free of it. What happened to her that day? Why was she chosen, and not me? Has she suffered? Has she endured—' The words caught in his throat. 'These questions haunt me.'

Dee snorted. 'You speak as if these things matter.'

Will's head whipped round. 'They matter to me.'

The old man swept out an arm to indicate the sea and the island. 'All this is illusion, this world, a stage on which we play out parts assigned to us. We wallow in the mundane detail of our life, all the petty hardships and the struggles that occupy our every waking moment, and we lose ourselves in them. They take on an import that far exceeds their worth. They are a distraction, no more, and we are complicit in allowing ourselves to be distracted because those things, however hard, are easier to comprehend than the greater questions that hang over us. Who plays the fiddle and pipes, and why must we be forced to dance? The answers we seek are here, but they are hidden amongst the illusion, in the smallest detail.' He snatched up a handful of sand and let the grains trail out of his clenched fist. 'We only have to sift and look and pull the jewels from the mud.'

'And yet these things you dismiss so easily cause us so much pain. That cannot be discounted so readily, doctor. Though all be illusion, we still hurt.'

Dee smiled. 'Perhaps that is one of the jewels. When you hurt, you are forced to look more closely. The mundane details . . .' he snapped his fingers, 'dissolve.'

'Perhaps.' Will turned his face to the sun, enjoying the unfamiliar warmth on his skin. 'But I know this, doctor. When you look away from that mortal suffering, you become inured to it, and thereby allow it to endure. Indeed, if there is no substance to it, only one further step is needed to perpetrate that hurt, for it is like the mist, insubstantial and soon gone.' He waved his fingers in front of him. 'There are dangers in thinking too much and removing yourself from human concerns, doctor.'

'And you feel too much,' the alchemist snapped before catching himself. 'Perhaps the true path lies somewhere between, I give you that. I am not blind to my many and varied flaws, Master Swyfte, though you think me as hard-hearted as the rocks of that reef.'

'I know the true nature of the Mooncalf.' Will found

298

himself unable to keep the cold tone from his voice.

After a long moment, Dee replied, 'In my defence, I can only say that I was in the throes of my self-inflicted madness.'

'You destroyed a man's life to provide yourself with a guardian.'

The alchemist sighed. 'You know as well as I that this business makes monsters of all of us. We each do things we never dreamed of in the days of our youth. You say I am too distracted by scholarly pursuits, but I have devoted my life to this long battle with the Unseelie Court, to keep men safe and dreaming sweet dreams in their beds at night. I have sacrificed my youth, driven an ache deep into my bones and shattered my mind. Sometimes we are forced to do terrible things to prevent even greater atrocities. Should one man suffer to prevent the deaths of a hundred? A thousand? These are questions we should not have to ask ourselves. Most men can hide away and pretend such dilemmas do not exist, or turn up their noses and pass judgement upon those forced to make sacrifices to keep the realm secure. We are faced with the harsh reality every day, and we cannot flinch from its glare.'

When they reached the end of the beach, Will perched on the rocks where he had peered into the devil's looking glass the previous night. He felt a troubling confusion. 'Not too long ago, I might have agreed with you, doctor. But now I wonder if we should hold ourselves to a higher standard. The question you ask – should one man die to save a hundred? – is too simple. There is comfort in making the choice so easy, but good men should always suffer to uncover the more challenging but truer course.'

With the toe of his shoe, Dee flicked a green-shelled scuttling crab into a rock pool. 'And I am not a good man, is that what you say? There is some truth in that. I was certainly a fool for losing myself in intellectual pursuit and failing to see that the angels with whom I thought I communed were in fact the Unseelie Court. How they must have laughed at my arrogance. Dr Dee, who thought he of all men had the power to speak with Heaven's messengers. How easy it was to expose my weakness and then play a game to try to twist me to their ends.'

'You were not unprepared, though.'

Dee smiled, rubbing his hands together. 'I knew the Fay would come for me at some point, just not in that way. Long ago, I built defences deep inside me that would come into play should they ever try to seize control of my wits. Madness would consume me and I would flee England to a place where the Unseelie Court could not find me and use me against the Queen and Albion.'

Will came to a halt, in awe of what the alchemist had done. 'Why here, so close to their home?'

'Because if all seemed lost, I would allow them to take me into their midst and thereby destroy them.' Dee stretched his arms wide as if rising from a deep sleep.

The spy's ears pricked up. 'How so?'

'By denying them access to our world and trapping them in their own miserable land.'

'But it is a place of wonder.'

'So they say.' Dee laughed. He waved his arm across the sunlit view. 'More wonderful than our own home? Why, then, do those fiends sweat blood to take our green fields from us? No, there are more wonders here than you realize, and all the secrets the Unseelie Court need to understand their own forlorn existence. They are lost, Master Swyfte, and sometimes I believe more lost than us.' He folded his arms, nodding to himself. 'The "angels" told me of a beacon that keeps open the way between our worlds—'

'The Tower of the Moon,' Will interjected, recalling what he had learned from his conversation with the Faerie Queen.

The alchemist eyed him askance. 'You are better informed than you appear, Master Swyfte. Yes, the Tower of the Moon. I would bring it crashing down and seal them in their dismal land for ever.'

'And you with it?'

Dee shrugged. 'A small price to pay.'

'You are a courageous man.' Will shielded his eyes from the sun as he looked out across the azure sea.

'I am a fool and never you forget it. Only one thing troubles me now: the devil's looking glass. Tell me you were not such a simpleton as to bring it here.'

'I left it in your chamber at the Palace of Whitehall,' Will lied. So Dee would not see his face, he ducked down to pick up a pebble.

'At least some sense resides in that thick head of yours. I have spent my life keeping that mirror out of the Fay's hands.' His face darkened. 'So much power resides in that thing it could change the course of this war in the blink of an eye.'

'You have mastered it?' Will asked. He threw the pebble out into the crashing waves.

'I have heard tales,' Dee mumbled, clearly knowing more than he was saying. 'It keeps its secrets well. But the Unseelie

Court could unlock it. Never must it be allowed to travel anywhere near those pale-skinned bastards.'

Will swallowed his guilt. Another gamble, worse by far than all the others. Yet the mirror was his only link with Jenny and he could no more give it up than his own life.

Reflecting on what he had learned, he lowered his eyes to watch the crab take shelter in a crevice in the rock pool. 'It is so easy to hate our eternal Enemy for the miseries they have inflicted upon us – upon me, and Jenny. The Unseelie Court think us the wicked ones in this game. And there are many times when I am inclined to agree.' He furrowed his brow, his voice reflective. 'We have committed some terrible crimes in pursuit of victory, doctor. Yet, what a mess this business is. How simple it all seemed when we thought we were on the side of the angels, fighting devils. Now we know there are devils masquerading as angels on both sides.'

Further down the shore, a longboat pulled up and two sailors clambered out and splashed into the surf. They began to haul their vessel up the sand. Amongst a group of on-lookers, Will saw Carpenter, Launceston and Strangewayes, and Meg and Grace.

'Here is my question, doctor,' he added. 'When we fight monsters, must we become monsters?'

Dee shook his head, his face preternaturally sad. 'Set me free from this damnable island,' he muttered. Without answering the spy's question, he strode across the beach towards those gathered on the shore. After a moment, Will followed.

Picking up her skirts, Grace hurried to meet him. 'It is true, then?' she enquired, her eyes gleaming with hope.

'You travel to the home of the Unseelie Court to rescue Jenny?'

'Do not think for a moment that you are accompanying me, Grace.'

'I am coming,' she snapped, her cheeks flushing. 'Do not try to abandon me here on the brink of discovering my sister's . . . my sister's fate, Will Swyfte.' She was close to tears.

'When I return—'

'And if you do not return? How can I live my life knowing I came so close to the answers I have prayed for and then walked away? No, I am coming too. And if you try to put me back on the *Tempest*, I will leap into the waves and drown myself.'

'Grace—'

'You have no power over me. I make my own decisions.' She glared at him.

After a moment, he nodded. Grace was no different from him; she deserved a resolution too, for good or ill. Over her shoulder, he saw Strangewayes look at him, his eyes daggers. Will knew he had made a bitter enemy in the younger spy, and he wondered if there was any way he could change that. Tobias was misguided, nothing more. He only wished to protect the woman he loved, but he could never understand the deep currents in Grace and Will, and the ties that bound them. 'And you?' he called over to the little group.

'Why, my sweet, I could not leave you to look after the children.' Meg blew him a kiss. Grace scowled at the other woman. Will recognized the truth, and the tragedy the Irish spy tried to hide. She had failed in her purpose and now was a woman without a country. An enemy in England, with Dee returned to London she had betrayed her chieftain and risked pain or death if she returned to her own home. And yet, knowing what was at stake, she had aided Will every step of the way. He walked towards them, relishing the sound of his feet scrunching on the sand.

'I wish you well,' Carpenter said, an unfamiliar smile of relief upon his lips, 'but I have no desire to die young. I will ensure the doctor reaches London safely, and then I will leave this mad world behind and find a new life, though Cecil and his dogs pursue me to the ends of the earth.'

'And good luck to you,' Will said. 'You have earned it.' He turned to Launceston, who was cleaning his nails with a knife-point. In the sun, his skin seemed paler than ever.

'John is incapable of looking after himself, and so it is my burden to watch over him,' the Earl said, his face expressionless, though Will thought he saw a surprising hint of humour in his eyes.

When the two men had walked back to the longboat, Strangewayes muttered to Will, 'I will accompany you.'

'Very well.' Will nodded. 'We are going to take the *Corneille Noire* and I have asked Captain Courtenay to supply a handful of men to crew her. Once we reach our destination I will send them home. I would not have their deaths on my conscience.'

'And how exactly do you intend to return?' Dee asked. He eyed Will from under his overhanging brows.

In reply, Will smiled tightly.

A cry from the longboat interrupted their debate. Carpenter was bent double, clutching his stomach. After a moment he appeared to recover. He exchanged a few words with Launceston and then the two spies trudged back along the sand to the others. Will frowned at the sight of Carpenter's ashen face and sweat-lined brow. 'What ails you?' he asked.

'My conscience,' Carpenter croaked. 'I cannot allow you to sail to your doom alone. Another sword . . . or two . . . might mean you return with your life. We will join you.'

Will grinned, shaking the other man's hand firmly. 'Brothers in adventure, then,' he said cheerily, adding in a more serious tone, 'I would thank you, John. With a man like you at my side, who knows what we will achieve.' Yet the compliment seemed to fall on deaf ears. Carpenter's expression darkened and his eyes skittered. Will thought he saw a hint of despair there, although he could not guess what it meant. He banished it from his mind.

'Then it is agreed,' he continued, looking around the assembled group. 'Put steel in your hearts, for this day we take the fight to the Enemy.'

CHAPTER FORTY-TWO

SUNLIGHT GLINTED OFF THE WAVES IN THE BAY. OUT ON THE rising swell, the *Corneille Noire* strained at anchor. The full-throated shanties of the seamen preparing for sail drifted over the water. Carpenter squatted in the thin shade of a barrel among the last few provisions on the beach, watching Strangewayes glowering at the galleon where his woman waited with that guile-filled Irish spy.

He shook his head, struggling to dampen his rising despair. A puppet, that's all he was, with strings tugged by the Enemy so that he danced when they played their tunes. Deep inside him, the Caraprix squirmed, flooding his head with its whispers. Why had he been so foolish? A new life free of worry had seemed close enough to grasp when Lansing had woven his deceitful promises, but in his weakness he had set in motion the events that would deny him his heart's desire. He'd been so close, too. One foot placed upon the longboat that would take him to the *Tempest* and the first leg of his journey back home, and then the hated thing inside him had snatched him back and propelled him in the opposite direction; away from freedom, away from hope, towards only doom.

He jerked his head up at the crunch of sand and saw Will and Dee deep in conversation, their heads nodding seemingly in time as they walked towards the cove where the *Tempest* lay at anchor. Carpenter noticed what seemed to be an unfamiliar bond between them, a new understanding, perhaps.

He overheard Dee saying, 'When you leave this island, you must pass through the Pillars of Medea.' Carpenter watched as the old man pointed out to sea, past the galleon to where two columns of black rock protruded from the waves in the hazy distance.

'Why there?' Will asked. 'Surely it is safer to sail around them.'

'They are a gateway. Once you have passed the pillars, you are in the territory of the Unseelie Court, may the gods have mercy upon your soul.'

As the two men made their way along the sand, Carpenter hauled himself to his feet and trudged towards the treeline where he had seen Launceston prowling earlier. He had begged the Earl not to accompany him on Swyfte's mad voyage of the damned, but the aristocrat would have none of it. Carpenter felt only more guilt at that loyalty. Not only was he dooming himself, he was dragging Launceston down with him.

When he stepped into the shade of the trees, he breathed deeply, tasting the sweet scent of the pink blooms. Unfamiliar birdsong rang out through the gnarled branches, whoops and cries that reminded him of the chatter of the women who hung the dyed cloth out to dry on the tenter grounds beside Moor Fields. A red butterfly as big as his hand fluttered by, the green eyes upon its wings mocking him.

Through the fronds, he glimpsed a grey shape: Launceston wandering among the flora, he guessed. But then a low whine rolled through the undergrowth and Carpenter stiffened. Fearing the worst, he dashed across the twisted roots and burst into a small clearing lit by a shaft of brilliant sunshine. Blinking, he discerned Launceston on the far side, hunched over something. He felt his heart sink.

As he edged round the clearing, the object of the Earl's attention fell into view: a wild pig, not yet fully grown. It appeared to be half stunned; a bloodied stick lay nearby. The Earl hovered over it, knife at the ready. Carpenter watched a look of disgust cross his colleague's face. When Launceston saw his friend, he murmured dismally, 'I thought I could still the urges within me with the life of a beast, but, God help me, it is not the same. I hunger still for a human life—'

His anger searing through him, Carpenter felt all control drain away. In a blaze of white heat, he flung himself at the Earl, knocking him to the tangle of half-buried tree roots. His blows rained down as he took out all his self-loathing and hopelessness upon the other man. Finally, he realized Launceston was not defending himself. Rolling off, he sat with his head in his hands, fighting to contain the rush of emotion and the sobs that threatened to follow.

'Damn you, Robert. Why can you not control yourself?' he croaked. 'Must I spend the rest of my days pulling you back from the brink of another atrocity?' He laughed bitterly. 'This is my life in essence.'

After a moment, he heard the aristocrat climb to his feet

and move to stand in front of him. Carpenter bowed his head, waiting for the blow. When none came, he looked up to see Launceston holding out a hand to help him to his feet. The pallid face was dappled with bruises.

'I realize this is a burden for you. I cannot control my urges alone,' the Earl said, his whispery voice almost lost in the rustling of the leaves.

Carpenter sagged, his guilt magnified. 'We are both lost souls,' he muttered. Dazed, the wild pig lurched upright and with a squeal crashed away through the undergrowth.

The aristocrat slipped the dagger into his grey breeches. 'The world can look as black as pitch, but there are things which bring a little light in. When I first recognized my desires, on the third night of my incarceration in the hole beneath the cellar, with the rats and the beetles scurrying around and my father above ordering the fiddler to play louder to drown out my cries, I thought I would follow a solitary path for the rest of my days. But when you offered me the hand of friendship in my bleakest moment, I realized there was still some hope, even for a rogue like me.' He hauled the other man to his feet. 'We are who we are, and we do our best to struggle down this long road, but the journey is better for having someone at your shoulder.'

Carpenter sucked in a calming gulp of air. 'Then I have a request, from one friend to another.'

'Anything.'

'If there comes a time when I ask you to kill me, you must do so without a second thought.'

Launceston blinked slowly, the endless depths of his pale eyes revealing nothing of his thoughts, nor any dismay he might have felt that such an act of friendship would condemn him to the life of loneliness he feared. Carpenter strode away, without waiting to hear if an answer would come.

Back at the beach, he helped load the remaining provisions into the rowing boat, sweating in the mid-morning sun. When they were done, the two men sat in silence for the journey across the waves to the *Corneille Noire*.

With everyone now aboard, the small crew spared by Courtenay prepared the ship for departure. Sails were unfurled and the anchor raised. An apprehensive mood seemed to have fallen across everyone, Carpenter noted. On the forecastle, Swyfte leaned against the rail watching the shore where Dee still stood. His mood seemed to have darkened. Was he now regretting taking a path that could only end in death for all of them, Carpenter wondered? Did he feel anything?

As the anchor burst from the waves trailing glistening diamonds, a low, plaintive howl rolled out across the lonely island. Carpenter felt the hairs on his arms prickle at that sound, and he shuddered. Had the Mooncalf somehow survived the destruction of the tower? But when he glanced to the prow, he saw a curious thing: Swyfte was smiling.

On the beach, Dee gave a slow wave and then turned and walked into the trees. Amid the cries of gulls, the *Corneille Noire* heaved away across the swell, and after a while steered a course for the columns of black rock protruding from the crashing sea. Carpenter felt the galleon judder as it slammed into the currents that swirled around the towering formation. There were easier routes away from the island, but Dee had been adamant.

Sanburne, the acting captain, was a seasoned voyager and had accompanied Courtenay on many a foray into enemy waters. Lean and weather-beaten, with a shaven head and a gold hoop in his ear, he was more taciturn than the *Tempest*'s captain, but he commanded no less respect. He kept a weather eye on their destination and the surging currents, shouting adjustments to the line of approach.

Carpenter gripped the rail as the ship bucked. How much simpler it would be to leap into that blue-green swell, he thought, but even if he found the courage, or the cowardice, he was not sure if the Caraprix would let him.

Salt spray misted the air. Above the white-topped waves, a haze hung around the looming rocks. The brassy light thinned, and the temperature dropped in the growing wind.

'There is no going back now.' Swyfte had appeared at the rail beside him, his gaze fixed on the Pillars of Medea.

'An ending is all I want,' Carpenter muttered.

After a moment, Will said, 'I would thank you for accompanying me, John. We have had our differences, you and I, but you are a good man.' Carpenter felt a spike of guilt in his heart at that.

And then the shadow of the basalt columns fell across them, and the sea heaved and they could only grip the rail and pray for the calm waters on the other side. In the boiling cauldron between the pillars, the haze closed around them, and the far horizon and the island both fell from view. Gripping on to the stays, Sanburne stood as if made of stout oak, unyielding in the face of the elements. His barked orders rose above the roaring of the ocean and rang out across the deck with the rhythm of a galley's drums.

Carpenter craned his neck to look up the length of the black columns. How unnatural they appeared. Through the mist, he thought he could discern carvings of grotesque figures and symbols etched into the rock face, but the tossing of the deck threw him so violently he could not be sure. He shivered in the chill of the shade, but then the *Corneille Noire* heaved one final time and swept them out of the most turbulent water. The wind subsided, the spray eased, and as the Pillars of Medea fell behind them, the sun beat down once more.

Swyfte was smiling. Carpenter noticed a faraway look in his eyes and wondered what was on his mind. Was he not afraid of what lay ahead?

As the galleon turned towards open waters, Sanburne strode up, frowning. 'Trouble, captain?' Will asked.

'You might say that, Master Swyfte.' In his right hand, he held out the ship's compass and with his left he jabbed a finger towards the sky. 'Though I be bound for Bedlam, it seems we now sail in a world where the sun rises in the west.'

CHAPTER FORTY-THREE

BLOOD PUDDLED ON THE STONE FLAGS. FIVE BODIES LAY SCAT-
tered across Queen Elizabeth's antechamber in the Palace
of Whitehall, all good men and true, all despatched in an
instant by the thing that had swooped through the open
window on leathery wings. Cecil hauled himself on to
shaking legs from the corner where he had cowered like a
frightened child. His white ruff was now stained, and more
blood speckled his right cheek, but he had survived, by little
more than the grace of God.

As he wiped his face clean with his kerchief, he looked
around the scene of slaughter and tried to compose himself.
How close they had come to disaster this time. The door to
Her Majesty's bedchamber flew open and a rush of bodies
swept out: the Queen herself, wrapped in a cloak of midnight blue, her frail body hunched over, her face hidden in
the depths of a cowl; Essex at her elbow, aglow in his white
doublet and hose as he guided her towards safety; and three
pikemen with faces like Kentish ragstone.

Essex flashed an anxious glance at the spymaster as he
went. What passed between them moved from desperation

to dread. How much longer could they carry on this way was the question they asked each morn when the sun finally rose. The threat crept ever closer to Her Majesty's door. Soon they would not be able to repel it.

Once Essex had led the Queen out of the antechamber, silence settled, but only for a moment. Raleigh slipped in, the pink lining of his half-compass cloak looking unnecessarily flamboyant in that butcher's shop. 'Gone, like the wind,' he said, going over to the open window and looking out across London. 'Our Enemy never fail to find inventive ways to make us suffer.'

'You speak as if you envy them their skill in murder,' Cecil snarled.

'I respect a dedicated foe. That is the only way to find a means to defeat them.' The adventurer inhaled a deep draught of the cool air, scented with the coal-smoke from the first home fires of the day.

'One day the Queen will find you skulking around the palace, and then your only view will be of the rats in your cell in the Tower,' the spymaster muttered. He joined the other man at the window, relieved to see the first silver streaks of dawn. 'Food is short and people starve. Fresh water is fouled and cows deliver young with two heads. We are assailed on all sides.'

'But spring is here. The winter cold is gone,' Raleigh replied wryly.

'At least the damnable plague has finally departed. The order has been given to open the playhouses and inn yards so the Queen's subjects have something to take their minds off their miseries.'

Raleigh closed his eyes, enjoying the breeze. 'This play

would have long since ended if not for the School of Night, you know.'

Cecil gritted his teeth. Loath as he was to give any credit to the secret society, he knew the other man was right. 'But still no news of Dee from Swyfte and his band. Even the great resources of the School of Night cannot keep us alive for much longer.'

'You plot and scheme from the shadows, as Walsingham did before you, seeing only the ends, but not the road that takes you there. How has that served you?' The adventurer pulled the casement window shut and turned to inspect the bodies, his expression grave. 'You and all your kind have lived a life of compromise,' he continued, moving to each corpse in turn. 'You said, not long ago, that the Unseelie Court whittled us down by degrees. But you and Walsingham have done that to yourselves.'

'Watch your tongue, sirrah.' Cecil glanced at the kerchief in his hand and, disgusted, threw it away as if it had burned him.

'I know the agreement Walsingham made, which you perpetuated,' Raleigh said in a cold voice. The spymaster flinched. 'You think one life here or there makes no difference when weighed against the security of the Queen and all England?'

'All is a balance—'

'Look here,' Raleigh said with passion, sweeping his arm across the fallen guards. 'Where is your balance? Where is your security? Those poor souls you sacrificed suffered for naught. And the ones who were stolen, they suffered too.'

Cecil cast his eyes down.

'As for Swyfte, why, no better man has served you,' the

adventurer continued. 'Yet neither you nor Walsingham could find it in you to tell him what happened to the woman he loved? No, because then you would have had to explain why you allowed her to be taken, and for what reason. And the others too.'

'It was a gamble,' Cecil snapped, rage born of guilt rising inside him. 'If it kept us safe, it was worthwhile.'

'It did not.' The adventurer took a deep breath to calm himself and walked to the door. He paused on the threshold and looked back. 'Your compromises have failed to deliver what you hoped. You have failed. This world is changing fast, Sir Robert, and you are yesterday's man. This new age demands better principles. Sooner or later it will be time to step aside and let those who measure themselves by a higher standard guide this nation to glory.'

Raleigh fixed his penetrating gaze upon the spymaster for a long moment, and then, with a flamboyant sweep of his cloak, he strode out. Cecil watched the space he had left behind as the shadows in the room slowly melted in the thin light. After a long moment, he strode to the door and called out. Two pikemen came running.

'Find Sir Walter Raleigh,' he ordered. 'Tell him the Queen says he is no longer welcome here and escort him from the palace grounds. Should he resist, take him to the Tower.'

CHAPTER FORTY-FOUR

LANTERNS GLOWED DEEP IN THE HOT NIGHT. SPIKES OF RE-flected light shimmered across the black waves as the silent fleet sailed towards the east. Haloes of green and red flickered around the grey-sailed galleons, the otherworldly illumination fading like marsh lights. Will watched the Unseelie Court ships, feeling troubled by the display of firepower.

'Extinguish the lights, Master Dusteby,' Captain Sanburne called. The lanterns winked out one by one and the *Corneille Noire* sailed on westwards, wrapping herself in the dark. Tense moments passed as Will and the others aboard held their breaths, but the Fay cannon was not trained upon them.

'Even if they glimpsed us, we are insignificant,' the spy said with a nod. 'They have more pressing matters to hand.'

'Dee,' Launceston whispered, spectral in the gloom.

'When you sent the magician back to England, you knew the Enemy would pursue him.' Strangewayes narrowed his eyes accusingly. That gaze had barely left Will since the galleon had departed the island.

'Was there any possibility that the Unseelie Court would let the prize they valued more than anything in our world sail away freely?'

The younger spy snorted. 'And in no way did this enter your calculations as you dragged us all on your personal quest for destruction.'

'You chose to come,' Launceston interjected. 'No one forced you. Indeed, we might have found more joy on this voyage if you had been left on that island.'

Strangewayes glared at the Earl.

'To answer your question, Tobias, of course I knew the attention of the Unseelie Court would be drawn to Dr Dee, allowing us to sail quietly by,' Will said with a grin, seemingly unruffled.

'Then should we not have accompanied him? Two galleons could better fight off—'

'Two galleons are neither here nor there against the overwhelming power of the Enemy.' Will leaned on the rail, staring into the night. 'The *Tempest* is the finest galleon in all the world, race-built and fleet. We would only have slowed her down.'

Gnawing on a ship's biscuit, Carpenter added, 'Courtenay has four days' start, and he will give them a good fight if they want one—'

'Against the Unseelie Court fleet?' Strangewayes interrupted, incredulous.

'—and with Dee in his right mind once more,' Carpenter continued as if the younger spy had not spoken, 'there will be magics and trickery aplenty if battle is joined. In truth, I would not wish to be on a Fay galleon.'

Will watched Grace walk up to the clutch of men, her

brow furrowed in suspicion. 'Why do you argue?' she asked. She kept her voice light, but Will sensed in it a hint of caution for the one who professed to love her. She was more than aware of Strangewayes' loathing for Will, and she had taken it upon herself to prevent any trouble from developing between the two men.

'Nothing,' Strangewayes muttered. He turned away, seeing the other men were closing ranks against him too. But Will sensed that not only Strangewayes but all there recognized that he had taken a gamble with the lives of men he knew; and indeed with England itself, for if he had truly sacrificed Dee to gain an advantage, all would be lost. They still trusted him, for now, but he wondered when they would begin to suspect he would sacrifice even their lives to bring Jenny home.

Will watched as the Unseelie ships disappeared into the night. 'Enjoy this moment of peace. The Unseelie Court will become aware of us soon enough, and then we will feel the full force of their fury.'

'You have a plan?' Carpenter asked.

'I always have a plan.'

For near three weeks, with the crew surviving on meagre rations, the *Corneille Noire* seethed under a merciless sun, heading towards the west away from the main trade routes. Though the compass remained reliable, Captain Sanburne would scowl and stare up to the heavens as the sunrise flipped from west to east and back again with no rhyme or reason. Will wondered if the land the Enemy called home was like the autumn mist on the Thames, flowing in and out of every nook and cranny along the crowded banks of the city. He took comfort from the fact that they sighted no other Fay vessels, and that only one Spanish treasure galleon crossed the blue horizon.

As they neared the New World, Will felt the obsidian mirror calling to him. Time and again, he found himself in one of the cabins with the looking glass on the trestle in front of him, hoping against hope that Jenny would appear before him. Only once did he catch a fleeting glimpse of her face. Her eyes seemed heavy with worry, and that only spurred him on. She lived, and that was enough. And soon he would bring her home or die trying.

As he climbed back into the sweltering sun from his latest attempt to use the looking glass, he glimpsed Meg watching him with a curious expression from the narrow strip of shade near the forecastle. It was as if she knew every doubt that plagued him. He turned away, pretending not to see the beautiful Irish woman's searching gaze, but she glided over and hailed him in a jaunty manner. 'Such a handsome face should not be troubled by a brooding look. You need good company to raise your spirits,' she said with a smile, flapping a hand to cool her flushed brow. 'Indeed, we both do. Life aboard ship has little in the way of excitement, or comfort, and it seems I have been looking at nothing but blue waves for a lifetime.'

'I fear I would be poor company,' he replied, putting on a practised smile. 'My mind is weighted down by plans and strategies.' He heard a splash and watched Carpenter draw up a flapping silver fish on a line at port. As if standing guard, Launceston stood nearby with his arms folded and a blank expression, studying his colleague.

Meg cocked her head to one side. 'There is still time to

turn this galleon round and sail for more entertaining climes.' When she saw he lacked enthusiasm for her suggestion, she sighed and added, 'But no. There will be no turning away while the memory of your long-lost love has its hook in you.'

'I have waited too long to discover the truth, Meg. I would have some peace in my life.' He grabbed a stay and looked up to the yards and the blue sky beyond, but the intensity of her attention drew his eyes down to her once more.

'You would have her back beside you, more like.' Her features softened briefly and he glimpsed some honest concern there. 'I hope you gain your heart's desire, I truly do,' she added on a wistful note.

Her words struck too close to home and he changed the subject, nodding towards Strangewayes and Grace locked in intense conversation by the mainmast. 'I have a favour to ask. Grace is not accustomed to the life we lead. I allowed her to accompany us against my better judgement, but she deserves her answers and her own peace, and I know she would rather die than live the way she has been.' He ignored the Irish woman's searching gaze. 'If you could do all within your power to keep her safe, I would be in your debt. Should we return to England, I will find as much gold as you require.'

'It is not gold I need,' she replied with a teasing smile. 'Sometimes she buzzes like a fly, and I must resist the urge to swat her, but I will do as you ask.'

'I fear I cannot trust Tobias to protect her. He is too raw, too fired by his passions.'

Meg's eyes narrowed as she flashed a glance towards the younger spy. 'You cannot trust him at all. He is a lovesick fool who can only see the world with the simple eyes of a child. Black and white, good and evil. He thinks you place his girl in danger and so you are his enemy. If only he knew the truth. How much you harm yourself—'

'Enough.' Will waved a dismissive hand. 'Let us not wish upon him this grey world of compromise. He will arrive here soon enough.'

He saw a softness in her look, but she hid it quickly. 'And yet there is some truth in what he says.'

Will watched the cut and thrust of dolphins' fins slicing the waves alongside the galleon. He sighed. 'I presume you are going to tell me your thoughts, whether I wish to hear them or not.'

Meg leaned in close so no one could overhear. 'Your desire to save your lost love has consumed you,' she said. 'I understand that it is driven by more than just the heart, and that for long years now the wound has festered.' He felt that she wanted to hold his hand, to comfort him or to share their hidden bond, but she restrained herself, knowing it would be unseemly. 'But young Strangewayes sees your blood quicken as you perceive the end of your long quest, and how in your eagerness you are prepared to risk others' lives to achieve your ends.'

Will rested on the rail, not meeting her eyes. All she said was true, he knew, but he had reached the stage where no gamble was too great.

The Irish woman smiled to soften her words. 'I care little. John and Robert too, I feel, and even young Grace. We are with you in this and do not mind your . . .' she fluttered a hand while she searched for a word that carried no poison, 'insensitivities.'

322

'Insensitivities.' He nodded, smiling wryly.

'But all men can be pushed too far, and you must remember who your friends are,' she continued. 'They will walk through fire, if you would but ask them.' A shadow crossed her face as she leaned against the rail, watching the waves. 'This long war kills us all by degrees. We begin as good and decent but gradually edge away from the light, so slowly we barely notice, until one day we look up and we are surrounded by night. Do not let that happen to you, my sweet.'

Before he could respond, she turned and walked towards the forecastle. But after a few steps she paused as if she had recalled something vital, and then turned back, her expression sad. 'You have more faith than any priest,' she said, 'more hope than I could ever have, but think, Will, what has happened to every soul ever taken by the Unseelie Court?' He showed her his back, not wanting to hear, but she continued. 'Men lured under hill by the sound of fiddle and pipe, only to crumble to dust upon their return to the daylight world. Knights and dancing maidens turned into stone. Others twisted into straw men, or bound by unbreakable briar, or dissolved into water. You must ask yourself how many have survived contact with the Unseelie Court.'

None, he knew. None, damn her.

'You must prepare yourself,' she said quietly. 'I do not wish to be cruel, but I would not see your heart broken when we reach our destination. Do not hope too much.' And with that, she walked away.

Two more days had passed when the lookout bellowed that land had been sighted. Soon gulls were wheeling across the blue sky, their hungry calls filling every heart with relief that the days of endless blue had passed. A line of green smudged the horizon. In the cabin, Will and Sanburne pored over the pirate captain's charts and the one that Courtenay had given to them, which showed all that was known of the New World coast. Will thought back to everything he had gleaned from the Faerie Queen of her distant home that night so long ago in the Lantern Tower. Legends of the Unseelie Court's bastion had circulated since the first European had set foot upon that mysterious land. The City of Gold. Manoa. The Fortress Crepuscule. The home of all wonders and terrors.

The chart showed a river system reaching out from the dark interior like a skeletal hand. From his discussions with Raleigh, Will knew some of the tributaries had been partially explored, but the land was wild and inaccessible, heavily forested and filled with villages of brown-skinned people who hated strangers after so much of their blood had been spilled by the Spanish over the years. Sanburne traced one dirty-nailed finger along the main river. 'Then we take the Orinoco to here, and then the Caroni?' he said. 'The river is navigable for a ship of this size?'

'So I am told.'

'And then?'

'Then, Captain Sanburne, your passengers will be set ashore and you may depart this devil-haunted land and anchor offshore where we now sail. Should we survive, we will find a way back to you.'

'And how long should we wait?' Sanburne said in a dis-missive tone that suggested he did not expect any survivors.

'Take on fresh water and sit here for no more than two

weeks. And if you come under attack from the Unseelie Court, leave immediately.'

Sanburne nodded, hiding his apprehension. Nor did he show any sign of fear to his men as he ordered them to steer the galleon into the mouth of the wide river; a brave man, as were all of them, to risk so much in the service of the Queen, Will noted. He joined Carpenter, Launceston, Strangewayes, Meg and Grace at the rail, where they watched the nearing land with some trepidation. Hardened by the long struggle, they had become adept at putting on brave faces, but here, so close to the source of their worst fears, they could no longer hide the truth in their hearts. Only Grace held her chin up as she studied the verdant line with an unflinching gaze. Will understood her hope – that whatever waited there was better by far than the endless hell of not-knowing that she had lived through for so long. As if she could read his thoughts, she suddenly turned towards him. Their gaze locked in shared understanding. She smiled and nodded.

'Is this our world or the Unseelie Court's world, or something of both?' Launceston asked.

Carpenter rubbed at the scar under his lank hair. 'That is the damnable thing about those foul creatures,' he growled, his eyes darting. 'They play so well with illusion that nothing can be trusted. One moment you think you are on solid ground, the next you are sucked down into the bottomless bog.'

'We travel into the very heart of madness and death,' Strangewayes muttered, crossing himself. 'God save our souls.'

As the *Corneille Noire* entered the river mouth, the dense

forest loomed up, a blanket of green stretching towards purple, mist-shrouded mountains far to the south. In the sweltering heat, stillness lay across the wild country. For all they could see, no human had ever walked there, nor within a thousand miles. They felt alone. Unfamiliar birdsong echoed all around, whooping cries and staccato clicks, punctuated by the low roar of some wild creature that sent shrieking rainbow flocks swelling into the blue sky. River dolphins stitched the shimmering water alongside the hull, and what they had perceived to be a log slipped off the muddy bank with a yawn of a wide mouth revealing rows of ferocious teeth.

'Paradise, the first explorers called this place,' Will remarked as he surveyed the lush countryside.

'Hell, more like,' Carpenter muttered. 'Give me the Mermaid and a cup of sack any day. That is my paradise.'

As the galleon sailed on along the twisting river, the stifling forest closed around them and the sea and the freedom it promised fell away from view. Though they kept to the centre of the channel, Sanburne plumbed the depths regularly, afraid that his ship might become beached. As the day drew on, the mood of unease became more oppressive. Silence enveloped the deck, all eyes flitting towards the trees. When night fell, the captain ordered that the anchor be lowered and no naked light be allowed on deck. The watch changed every hour so no lookout had the time to be lulled to the edge of sleep by the gentle lapping of the river and the breeze through the swaying branches. In the choking heat of the berth, the light of a single candle flickered across Sanburne's grim face as he told them, 'We are at war. Let no man lower his guard. Our Enemy could come at any time.'

At first light, they raised anchor and set sail once more. Will watched the tree-lined banks press closer with each turn of the river. When the narrow Caroni river appeared in the wall of vegetation, the birdsong died away and the wind dropped. The water frothing around the ship's hull looked almost black. Climbing up to the forecastle, he searched for the landmarks the Faerie Queen had shown him. When he glimpsed a familiar range of hills rising up above the tree-tops, he felt a chill. Here was the stuff of nightmares, the haunted realm of the Unseelie Court.

He waved a hand to Sanburne, who ordered the anchor to be dropped. 'We continue the rest of our journey on foot,' he said when the other spies had gathered around him by the mainmast. He added wryly, 'Will it not be good to stretch our legs after so long on ship?' Only Meg and Grace smiled. They had dressed for the hard trek to come, and were wearing rough woollen kirtles of the kind a country girl might own, with the sleeves of their chemises rolled up.

The longboat was loaded with a small sack of ship's biscuit and skins of water attached to twin staffs for ease of transport. Within the hour, the four men and two women had said their goodbyes and stood on the bank watching the *Corneille Noire* sail out of view round the bend in the river.

After a moment Will turned and strode into the dark among the trees. There was no going back.

CHAPTER FORTY-FIVE

FOUR BLACK BASALT TOWERS PUNCHED THROUGH THE SEA of green. Blades of light stabbed out from the gold roofs, each one burning like the sun. As he pressed aside the thin curtain of leaves, Will shielded his eyes against the glare. The narrow branch bounced and shook under his feet and threatened to hurl him down the dizzying drop to the forest floor far below. Steadying himself, he screwed up his nose at the bitter taste of sulphur on the wind, but though he strained he could hear no sounds echoing from the fortress. Truly, it seemed a city of the dead.

He let his gaze run down those grim towers, noting the proliferation of grotesque carvings silhouetted against the silver sky, and the bands of gleaming gold encircling each column at regular intervals. He saw echoes there of the Pillars of Medea, those towering columns through which they had sailed to reach this mysterious place. Surely there could be no doubt that this was the Unseelie Court's fortress? He felt a seething power radiate from it, prickling the skin on his bare forearms into gooseflesh. His nose began to bleed.

Will bowed his head, peering through the branches to

where the others waited below. He felt proud of the way they had coped with the hardships he had thrown in front of them. The trek from the river had been harder than any of them had anticipated. Under the forest canopy, the heat sweltered like a baker's oven. Over tangled roots they scrambled, sweat stinging their eyes and plastering their clothes to their bodies. Buzzing insects with wingspans as large as their hands hunted for exposed skin to bite and draw blood. No amount of water seemed to ease their thirst. Yet tempers had not frayed. As they struggled steadily uphill from the river, hands never strayed far from weapons and eyes continually searched the green world all around. Will had seen the strain in every face and had marvelled that he could not hear the throb of their hearts.

While they had rested, Carpenter had sidled alongside him and whispered, 'When will you reveal your plan?' With a reassuring smile, he had replied, 'In good time.' The response seemed to satisfy the other man, at least temporarily, but Will knew that soon the questions would become more pointed. What could he say? That he needed them to help him survive the forest trek, but then he planned to abandon them and sneak into the fortress alone? They would never let him go. Yet for all that he had manipulated them to his own ends, it was time for him to stop risking their necks, and once inside that merciless fortress there was little chance of emerging alive. It was his burden alone, his misery and suffering, his one chance of redemption.

Edging back along the branch, he swung down the towering trunk and dropped the final few feet to the mossy ground with feline grace. 'We should be there by dusk,' he said. 'Steel yourselves.'

Launceston's whistle rolled out of the undergrowth. The others darted through the trees to where the Earl waited on the edge of a clearing. Sallow-faced and seemingly unruffled by the heat, he waited by a broad-trunked tree, immobile. His eyes flickered towards them and then he nodded towards the clearing.

Dropping to his haunches, Will crept forward. The aristocrat had been scouting ahead for signs of the routes the Enemy took through the forest. What seemed to be a village stood on the other side of the clearing, ten or so log dwellings on stilts beside a creek. Several hide-covered boats had been dragged up the bank. Nothing moved. Will sniffed the air, but could smell no smoke from cooking fires. He had heard tales of the forest folk who, armed with bows and arrows, moved like ghosts among the trees. He gestured left and right. Drawing their daggers, Carpenter and Strangewayes loped in opposite directions round the clearing, then hunched down behind trees and watched and waited.

Long moments passed. Will spied no hint of movement, nor heard any sign of life. The inhabitants of the village could have overheard their approach and be waiting to strike, he knew. But he noted the straggly, unbroken grass around the wooden buildings and the holes in the boats where the hide had rotted, and he chopped his arm forward. The spies edged into the clearing, eyes flashing all around. When no arrows struck Will felt the tightness in his chest ease.

Launceston ghosted to the nearest house, slipping inside with his dagger raised. He moved on to the next, and the one after, and returned, sheathing his blade. 'Long since deserted,' he said, with a shrug. 'Rats as big as cats in there, and spider-webs trailing from every corner.'

'If all you have told me about the Unseelie Court is true, surely they would never tolerate any human village within their purview,' Grace said, showing not a trace of fear. Will felt proud of her.

The Earl grunted. 'I still cannot tell if I am in their world or our own.'

'Wherever we are, it is our world, because we make it so.' Meg strode past the men, tossing her red hair. 'Are we to stand here gossiping like maids, when there is work to be done?' Grace followed her.

'Gentlemen, we are put to shame,' Will said with a sweep of his arm.

Carpenter bowed his head and followed, muttering, 'Will they jump in our graves afore us too?'

In single file with Meg at the head, they made their way across the clearing and past the silent houses. As they reached the treeline on the other side, Will frowned. Something had made the hairs on his neck prickle, though he could not tell what. He called for the others to stop and turned slowly in an arc, scrutinizing everything that fell before his eyes. A faint movement on the trunk of a golden-leafed tree gripped him. Still unsure what he was seeing, he felt the hairs on his neck prick erect as he eased past the others to investigate.

White eyes blinked in the brown bark.

Carpenter and Strangewaves leapt back in shock, daggers at the ready. A figure was submerged in the trunk, a man, with brown skin, a broad nose and black hair. Will thought he looked as if the tree had grown around him, so that it was impossible to tell where flesh ended and wood began. And yet he was still alive. The eyes blinked again, and as the

331

lips twitched a dark hole appeared where the mouth would have been.

'Put him out of his misery,' Carpenter growled. 'No man should have to live like that.'

Grace's hand flew to her mouth when she realized what she was seeing. 'Oh,' she exclaimed, blanching.

'Do not look.' Meg caught the other woman's arm and tried to turn her away.

'I would know what monsters we face,' Grace said, resisting. Her expression hardened. 'If we flinch from the truth, we cannot be prepared for what is expected of us.'

'Kill him,' Carpenter pleaded, his face contorting. 'Let him suffer no more.' Will was surprised by the vehemence in his voice.

Launceston slid his dagger out of its sheath once more and stepped forward, his face impassive. Will wondered if it was even possible to kill the poor soul, short of chopping down the tree that contained him. But as the Earl raised his blade, those lips in the wood finally recalled their ability. With a twitch, they formed an O. Caught by the sight of that dark hole in the trunk, the spies recoiled in shock when a rumble reverberated deep inside the wood, rising up until it burst free as a high-pitched squeal of alarm. Clear and unending, it soared up above the treetops. Even as the aristocrat struck out with his dagger, other voices picked up the sound until the forest rang with warning shrieks.

'What do we do?' Grace cried.

'Run.' Will beckoned for her to follow as he turned to dash into the trees.

As if in answer to the cries, the air filled with the sound of mighty wings. Black shapes wheeled across the brassy sky. Will squinted, unable to tell if they were winged men or giant birds, but he had already guessed before Meg spoke. 'The Corvata,' she said, her features darkening. 'The eyes and ears of the Enemy.'

The spies darted beneath the verdant canopy, hoping they had been quick enough to avoid being seen by the flying sentinels. As they stumbled through the thick forest, tripping over roots and crashing into trunks, Carpenter snarled, 'We were fools to think we could approach the fortress without discovery. We were fools, and now it will cost us our lives.'

CHAPTER FORTY-SIX

SHAFTS OF SUNLIGHT PIERCED THE CANOPY OF LEAVES. Branches lashed the faces of the six humans as they raced over the soft, treacherous, mossy ground. All around them, screams rang out through the hot, humid air, offering no respite or chance to catch a breath. High overhead, mighty wings beat like the sound of rending sailcloth. Will glanced up, but he saw nothing and hoped that meant the things could not see him.

Strangewayes ran up to Will. 'We cannot outrun them. Let me take Grace and return to the river,' he gasped. 'We can follow the course more easily.'

'Fool,' Launceston breathed. 'That is the first route the Fay will investigate.'

Will raised a hand to bring the group to a halt. As they gathered around him, eyes searching the green world, Strangewayes cried, 'What, then?' Tears of desperation stung the corners of his eyes. He let his gaze fall upon Grace as he blinked them away. 'Do we run wildly like stags before the hunt until the Enemy bring us down one by one?'

'This forest is vast and the Unseelie Court few,' Will

replied. 'Even with their vaunted supernatural powers, we can evade them.'

Meg's green eyes glinted, her face now as hard as marble. 'Take heed of Will,' she said. 'Anything but a calm head will lead us into the Enemy's hands.'

'His recklessness and wilful disregard for our safety have brought us to the brink of disaster,' Strangewayes protested. 'And you say we should follow him still?'

'If he makes much more noise, I can silence him with one stroke,' Launceston volunteered, his stare unwavering.

'Tobias, you must listen to Will.' Grace clasped his hands in hers as she addressed the youngest spy. 'I know you fear only for my safety. But Will has never failed us—'

'How can you say that?' Strangewayes threw his hands wide.

'The Fay will expect us to flee in panic,' Will continued in a calming tone. 'In their arrogance, they think us weak, driven by our passions, our fear. We must show them we are better than that. If we run like rabbits, you are right, Tobias, they will hunt us down with ease.'

'What do you suggest, then?' Carpenter sucked in a deep breath to calm himself.

'Stealth is the only way we can win this fight,' Will replied. 'We continue towards the Fortress Crepuscule—'

'No.' Strangewayes shuddered. 'Into their very arms?' His hand slipped to the hilt of his dagger.

The unearthly shrieks had ebbed away, but the beating wings still circled overhead. Will held up a hand. 'We must keep our wits about us, and maintain a clear head. While they look for us running towards the river, we can steal to the very walls of their home, unseen, unexpected.'

'Please, Tobias, listen to him,' Grace implored.

The hot-headed young spy seemed agitated still. 'I will not stand idly by and watch him lead you to your death.'

Strangewayes was acting like a fool, but Will pushed aside his irritation; he had seen this behaviour too many times before. When the Unseelie Court entered someone's life, the world suddenly looked strange and terrifying. Men coped with it in different ways, and some, like Strangewayes, were driven to extremes to try to hold on to things they valued and people they loved. It was a kind of madness that oft-times passed, if the person was given space to recover. The ground had moved rapidly under Strangewayes' feet, and Will only hoped the young man could find the strength within him to survive this turbulent time.

Carpenter and Launceston were less tolerant, Will knew. They exchanged a quick look and he could see they were poised to act. 'We must not fight,' he insisted, trying for a calming note. 'They are listening for us. That is why the warning cries have stopped.'

Then, just when Will thought he was about to relent, Strangewayes lunged with the dagger. As Grace cried out in shock, Will threw himself back, feeling the blade whisk past his neck. He sensed that the younger spy had been waiting for a long time to make his move. As he regained his balance, Strangewayes' fingers closed on Grace's slim wrist and he dragged her with him through the undergrowth. She struggled to free herself.

'Tobias, do not do this!' she cried out, turning to look back at Will with pleading eyes. In that glance, he could see she was torn between the man she loved, though she knew he was a fool, and her belief in Will himself.

Cursing, Will dashed after her, the others close behind. Each moment increased their risk of being heard. '*He* will be the death of us, not you,' Launceston hissed through clenched teeth.

'Do not hurt him,' Will ordered. 'He is deluded—'

'And dangerous in his foolishness,' Meg said. Her eyes narrowed, her patience exhausted.

Through the curtains of low branches, Will glimpsed Strangewayes twisting and turning. Grace was now stifling her urge to call out so as not to attract attention, but he could see she was struggling to break free. As the younger man stumbled over a fallen tree, Carpenter, Launceston and Meg circled him like a wolf pack.

Drawing his rapier, Strangewayes levelled it at the other spies. He clutched Grace to him. 'You waste precious time,' Will cautioned, unable to keep the crack out of his voice.

Strangewayes took a step back, his heel pressing against a moss-covered mound. White eyes snapped open in the green, a black mouth tore wide, and the buried man screamed. The call was picked up in an instant. Shrieks rang out from trees and grassy banks and bubbling streams as the lost inhabitants of the village summoned their masters. The blood drained from Strangewayes' face as he realized that through his own naivety he had put Grace's life at more risk than Will ever had.

Cursing, Carpenter whirled, looking for a way out. Before any decision could be made, the screams stopped, leaving an unnatural silence that was even more chilling. 'What have you done?' Carpenter croaked.

From the direction of the fortress, the mournful sound of a single bell rang out.

'The first alarm prepared them,' Will growled, trying to pierce the forest gloom. 'Now they are coming.'

A tremor ran through the leaves above his head; the branches began to sway. After a moment, a tremendous wind tore at the branches like a herd of wild beasts marauding through the forest. The angle of the sunbeams shifted as if the sun had been hurled towards the horizon, and a deep, abiding gloom began to unfurl among the trees.

Will grabbed Grace's wrist and wrenched her out of Strangewayes' grasp. 'They took Jenny. They will not take you,' he snarled. Beaten, the younger spy cried out in impotent fury, but Will was already picking a path away from the gathering dark. A drumbeat began to roll out deep in the forest at his back, the pounding growing louder by the moment. It was the sound of pursuit.

'Will, do not fear for me,' Grace cried out. 'I chose to come with you in the full knowledge of the dangers that awaited.' Her breath caught as they scrambled up a steep bank. 'I am not afraid to die,' she gasped.

'Death is the least of our fears,' Will growled. Forcing aside what might lie ahead, he thought back to the charts he had studied on the *Corneille Noire*. The vast Caroni river's meanderings had been punctuated by falls and rapids, fast water gushing by high banks. There lay the one chance of escaping their pursuers.

Crashing through the branches with one arm thrown across his face, he yanked Grace along so hard her feet barely touched the ground. The drumming swelled behind them. Out of the corner of his eye, Will spied Meg, Launceston and Carpenter pushing through the undergrowth in the same direction, but the young fool Strangewayes was nowhere to be seen. He glanced over his shoulder and instantly regretted it.

Spectral, cadaverous faces snarling like wild beasts were emerging from the gloom. The pursuers thundered ever closer, bounding like hounds on all fours or swinging off branches and springing from tree trunks. Some were shaven-headed and bare-chested, with belts crossed over their torsos and axes or swords strapped to their backs. Others were ghosts in grey and silver doublets, white hair streaming, wicked-looking blades clenched in their fists. Will counted at least twenty of them: the Unseelie Court's dreaded Hunters. Never slowing, never stopping, until they had their quarry; no more ruthless predators existed on the face of the earth. He had confronted them before, in the dark of an Edinburgh night and on the rain-lashed roof of Nôtre Dame cathedral in Paris, and it had taken all of his skill and experience and a dose of good fortune to survive.

Twenty. Will's blood ran cold.

The glowing green world darkened as if storm clouds had swept across the sun. The suffocating heat of the day gave way to an unnatural chill. On the breeze rode the loamy stink of the grave. The drumbeat turned to thunder and Will knew their time must be near. Yet ahead the gloom looked a little brighter and he thought he could hear cascading water. *So near*, he thought. Grace was trying to hide her fear and in that moment he loved her more. He raised his head, showing his defiance.

On the edge of his vision, a flash of movement. Carpenter sprawled across the forest floor, one of the Hunters clinging to his back like an ape. Clawed hands rose and fell. There was blood. Realizing his friend had fallen, Launceston skidded to a halt. Whirling round, he drew his rapier and ran towards his companion.

Will ran on, feeling the ground shake under his feet. Grace's hand was, it seemed, his only link with life.

Skirts held high, Meg danced through the undergrowth to his left, her red hair flying. With a frustrated cry, she flung her back against a tree and waited. Will locked eyes with her, and for one moment she smiled defiantly before her features hardened and her gaze flicked back to the approaching threat. As one of the Hunters leapt at her, she slashed at the thing with her dagger. Will felt grim pleasure as the agonized cry rang out.

Meg slipped from view. The gloom closed all around until he could see only that small circle of bright light ahead, drawing him on. Grace gasped and sobbed for breath, trying to keep a brave face. Behind him, more screams rang out – man or woman, he couldn't tell – and the sound of rending and tearing, like a pack of dogs fighting over a ham bone. For Grace's sake, he hid his growing despair.

Through the thinning screen of leaves and branches, the sunlight blazed brighter. He could smell the dank aromas of the river, and over the pounding of his own feet he could clearly hear the rush of water.

As he broke out of the gloom under the trees into the hot sun, he felt a weight slam into his back. Losing hold of Grace, he pitched forward and hit the ground hard. Skidding across the sward, he rolled over and then felt his legs swing out over a drop. He kicked wildly and dug his fingers into the turf as he slid round, and down. The roar of the rushing river rose up from somewhere beneath his boots. He forced himself not to look down. Saving Grace was now all that mattered.

As he tried to haul himself up on shaking arms, he caught sight of her terror-stricken face. She lay sprawled, two sword-lengths away from him, one desperate arm outstretched. From the dark around her head, ghastly faces appeared, baleful eyes fixed upon Will. Bony hands clawed out of the gloom, snatching her hair, pulling at her arms, her kirtle. Grace screamed, the sound drowning out Will's cry.

His clutching fingers failing, Will felt leaves, twigs, slide under his nails as he scrabbled desperately to hold on. He called again, his voice cracking as those ghostly hands dragged Grace back into the dark.

And then his fingers tore free and he felt himself falling, Grace's expression of sheer terror branded on to his soul.

CHAPTER FORTY-SEVEN

WILL PLUNGED INTO THE ICY TORRENT. THE BLACK WATER closed over his head. Muffled booms rumbled in his ears, and then he kicked out, grabbing one precious gulp of air before the flow wrenched him along. The roar of the crashing river engulfed him. Spun round, he slammed against a rock, and another, almost dashing his wits from his head. His chest burned as he fought to savour his last breath. Snatches of the world around him flickered through the constant dunkings: soaring banks of grey rock, overhanging trees against blue sky, spikes of sunlight punching into the water, but no hideous white faces peering down at him.

After what felt like an eternity, the flow eased. The narrow gorge gave way to low, tree-lined banks as the river broadened. With the last of his strength, Will crawled towards the shallows, stumbling out of the lapping black water to crash down on the muddy bank. As he heaved in great lungfuls of air, the thunder of his heart subsided and the realization of his grim situation settled on him. He shook his head and tried to drive that last sight of Grace's dread-infused face from his thoughts, but it lingered, haunting him. The cries of his companions still rang in his ears too, and he felt a deep guilt that he had brought them all to this terrible point. But then he shook his head and sat up. Nothing would be gained from wallowing in self-pity. Rescue or revenge, those were the twin paths that lay ahead of him now.

Soaked to the skin, he rose on shaking legs and checked he still had his dagger and his rapier, and that the velvet-wrapped mirror was still safe in his pouch. Once he had recovered, he forged on into the trees.

The sun was slipping past its highest point by the time he had followed the course of the river back to where the Unseelie Court had mounted their attack. He cocked his head, listening for any sound of the others, but heard no human voice. Stealth was the only way to proceed, however long it took. He would not make Strangewayes' mistake. His eyes grew accustomed to the strange world of leaf and moss, slanting sunbeams and whirling insects, and whenever he encountered any misshapen tree or hummock that might hide one of the subsumed people he gave it a wide berth. There in the glade he saw signs of struggle, the odd spatter of blood, but no worse. That meant there was still hope, he told himself, though a part of him feared the opposite.

Will ignored the growling of his stomach; it had been almost a day since he had gnawed on the last of the ship's biscuit. He pushed and hacked his way through trailing vines and thorny bushes in the direction of the Unseelie Court's Fortress Crepuscule.

For the rest of the day, he weaved through the thick forest, occasionally pausing to clamber up the soaring trees to get his bearings. The gold caps on the black basalt towers were like beacons, drawing him inexorably towards them. It was as shadow slid into dips and hollows, and the bloated red sun settled down on the horizon, that he reached his destination.

He felt a chill as he crept to the treeline and looked down the slope into a hollow where the massive fortress stood. The Unseelie Court's dwelling place dwarfed any he had seen, even the Escorial of Philip of Spain. Towering black walls enclosed a lake of shimmering gold covering every roof and dome of the castle buildings. In the ruddy light, it glowed like fire. Along the battlements, nothing moved. Will scanned the walls, frowning. When it came to the Unseelie Court, human eyes could never be trusted, and he suspected unseen sentinels would be looking out over the surrounding forest.

As Will gathered his thoughts a low groan disturbed the eerie silence. The main gate – the height of six men – ground slowly open and a column of figures moved out into the fading light. At the front was a Fay on a black stallion, his head raised as he surveyed the darkening forest with slit eyes. He wore a silver helm and armour with whorls etched on it in black filigree, and in his right hand he held upright a silver-tipped spear. Behind him marched a raiding party of around twenty armoured Fay, bristling with swords and axes. Flanked by four others holding sizzling torches aloft, the column moved across the cobbles and on to the broad path leading into the forest. The gate shuddered shut.

A search party? Could any of the others yet live? However powerful the Fay were, they still could not see or know all. Perhaps one man could creep under their noses like a spider entering the Queen's bedchamber.

Once darkness had fallen, Will left his hiding place and crawled down the incline among the thick, spiky-leaved bushes. Around the fortress perimeter he crept, until the full moon cast long shadows over silvered ground. The rear wall was cut off by a dense barrier of thorny bushes. When he tossed a stone over the top, but never heard it fall, he guessed the fortress sat on the edge of a sheer drop. His heart sank as he concluded there was no obvious way to steal inside, no drainage tunnels, no sluices, no handholds on the soaring glass-smooth walls. Returning to the main entrance of the colossal fortress, he sank into the shadows at the foot of the wall and pondered his options. Determination gripped him; he would not be defeated.

Barely had the thought crossed his mind when he caught sight of a lone figure stumbling along the road out of the forest dark. No Fay this, Will saw from the rolling gait, but he still felt shocked when the moonlight revealed Strangewayes. The young spy looked broken, shambling like a man in his cups, his head bowed, his shirt torn, his face streaked with dirt and blood.

Will wondered if the torment of what he had done had driven him mad. Why else would he be stumbling up to the gates of Hell, alone and unarmed? Will pressed himself against the wall, which felt icy against his skin despite the heat, ready to drag Strangewayes off the path when he neared. But a stone's throw from the vast door the younger man shuffled to a halt and raised his head, looking up at the dizzying height of the imposing edifice. Before Will could move, he shook his fist at the fortress and roared in a cracking voice, 'Give her back to me.'

Will stiffened; it was too late now.

'You cannot have her,' Strangewayes raged. Spittle flew from his mouth. 'Take me instead. I deserve to die. But set her free, I beg of you.'

With a resonant rumble, the gate began to grind open once more.

Strangewayes, you fool, Will thought. *You have ordered your own death — or something far, far worse.* If he tried to save the other man, he knew his own life would be forfeit. Then what of Jenny, and what of revenge for whatever had happened to the others? Sickened by his powerlessness, Will could only watch as the younger spy peered into the black maw of the gates. After a moment, the blood drained from his face, but he didn't run and Will admired him for that.

Two figures walked out, their faces obscured by shadow despite the moonlight. Guards, Will guessed, dressed in out-of-time grey bucklers and breeches. Their too-pale hands rested on the sculpted silver hilts of their swords.

'I am not afraid of you,' Strangewayes shouted, his voice cracking with fear. 'Take me . . . to Grace.'

Will's hand hovered over the hilt of his own blade. His every instinct told him to rush to Strangewayes' aid, but he forced himself to hold back: this was his moment. Sneaking along the wall while the guards were occupied, he slipped round the door and darted into the dark interior. Yet as the shadows swallowed him, for all Strangewayes' folly, he couldn't help but feel guilt that he had turned his back on a companion . . . and so consigned him to death.

CHAPTER FORTY-EIGHT

BLOOD DRIPPED FROM WILL'S NOSE AS HE STEPPED FROM THE grim darkness of the gateway into a soft glow. He felt shock at the stark transition, as if he had stumbled into a half-remembered dream. Gold sheathed the walls of soaring halls, gleamed off statues of slender figures with severe features, and glittered in the swirls and knots of finely wrought screens and porticos. Along paved walkways running between the jumble of buildings torches hissed and spat, bathing the entire scene in a rippling, flickering light. Drifting from the windows and doorways came the delirious whirl of fiddle and pipe, and when Will inhaled, the heady scent of sweet honeysuckle swaddled him. He felt light-headed at such a rush of sensations.

For a moment, the spy marvelled at this magical world. Slowly, though, the brooding sense of menace that lay behind the glitter began to envelop him like an encroaching tide. He must never forget that whatever charm and beauty danced before his eyes he was in Hell, and no man could survive here for long. He shook himself and tensed, every sense afire for a sign of threat. Drawing his sword, he padded along the pathway to his left, seeking out every pool of shadow as he slipped from doorway to doorway. He looked up the vertiginous walls and wondered once more at the vastness of the Unseelie Court's home. How could he expect to find Jenny before the devils found him and tore him limb from limb?

Yet he refused to be daunted. He eased open the nearest door and slipped inside. In the hallway of gold and stone, the music throbbed so loudly that his ears rang. Now he heard a frenzied edge to the jig that spoke of madness. Buried behind it rumbled a low pulse that reminded him of the pounding of a blacksmith's hammers. He traced his fingers down the cool wall and felt the vibrations running through the stone, seemingly rising up from deep underneath the castle. An oppressive heat seethed through the building as if mighty forges were being stoked under the floor.

Crossing the entrance hall to the next door, he opened it a crack, taking care that he would not be seen. He peered into a great hall, lit only by the ruddy glow of a fire. Long tables creaked under platters of meats and pies and bread, silver goblets and wooden flasks, and tall jugs of drink. Around the trestles, the Fay were at play. They whirled around to the wild music of the fiddler and pipe player, or tore at meat and swigged down mouthfuls of wine, the red liquid spilling down their chins. Others fornicated in full view, the women sprawled on their backs on the tables or on all fours, while the men thrust into them.

Will pulled the door shut with great care, his head swimming from the sights, sounds and smells. Once back on the pathway, he sucked in a deep breath, feeling as if he had spent a night drinking in the Mermaid. He could now feel the dull, deep rumble everywhere he went. It ran up through his legs and into the pit of his stomach. He forced himself to move further into the heart of the castle, though every sense rebelled. After a while, he began to feel that all he saw was illusion, created by his own wits to hide the true madness and rot that lay behind it. Was that a keep, or a hellish pit where foul things writhed? If the walls were really gold, why did he keep smelling the reek of spoiled meat when he brushed by? The world he remembered back in England receded into the depths of his mind, and that sickening place became the only thing he knew, as if he had always lived there and always would. And the music roiled wherever he went until he could no longer trust his own thoughts.

In one chamber he found a strange creature like a shaven ape throwing dice on a long table. When he entered, it stared at him with golden eyes that contained an unsettling intelligence and then proceeded to mimic every movement he made as if it were his mirror image. In another chamber, ten pendulums as long as a ship's mast swung from the high, vaulted ceiling. In the gloom, Will could just discern on each one a long-beaked figure, seemingly asleep, strapped upside down, hands crossed on its chest. As he moved deeper into the fortress, the sense of being part of a troubling dream swallowed him whole and he had to fight to keep his hold on his purpose there. How easy would it be to give himself up wholly to these wonders and mysteries?

Again and again, as he made his way through the fortress, Will had to duck into doorways to avoid the Fay themselves as they moved silently through their realm. The air of corruption heavy around them, males and females walked side by side like courting couples, heads bowed yet occasionally glancing at each other as if they communicated without words. Some Fay passed on horseback, their silvery cloaks and helms suggesting a higher status. Occasionally, their heads would turn, their eyes wide and staring as if they could see him in his hiding place, but they rode on without a sound.

It was as if time had no meaning there. It felt as if the walls, the paths, the vast hallways, went on for ever. Will paused and leaned back against a golden wall. Though Dee's warning still rang in his mind, he found himself reaching into the pouch that rested on his hip. After a moment fighting with his conscience, he pulled out the obsidian mirror. Even knowing all of the Unseelie Court could swoop down upon him in an instant, he was so lost that he felt he had no choice but to use the looking glass if he were to find Jenny.

As he hunched over the mirror, the mist in the glass cleared and Jenny appeared. Her face looked uncommonly pale in the gloom, and though she gave a faint smile when she saw him her brow was furrowed. Despite the dangers, Will was overjoyed to see her. He could scarcely believe he was so close now after so many years of wondering whether they would ever meet again.

'Where are you?' she asked, squinting. He knew she could see the gleaming gold on the halls around him. 'Will,' she exclaimed, her eyes widening. 'I told you not to come.'

'That conversation has long since sailed, Jenny,' he replied, his eyes scanning his surroundings. Would he even hear a footstep when they came for him? 'Quickly now, tell me where I can find you, afore I feel a dagger at my neck.'

She hesitated for an instant, then said, 'The highest hall is always lit by moonlight. Turn to the left once you enter and climb the steps. On the third floor, behind the third door, you will find me.' She flashed the smile that he remembered so well and then whispered, 'Take care, my love.'

Will felt his heart swell. So close now, so close. He darted ahead, looking up the towering walls every time he reached a courtyard. At the centre of the fortress, the highest hall was indeed silvery with moonlight, the shadow of every grotesque carving stark on the upper reaches. With each step, it loomed ever closer.

His heart pounded fit to burst. If the Fay discovered him when he was so near to the prize he had desired for so long, he thought his spirit would be broken for ever. Silently, he prayed that his enemies would continue to search beyond the fortress walls, but he knew the time must surely be near when they would turn their cruel eyes towards the dark streets of their home. When he reached an arched doorway at the base of the highest hall, he finally sucked in a deep draught of hot, fragrant air. His head was spinning with the rush of conflicting emotions. All he wanted now was to feel Jenny in his embrace. Steeling himself, he eased open the heavy gold and jet door and stepped into searing heat. The deep rumble of hammers rang through the walls louder still, reverberating in the pit of his stomach.

His pulse racing, the hand that held his sword now clammy with sweat, England's greatest spy took the steps two at a time. Fiddle and pipe music swirled dimly from the chambers below, but above him all seemed still.

At the top of the steps on the third floor, he leaned against the throbbing wall and drew in a deep breath to steady himself. Ahead lay a corridor lit by a single torch with doors

351

along the right wall. Will noticed his sword hand trembling as all the years of yearning for this moment rushed out of him, and he knew he had to steady himself.

Calm descended on him. He was ready. He crept along the corridor, his senses alert to the slightest sign of danger. At the third door, he raised the latch and pushed gently with his shoulder. It didn't move. It was locked.

His heart beat faster. He pressed his ear against the rough wood, listening for any sound from within. All was quiet. Visions of what horrors might lie on the other side of that door flashed through his mind. He hesitated for a long moment, his chest tightening. Dare he call out?

When he had weighed his choices, he leaned closer until his lips were almost brushing the timber and whispered, 'Jenny. It's me.'

Silence followed, and his heart grew heavy. But then he heard movement on the other side of the door, drawing closer. He held his breath. After a moment a woman's voice hissed, 'At last.' It was Jenny.

The hairs on the nape of his neck tingled with antici-pation. How much richer her voice sounded in life than coming through the glass of the obsidian mirror.

A bolt was drawn. The door swung open.

The only light came from the ruddy glow of a hissing brazier in one corner of the chamber. Will's eyes slowly adjusted to the gloom. A figure loomed in the half-light: tall . . . much taller than he remembered. He saw the silhouette of a staff, pale fingers wrapped around it. They looked unnaturally long, the curved nails sharp, like talons. Other details emerged as if a curtain were being drawn back. Robes, seemingly too thick for the unbearable heat, a faint gold filigree glinting in the brazier's light. Yellowing skulls of birds and mice, and trinkets, all braided into gold and silver hair. And finally the face appeared from the shadows, hollow-eyed and sunken-cheeked.

Deortha, sorcerer to the Fay High Family, reached out his right hand, palm up. With a sly smile, he murmured, 'The looking glass, if you will.'

CHAPTER FORTY-NINE

THE BRAZIER'S ACRID SMOKE DRIFTED ACROSS DEORTHA'S COLD features. Will's mind reeled as he watched the shadows play on the Fay's face in the incarnadine glow of the chamber. 'You made a play of being Jenny all along?' he croaked. Despair flooded him.

He remembered the first time he had ever cast eyes upon the Unseelie Court's sorcerer, on that awful moonlit night on Dartmoor six years gone. It was after Deortha had departed that he had found Jenny's locket upon the grass, his first real evidence that she was still alive and a prisoner of the Unseelie Court, or so he'd thought. At the time he should have questioned the coincidence, but he had wanted to believe it so much it had clouded his wits.

There had been so much more: the whispered words of Christopher Marlowe's devil telling him Jenny still lived in a hot land across the sea; his love's face in that devil's looking glass, insisting he ignore her while encouraging him to do the opposite, all of it luring him to this place, this moment. And all of it a play, an illusion. He was a fool to have believed so easily, because he wanted to, because he loved, and the Unseelie Court were nothing if not expert in finding the flaws in every man. Time meant nothing to them. They wove their schemes across the years, not caring how long it took to achieve their aims. And in his weakness he had delivered into their hands the one thing they wanted: that terrible mirror.

Deortha smiled as if he could read all his thoughts.

'Where is Jenny?' Will asked in a low voice. Yet he was afraid to hear the answer. He raised his rapier until the point quivered over the sorcerer's heart. 'Where is she?' he asked again, this time raw anger flaring from the embers of his dismay.

'You wish to know if she is alive or dead.' Will sensed mockery in Deortha's calm tone and felt his anger grow hotter still, but the sorcerer only gave a low laugh.

Will snatched the devil's looking glass out of the leather pouch and held it high, ready to dash it on the flags. 'I will destroy this before I would ever let you use its power.'

'And you think that here, in our home, at the very heart of our authority, you have any control over your own actions? Here you are a puppet, no more than that, and I hold your strings.'

Will's sword arm felt as heavy as stone. He thrust his blade at the sorcerer's chest, but something unbidden stayed his hand. However much he tried, he was powerless to drive the point home.

He felt the chilly touch of despair caress his spine. 'Tell me now,' he said, his voice low and hard, 'what befell her?' And as the words left his lips he realized how afraid he was of the answer.

Deortha eased the obsidian mirror from his fingers.

Peering into the glass, the sorcerer nodded and caressed the black rim. 'She lives,' he said, distracted. 'She is here.'

All thought of the mirror vanished. Will's breath left him in a rush, but he hardly dared believe the sorcerer. 'And you have not harmed her?' he demanded.

Deortha raised his head and gave a strange smile. 'She is safe. She is an honoured guest of the Unseelie Court.'

'Take me to her. Please.'

'That was always my intention.' The pale eyes glinted. 'It was my intention from the moment we met upon the moor.'

'What trick are you playing, devil?' Will's voice was hoarse with grief, anger and hope.

'All life is illusion,' the sorcerer replied, echoing the words Dee had spoken shortly before the *Corneille Noire* departed the island for the New World. 'And in the midst of that, all appears trickery when the truth is hidden.'

Will's eyes narrowed. There was no gain in showing the pain he felt, he knew – he might as well bare his throat to the cruel Fay – and so he forced himself to put on a grin, and with a swagger that he didn't feel he sheathed his rapier. 'Then I can take from your words that it is not your intention to kill me yet,' he said. 'I would see Jenny, now.'

'All in good time.'

Will nodded, trying to seem unruffled. 'What plans do you have for the mirror you have fought for for so long?'

Deortha turned over the mirror as if it were unimportant. 'For those who know how to use it, this mirror reveals all places, all times. No secret can ever be hidden. Whoever wields this mirror controls everything.' Waving his right hand as if wafting away a foul smell, he added, 'But for now that is of no interest.'

The spy frowned. 'Of no interest? A weapon that can uncover the flaws in any enemy's defence, and divine future plans? The world is now yours.'

'The world always was ours.' Deortha stepped towards the door and beckoned for him to follow. 'Will Swyfte, I have work for you.'

CHAPTER FIFTY

THE TORCHES SIZZLED AT THE BOTTOM OF THE VAST GULF OF dark. In the pool of light, pale faces gleamed, eyes frozen wide in terror. Captain Sanburne showed a cold face to the ones who waited in the shadows, but his men shook as the deep rumble of mighty hammers enveloped them. High above the knot of frightened sailors, Will gripped the stone wall of the gallery whither Deortha had brought him. As he peered down the well of the great hall, he wondered how the captain and his crew had been seized. He felt relieved that they were all still alive, but he feared for their future.

Deep grinding echoed all around. Disoriented, he felt as if the basalt and gold of the hall were revolving like a millstone, crushing the husks of the men cowering below. More torches hissed into life, widening the circle of light. The hidden figures flickered into view, a near-army of Fay guards surrounding the men. Grey and indistinct, their faces were cloaked by shadow. Silver breastplates and helms glinted in the dancing flames. The guards bristled with cruel weapons: spike-topped halberds, double-headed axes and broadswords.

The circle of guards parted to allow four figures entry. Will's heart thundered with joy as he watched Meg, Carpenter, Launceston and Grace step forward. He could scarcely believe they lived. Bloodied and bedraggled, they still held their heads up defiantly, he saw.

Halberds levelled at their necks brought them to a halt, and Will's jubilation drained away. He looked back at Deortha, but the brooding sorcerer gave no sign of what was to come.

A distant door slammed shut, the echoes rippling through the hall. A moment later he heard another door, and then another, the successive booms growing louder as they approached until the hall rang with the steady beat of a funeral drum. The sailors' heads turned in the direction of the sound, the men fearful at the thought of what was approaching.

Finally the Unseelie Court circle parted once again. Agleam in a silver winged headdress, glistening robes and a white cloak that swept the flagstones, a tall, slender Fay stepped forward. Will leaned over the stone wall, squinting to get a better look. Here was a leader of sorts, perhaps even a King, he thought, his eyes narrowing; the architect of all their suffering.

The regal Fay glided towards the Englishmen. Beside him came a smaller figure, and Will gasped. His memory reeled across the vast ocean of years to the day when Jenny had been swept away into mystery. Her face as she had crossed the cornfield was burned into his mind's eye, every moment they had shared, the depth of the emotion he had felt, all wrapped up in that single sunlit image. Could this be another of the Unseelie Court's cruel tricks, he thought, as he peered down at the woman who stood beside the King?

Cold breath chilled his ear. 'Yes,' Deortha whispered, 'it is she.'

Jenny. His heart pounding, his thoughts awhirl, he drank in every familiar movement, feeling a pang of bittersweet remembrance. His gaze drifted to her white skirts edged in gold, and the gold at her wrists and in the band snaking around her forehead, and he saw that she walked at the King's side without any sign of defiance or resistance. As far as he could tell, she seemed to look on the Englishmen without compassion or recognition. *No prisoner this*, Will thought, growing cold. *She accompanies the Fay willingly.*

'You have spun your magics to seduce her to your side,' he snarled into the dark of the gallery. 'For that you will pay a harsh price, I vow.'

'There is no glamour. She is what she seems,' the sorcerer replied.

'You lie, as your kind always lies,' Will spat. Yet he knew there could be no other explanation. His knuckles whitened round the hilt of his rapier as he fought the desperate urge to rush down to the floor and tear Jenny – his Jenny – away from those foul creatures.

Until then Grace had remained silent, head bowed, eyes fixed on the stone floor. Now, as if waking from some deep slumber, she twitched as if someone had called her name, and looked up. When her gaze alighted on Jenny, her mouth fell open and tears flooded her eyes. Arms outstretched, she rushed to embrace her, and would have fallen under the Fay guards' halberds had Meg not lunged to stop her.

She staggered back with Meg's arms wrapped round her, incomprehension turning to devastation when Jenny turned her calm, cold face towards her. No sign of recognition flickered in the elder sister's hard features.

The Fay King looked down on the tableau before him, the group of confused and frightened humans caught in the small circle of light, and said, 'I am Mandraxas, highest of the High Family. In my sister's absence, the Golden Throne is mine, here in this place beyond places that your kind call Manoa. It is my word that rings out across this world, across all worlds; my design which shapes this war; my judgement that hangs over all the heads of your people. Do you fear me, men?'

Sanburne showed a defiant face, but the other seamen cowered.

From a pouch, Mandraxas pulled out a black oval stone on a silver chain. He let it swing in front of him like a pendulum. 'We are the oldest beings in the great sweep of existence. We are the silver of the moon and the cool mist of dawn and the dark shadow of night. And we are the gold of the sun and the searing heat of the forge. And we will no longer be defied.' He paused and looked around him, still swinging the stone from side to side. 'In that time before times, we knew only beauty, only wonder. And then your infestation spread across the fields in which we played. Your urge for blood, and power, consumed you and corrupted all that had been made. And then you sought to challenge us. Is there no end to your arrogance? Now, though, the age of man is passing.'

Launceston raised his head, a finger's breadth from an axe's blade. A trickle of blood on his pale skin gleamed in

361

the torchlight. 'I know you,' he said, fixing an eye on the Fay King. 'I know you as I know myself, for we are much alike. A pale shell hiding a monster. For all your high words, you are the parasites, preying upon the flesh of the world. Creatures like us, we cannot survive for ever, for we are against nature. The things I see in other men, the small kindnesses and the great loves, they cannot be crushed by the millstone of your midnight power. They will survive. You will not.'

A hint of a smile ghosted on to Mandraxas's lips. He allowed the pendulum to come to a halt and stared at the stone for a moment, as if weighing his next words.

'And yet, for all your deceit and your cruelty and your brutality, you are fools. Poor, witless sheep,' he continued as if he had not heard the Earl, his voice so low it was almost lost beneath the deep rumble. 'You dared to trespass on the province of the Unseelie Court. You thought you could wander here, in the borders of the Far Lands, with impunity. This is not your world, mortals. This is a land of madness and terror beyond imagining.'

Shadows raced across his face as he began to swing the stone on its length of glinting chain just above his head. A low whistle echoed through the vast space, growing louder the faster Mandraxas whirled the sable stone. Will felt a corresponding queasiness in the pit of his stomach. He watched the Fay King's smile grow.

'The Spree-birds are coming,' Mandraxas said.

Deep in the shadows high overhead, a shrieking rang out from all parts of the hall. Will was reminded of the haunting cries of hungry crows on a grey autumn morn. A moment later, the beating of wings filled the vault with thunder. The spy looked up, shocked by the thought of how many birds it would take to create such a roar.

Wind rushed by his face, the draught of that swooping flock as it passed, and his ears rang with the piercing shrieking. He clutched the wall and peered down, the circle of light now hidden behind a swirl of black bodies. Torchlight flickered through the flapping wings. When the shrill human screams soared up to the roof, Will tore out his rapier. Deortha grasped his shoulder to restrain him and whispered in his ear, 'I have ensured your friends will be safe. Reveal yourself and they will surely die, as will you.' His breath was icy.

Will felt sickened by what he saw, but he fought to contain himself. After a moment, he sheathed his blade and turned back to the carnage. The Spree-birds were feeding. In the torchlight, their black feathers gleamed, but their heads were little more than skulls. Most of the flock wheeled around the hall above, but many perched on the thrashing sailors, their long bony beaks stabbing like daggers. Blood pooled across the flagstones. Amid the cacophony of bird-cry and dying screams, Meg, Grace, Launceston and Carpenter looked on in horror as one by one the hellish birds rose and flapped away, white skulls stained red. A picture of starkest horror revealed itself. Where Sanburne and his crew had huddled, now only bones clotted with chunks of meat remained. As the last bird disappeared back to its hidden roost, a sickened stillness fell over the surviving mortals.

His anger boiling, Will turned to Deortha and whispered, 'You have shown me this savagery so that I would know it hangs over the heads of my friends. Another way to bend me to your will.' He glanced down to that bloodied circle of light and saw Jenny studying the scene without a trace of emotion. How far the Unseelie Court had twisted her away from the innocent woman he had known.

'Come with me,' Deortha demanded.

Will followed the sorcerer down flight after flight of steps until he found himself in a small, bare antechamber lit by a single torch. The Fay left him there, alone, for what seemed like a lifetime. He paced and brooded and made silent vows until he heard the door creak open.

Turning, he stared into the sorcerer's pale eyes. Deortha stepped aside with a sweep of his arm to reveal Jenny, her expression dark with suspicion. Will felt his heart leap. His head spun with the thousand imagined speeches he had dreamed of making when they met again, but he uttered none of them. Instead, he found himself transfixed by the luminescence of her youth and beauty.

She had not changed in the fifteen years they had been apart. Her milky skin was smooth, her brow unlined, her cheeks full and her eyes bright. Unconsciously his fingers crept to his own unkempt, unshaven face, tracing the pattern of years, the wrinkles round his eyes from long spells under a mediterranean sun, the laughter lines bracketing his mouth from lush days in the Mermaid with Kit Marlowe and spicy nights with the doxies in Liz Longshanks's stew. There was the true tragedy. He had thought her only a prisoner, but trapped in this timeless place she had drifted away from him in years and experience, the commonality of their life and the bonds forged by being in the same place at the same time shattered for ever. Though she stood only a sword's length from him, she might as well have been a thousand miles away.

And yet it was still Jenny. He refused to allow sour thoughts to tarnish the moment, and moved to embrace her.

Sharper than a slap to his face was Jenny's cold look. She half turned to the sorcerer and demanded, 'Who is this?'

Will recoiled. In her eyes, he could see no trace of the Unseelie Court's taint. Jenny truly did not recognize him.

His voice barely a whisper, he said, 'This dark place has swallowed your memories. Cast your mind back to England, to Warwickshire and the village of your birth. Remember the hours we walked in the woods together, or dallied on the banks of the millstream.' He watched her brow knit, but no recognition sparked in her features. 'I am Will.' He felt a lump rise in his throat.

She shook her head. 'If we knew each other once, it is long gone. This place is all I remember. How could it not be? I have dwelled here now these past thousand years.'

CHAPTER FIFTY-ONE

SILENCE LAY LIKE A SHROUD ACROSS THE ANTECHAMBER. In that emptiness, Will could hear his world crumble and fall away. At the door, Deortha listened for any intruders. 'Dreams are elusive,' the sorcerer said without emotion. 'And sometimes the most fervent wishes float out for long years and return like an arrow through the heart.'

'No,' Will snapped. 'I will not accept that.'

'And what will you do? Stab it with your dagger? Plunge your sword through its heart?' Deortha turned back to him, his pale eyes glowing in the gloom. 'Here is an enemy that is immune to all your vaunted martial skills.'

Reaching out one imploring hand, Will stepped towards Jenny. She near-leapt away from him. 'Stay back,' she said. 'No stranger can approach the King's consort.'

Will felt his blood run cold.

'And there lies the heart of this great tragedy,' Deortha said with a sour undertone. 'We are thrust together in a bitter struggle of monumental proportions. Many lives hang in the balance, and power, and the very shape of what has been and what will be. And all that we fight to achieve has been placed at risk. By this.' He waved a contemptuous hand towards Will and Jenny. 'By the insignificant desires of three lovesick fools.'

'Enough,' Will said. 'Tell me some truths.'

'Truths?' Deortha glowered. 'Do you remember aught of how you came to us?' he asked Jenny.

'I have always been here,' she replied, her chin raised defiantly.

'You are not one of us. You are a mortal.'

'And you have always despised me for it,' Jenny snapped.

Will was surprised to see anger in the sorcerer's face. 'If you have only contempt for humans, why did you steal Jenny away?' he asked.

'We are strong and you are weak,' Deortha replied, pursing his lips, 'but sometimes . . . some of my kind . . . are infected with a flaw of the spirit. A black corruption that eats away at their hearts. We keep our secrets well. We lie to ourselves and pretend. But our history is littered with the failures of those who have turned their affections towards your kind.'

Will watched Jenny's face, a chill rising as he began to understand.

'Our King . . .' Deortha formed the word as if he had a pebble in his mouth, 'came across this woman while at play in your land. It is in his nature to give himself to foolhardy pursuits. Day after day, he watched her, until he believed his heart held affection.' He waved a hand as if dispelling a stench. 'Love.'

'So he took her,' Will said with quick anger. 'He forced her to submit to his will.'

'We have nothing but time.' A cruel smile flickered

on the sorcerer's lips. 'We can wait for the waves to turn the rocks to sand if we wish. Time does our work for us. Mandraxas only had to wait. Here in this place, the years eroded her resolve, which at the beginning was great indeed. Removed from the comforts of her own life, it became like a half-remembered dream. She saw only our home, and the wonders it contained, and slowly she fell into its embrace.'

As she listened to the sorcerer's words, Jenny hung her head, a faraway look in her eyes as if something deep was stirring inside her.

'How can it be,' Will asked, 'that only fifteen years passed in our world and a thousand here?'

'The rules of existence are not as simple as your "wise men" would have you believe.'

Will felt hollow. He had always believed the solution to his suffering was simple – to bring Jenny home. But this . . . this seemed insurmountable.

'And still you think us devils, even though we show love for your kind,' Deortha said. 'Let me reveal one more secret. Then perhaps you will see who are the true devils. Your own kind knew where this woman had been taken, and why. Indeed, they encouraged it.' The contempt was barely restrained.

'Why would they?' Will snapped, all his long-held suspicions turning to hot anger. This must have been what Grace overheard Cecil and Essex discussing as the court left Nonsuch.

'A good question. Yes, why?' The sorcerer smiled, but his eyes remained icy.

'Tell me!' Will fought the compulsion to beat the answer out of the Fay.

'In good time.' Deortha raised an index finger. 'Firstly, nothing is ever lost. You must know that this is true. What was still stirs within her, if you can but find it.'

Will saw Jenny studying him. When he smiled, she did not look away. Perhaps there was hope yet, he thought. 'And you tell me this out of the goodness of your heart?' he said to the sorcerer sardonically. 'What is it you require in exchange?'

'I wish you to take this woman away from here.'

'What gain is there for you in that?'

'He would not have me whispering in the King's ear,' Jenny said acidly.

'She has stolen what little steel Mandraxas had.' Deortha ignored Jenny's glare. 'We cannot win this war while she sits beside the Golden Throne. And we will never have our Queen returned to us.'

'How so?'

'The King does not want the Queen returned from her imprisonment at your hands.' Deortha circled Jenny like a carrion crow eyeing a wounded rabbit. She stared at the torch through heavy lids, pretending to ignore him. 'He would lose both the Golden Throne and this woman he loves so much. The Queen would never allow such an abomination to continue. If she knew a mortal sat as King's consort beside the Golden Throne, her fury would be terrible indeed.'

Will paced beside the black basalt walls, weighing the Fay's words. His thoughts raced, confused by the revelations, and he fought to make sense of everything he had heard. After a moment, he smiled to himself. 'Mandraxas does not want to free the Queen for he would lose what he cares for most,' he mused. 'And so the plots of Elizabeth's court are reflected here. You are more like us than you realize.'

'The King plays his games.' Deortha nodded. 'He shows the face of a determined ruler who will do all within his power to free our Queen. And yet he undermines every attempt, and obfuscates, and delays. Some would even say,' the sorcerer said with studied disinterest, 'that he plots to have the Queen, his sister, killed while she is in your hands.'

'And to blame us for the murder. And thereby unleash an even greater fury among your people, a greater desire to commit atrocities against us.'

Deortha shrugged. 'Perhaps. I would not pretend to know the King's mind.'

'You speak of love between Fay and man.' Walsingham, the long-dead spymaster, and Cecil, the present one, and the grey faces of the Privy Council, paraded across Will's thoughts, and his anger burned hotter still. He felt that at last he was beginning to understand. 'Your King reached some agreement with my masters,' he said finally.

The sorcerer steepled his fingers in front of him. 'Mandraxas was allowed to wander your land with impunity to find a woman who met his desires. And then he was permitted to spirit her away, with no questions asked and no effort made to recover her.'

Will clenched his fist in anguish.

'And she was not alone,' Deortha continued. 'We have been granted the right to take whom we wished from your people. Not many, not near as many as we stole before you built your defences. A child here, a wife or husband there. For the sake of love, in the main.'

The spy seethed. All those years of lies and deceit, all the pain he had suffered with the connivance of those he served. 'And in return?'

'The King agreed to contain those of the High Family who demanded slaughter on a grand scale to regain our Queen. His work has become more difficult in recent times. His brothers and sister have grown impatient with his failures and so his attempts to undermine their best endeavours have grown more determined.'

Will bowed his head. He felt devastated. Hearing the truth in the sorcerer's words, he now understood so much. Deortha had been right. The epoch-shaking clash of high power between England and the Unseelie Court that had been rolling across the world with increasing brutality was little more than an illusion. In truth, the high drama of vast sweeping schemes and strategies came down to nothing more than raw emotions: passion, and yearning, and two suitors aspiring to the hand of one woman. He laughed bitterly at the irony of it.

'Though you keep your teeth hidden, I suspect you have venom enough,' he said, eyeing the sorcerer. 'I would have thought if such an obstacle existed to the great plans of the Unseelie Court, it could be solved with a dagger in the night.'

'And risk the terrible wrath of the King? Only a fool would follow such a course.'

While the Fay and Jenny glared at each other, Will slipped his fingers into his boot and withdrew his dagger. He hid it behind his back as he circled towards Deortha. Yet he felt the sorcerer's words lying heavily on him. 'If I take Jenny away from here, the King will be forced to act to reclaim her. You will find whatever it takes to win this war and bring about the destruction of humankind.'

'If you leave her, you destroy yourself. Can you bring yourself to do that?'

'You cannot take me away,' Jenny said, her tone dismissive. 'My King would never allow it.' She clasped her hands behind her back, showing her face to each male in turn.

Will studied her features, seeing the fire he had admired so long ago. 'You love this King?' he asked.

'I am his consort,' Jenny replied, as if that explained everything.

Will stepped in front of Deortha, the unseen dagger cold in his hand. 'And there is the difference between our people. Your King steals Jenny from her life because he sees something he must have, with no more thought for her than a beast in the field. And you expect me to take her back in the same way – because I want her more than the world itself. But she is no rag doll to be torn between warring children. She commands her own life and she must decide her own path.'

'And you would allow her to choose life here in this fortress of madness and dark? Even after you have sacrificed the years of your youth to find her?' Deortha asked, uncomprehending.

'All I want for her is joy and peace. I would not see her heart broken to salve my own ache.'

He watched Jenny's face soften at his words. Her gaze flickered across his features, a question in her eyes.

Will stifled his swirling feelings for her, ready to plunge the dagger into the sorcerer's chest. If nothing else came of this dismal affair, the death of the Unseelie Court's scheming adviser would strike at the heart of their aspirations.

Before he could decide, the door crashed open. Jenny cried out in shock, her hand flying to her mouth. In a flurry of snow white, Mandraxas swept into the antechamber, eyes afire, with three Fay guards at his side. The sorcerer's eyes widened with fear, and in an instant he had pressed something hard into Will's hand. The King hurried to Jenny to see she was well. As the spy slipped the object under his shirt and into the waist of his breeches, Deortha whispered an instruction. He had barely finished when Mandraxas turned his coruscating gaze upon them.

At the King's order, the guards forced Will and Deortha against the stone wall with the cruel blades of their halberds. Will felt the tip of the spear dig into his neck; one thrust and his head would be gone. He cursed.

Mandraxas fixed his attention on Deortha and intoned, 'Take the traitor to the Scalding Rooms.'

Horror flitted across the sorcerer's face, but he fought to retain his composure. He glared coldly at the King, but reserved a more lingering glance for Will, urging, perhaps, that they had business in common. He strode out with a halberd pressed against his back. The King stepped to Jenny's side, and placed one slender finger under her chin to raise her head. He gazed into her eyes for a long moment and then brushed his lips against hers.

Will felt a flare of fiery anger, and jealousy too, he could not deny that. He struggled to reach the Fay King, only for the remaining guards to press their halberds harder still. He felt sticky blood trickle down his neck. And yet, as Jenny's lips met her master's, he swore he saw her eyes look towards his own.

Leaving her at last, Mandraxas strode towards him with a

triumphant grin. 'I saw you once, long ago in your terms,' he said with contempt. 'A callow youth. Not fit to dally with this proud woman, my consort.'

Though the King held the upper hand, the two faced each other as equals in love, their faces cold. 'I have sailed across an ocean of years and half a world to find Jenny,' Will said. 'I have sacrificed my youth, my innocence, my dreams, my morals, to get her back. I have turned my skin to flint and my heart to steel. There is nothing I would not do to free her from your cruelty.' He could feel Jenny's eyes upon him, but he kept his gaze upon the King.

Mandraxas's face loomed a finger's width from Will. His eyes gleamed golden, his pale skin almost translucent, his breath ice-cold. 'I always knew you would come for her,' he whispered. 'I welcomed it. I needed you here, in my hands. You were always the one who might waken her from this long, peaceful sleep, even after a thousand years, but now I have you she will be mine for ever. And you will suffer a thousand hells for your failure.'

CHAPTER FIFTY-TWO

THE FIRE ROARED IN THE GRAND STONE HEARTH LIKE A blacksmith's forge. Golden sparks surged up the chimney as shadows fluttered across the whirling figures. Dresses of mildewed grey swirled around in furious dance to the delirious rhythm of fiddle and pipe. Their cloaks flying, the Fay males caught the hands of their partners and whipped them around faster still. And with every spin the faces altered, hauntingly beautiful one moment, cadaverous the next. With the music ringing up to the vaulted roof, the fiddler and the piper danced along the twin tables running the length of the hall, deftly avoiding the platters of meat and bread and cheese which seemed at once both bounteous and corrupted by rot. On the Golden Throne, Mandraxas steepled his fingers and watched the Unseelie Court at play with the easy eye of a victor. Beside him on a smaller throne, his consort folded her hands in her lap, unable to bring herself to look upon the knot of prisoners who huddled at the heart of the madness.

Meg held up her head defiantly, refusing to reveal the terror she felt in that hell. Amid the choking heat, she sucked in a deep draught of air, the sickly-sweet smell of honeysuckle and rose so strong she felt as if she was in her cups. Surely the end was not far away now. It would not be pleasant, she knew, and there would be agonies aplenty for a time. But it would at least be an end.

The Irish spy saw Grace kneading her hands as she watched her sister beside the Fay King. 'She lives, and for now that is enough,' Meg shouted above the din. A little comfort in the final hour was no bad thing.

'She is remembering, can you not see?' Grace replied. 'The coldness has drained from her face. Soon she will know me, and then she will save us all.'

'We are fortunate indeed,' Meg lied. She studied Jenny with a sharp eye. A country girl, nothing more. Was this really the one who had filled Will with such passion that he had travelled to death's door to bring her home? She shook her head, unable to comprehend how Swyfte could prefer that child when she herself offered passion and life and experience.

As the wild music reached a climax, Carpenter clutched at his head as if something squirmed in his skull. Meg had sensed that something was wrong with the spy ever since they had left the island, but what it was she could not guess. She saw that Launceston was concerned for his friend too, his raptor eyes rarely leaving the other man.

The Fay swooped closer as they whirled, white faces flashing past in a blur of mad, staring eyes. Jagged fingernails caught in Meg's hair and raked across Grace's breast. The two women pressed back to back against Carpenter and Launceston, all of them determined to fight to the last when the ravenous pack fell upon them.

It was then, just as the Irish spy began to fear the worst, that a bell rang, its tone crystal clear. The dancers swept to the perimeter of the hall where they continued to circle, and the music quietened a little as the fiddler and pipe player retreated to the hearth. When the door flew open, two guards in winged helms dragged Will in. Meg felt a rush of joy to see him still with the living, and, despite everything, a flicker of hope warmed her heart. Blood caked the edge of his left eye and a bruise swelled on his cheek, but he flashed a grin when he saw her. Even at the last, he knew how to make a girl's heart beat faster, she thought with a quiet laugh.

The guards flung Will on to the flagstones in front of Mandraxas. Climbing to his feet, the spy brushed the dust from his shirt with lazy strokes. He paid no attention to the Fay King. Yet when he was done, he locked eyes with Jenny in a gaze heavy with emotion. In that look, Meg saw such depth of feeling that it touched her heart.

'You are creatures of few days,' Mandraxas said, looking down upon Will, 'and they pass in a blink of an eye. We, however,' and he gestured to those around him, 'we continue for ever. You move slowly, through a fog of ignorance. We race across fields of wonder. How high you raise yourselves up, insisting you are not beasts of the field. How pitiful you are in truth.' The King reached out his left hand for Jenny to take, no show of affection but one of ownership, designed to wound. 'Shall we see how little you mean to us? Shall we have fine sport? For now your days are truly at an end.'

Will drew himself up and spat a mouthful of blood on to the flagstones. 'You think you have our necks upon the block, but we are exactly where we wish to be.' He turned to the spies and flashed Meg another grin. She recognized the familiar heat in her belly. Could he really have a plan, even here in the heart of Hell, friendless, weaponless and surrounded by an army of enemies? She would have mocked the suggestion if it were any other man, but Swyfte, he was a schemer and a gambler, perhaps the greatest one she knew. *England's greatest spy.* How the other rogues in Cecil's service laughed at the sobriquet concocted to assuage the fears of the good men and women of England. And yet it was true, it was true.

As if unsure of what he was hearing, Mandraxas's eyes narrowed. 'We are masters of torment and suffering. We can pluck agony like the string of a lyre and sustain it for eternity. Do you doubt me?' He clapped his hands once and the musicians stepped in front of the throne. The fiddle player began to increase the tempo until the music whirled into a frenzy, his silver hair lashing the air with his passion. The piper spun round and round, atonal notes seemingly in opposition to his partner's melody.

The din set Meg's teeth on edge at first, but gradually she felt her heart begin to beat faster, and her cheeks flush, and euphoria begin to burn inside her. Under the clashing tunes, she thought she could hear another song being played. Despite herself, her feet and hands began to twitch to the rhythm.

And yet it was Grace who seemed most affected by the music. Carpenter clutched for her, but she danced away from his fingers, spinning on light feet into the space in front of the musicians. Sweat glistened on her brow as she turned faster and faster still, her brown hair flying. Yet Meg saw none of the joy the girl would have exhibited at one of the court masques. Instead, her eyes were wide with fear, her expression fixed.

'She cannot stop,' the Irish spy murmured with dawning realization.

'Dance your hours away,' Mandraxas called. 'Dance until your flesh withers and falls from your bones.'

When Meg heard the piper alter his tune once more, she saw shadows cross the faces of Carpenter and Launceston. Their eyes gleamed and faint, beatific smiles flickered on their lips. It was as if they had forgotten all that transpired in that hall and were instead looking deep within themselves to some glorious time of their youth. Gradually Meg noticed that it seemed as if a light was slowly going out in their features.

Will's expression darkened, but he held firm. Meg saw his hand reach behind his back where his shirt hung loose above the waist of his breeches.

'Do not harm them.'

Though the voice was quiet, it rang out with such intensity that it cut through the raucous music. Mandraxas recoiled as if he had been slapped. It was Jenny who had spoken. Tears glimmered in the corners of her eyes, but her expression was fierce. And Grace's mad dance began to slow.

Meg looked from the woman to Will. He was smiling in triumph, and she knew that he had gambled on his love's awakening.

'It seems your Queen disagrees,' he said. 'Spite her and show we mortals mean nothing to you. Or accede to her request and accept that our kind, in certain circumstances, have power over you.'

Meg watched Mandraxas wrestle with the net that

seemingly snared him. The dancing of the Unseelie Court slowed and all eyes turned towards their King. They had the look of a hungry wolf pack ready to pounce, the Irish spy thought.

'You have not forgotten,' Will continued. He swallowed, nearly choking on his passion as his gaze locked upon Jenny. 'One thousand years may pass, but still the heart calls out.' Her cheeks flushed. 'You remember your sister, Grace, who whispers a prayer for you to return home every day. And you remember me—'

'Enough,' Mandraxas snapped. Gone was the striking, regal face, replaced by a death's head of sunken cheeks, thin lips and hollow eyes.

Meg brushed the hair from her face, standing taller as she looked with hope to Will. A faint but familiar smile played on his lips. It was the smile of a man who saw his carefully laid snare tightening around his prey's neck. 'There is one way to solve this knotty affair of pride and human emotions,' he said, as if the notion had only just come to him. 'A duel.'

The King snorted with derision. 'Between you and me? But a duel is a fight between equals.'

'Before I left London, I visited your Queen.' Will raised his voice so the other gaunt-faced members of the Unseelie Court would focus upon his words. 'The true ruler of this place and people. She yearns to return to the City of Gold—'

'And so she will,' Mandraxas said, too quickly.

'She spoke to me of your people, of the rules that bind you, and the beliefs, and she told me of honour,' Will pushed on, his voice louder. 'You believe mortals are a dishonourable breed, yes? That our kind are filled with deceit, shaped for betrayal. Honour is what separates your kind from ours, that is what your Queen said.'

'And she spoke true.'

Meg smiled as she watched the Fay King move towards the trap step by step. Seemingly unable to look away from the dancing fire, he appeared oblivious of what lay in the dark around him.

'Then we duel, you and I,' Will said, his tone lazy. 'And honour dictates the outcome. If you win, you will have your cruel sport with us. And if I win, we have safe passage to leave this place and return to the world of men, my friends and I.' He paused, for effect. 'And Jenny.'

Mandraxas's eyes widened for a moment, but then he settled back into his throne and folded his hands in his lap. His smile was corpse-cold. 'But you cannot win. I am faster, stronger, more skilful than even one of our Hunters. Will you brag as much when you wriggle on the end of my cold steel?' He threw his arms wide, looking around his court with a wolfish grin. 'A duel, then. Fine sport for all.'

'A duel conducted with honour,' Will said. 'You will use no magics or illusions to turn my head. No music to make me dance like a fool. No whispers that turn my bones to straw or whisk my wits away to Bedlam.'

'Rest assured, all I need is my rapier.'

'I have your word?'

Mandraxas nodded slowly. 'You have the word of the King of the Unseelie Court.'

Had Will truly lost his mind? Meg was torn between apprehension and belief in the man she now realized she loved. His plan remained hidden, but with Will Swyfte that was always the case.

With a deep bow, Will said, 'Then let our dance begin, and may the devil take the loser.'

CHAPTER FIFTY-THREE

WILD SHADOWS DANCED ACROSS THE STONE WALLS. BEYOND the crackle and spatter of the flames in the hearth, silence lay heavily across the hall. Feeling bruised and battered but ready for a fight, Will weighed the rapier in his hand, checking that it was indeed the one that had been taken from him when he and Deortha had been captured. He whisked the tip of the blade through the air, making a play for the eyes of the Enemy he felt upon him. He glimpsed the Fay's cold, haunted faces. Were they hungry for his death, fired at the prospect of bloody entertainment, filled with loathing for one of the men who had taken their Queen from them? Of one thing he was certain: none of them could countenance anything but his defeat.

Mandraxas shrugged off his white cloak and pushed his shoulders back. For a moment he watched Will with undisguised contempt, then drew his own rapier and flexed the tip against the flags. Will ignored him, looking instead at Jenny, drawing strength from the concern he saw in her face. She leaned forward on her throne, and her eyes did not waver when they met his. She remembered him now, and what they shared, he could see. If he were to die there and then, that would be reward enough for all the years of searching and striving and disappointment.

He bowed. 'Consider now what we fight for,' he said, levelling his blade at the King. 'This is not man against Fay, or two bitter enemies waging war for the good of their country. No, we are rivals of the heart, about to clash swords for the hand of the woman we love. No great affair, this. Indeed, 'tis a private matter.'

Mandraxas all but snarled. 'Like all your kind, you are deluded. That matter has already been decided. I have my Queen and you have nothing, and soon less than nothing.'

'Look in your Queen's face, Your Highness, and repeat your words with conviction,' Will taunted, enjoying the anger that sparked in Mandraxas's features. In any sword fight, such emotion was weakness.

'Let us be done with this,' the King said with a theatrical sigh. He levelled his own rapier and gently tapped the end of Will's blade.

And the storm broke. The cold sea of predatory white faces seemed to fade away as Will's vision closed in upon his opponent. Barely had their swords clashed before he found Mandraxas as threatening as he had boasted. Will moved with the speed of a snake as the Fay struck with quicksilver strokes. The King's rapier glowed with the reflected flames from the hearth, slashing high, for Will's throat, then low, to disable. A thrust to the heart ripped open the spy's shirt, drawing blood on his chest. Unable to anticipate the rapid strokes, Will knew he must rely on instinct.

And yet when he looked past Mandraxas's lupine grin into those haunted eyes, Will thought he understood his foe. The Unseelie Court always found the flaws in men's hearts, but now he had discovered the Fay's weakness. No monster of the night, this. The King was weighted with all the fear of any man afraid of losing the woman he loved.

As if he could sense Will's probing of his vulnerability, the Fay snarled in fury and suddenly lunged at his opponent's face. The spy skipped back a step, feeling his cheek bloom hot from the steel's breath. Will knew he would not last much longer in the face of such an onslaught.

The time had come.

Parrying another lightning thrust from the Fay King, Will reached behind him with his left hand and withdrew the object that Deortha had pressed on him earlier, and he'd hidden under his shirt. In the firelight, the devil's looking glass burned like the sun.

Mandraxas hesitated, suddenly unsure. Will sensed the rest of the Unseelie Court bracing itself, claw-like hands clutching, barely resisting the urge to fall upon him and tear him apart. He refused to acknowledge the threat, and glanced into the smoky depths of the obsidian mirror.

The mist cleared, and there was the hooded gaze of the sorcerer. Deortha's whispered words sizzled in his head: 'Fulfil our agreement. Slay the traitor.'

As Deortha's lips shaped some silent incantation, his visage faded. It was replaced by Mandraxas, as though the mirror was but a window on the scene in front of him. Yet the mirror-King thrust upwards a moment before the real King, and as Mandraxas struck the spy stepped aside. Will smiled as a flicker of surprise crossed his opponent's face. How the sorcerer must hate his King, to give up such a prize so readily, a mirror which could see across all time, even if it were only one moment from now.

As Will parried each of his foe's strikes with ease, so the triumph ebbed from the Fay King's face. Balancing on the balls of his feet, the spy danced around his foe, making his opponent look a fool. As the looking glass revealed the weaknesses in Mandraxas's defence, so Will jabbed and thrust with growing confidence and fervour. He slit the King's doublet, his breeches, his silk sleeves, then nicked his cheek. And each strike could have been a killing blow.

The Fay stumbled back under the relentless assault until he sprawled against his throne. A murmur rippled through the Unseelie Court. Mandraxas's features grew taut with shame.

'Herein lies a lesson,' Will said, the tip of his rapier hovering over the King's heart. 'Pride comes before a fall.'

'Deceit and trickery,' the King snarled. 'Your nature remains true – your kind are lower than snakes.'

'I would not wish to disappoint you, Your Highness. And yet, in your arrogance, you saw no need to define the rules of my engagement, as I did of yours.'

His face twisting with rage, Mandraxas flung himself forward. Almost lazily, Will stepped aside, and tripped his opponent. The Fay King tumbled across the flagstones. The spy could feel how close he was to being ripped limb from limb by the ghastly figures hovering close by, and he spun away from the duel to the huddle of his friends.

'Be prepared,' he whispered. 'When I give the signal, we make our move.'

'You are as mad as always,' Carpenter snapped, nearly hysterical. He frantically raked his fingers through his hair as though his head was fit to burst. 'Those pale bastards will be on us like wolves before we have taken a step.'

'John, you must trust Will,' Grace implored. Though her hands trembled, she kept a brave face.

Will heard Mandraxas scramble to his feet, but before he could turn Launceston caught his eye with his unsettling gaze. 'What deal have you made to gain the advantage that mirror gives you, I wonder?' the Earl hissed.

'I have agreed to kill the King,' Will replied without emotion, 'thus damning all mankind to immediate destruction at the hands of a vengeful Fay army.' Sweeping out one hand, he added with a sardonic smile, 'But at least we will be allowed to leave unharmed, with Jenny.'

Grace's face drained of blood. 'No. Will, you cannot.'

Will felt a twinge of hurt when he saw Meg's face harden. 'Some would say that is too high a price, even for the love of your life,' she said with faux-sweetness. 'I would think again, my darling.'

'The only choices worth making are the hard ones,' he replied, turning back to Mandraxas. Clearing all extraneous thoughts from his head, he added, 'And I would have an end to my suffering, one way or another.'

When Will raised his rapier, the King feinted and thrust, though his attack lacked guile or power. His confidence was ebbing, the spy saw. It was time to finish this play. As Mandraxas searched for an opening, Will wiped the sweat from his brow. He had been delaying that moment of no return, he knew.

The mirror glinted, and once again he glimpsed Deortha's cold, watchful eyes urging him on to damnation. He dealt a flurry of ferocious blows, catching the King off guard and driving him back. With a flick of his wrist, he whipped his foe's blade from his hand and thrust his rapier towards the Fay's throat.

Jenny leapt from her throne. 'Do not kill him,' she cried. Will ignored her, though his heart ached at her concern for his foe.

The Unseelie Court surged closer, white faces contorted with bestial rage. Sword poised to strike, the spy thundered, 'Stay back. I will slay your King without a moment's thought for my own safety.' Hands hooked, the Fay slowed close enough for Will to smell their loamy odour. 'Meg. Robert. Some help, if you will.'

Launceston and the Irish woman grabbed daggers from two of the nearest Fay and held the blades against the King's neck. Stepping back, Will sheathed his sword and then held out his hand. After a moment's hesitation, Jenny took it. He could feel the fury of Mandraxas's gaze upon him as Carpenter and Grace hurried to his side. The Fay surrounded them and, Will guessed, countless more were gathering in the fortress beyond.

'How can we ever escape?' Grace whispered as if reading his thoughts.

'Deortha, show me the way out,' Will commanded into the looking glass.

The surface cleared and he heard the sorcerer speak: 'First, kill the King.'

'Do you take me for a fool? Once we have our freedom, you can have your monarch's life.' After a moment's hesitation, the sorcerer uttered the words Will needed to hear. He grinned at the others, a reassuring show of bravado. 'Stay close at my back. And if any here dare threaten you, prick the King till he squeals. Our Enemy will think twice before daring to lay a hand on you.' With Launceston and Meg guarding their prisoner, Will slid out his rapier and brandished it in front of him. The wall of Fay parted and he began to lead the way through them. Cadaverous faces loomed from the half-light on either side, hungry eyes staring and jaws snapping. A choking sense of dread enveloped him.

At the hall's great door, he turned back and looked across the Unseelie Court. Waving the tip of his rapier towards Mandraxas's face, he announced, 'Your King has betrayed you. He has conspired to leave your Queen a prisoner of men so that the Golden Throne can be his alone.'

'Lies,' Mandraxas bellowed.

With a smile and an arched eyebrow, Meg dug her blade deeper into the King's neck and breathed into his ear, 'Quiet now, my sweet. I can cut out your tongue and still keep you alive. For a while.'

'Trust not my words,' Will continued, his voice clear and strong. 'Seek out your court's wise adviser, Deortha, who is now incarcerated, upon your King's orders. Free him from his cell where he has been locked away along with the truth and listen to what he has to say. Then you will learn that we are not so different, Fay and men.'

Will turned to Jenny and drank in all the things he had missed, the sparkle in her dark eyes and the way her brow knitted as if she was always questioning, and the colour in her cheeks and her lips, in case this was their last moment. Gently, he cupped the back of her neck and pulled her to him. She showed no resistance. He closed his eyes. Their lips met and he felt a jolt run through him, and all the lost years melted away. Once again he was in Warwickshire with the sun on his shoulders and the future ahead of him. Blood throbbed through his head, driving out all thoughts. And when he opened his lids, he watched a light appear in her face as if she were waking from that dream. *All is illusion, and sometimes the truth is hidden*, he thought with a surge of pure joy, the first he had felt in many a year. *But it is here, now.*

Turning back to the ranks of glowering faces, he called, 'Our time here is done.' He bowed deeply, flinging out his left arm with a flourish. 'And so I bid you farewell.'

And with that, he pushed open the doors and led the others out into the dark alleys of a fortress teeming with the Enemy.

CHAPTER FIFTY-FOUR

TORCHES HISSED ON THE BLACK BASALT WALLS. IN AND OUT of swooping shadows, six figures ghosted along the narrow, labyrinthine ways, bundling a seventh. Darkness as thick and impenetrable as the grave shrouded the spaces in between the too-small pools of light. Will ran a hand through his sweat-soaked hair, wondering how long they had before their pursuers caught them.

At a crossing of the ways, the fleeing figures pressed back into an archway as two grey sentries marched past. Once they had gone, the spies slipped by, but at every turn more Fay drifted like ghosts emerging from churchyards at dusk. Will's chest tightened. It was only a matter of time until their escape route was discovered.

'Can you not use the mirror to predict where these foul things lie in wait?' Meg hissed as they huddled by a wall.

'Without Deortha's guidance it is useless to me,' he replied, 'but to keep it out of their control is victory in itself.' He squeezed Jenny's hand, never wanting to let it go, and she returned a wan smile, but the light of recognition gleamed in her eyes with increasing brilliance.

'You damn yourself with each step you take,' Mandraxas snarled. His head was pulled back, his long hair held in Launceston's fist, his throat bared for a simple, swift slash of a blade. 'Your agonies will be never-ending.'

'Keep a close eye on our guest,' Will warned the Earl. 'Given half a chance he will violate your wits with his whispered words and turn you upon yourself, or he will use his magics to leave you nothing but a straw man ripe for the harvest bonfire.'

It was then that he noticed Carpenter. The man was tearing and scratching at his face as if insects crawled there. 'John? Are you sick?'

'He is well enough,' Launceston cut in, too quickly. 'I will watch over him. Your task is to guide us safely through this hell. Or lead us to a quick death, at worst.'

Barely had the words left his lips when the funereal tolling of a bell tore through the hot dark once again. Will felt the hairs prickle on the back of his neck.

'The night unfolds and releases its terrors,' Mandraxas whispered with a low laugh. 'Run. Run.'

Across the City of Gold, they could hear the wind rising. In the high eaves and along the twisting alleyways it moaned. Doors crashed open. Feet pounded on stone. A high keening, of inhuman voices raised in anger, tugged at their ears.

'The sands have run out, my love,' Meg said with an edge to her voice. 'This is no time for caution.'

Urging the others to follow, Will broke into a run, following the directions Deortha had whispered in his head. But the alleyways twisted and turned in a confusing manner, and the dark lay heavy around them.

Running feet echoed on all sides. Will could feel the rising anxiety of his friends as the activity milled closer. But just as he feared the worst, he saw the landmark he had been searching for, a golden globe spinning with no visible means of support at the centre of a small courtyard. He ran forward, only to be confronted by a high, black, featureless wall. Despairing glances darted among the others as they realized they were trapped.

Footsteps and calls echoed all around. The Unseelie Court were drawing near.

'Why do you tarry?' Carpenter barked. 'Make haste before we are undone.'

Jenny squeezed Will's hand as he scanned the length of the wall. 'What is it you search for?' she asked.

'A door. Deortha told me our path of escape would begin here, at his chambers.'

'The sorcerer has betrayed us,' Launceston snarled, glancing back.

'Deortha keeps his secrets well,' Jenny said. 'With him, nothing ever lies in plain sight.'

Will weighed her words. After a moment he snatched a sizzling torch from the wall and reflected its ruddy light with the obsidian mirror. Lines of silver filigree glimmered on the basalt: stars, a moon, a sun, a host of magical symbols of the kind he had only ever seen before in Dee's shadowy chamber in the Black Gallery. And there, at the centre of them, the faint outline of an arched door shimmered. Handing the mirror and torch to Grace, Will pressed round the edge of the shape until he heard a click and the hidden door slid open.

The spies dragged their prisoner into the dark space. It

was not a moment too soon. The tumult crashed against the edge of the courtyard as the door whispered shut behind them. His hand trembling, his face pale, Carpenter levelled his rapier, ready to repel any who followed. Shrieks and cries rang through the stone wall, but after a moment they began to pass by. Carpenter exhaled, his shoulders sagging as his blade fell.

Will took the torch and held it high to reveal a flight of stone steps disappearing down into the dark. As they paused to catch their breath, Grace could contain herself no longer. She threw her arms round Jenny, burying her face in her sister's shoulder. Awkward and unsure, Jenny's hands wavered over the younger woman for a moment before she returned the embrace.

'Do you know me yet?' Grace said between juddering sobs. 'My heart will break if you remain a stranger. So long have I yearned for your return.'

Jenny held her sister's tear-streaked face between her hands and gazed into the young girl's eyes. Her brow cleared, and she smiled. 'I remember holding a little girl's hand as we searched for wild flowers in the wood. And telling stories under the covers when we were supposed to be asleep.' She stroked the centre of her forehead. 'I thought it a dream, insubstantial. But now I see you here, the visions grow clearer by the moment.'

As she pulled back, Grace bit her lip. 'I feared you dead. Oh, I lost faith, Jenny. Only Will . . .' She choked back the words. 'Will never lost his belief that you would return to us. Even in the darkest days, he kept a candle in his heart, and that in turn brought comfort to me.'

Jenny looked beyond her sister's shoulder to where Will

394

was beginning to descend the stone staircase. While Meg and Launceston pricked Mandraxas with their daggers to follow, Will sensed Jenny hurrying to catch him up. Looking back, he saw her glance at the Fay and whisper, 'I beg you not to hurt him.'

'He is our foe and I have reached agreement with Deortha to take his life in exchange for our freedom. Your freedom,' Will replied, ignoring a pang of jealousy.

'Whatever you might think of him, he has shown me many kindnesses during my long years in the City of Gold.' He felt her breath on his ear as they descended into the dark.

'You love him? Even though he stole you from all you knew?' he whispered, his voice sounding too harsh in the stillness.

'When I was first brought here, I cried every day. I cried for the man I had lost.' She swallowed and added quietly, 'And you?'

He nodded, feeling the rawness of the memory, even after all the time that had passed.

'But over the days and years, the life I had faded like a dream,' she continued. 'Soon this place, and Mandraxas, was all I knew. And he was gentle and caring, and he showed me love—'

'They are not capable of love,' Will interrupted, his voice hard. Moisture now glistened on the walls.

'They are,' she protested. 'They are no different from us.'

'And did you love *him*?' Will asked coldly. He paused, looking into her face. From further up the steps, he heard the shuffle of feet as Grace, the other spies and their prisoner descended cautiously.

'You must understand, it was all I knew—'

Will turned away and continued his descent, his expression unreadable. 'My plans for the King's future were made long ago. Nothing will alter them.' He increased his pace before she could protest.

The staircase opened out on to a long, low-ceilinged chamber barely lit by the glow of four candles arranged on the cardinal points of a circle inscribed on the dusty flagstones. Along the walls, a multitude of gilt-framed mirrors each as big as a man glittered in the reflected light. As Will stepped into the room, rapier drawn, shadowy figures formed in several of the mirrors, each one growing more distinct as if they were stepping out of a thick fog. He recognized several members of the Unseelie Court's High Family, including Malantha, seductive and cruel, the silver-haired Lethe, a grotesquely fat, bald Fay he had glimpsed in Paris the previous year, and others he did not know. Each seemed to be standing in a different chamber, at courts across the world, Will guessed, where they wove their manipulations of men. And among them stood Deortha, his eyes ringed with shadow, the bird and mice skulls braided into his hair trembling with each faint movement.

'What is this?' Carpenter muttered, shuddering. 'Are we betrayed?'

'I am sure the High Family care little for us at this moment,' Will murmured in reply. 'Greater matters must now occupy their minds.' He nodded to Meg and Launceston, and they forced Mandraxas to his knees in front of the mirrors. The Earl pressed the tip of his dagger against the nape of the King's neck.

'They are here to pass judgement,' Will said to Carpenter. And to witness an execution? He wondered how much

Deortha had told the other members of the High Family. He watched Jenny look along the row of Fay lords, her face cold, and knew there was no love lost there. She took Grace's hand in her own, perhaps an unconscious desire to protect her sister from these predators.

A faint click echoed from the shadows behind them, but as Will peered into the gloom Mandraxas turned his face towards his siblings and uttered, 'You will not judge me. I am King.'

'King.' Deortha shaped the word with cold precision. 'You keep the Golden Throne safe for our Queen at the pleasure of the High Family. It is a privilege.'

Mandraxas's brow knitted as he looked along the row of emotionless faces. Silence swaddled the chamber. After a moment, Will realized that the cold-faced Fay were communicating in some manner beyond speech. The King's features darkened, and he flashed a threatening look at Deortha before he glanced back at Will.

'I will not be *your* prisoner,' he said.

It was then that Carpenter cried out, stifling the sound with a trembling hand. Will turned to look at the man. It was not in his nature to be scared of any Fay, Will thought, not even one with the power of a King. Yet tears now streamed down the man's face, and his brow was beaded with sweat. Muttering under his breath, he lurched out of sight behind Will as the latter turned back to the mirrors.

Deortha's pale eyes shone like the moon, urging the spy to complete their agreement and take the King's life. Will felt Jenny's apprehensive gaze heavy upon him too.

With a hard smile, Mandraxas was saying, 'Nothing is left to chance.' As Will struggled to understand the context of the King's words, he glimpsed Meg's brows snapping together and heard Grace's startled gasp. Movement flashed on the edge of his vision.

Dagger drawn, Carpenter lunged. The blade shimmered as he thrust it towards Will's right eye.

CHAPTER FIFTY-FIVE

THE GLINTING STEEL FILLED WILL'S VISION. AND ONE THOUGHT seared: Carpenter's great betrayal had doomed them all. He jerked back in anticipation of the blade's sinking into his skull, just as he sensed a flurry of movement and a sudden impact. His attacker spun away. The deflected blade ripped through the flesh above his cheek and tore into his tangle of black hair. Blood dripped on to the flags.

In agony, he stumbled back, wiping at the burning wound with his sleeve. His gaze fell upon Carpenter, who was sprawled across the stone floor, pinned down by Launceston. 'Kill me,' Carpenter pleaded, staring into the aristocrat's pale, impassive face. 'Do it now, as you vowed.' When the Earl didn't respond, Carpenter blinked away tears and wailed, 'If you do not end my life, I will betray you again and again until I have slain you all. You will not leave this place.'

Will saw Meg hovering over Mandraxas with her dagger drawn, Grace and Jenny beside her, all of them gripped by Carpenter's plight. Blood trickled between his fingers. He saw the truth in the treacherous spy's words. Sooner or later,

Carpenter would attack them again. With a surge of bitter regret for the friend he once knew, he drew his own dagger from his boot.

As he levelled the blade, Launceston caught his wrist to block the strike. 'Let him live,' the Earl said, his voice quiet but his eyes flashing a warning.

'From his own mouth he has damned himself, Robert. We will never escape with a traitor in our midst.'

'He is no traitor.' The aristocrat pointed a wavering arm at the ghastly figures watching from the mirrors. 'They have infected him with their vile magics.'

'Is this true, John?' As he spoke, Will winced in pain from his wound.

'Some foul creature crawls inside my head,' Carpenter replied, his voice a ragged whine. 'It rides me like a Barbary mare, forcing me to do its bidding, and, God help me, I cannot resist. Whatever it demands, I must do – even murder my friends.' He screwed up his eyes to hide the tears of shame and regret.

'It seems our King has long since set his own schemes in motion,' came Deortha's voice. 'The Caraprix can only work its spell when it has been accepted freely.'

'They tricked me,' Carpenter raged. His voice caught and he choked, 'I am too weak. I wanted an escape from this life. I should have resisted.'

Will sighed. More than anyone he understood the manipulations of the Unseelie Court. 'Robert, the outcome is still the same. John cannot be trusted. We cannot take him with us.'

'No,' the Earl spat, his face alight with a rare show of passion. 'I will be his keeper.'

'That burden may be too great, even for you, Robert.'

'I will watch him like a hawk, and whenever that enchantment drives him to commit traitorous acts I will be there,' Launceston said, his grey, blank eyes fixed on Will.

'Take my life, I implore you,' Carpenter begged again, his voice cracking. 'I cannot bear to live this way, with a life that is not my own.'

The Earl peered into his friend's tear-flecked eyes for a long moment. Will wondered what thoughts turned in that unreadable mind. He could barely hear when Launceston spoke. 'You have saved me. I will save you. I can do no less.' Turning back to Will, he added, 'This is my burden now, for all our days if necessary. I am prepared. You must trust me.'

Will watched Carpenter in his torments and nodded. 'You are a good man, Robert, for all your weaknesses.'

A sharp cry of pain echoed across the chamber. Will whirled round. He was a fool; he had allowed himself to be distracted for too long. Mandraxas had made his move and taken Meg by surprise, knocking the dagger from her grasp, and now his long fingers were clamped around her wrist. One touch, no more. But it was enough. The Irish woman's face had drained of blood. Where the King's hand gripped, her skin was marbling. Mandraxas smiled in triumph at Will, knowing he could never reach him before the graven transformation had spread to the point of death.

Will drew his sword as the beautiful Irish spy swooned. Yet he had barely moved when shock flared in the King's face. Meg tumbled from his grasp. The Fay King staggered back, grasping at the dagger embedded in his thigh.

Ashen-faced, Jenny stepped back, her hand shaking.

Mandraxas stared at her, a look of such sadness and disbelief that it could only have come from a broken heart.

When Will reached him, the King had barely moved, seemingly drained of all resistance by his love's blow. One clout from the hilt of the spy's rapier and he fell to his knees once more. 'Stay back,' Will warned Meg, who had staggered to her feet, shaking her head as she fought to gather her thoughts and rubbing furiously at the skin on her arm. 'He is mine and mine alone.'

Yet the Fay's gaze remained fixed on Jenny, weighted with infinite grief. Will hated what he saw there. He thought of Mandraxas and Jenny's long years as consorts, of caresses and shared moments, of gentleness and intimacy and joy. And love. How much easier it had been when he had thought his love simply stolen. What a stew of confused emotion this was; how bitter it tasted. His sword at the ready, he circled the stricken King, imagining what it would feel like to skewer the one who had torn the heart out of his life so long ago. In his mind's eye, he saw the gout of blood and the death-rictus on Mandraxas's face. Hatred seared his chest. He wanted vengeance.

Around them, the chamber had grown silent. He could feel Deortha's gaze upon him, willing him to complete their pact: execute the King who had betrayed his own people, for power, yes, but for love too.

'Deortha. Once the deed is done, I would not wish to tarry here. Which way?' Will called, his eyes not leaving the Fay King.

'On the far side of the chamber there is a door,' the sorcerer replied, triumph creeping into his voice.

Will's hand shook. The tip of his rapier nicked the

King's flesh. For a moment, simmering rage hardened his face and then he sucked in a deep breath and calmed himself. Jenny turned away, sickened by what she feared was to come.

'You can keep your worthless life,' Will growled, putting up his sword. Mandraxas twitched. Incomprehension crossed his pale, refined features. From the corner of his eye, the spy glimpsed cold rage beginning to glow in Deortha's face. 'I am not you,' he continued. A deep calm settled over him, and his sombre words were tinged with sadness. 'Nor am I the man that others think me. Not England's greatest spy, nor the rake driven solely by selfish urges. The truth is harder to define, even for me. More than anything under Heaven, I want my revenge for what you did. But that would sacrifice all men and women to the righteous fury of the Unseelie Court, and even as cold-hearted a knave as I could not plumb those depths. And yet . . .' He waved his index finger in the air. 'And yet . . . I saw an opportunity here for a clever man . . . or a reckless gambler, one or t'other.'

'And you were always both,' he heard Meg whisper.

Still clutching at the wound in his thigh, Mandraxas looked bemused. Will turned to Jenny, his voice growing more intense. 'A slim chance to achieve the two ends to which I have dedicated my life – to save you and to deal the Unseelie Court a crushing blow that might set them back years, if not for ever.' He took a deep, juddering breath and smiled at his love. Returning his attention to the Fay, he raised the tip of his sword and held it against the King's chest. 'If you are allowed to live and return to your people, the Unseelie Court will be riven by strife as factions battle for supremacy. Those who support you, and those, like Deortha, who wish to see the return of their true Queen. For how long?' He shrugged. 'For those such as you for whom time is meaningless, it may well be an eternity. Divided, you would have little time for your war against men.'

'You are mistaken,' Will heard Launceston's hushed voice. 'You are indeed England's greatest spy.'

Her eyes sparkling, Meg beamed. 'You might well have ended this war we all thought would last for ever.'

Will held up a bloodstained hand, hardly daring to believe it himself. He looked round. Jenny and Grace were both smiling in disbelief, tears of relief glistening in their eyes. Jenny mouthed, 'Thank you.' He refused to consider why she was thanking him. There would be time for that conversation later.

Fury finally ignited in Deortha's face. 'Lies and deceit. I should have expected no better from a man.'

'True,' Will replied with a shrug. 'We are worse than beasts in the field.'

'Have you no honour?'

Placing a finger on his chin, Will feigned a moment of reflection. 'Honour? What is honour? Does it buy me good sack in the Mermaid? I have saved my love and ended a war. I leave honour for better men than I. I am happy to remain a bastard.'

Deortha's snarl echoed across the chamber until it was drowned by Mandraxas's laughter. He stood, pushing away the tip of Will's rapier with a slender finger. 'So you refuse to kill. And yet on that hot night soon after I took from you the thing you valued most, I saw you slay an innocent man.'

Will felt the eyes of all there fall upon him. His breath caught in his chest as years of self-loathing bubbled up. Finally he nodded. ''Tis true, though I have never spoken of it to anyone.' He glanced at Grace, noting the lines of worry in her face, and sighed. Bowing his head, he confessed, 'When Jenny disappeared that afternoon, I barely held on to my wits. I searched every byway around Arden and in the depths of night came across a man struggling with Jenny beside a hedgerow. Blinded by fury, I leapt from my horse and beat him to death with my fists.' His head flooded with the sensations of bones breaking under his knuckles and blood flowing over his fingers. He felt the weight in his heart that he had carried since that night.

'But when he lay lifeless at my feet and I turned to embrace Jenny, I saw it was not her,' he continued. 'It was one of the silly village girls, known for her easy ways. The man was a footpad, so not a good man, and the girl was grateful that I had saved her from the fate he had intended.' He swallowed. 'But in truth, yes, I had killed an innocent man.' He looked to Grace, expecting accusation or disgust, but he saw only pity. 'That night when you came to me at the well I was washing the blood from my hands, though I could never clean the stains from my mortal soul. That night . . . the course of my life changed. I learned that I am not a good man. And though I have tried to make amends for my crime, I know I never will.'

Grace ran to his side. 'It is not true. You are a good man and you have proved it time and again.'

Mandraxas gave a cold laugh at the subtle blow he had struck. But as his amusement drained away, he pointed a threatening finger at Will. 'You think yourself clever, but the schemes of mortals rarely turn out as planned. And I have nothing but time to take the prize.' He glanced at Jenny, but turned away quickly so Will could not see his expression. Then he grasped the hilt of the knife in his thigh, and, with a grimace, slowly withdrew it. Tearing off a strip of cloth from the hem of his cloak, he began to bind the wound. Jenny hesitated, glancing at Will, and when he nodded she hurried to help the one who had been her consort for so long. The Fay King watched her as she tenderly tied the cloth round his thigh, but if he felt anything it did not show on his face. When she had finished, Mandraxas muttered something that Will could not hear, and then turned quickly and limped towards the stone steps leading out of the chamber of mirrors.

As if in a trance, Will watched him go, still barely believing that he had plucked some kind of victory from the direst of situations. Once the King moved into the penumbra beyond the circle of candlelight, he turned, beckoning the others to follow him. 'Come, my friends, we must make haste,' he said.

Yet barely had he taken a step when a sharp gasp brought him to a halt. He spun round to see Mandraxas staggering back down the steps, one hand clutched at his chest as blood fountained between his fingers. Will gaped in shock. The King half turned, his yearning gaze finding Jenny for one moment, and then he fell to the flagstones, dead. Jenny rushed to him with a cry of despair.

In his mirror, Deortha was smiling.

'What is this treachery?' Launceston said, menace curdling his voice.

A figure stepped out of the shadows from the foot of the stairs, holding a blade that dripped gore. It was Strangewayes. The red-headed spy looked across at his companions with a cold face and said, 'The only treachery here is yours. And now there is an end to it.'

CHAPTER FIFTY-SIX

'OH, TOBIAS, WHAT HAVE YOU DONE?' GRACE CRIED WITH A sob, running to where Jenny knelt by Mandraxas's lifeless body.

Strangewayes stepped over the King and swaggered towards the guttering candles. He pointed his rapier towards Will. 'You, sirrah, should not have ignored me when there was an opportunity to prevent this outcome,' he said in an icy voice. 'Too long have you placed Grace's life at risk with your reckless behaviour. But no more.' He beckoned to Grace to join him. 'Come – I will take you away from here.'

Dismay spreading across her face, the young woman shook her head slowly, taking a step back.

'Come to me,' Strangewayes snapped. 'I am here to make you safe.'

'No, Tobias, not safe,' she said in a small voice, 'for you have doomed us all.'

Stung, Strangewayes glared at Will. 'She is still under your spell, I see, but soon she will learn.'

'You know not what you have done,' Will began, his

voice hushed. He shook his head, appalled, then let the words drain away. 'We thought you dead.'

'You wished me so.'

'Never, Tobias—'

'I have saved Grace. From you.' The young man's gaze skittered towards Deortha, and in the look that the two exchanged Will glimpsed the truth. It must have happened when Strangewayes was taken prisoner at the fortress gates. The scheming sorcerer had seen an opportunity to use the pitiful spy in case Will should fail to kill Mandraxas. He cursed himself for a fool. If only he had heeded the click of the door opening into that chamber before Carpenter's attack.

'Whatever the conjurer has promised you, it is a lie—' he began.

'Quiet,' Strangewayes roared. He wiped the sweat from his brow with a trembling hand. Will saw only a boy, reeling from events far beyond his ability to deal with them. 'The King is dead,' the red-headed spy said to Deortha. 'I have done all you wished. Now let me take Grace away from here.'

In the strange mirror, they saw the sorcerer steeple his fingers, thin lips twitching. 'Ah, but the terms of our agreement have been breached.'

Strangewayes gaped. 'What is this trickery?'

'Unless you reached another deal with this devil,' Will said, 'the agreement was free passage if I killed the King. I did not.'

'You fool,' Carpenter roared suddenly, turning his hopelessness into rage. Pushing Launceston to one side, he snatched out his rapier. 'We were free. And now you . . . you . . . have doomed your girl as surely as if you wielded the dagger yourself.'

'No,' Strangewayes croaked, his face pale with disbelief. 'I saved her.' He looked to Grace for support, for her to confirm that what he said was true, but found only dismay and disillusion. He sagged, his rapier loose in his hand. A last drop of the King's blood fell from the tip, colouring the stone slab.

'The traitor has been deposed.' In a triumphant tone, Deortha addressed the other Fay in their ethereal mirrors. 'Though the passing of a brother is a time of sorrow for the High Family, now we may achieve what we have desired for so long, the return of our true Queen. Let our vengeance rain down on the world of men. Bring fire, and blood. Cleanse this world of the corruption of man, and bring our Queen home.'

One by one the mirrors misted as the Fay of the High Family departed until only Deortha remained. Will felt chilled. Only horrors beyond imagining lay ahead. Realizing what he had done, Strangewayes dropped his rapier with a clatter. He held Grace's gaze for a moment, perhaps hoping for forgiveness, and when he saw none he turned and ran into the shadows.

'Tobias, come with us,' Grace called after him, but Will caught her arm.

'You cannot save him, and you will only condemn yourself,' he said, wincing at the hurt he saw in her face. But she stifled her grief and nodded, allowing herself one last glance into the gloom as she went to her quietly sobbing sister where she knelt beside Mandraxas's body.

From his mirror, Deortha levelled his gaze at Will. The spy saw no triumph there, no contempt, not even superiority, only the icy satisfaction of a long-gestating plan finally come to fruition. Breaking the stare, Will looked from Meg to Launceston and Carpenter and nodded. The silent communication was more than enough and his three colleagues went in search of the door out of the chamber.

Will hurried to the two sisters. 'Jenny, I am sorry. Truly I am,' he said, his voice gentle. She looked at him. Her face was unreadable – pale, tear-stained. 'And for you, Grace. But we must all grieve later.' He swept his left arm out to direct them to the end of the chamber. Grace ran ahead, but Jenny turned back and pressed her lips close to Will's ear. 'I remember . . .' she breathed, and paused. 'I remember a kiss. Under the great oak on an autumn evening when the leaves were turning gold. Our first kiss.' And in her eyes he saw the Jenny he knew. She hurried after her sister before he could respond.

Carpenter and Launceston waited either side of a low, arched door. In a tunnel beyond, Meg had found and lit a torch and was beckoning to Grace and Jenny to join her. Will saw unease in the Irish woman's stare. So close to victory they had been, and now they could all feel the winter chill of impending doom enveloping them, he thought bitterly.

He turned to Carpenter, but before he could speak the other man snapped, 'No pity. For now, I have my own wits about me.'

'Good. Then it is like old times, John.' Will touched his torn cheek before clapping a friendly hand on Carpenter's shoulder. He flashed a searching glance at Launceston, who gave a curt nod of reassurance. Ahead, the golden glow of

Meg's torch washed across the glistening stone walls, and the three men plunged into the gloom in pursuit.

As they scrambled along the low-ceilinged tunnel, they could hear the dull tolling of the alarm bell reverberating ever more clearly, each throb seeming to match the beat of their hearts. Torchlight flickered across faces struggling to contain hopelessness and dread.

'Why run when those bastards know which path we take?' Carpenter growled. 'They will never let us leave. We are already dead.'

'It is the only way out of here,' Will replied. 'And we died a long time ago — the moment we set foot in this cursed place. Every breath we take now is a boon.' Visions of Unseelie Court galleons sweeping out from the New World flooded his mind, each one filled with more horror than any man could bear.

'And if we escape,' Carpenter continued bitterly as if he could read Will's mind, 'what do we escape to? An England made Hell? Better we die here.'

Will stopped suddenly, catching the other man's arm as he turned. 'Is this the John Carpenter who fought his way out of Muscovy alone, after I had abandoned him to a fate worse than death? In all our time in service to the Queen, we have never given up, though we faced overwhelming odds. Even if all the Unseelie Court and their night-terrors snap at our heels, we fight on, until the last drop of blood flows from our bodies and our rapiers fall from our dying hands.'

At first Carpenter would not meet Will's eyes. But then he nodded in apology. 'Aye, Will, let us die as we have lived. For the Queen, for England. Let those pale bastards come and we shall see how many I send to Hell afore me.'

Will nodded in approval. As he turned to continue along the cramped tunnel, Meg called back, 'I see light ahead.'

Moments later, they stepped out on to a wide stone balcony protruding from a sheer cliff face towering above their heads. Will saw it was a lush garden of some kind, with creepers, shrubs and blooms in sickeningly unnatural blues, blacks and purples clustering around the low enclosing wall. He forced his way through the vegetation to the edge and peered over. A series of further gardens cascaded down the cliff into the mist far below. In the distance, he could just discern a black basalt tower thrusting up from the dense forest with a glowing orb on top of it. It could only be the Tower of the Moon, the beacon that kept open the way between worlds.

As he turned back, he saw the others looking up to the sky. It could have been on fire. Flames rolled out across the arc of the heavens, the horizon burning a deep shade of crimson. Silhouetted against it, Manoa, the Unseelie Court's City of Gold, seemed to transform. Will blinked, attempting to comprehend what he was seeing. For a moment, the fortress appeared to be surrounded by massive, circling, grinding rings of iron. Was this the true form of that foul place, he wondered, as the Fay hid their own ghastly appearance behind illusions of beauty?

All life is illusion, Dee had said. If that was so, what could they truly believe?

As the tolling of the bell boomed out into the burning sky, shapes flooded out of the fortress and began to descend the cliff. Realization dawned on Will, and he yelled, 'The Hunters are coming. We must flee. Now.'

Yet even as they raced to the edge of the balcony and

searched for a way down, another noise tore through the hot, still air. Will frowned, trying to place the origin of that teeth-jarring whistle. And then he had it: it was the sound made by the black stone Mandraxas had whirled around his head in order to summon those flesh-eating predators, the Spree-birds.

Barely had the thought come to him before a black cloud swept out of the fortress. It circled for one moment and then swooped down. The air was torn by the thunder of a multitude of wings, and a shrieking as if Hell had given up its lost souls.

CHAPTER FIFTY-SEVEN

THE SEETHING, ROILING MASS BLOTTED OUT THE FIERY SKY above Manoa. Like a tropical storm the Spree-birds swirled, their shrill shrieks tearing across the treetops. Will glanced from the avian predators to the Hunters swarming down the cliff face, like angry ants spilling out of a disturbed nest. He breathed in the acrid stink of burning and heard Grace's whispered prayer caught on the wind. Taut faces turned towards him; only Launceston seemed unruffled.

But then, when all hope seemed to have departed, he felt a surprising calm descend upon him. He ran back to the dense vegetation edging the spacious stone balcony, ignoring all the sounds of Hell, the cries of the blood-crazed birds and the grim tolling of the bell and the grinding of revolving iron, and studied the strange blooms and dry, thorny bushes.

'Our steel will be of no use against those birds.' Meg's voice was ragged. The others stood beside her. 'And we cannot outrun them. They will have the flesh from our bones in no time.'

'We could hide in the tunnel,' Grace ventured.

'Of what use is that?' Carpenter turned his back to them, watching the skies as the black cloud wheeled above them. 'They will come for us soon enough. No, better to make our stand here, and die like men.'

'We are not finished yet, John,' Will said as he plunged into the vegetation and bounded on to the stone wall edging the balcony. Balancing on his precarious perch, he snatched up a handful of trailing creeper and pulled hard, testing its strength. With a satisfied nod, he said, 'Quick, now. Take these and climb down to the garden below. If fortune is with us, we can make our way down to the ground.' They thought it a futile gesture, he saw in their faces, but they trusted him enough to comply.

Grasping a vine, Carpenter went first, seemingly uncaring if it snapped and he plunged to his death. Meg handed Will her brand and blew him a kiss as she followed with Launceston beside her. Grace and Jenny looked down at the three spies suspended in the gulf above the next balcony and then exchanged a reassuring smile. Will bowed, holding Jenny's gaze for one moment before the two sisters disappeared from view.

A shadow engulfed the balcony.

The shrieks of the Spree-birds rang in his ears, and he knew if he looked up he would see their skull-heads and cruel beaks still stained with the blood of Sanburne and his men. Will thrust the torch into the vegetation and the tinder-dry bushes caught alight. The thrashing of wings stirred his hair as the vermilion flames roared up. He grabbed a vine and threw himself back over the low enclosure.

Only then did he look up. A wall of fire raced around the edge of the balcony. Black smoke billowed into the dense flock of birds so that it seemed like night. As Will had hoped, the heat drove the vicious creatures back. They screeched around in circles above the balcony, frustrated that their prey had been denied them. He squinted, peering through the cloud at the Hunters still far behind, climbing down the sheer cliff.

Some of the flock spotted Will lowering himself down the creeper and swooped past the crackling bushes and shrubs. Coiling the vine round one arm, he wrenched out his rapier and lashed the air. A burst of black feathers and a spray of blood trailed in the sweep of his blade. The skull-headed birds wheeled around him, searching for an opening. As he ripped through two more, the other Spree-birds swept in. Beaks like fine Spanish steel stabbed into his flesh, staining his undershirt brown with his blood. Pain seared through him, but still he struck out.

The creeper jerked in his grasp, and when he glanced up he saw flames licking at the top of it. A moment later, the vine snapped. Will hurtled down, slamming into the hard, dry soil of the garden below. Winded, he watched the Spree-birds circle before swooping down towards him.

Flashing steel glinted in the ruddy light above him. Carpenter, Launceston and Red Meg hacked and slashed, blood and feathers spraying across the vegetation. Will scrambled to his feet and looked up at the chaos overhead. Driven back by the heat and confused by the billowing black smoke, most of the Spree-birds had turned on the Hunters, tearing them apart as they crawled down the cliff face. But it was only a momentary respite, Will knew. There were too many of the Fay stalkers, and they were too relentless, too brutal.

All around the dry vegetation was burning, set alight by smouldering vines falling from above. Ordering the others over the side once more, he followed them down, swinging and falling to each new level of the hanging gardens, until their joints burned and their chests were seared from the exertion. And the flames leapt up the cascading balconies, the pall of smoke obscuring the Unseelie Court's grim fortress.

A sea of grey mist washed over the treetops below the final garden. The drop here was the longest. Will clambered down the vines first, letting the last of them slip through his fingers long before he could see the ground. Branches battered his body as he fell. He hit the softy, loamy soil of the forest floor, rolled and sprang to his feet. Every muscle burned. The others rained down around him in a shower of shattered branch and twig and leaf. Once they were sure no bones had been broken, they stopped and listened.

An eerie silence lay beneath the protective blanket of mist. Taking a deep draught of the hot, humid air, Will advanced with slow, careful steps, blade at the ready. A high stone wall stretching deep into the forest on either side appeared out of the folds of grey. An arched opening loomed ahead of them.

'This has to be the labyrinth that leads to the outside world,' Jenny whispered at Will's side. 'I heard Mandraxas tell of it. Many have been driven mad when they became lost in its depths as they sought to reach the riches of the City of Gold or flee the horrors they found there.'

As he looked around them, Will allowed himself a tight smile. The message in the captain's journal on the abandoned Spanish galleon now made perfect sense. He reached into the battered leather pouch at his side and pulled out the torn page, reading again those scrawled words: *Twice stare into the devil's face, then bow all heads to God. Thrice more the unholy must call. Again, again, again until the end.*

'Two left turns, then a right, then three left turns. Count carefully: this sequence must be repeated until we reach the other side.'

The sound of crashing from above reached them through the mist. He guessed the Hunters were dropping from the cliff face into the treetops. Beckoning to the others, he hurried through the arched door. It was cooler in the deep shadow of the high stone walls, and the six fugitives seemed to shudder as one. The way was narrow, barely more than a sword-length between the lichen-crusted walls.

'At least there is only space for those fiends to come at us one at a time,' Carpenter growled as he ran.

'Stay close, and watch your backs,' Will called. At each junction, he mouthed the count to himself, and so they twisted and turned deeper into the heart of the labyrinth.

Soon the thump of feet on hard-packed earth rang off the walls. Their pursuers were closing fast. Will beckoned for Meg to join him, and slowed to whisper in her ear, 'Lead Jenny and Grace ahead. And I beg of you, do not stop, whatever sounds you hear behind you.'

'I am as good with a blade as any man,' she replied, her green eyes flashing. 'Better. You know that.'

'I do, which is why I entrust such valuable lives to your care.'

The beautiful woman's features softened. 'Very well. But do not risk that handsome neck, my love. I still have plans to win your heart.' Blowing him a silent kiss she waved the two other women ahead. Once they had disappeared along a branching path, Will said, 'We take turns to hold the rear. When we tire, we make way for a fresh arm, yes?' The other two spies nodded, their faces grim.

The footsteps at their backs now echoed with the relentless rhythm of driving rain on wood. Steel scraped on stone. Will wiped a trickle of blood from his nose, trying to imagine how many were in pursuit. After a moment, he pushed the thought aside. It was not good to dwell upon such things.

Left, left, right, left, left, left. The high stone walls sped by in a monotonous blur. Will found it impossible to tell if they were close to exiting the labyrinth or still meandering in the centre.

The feeling of iron nails rattling in his skull alerted him a moment before Launceston's hissed warning. Glancing back, he glimpsed a bloodless face floating in the gloom. The unflinching gaze fell upon him. Out of the murk, the Hunter bounded like a wolf, silver hair streaming behind him. His hollow chest was bare, with leather belts strapped across it, his breeches grey and loam-stained. Clutched in the long, thin fingers of his right hand was a glinting sickle. Other shadowy figures loped behind.

Will's chest burned as he stepped up his pace. Snatched looks caught flashes of steel and bared teeth, and the ghastly figure looming closer with each step. Launceston held the rear, seemingly oblivious of the thing drawing close to his back. When the sickle swung towards his neck, the aristocrat ducked at the last moment. As the curved blade whistled over his head, he half spun and plunged his sword into the Hunter's right eye socket. The Fay spun backwards in silence, trailing a stream of bloody liquor. His fallen corpse slowed the progress of the pursuers behind, but it would not be for long, Will knew.

Within moments, Launceston had slashed his blade across another face before allowing Carpenter to drop back and impale a third Hunter upon his rapier. Blood spattered from wounds on both spies.

When Carpenter had despatched another, Will moved swiftly to the rear. A wall of snarling faces hovered before him as the predators pressed forward, sheer weight of numbers eliminating the advantage the three spies had maintained in the cramped space. Gritting his teeth, he whirled his rapier back and forth, peeling open white flesh in an arc. Bodies fell with each thrust, but the Hunters cared little about their own lives, he saw.

For a moment his vision swam with those hideous faces. As the stink of their meaty breath washed over him, he knew his time was done. Determined that he would not go down to Hell alone, he snatched one final thrust with his blade, then waited for the wave to break upon him.

Instead, he felt a hand grab his shirt and pull him back so hard his feet left the ground.

Will lay sprawled across the hard earth. Shafts of sunlight punched through a canopy of leaves rustling high overhead. Lurching to his feet, he saw it was Carpenter who had dragged him from certain death, for that moment at least. He was out of the labyrinth in a clearing in the dense forest. Grace, Jenny and Meg huddled together at the edge of the trees. Launceston waited nearby, his rapier point dripping gore.

Anger born of desperation surged inside him. Why were

they not running? But then he followed their gaze, and turned to face a vast arc of Hunters, a grey army, with more still flooding out from the labyrinth. Silently, they waited, a thunderstorm about to break. All hope was gone. Now there was only time for dying.

CHAPTER FIFTY-EIGHT

'STAY YOUR GROUND. I AM YOUR QUEEN.' JENNY'S VOICE
rang out across the still clearing, suddenly imperious,
commanding. Holding her head high, she broke away from
the others and strode out from the shadows to face the line
of waiting Hunters. Will's chest tightened. He watched the
Fay, wondering if they would heed her words or fall upon
her first. In their cruel white faces, their eyes looked like
chunks of coal.

After a moment, he realized they were not going to
attack, but nor were they retreating. 'Jenny,' he whispered,
his voice hoarse, 'take no risks, I beg you.'

When she turned her face towards him, he almost cried
out at the sadness he saw there. She forced a smile. 'There is
no risk here, my love. They will not harm their Queen. As
long as I remain their Queen, upon the soil they call their
own.'

Will felt a chill run through him as the meaning of her
words slowly settled on him. 'No,' he whispered. 'You
cannot . . . I will not allow it.'

'We were lost the moment your fellow slew Mandraxas,'

she said in a soft, desolate voice, still smiling in an attempt to soften his pain.

'There is another way,' he protested. 'There must be.'

Jenny – his Jenny – shook her head, glancing back at the cold ranks of the Fay. 'If I walk with you into the human world, I abdicate the throne and they will destroy us in an instant. All of us, doomed. If I return, at least I can ensure you leave with your life. All of you.' Her voice rose and she looked at Grace. 'Including my sister, whom I treasure more than life itself,' adding so quietly he could barely hear it, 'as I treasure you.'

'I will not allow this sacrifice,' Will protested, clenching a fist impotently.

'Ah, but it is not for you to say.' She swallowed. 'There is more at stake here than you and I. We are as nothing compared to the devastation that would be wrought on all men by an Unseelie Court bent on avenging that which you – we – have meted out to their true Queen, and now their King.'

'Then let all the world be damned,' he uttered, his voice breaking. 'If I could walk away with you, I could live with the world burning around us.'

'No,' she interjected quietly, 'you could not.'

'I would sacrifice anything for one more day with you.'

'No,' Jenny repeated, 'you would not, though your heart were shattered into a thousand pieces. I saw inside you on that very first day we walked together, Will Swyfte. I know your true worth, perhaps more than any other person you call friend or lover. I see how the suffering of your last few years has formed a callus around you, but the good man within remains unchanged.'

'You cannot return,' Will whispered, his despair growing, 'not now that I have found you again.'

Jenny took his blood-encrusted hand in her cool fingers. 'And I have found you again,' she murmured. 'I remember everything. I feel all that I felt on that day I was stolen from you. If there was some way we could be together I would seize it with both hands. But Mandraxas's death could unleash a hell upon earth. If I can prevent that, I will.'

'You truly think the Fay will obey a mortal?'

'They must. I am their Queen.'

'And how long before you meet the same fate as Mandraxas? A dagger in the night? Poison?' Will felt his eyes sting with tears.

'I am no weak child. I will keep my wits about me at all times, and watch the shadows, and find allies, and plot and scheme as befits a true monarch,' his lost love said, narrowing her eyes. When he saw the defiance in her face, Will recognized a steel he had not encountered before. 'And I will keep heads spinning, and encourage factions and machinations and ruses so that the Unseelie Court will have no time to look out into the world of men, for they will be consumed by themselves.'

'How long, Jenny?' He felt hollow, numb.

She blanched, but kept a brave face. 'As long as I can.'

'I will not allow this,' he cried, snatching up his rapier from where it had fallen. Anger and despair roared through him. He only had eyes for the cursed Fay, who still had their talons embedded in the one thing he valued. As he lunged towards them, Launceston and Carpenter grabbed his arms and struggled to hold him back.

'Would you rather we all died here and now?' the Earl whispered. 'What good would that do?'

'Listen to her, Will,' Carpenter added with surprising tenderness. 'Her heart is breaking, but she does this for a greater good. She shames us all with her strength.'

Still struggling, Will blinked away hot tears of anguish until Grace stepped in front of him and held his face in her hands. She leaned in, filling his vision and holding his attention. Tears streamed down her cheeks too. 'No one wants Jenny home more than I,' she whispered, 'not even you. And it will destroy me by degrees to know she is a prisoner in this land of horrors. Though it is terrible to us both, you know in your heart that what my sister suggests is the right course. Think of the lives that will be saved, Will. Jenny is right – all of us mean nothing compared to that.'

'And you can live with that?' he snapped.

'As I have for these last fifteen years. But now I know that she still lives, though we are separated by oceans, by worlds, by time itself. I know! And I will carry her in my heart for as long as I live, and never lose hope that one day we will brave the terrors of this place once more and bring her back to where she is loved and cherished. We will bring her home, I promise.' She sucked in a deep breath to stifle a sob. 'You must let her go, Will.'

He steadied himself, wondering how it could be that these two women were stronger than all of them. Running a hand through his hair, he nodded and moved to stand in front of Jenny. It felt as if sadness must fill every part of her, but still she smiled, for his sake, and that broke his heart. 'It seems you have won this battle of wits,' he said, grinning, for her sake.

Her eyes sparkled as she held his gaze for a long moment. No words were necessary. Then slowly her face hardened with the weight of her responsibility. She glanced up to the heavens. 'You know what you must do.'

His chest tightened. He understood; it was what he had long planned. But with all of them free and sailing home to England; never like this. 'No,' he said, 'I cannot. Leaving you behind is torment enough.'

'If we are meant to be together, Will Swyfte, we will find a way.'

It felt too final, as if he were consigning her to the cold earth, but he knew she would never change her mind. 'No ocean is too wide, no walls too strong, no danger too great. I will be back for you, Jenny.' With trembling fingers, he felt under his shirt for the locket he had worn against his skin since Deortha had first dropped it in order to lure him here. Removing it, he gently fastened it round her slim neck, as he had done that day when they had sealed their love so long ago. 'Wear this as I wore it: to remind you never to lose hope. Cradle it in your hands every night and know that I will be searching for a way back to you. Know that one day we will be together again.'

Her eyes glistened. Bowing, he took her hand and kissed the back of it. When he raised his head, they held each other's gaze as they struggled to suppress all the hurt and the yearning, and then he took a step back and nodded. 'Soon,' he said.

'Soon,' she replied. She closed her eyes for a moment, and slowly her face transformed into that of a ruler, a Queen. Then she turned away from Will, from her sister, from Meg, Carpenter and Launceston, and walked back towards the labyrinth. Heads bowed in deference, the Hunters parted to let her through, and then turned to follow her. Will watched until he could see her no more.

When Grace reached out a hand to comfort him, he shook his head. 'We are done here,' he said, each word rolling out like a pebble falling upon wood. 'But this is not yet over.' Taking his bearings, he ignored the questioning gazes and moved to the trees. Looking up, he caught a glimpse of their destination through a gap in the canopy, and broke into a run. By force of will, he drove all his churning emotions deep inside him. Completing the task he'd set himself was now his sole aim. A memorial to Jenny.

The Tower of the Moon soared up through the trees, a cold sliver of grey stone with a bright white light burning at the summit. At its base, he halted to catch his breath and waited for the others. Meg was the first to arrive. 'Whatever plan has gripped you, take care. I fear for you.' Her voice was warm with concern.

'You worry needlessly,' he replied, his face betraying no emotion. 'Stay here and ensure our Enemy does not have a change of heart.'

'Where do you go?'

In reply, he simply raised his hand and pointed to the top of the tower high overhead.

Before the others had caught up and could question him further, he began to circle the base of the structure. As far as he could tell, there was no entrance. Only a series of stone footholds barely a finger's length wide protruded from the walls, spiralling up towards the top. Setting down his rapier, he took off his boots to get a better grip and hauled himself on to the lowest step. Pressing himself tight against the wall, he felt for small clefts that seemed to have been made as fingerholds. The others called out, urging him not to risk such a precarious climb, but his head felt numb and their words faded away. Gingerly, he shifted his weight from one step to the next, and then the next.

As he clawed his way around the tower, his nose wrinkled at the smell of the warm stone against his cheek, and the wet-wood aromas of the forest, and the hint of brine on the breeze blowing in from the coast. Sweat slicked his body in the day's heat. He balanced on the precarious footholds, clutching on to the wall until his finger joints screamed with pain. When he sensed the quality of light change as he rose above the treetops, the bird-cries rang in his ears as the shadows swooped across him.

And higher still he climbed, into a world of grey stone, blue sky and golden sunlight. He felt the suck of the dizzying drop as the wind tugged at his limbs, and the queasy twist in the pit of his stomach, but not for a moment did he look down. His legs and arms shook. The slightest misstep would send him plunging to his death. But then a soft white glow enveloped him and he realized he was nearing the summit.

A moment later he hauled himself over the edge, and rolled on to his back, filling his tight chest with clear, sweet and untainted air. He blinked, unable to see the sky any more for the moonlike luminescence. Yet it was not a harsh light; he felt as though he was swathed in down. Something about this strange light reached inside him and plucked at his grief, and for a moment he felt overwhelmed by the sense of loss and despair. He shook himself, gritted his teeth and clambered to his feet. He would not give in.

The top of the tower was flat and fixed upon it was an

iron plinth topped by a blue-green copper bowl. In it, what seemed like a glass sphere the distance of fingertip to elbow in diameter floated an inch above the surface, turning slowly. It was from this that the white light washed out.

Will leaned over it, studying the gently pulsing light, but as he reached a hand across the bowl the light wavered, then dimmed. Now was the moment. Steeling himself, he gripped the glass globe between his hands. His skin tingled at its strange, almost living flesh-like warmth. One act to change the world, he thought. One act to save England. One act to break his heart.

And he wrenched the sphere away from the bowl in a fizz of golden sparks and in a single movement hurled it over the edge of the tower. The soothing, pale light swept down in the globe's wake and he was left with a view across that verdant corner of the New World and the shadowy world beyond. A veil appeared to be hanging above the labyrinth from horizon to horizon. Through the shimmering haze, he could just discern the black bulk of Manoa, still turning against a fiery sky, but as he watched the mist slipped away, and with it all sight of the Unseelie Court's strange, twisted world.

The door upon the Fay had been slammed shut. In their crepuscular land, cut off from the realm of man, the Unseelie Court could scheme and fight among themselves until the stars fell from the heavens. And what few of the damnable Fey still moved among mortals would be lost here.

Will heaved in a deep breath, still peering towards the blue horizon as though he could pierce that veil by will alone. And he blinked away the tears.

And somewhere the loneliest woman in all Christendom

sat upon a golden throne, trapped in a world not her own and without end.

Jenny had given up everything to save this world, and beyond the few of them there, no one would ever know of her courage. Her sacrifice shamed them all. Will shielded his eyes. This would not be an end, he vowed silently. 'I am coming back to get you, Jenny,' he whispered. 'Though all the hordes of Hell stand in my way, though oceans swell and conflagrations rage, I will find a way to reach you. And I will finally bring you home.'

For another moment he waited, caught in the mournful cry of the gulls, and then he began to make his way down to earth.

CHAPTER FIFTY-NINE

SAPPHIRE GHOST-LIGHTS SHIMMERED AROUND THE MASTS OF the galleon tossing on heavy seas towards England. On the forecastle, Dr John Dee, alchemist, scholar and spy, stretched out his arms to the lowering sky and muttered his incantations. The heavens crashed in response. Sheets of white lightning flickered along the western horizon. The long night was coming to an end.

Wind lashed his silver hair, but he stood like an oak against the rising gale and fixed his stony gaze upon the grey-green smudge of land ahead. If war was coming, he would not turn away. Come hell or high water, he would drive those devils out of England.

On the main deck, Bloody Jack Courtenay roared with laughter as the storm swirled around him, and the crew bellowed their songs of death and blood and wine and women. The *Tempest* heaved across the turbulent waters towards home.

Louder and louder still, Dee howled his invocation, until his throat was raw and his ears rang. But then shafts of sunlight punched through the thick bank of grey cloud to illuminate the green fields of England, and for a moment he thought he saw a multitude of shadows take to the air like a murder of crows.

Flee, he thought with a grim smile. *Flee and never return.*

The wind dropped. The thunder rolled away. And the galleon sailed into calm waters.

On the quayside at Greenwich, Sir Walter Raleigh waited, the silver thread in his jerkin a-shimmer in the morning sun. 'Doctor,' he boomed in greeting, as Dee strode down the plank on to dry land. 'You have been sorely missed.'

'I have not missed you, you preening popinjay,' the alchemist barked. 'Now let us away to London. There is still desperate work to be done. We are not out of deep water yet.'

The two men climbed into the waiting carriage, and as it trundled on to the rutted road leading west the adventurer recounted his tale. 'Cecil is a fool,' he muttered, 'and a prideful one at that. Though it opened the door to disaster, he refused all aid from the School of Night and sent me away from the palace. The price has been high. Many have died during the long siege.'

'Her Majesty?'

'She is safe, for now. But I fear Cecil would sacrifice even her rather than give up his hold on power.'

Dee nodded. 'He is a dangerous man, and desperate with it. He will never turn his back on his dark games of deceit and treachery, though we now face a new age, and a better one, in all hope. We must see what we can do.'

'He will not rest until the School of Night is broken on his rack,' Raleigh said. 'We have a long fight upon our hands.'

'We always have had, and always will,' the older man replied.

The adventurer leaned in close, his face darkening. 'We should all watch our backs. I fear Cecil will go to any lengths now. He has already vowed to see Swyfte dead, should he set foot upon English soil again.'

Dee's face hardened. 'Then let us make haste!'

The carriage clattered through the gates of the Palace of Whitehall in the warmth of the afternoon sun. As the alchemist clambered down, he cast one eye to the top of the Lantern Tower. All was still. The Faerie Queen would enjoy her grim cell for a while yet.

Once Raleigh had departed, Dee strode through the dusty, echoing halls, sensing the wretched atmosphere that hung over all. Guards leaned on their pikes, faces drawn. The sour reek of sweat pervaded the silent galleries. The court clustered together for safety in the halls surrounding the innermost ward, where the Queen's own chambers lay. The black-robed Privy Councillors drifted around, whispering and ashen-faced, as they waited for yet another futile meeting to begin.

As the Queen's sorcerer entered the hall, eyes looked up in shock and a slow murmuring begin to spread outwards, growing louder until it broke into a resounding cheer. Dee glowered at them all. *Fools*, he thought. *You are your own worst enemies*. He glimpsed Cecil watching him through the throng, as conflicted as ever. Relief and loathing struggled for supremacy in the spymaster's features.

Dee had a long night of incantations and spell-casting ahead of him in order to shore up England's beleaguered defences, but first he had more pressing business. He pushed through the pathetically grateful courtiers and strode towards a young man who had arrived to investigate the tumult. Dee saw in an instant the worry etched into the face of Swyfte's faithful assistant, Nathaniel Colt. Sensing news, the crowd fell silent in order to hear what the old man had to say. Kind words rarely came to the alchemist's lips, but he felt bound to summon them.

'Your master yet lives, and if the gods are willing he will be home soon.' Dee's spindly hand clutched the young man's shoulder. 'Pray for his safe return. The perils facing him are great indeed, but Albion has never had a sword like Will Swyfte, and perhaps never will again.' This was a message that would reach far beyond the fellow's ears, he knew.

Nathaniel smiled with relief, stuttering his thanks. Dee glanced around and saw Cecil glowering. He bared his teeth at the spymaster, then bellowed to the crowd, 'Clear the way. I have important news for the Queen alone.'

CHAPTER SIXTY

LONDON WAS AGLOW IN THE LATE AUTUMN SUN. THE ELMS and cherry trees shimmered with golds, oranges and browns along the garden walks of the Palace of Whitehall. The air was smoky from new fires stoked against the growing chill, while the gardeners pruned the dead heads off the roses and cut back the woodbine ahead of the festivities to come. Will paused at the end of the avenue and raised his eyes to the lightning-blasted spire of St Paul's to the east. It was where the beacon used to be lit whenever the realm came under threat from the Unseelie Court. He allowed himself a brief smile of satisfaction. Near six months had passed since he had made his vow on the Tower of the Moon, yet he found he could recall it in his mind as if it were yesterday. A new door had opened that day, on to a new world, a new future.

He wore his best black and silver doublet and had bought a new velvet cap for the celebrations. Nathaniel too had dressed in the closest he had to finery, a plain green doublet and brown cloak, though Will felt the young man's angry expression rather spoiled the effect.

'They are a foul collection of disloyal, untrustworthy, clay-brained jolt-heads,' the young assistant muttered, kicking his way through the carpet of dry leaves.

'Why, Nat, is that any way to speak of Her Majesty's most senior advisers?' Will replied with a wry smile.

'You have risked life and limb in constant service to our Queen and country, and now they treat you with such ignominy? Dismissed? No recognition for all you have achieved, no pomp, no ceremony? Sent back to Warwickshire?'

'It is not the ends of the earth, Nat. And my pension will ensure I want for nothing while I slip into a life of serenity.'

'I know you,' Nathaniel grumbled. 'The boredom will be the end of you. You will be drunk or mad within days.' He eyed Will. '*More* drunk. *More* mad.'

'Ah, Nat, where would I be without your constant flattery?' In truth the decision to dispense with his services had not surprised him when he and the others had arrived back in England on the galleon despatched under Dee's direction. He had served his purpose. The realm was intent on looking to the future and he was only a reminder of unpleasant times.

Cutting through the walkways between the palace's grand halls, the two men arrived at the tilt-yard as a fiddle player in doublet and galligaskin breeches of crimson satin tuned his instrument. Servants scurried here and there with platters of meat, bread and cheese. Others suspended flags of red and yellow above the white tent that the Queen would occupy. None of them knew the true reason for the celebration, Will realized, thinking it was little more than another diversion like the coming Accession Day Tilt in November. But the

Queen herself, and all her Privy Councillors, would be united in their private festivities and the belief that the dark days were finally over.

Through the throng, Will glimpsed Grace walking with the other ladies-in-waiting towards the monarch's chambers. She was a picture of prettiness. Her hair was tied with a bow of eggshell blue that matched her skirts, and Will was pleased to see her laughing. For a moment their eyes locked. The bond between them was stronger than it ever had been, forged by determination and hope; not loss, never loss. In private, they plotted and dreamed of ways of crossing a gulf greater than any ocean, of breaking down the walls of Hell, then returning home in joy and triumph. She never spoke of Strangewayes, and Will suspected she never would.

Once she had moved on, Will and Nathaniel strolled to where Carpenter and Launceston were bickering in the shade of an oak tree while they swigged on flasks of sack. Wrapped in a scarlet hooded cloak, Red Meg pretended to ignore them, though they had all found some common ground in the hot days they had shared waiting to be rescued from the New World.

Carpenter looked up as Will and Nathaniel arrived. 'Tell this beslubbering beetle-headed flap-dragon I no longer need to be watched like a troublesome child now that the Unseelie Court are in no position to stir the foul thing that still resides within me.'

Launceston raised a single eyebrow, eyeing those who milled around them. 'I watch you because you are an accident waiting to happen, with or without your foul passenger,' he breathed.

Carpenter jabbed a finger at the other man. 'You are just trying to pay me back for all the days I had to prevent you from slaughtering for sport.'

'Are you the pot or the kettle, I forget?'

'Let them be married soon and be done with it,' Meg sighed.

Will bowed. 'Mistress O'Shee. You have found better lodgings than the Tower, I hear.'

'Your master feels I may have some knowledge which could aid him with his difficulties in my homeland.' Shrugging, she gave a sardonic smile. 'Why, I may be able to spin this out for many a month before he discovers that, although I am many things, I am no traitor. And then I may seek you out in Warwickshire, Master Swyfte, for as you know, I am not easily deterred.'

'Your company will be welcome as always, good Meg.'

Nathaniel tugged at his master's sleeve and pointed towards a black carriage waiting at the end of the tilt-yard. Standing beside its open door, Dr Dee glared at them, swaddled in his cloak of animal pelts.

'We will make merry later, my friends,' Will said. 'First I must take a draught of vinegar.' He strode over to the carriage, a broad grin on his lips in the knowledge that it would irritate the Queen's brooding conjurer. 'Finally,' he said, his voice brimming with cheer. 'You are as elusive as marsh lights. I have hunted you up hill and down dale since morning.'

'You find me when I choose to be found,' the alchemist growled. 'I have been summoned back to Manchester. The Queen insists I maintain the post of warden of Christ's College. It appears I am an embarrassment in this fine new world, a reminder of the terrible compromises we all made during the long struggle.'

'This world is changing.' Will shrugged. 'Now the threat of the Unseelie Court has been driven back into the shadows, a new dawn is breaking.'

'Or new threats may appear.' With claw-like hands, Dee tugged his cloak tighter around him. 'The Fellows of the college wish to consult me on a troubling matter which they feel is a good fit for my area of expertise. The demonic possession of seven children. Yes, the Unseelie Court may be gone, for now, but there are devils and there are devils, and do not forget it.' The alchemist glanced around him, and when he was sure they could not be overheard he whispered, 'You have it?'

Will nodded. From under his cloak, he pulled at a small object wrapped in a black velvet cloth. He thought he could hear the obsidian mirror sing to him, with stories of Jenny appearing in the glass whispering words of love. An illusion, like so many things. 'As promised,' he said, offering the looking glass to the older man. 'Did Cecil not insist this be delivered to his door, so his wise men could endeavour to unlock its powers for the benefit of England?'

'One cannot trust governments or authorities of any kind,' the alchemist snorted. 'That would be as foolish as trusting men. This looking glass will be conveniently lost until I can find the time or the inclination to probe its secrets once more.'

'It is not too dangerous?'

'No secrets are too dangerous,' Dee replied with a tight smile. 'We risk all for knowledge. It is the sunlit hill on which we build our dreams.' He allowed himself a brief smile before his features darkened. 'And speaking of devils . . .'

Will glanced back in the direction of the alchemist's glower and saw Sir Robert Cecil coming towards them with his rolling gait, two black-robed advisers following at a safe distance. Nathaniel had noticed the new arrivals too and was hurrying over, ready to defend his master should the need arise.

'Beware of him, Swyfte. There is much poison in his fangs.' The alchemist's tone was not unkind.

'That is not news, doctor.' Will eyed the spymaster and felt the cold weight of all the lies and the betrayals that had cost him so many years of his life. And Jenny. But he had long since decided not to let that wretched past taint his days to come. This would be a fresh start for all of them.

'Then consider this,' the alchemist continued. 'His hired blade was all but ready to slit your throat the moment you arrived in Tilbury. And yet that rogue was found floating in the Thames with the butchers' offal. How strange.'

Will and Dee exchanged a sly glance. 'Then I owe the School of Night my life,' the spy said.

'More than that, as you will soon discover. My friends in our society now have some influence with the Queen herself, but there has been a high price to pay.'

'Then I thank you, too, doctor, for all you have done for me.'

'I hope we will never meet again, Swyfte,' Dee grumbled, 'but I doubt the course of my life will ever run so smoothly.' As Cecil approached, he climbed into the carriage and shut the door, knocking on the roof to urge the driver to move away.

When the spymaster arrived, Will bowed so deeply that it could only be considered a taunt. 'Sir Robert. How fares the Queen's eyes-in-the-shadows?'

'Keep your sharp tongue in your mouth, Master Swyfte.' Cecil's eyes narrowed, but only for a moment, and then his gaze flickered elsewhere, his expression a combination of embarrassment and annoyance. 'It seems the decision to end your employment was . . . rash. I was, of course, preoccupied with the troubling business in the Low Countries and had no notice of this affair until the papers had already been issued. But know that the offending secretary has been reprimanded . . . most forcefully, I must add . . . and that the matter has now been resolved.'

As Nathaniel joined them, Will raised one eyebrow at the spymaster's bluster and lies. 'Then your signature and seal was a forgery? A conspiracy reaches to the very heart of England's security. Why, 'tis good I am away from this intrigue, Sir Robert, for if we cannot trust those in highest office, we are all at risk.'

The Queen's Little Elf glared, knowing he had no choice but to allow the other man his moment.

Will held out his hands. 'And yet, I have those papers, and my stipend, and Warwickshire has many comforts at this time of year—'

'Damn you, Swyfte.' Cecil flushed. 'The Queen herself has requested your continued service. Even you cannot refuse Her Majesty.'

'The Queen, you say?' Will glanced in the direction of Dee's trundling carriage.

'I have kept Her Majesty aware of your many successes,' the spymaster said, attempting to flatter though his expression was sullen, 'and she found your recent exploits in the New World of particular interest. You tweaked the beard of the devil himself, Master Swyfte, and returned from Hell to tell the tale. Any man who can achieve such a thing must surely be needed in the Queen's service.' He paused, moistening his lips. Will thought he saw a flicker of unease in his eyes. 'Particularly in the turbulent times that lie ahead.'

'Why, perhaps my master is England's greatest spy after all,' Nathaniel said, his nose in the air.

Cecil looked daggers at him, but Will cut in. 'What are these turbulent times you speak of?'

'While we dwelt on our all-consuming struggle with the Unseelie Court, other shadows were moving beyond our attention.' A strong wind blew, whipping the dry leaves into gold and brown waves. Cecil shivered. 'In Venice, across the course of this last month, six of our agents have been found floating in the canals at dawn, eviscerated, as if set upon by a wild beast. There is talk of an English spy turned traitor, a young man with fiery red hair who has spoken widely of his hatred for one Will Swyfte.'

Strangewayes? Could it be that he had somehow escaped Manoa before the way closed, and now, scarred by his failure, was seeking revenge for all that he had lost?

'In Muscovy,' Cecil continued, oblivious of Will's ruminations, 'the court of the mad Tsar is gripped with fear at tales that the dead have risen from the frozen earth, Mongols from the horde that swept across their land in times gone by. And in the far Orient, in China, comes word of something darker still, a plague of devils . . .' The words caught in his throat as he eyed Nathaniel. 'But that is a discussion for another time.' He watched Will's eyes for a

443

long moment and then smiled tightly at what he saw there. 'Very well. Assemble your men, Swyfte, and await further orders.'

When the spymaster had departed, Nathaniel sighed. 'I suppose this means I must unpack your boxes of doublets, cloaks and shoes, which only this hour I had finished packing.'

'No rest for you, Nat, and none, it seems, for the swords of Albion,' Will replied with a grin. As he watched the young man walk away, his thoughts abandoned Whitehall and London and journeyed across the world. Venice, Muscovy, China, one true road ran through all of them. From every fiend he encountered, he would prise the knowledge he required until he had found the key he needed to unlock that way between worlds.

'And then, Jenny,' he whispered to the wind, 'I will come to fetch you home, and no man nor devil will stand in my way.'

For a moment, he waited there alone in the golden autumn light, remembering. And then he turned back towards the throng. There would be blood, he knew, and strife, and there would be an ending. But not this day.

FINIS

Don't miss the first two in the
Swords of Albion series . . .

THE SWORD OF ALBION
Mark Chadbourn

1588. As the Spanish Armada prepares to sail, rumours
abound of a doomsday device that, were it to fall into
enemy hands, could destroy England and her
bastard queen once and for all.

Enter Will Swyfte. He is one of Walsingham's new breed
of spy and his swashbuckling exploits have made him
famous. However Swyfte's public image is a façade, created
to give the people of England a hero in their hour of need
– and to deflect attention from his real role: fighting a
secret war against a foe infinitely more
devilish than Spain . . .

For millennia this unseen enemy has preyed upon
humankind, treating honest folk as playthings to be
hunted, taken and tormented. But now England is fighting
back. Armed with little more than courage, their wits and
an array of cunning gadgets created by sorcerer Dr Dee,
Will and his colleagues must secure this mysterious device
before it is too late. Theirs is a shadowy world of plot and
counterplot, deception and betrayal, where no one – and
nothing – is quite what they seem. At stake is the
very survival of queen and country . . .

'Smart, fun, at times surprisingly moving, and occasionally
downright shocking . . . impossible to put down'
REALMS OF FANTASY

THE SCAR-CROW MEN
Mark Chadbourn

1593. Queen Elizabeth's trusted spymaster Walsingham
has been dead for two years . . .

As plague sweeps through the streets and stews of London,
so suspicion and mistrust sweep through the court and
government. No one feels safe. Even the celebrated
swordsman, adventurer and philanderer,
Will Swyfte, must watch his back.

It is when his best friend and colleague, the playwright
Christopher Marlowe, is killed in a pub brawl that Will
decides he must act. The murder has all the hallmarks of
an assassination. But in going in search of Kit's killer, he
discovers that there are those in positions of power and
influence who are not what they seem . . .

Against a backcloth of growing paranoia and terror, Will
detects the malign machinations of England's hidden
enemy, the Unseelie Court. With these devils at his back,
the country's greatest spy may find that even his vaunted
skills are no match for the supernatural powers arrayed
against him. The choice is simple: uncover the true
nature and intention of this vile conspiracy – or
face the executioner's axe . . .

'Pulse-pounding . . . combined with references to
myth and history, it's potent stuff'
LOCUS Magazine